Di

To Shelly

DIARIES OF AN URBAN PANTHER

AMANDA ARISTA

AVON IMPULSE

This book is a work of fiction. The characters, incidents, and dialogue are drawn from the author's imagination and are not to be construed as real. Any resemblance to actual events or persons, living or dead, is entirely coincidental.

DIARIES OF AN URBAN PANTHER. Copyright © 2011 by Amanda Arista. All rights reserved under International and Pan-American Copyright Conventions. By payment of the required fees, you have been granted the non-exclusive, non-transferable right to access and read the text of this e-book on-screen. No part of this text may be reproduced, transmitted, down-loaded, decompiled, reverse engineered, or stored in or introduced into any information storage and retrieval system, in any form or by any means, whether electronic or mechanical, now known or hereinafter invented, without the express written permission of HarperCollins e-books.

EPub Edition July 2011 ISBN: 9780062113160

Print Edition ISBN: 9780062114747

10 9 8 7 6 5 4 3

Diaries of an Urban Panther

Prologue

As I stepped into the crosswalk, the boy next to me ran across the white stripes to his mother's waiting minivan. His blue book bag danced wildly on his back as his hands waved in reckless abandon. Just down the road to our right, a car engine revved and the driver accelerated towards the crosswalk.

The space between my shoulder blades tingled and the scene before me slowed. The manic screams of the children on the playground across the street quieted. The breeze stopped carrying the sweet scents of fall. The police officer's stop sign rose slowly and froze just above his head. Everything faded into the background as my senses focused on what was going to happen. I knew that in five seconds, there was going to be a schoolboy pancake with a side of scrambled Violet.

Instinct took hold and I darted out in front of the car. Scooping up the small boy from the asphalt, I leapt onto the hood. The motion sent the two of us sliding, leaving a clean streak across the hot metal. We flew off the other side and tumbled to the ground.

I hit the pavement hard, almost on all fours. Kneeling, I held the boy tightly, his arms clutched around my neck. His little heart beat wildly, almost as fast as mine. I looked up to follow the driver down the street. It was the same car that had been parked outside my coffee shop. I caught a flick of blonde hair and a flash of white teeth as the driver laughed and sped around the corner out of sight. His parting shot echoed out his open window, "See you later, Leftovers."

The little boy began to wriggle in my tight grasp and pushed back to look up at me. I saw his doe-like eyes, his mouth in a small O, and the pulse in his neck. His little face puckered in panic and a small finger worked its way up to poke me in the eye.

That's when the world seemed to start up again. The wind swept through the trees carrying the scent of excited children. Doors slammed. People suddenly hovered all around us. "

"Oh my god, Tomas," a woman cried out and the boy was snatched from my arms.

I leaned against the car beside me, blinking rapidly to make the sting from his grubby little finger go away.

As I pushed myself to my feet, I caught my reflection in the side view mirror. Yellow eyes stared back. Crap. Guess if I saw a monster with yellow eyes, I'd poke her in the eye as well.

"You all right?" The police officer's musky cologne and the smell of leather from his holster drew my attention as he walked closer. He was a police officer. Just a public servant. Not a threat.

"Fine." I bent over, hands on my knees, hiding my face, simply taking in long deep breaths. In through the nose, out through the mouth. I'm just a writer. And I'm fine. Just fine. Everything's friggin' peachy in Violet-Land.

My hands were shaking; my knees were weak. I heard the

roar of blood in my ears and saw the pulse in my vision. My glance darted to the other side of the street where people had lined up to watch the show. Just people, I told myself. A boy nearly gets run down by a sports car and people are going to gawk. Nothing weird about that.

"I'm fine," I repeated, still taking in deep breaths, still processing everything that had flown by. Did the world actual stop moving? Had I actually just run out in front of a car? Who was that guy that called me Leftovers?

A slight chill ran down my body as the breeze cooled the sweat on my skin. My heartbeat slowed; my pulse less visible. As I turned back at my reflection in the car window, I looked like me again. Just Violet.

The boy's mother reached out and touched my forearm with cool fingers. "You saved my little boy's life."

I turned towards her quickly. I had. I had saved a life. Little Violet Jordan was a hero.

The woman hugged me, smashing the boy between us. It threw me off balance for a moment as her rose perfume assaulted my senses but I patted her back softly. She pulled away and, without meeting my eyes again, headed toward her car. Tomas's frightful eyes peered over his mother's shoulder and he stared at me until he was securely fastened into his seat.

The police officer watched silently as I tried to catch my bearings. I didn't know where home was. There wasn't a school anywhere near my house. I thought I'd run west, but with all the turns and shortcuts, I couldn't be sure any more.

"I've never seen anyone do that," the officer said with a smile as he scratched behind his ear, lifting up the edge of his hat.

"Adrenaline, I guess." I forced a half smile and watched Tomas and his mom drive away.

"You training for a marathon or something?"

"No. Why?"

"I watched you speed around the corner. It was like a woman with a mission."

I gulped. "Just running," I squeaked out.

He nodded and waved to the gathering crowd to disperse. As the people slowly retreated to their cars or back into the school building, five black dogs remained on the sidewalk, panting, staring at me.

Frozen, I stared at the motley group of mongrels. My skin crawled and the space between my shoulder blades tightened, the hair prickling down my neck. They'd found me. My vain attempt to blend into a crowd of schoolchildren three feet shorter than me hadn't worked as well as I thought and now they were waiting with baited breath.

"Is your ankle alright?"

"My ankle?" I looked down to see a gash just above my ankle soaking my sock with deep red blood. "Where's my shoe?"

The officer pointed to the middle of the street where my size ten rested like a big white speed bump. "You clipped the front; that's what made you spin."

"*I spun?*"

He nodded and looked at the dogs, then back at me. "Do you want me to call you an ambulance?"

I tried to put pressure on my swollen ankle and fire flew up my leg. Not just bleeding, broken. I gulped but tried not to show just how painful it really was. "I've survived worse."

He pulled out a small memo pad from his breast pocket. I almost expected him to lick the tip of the pencil like in the old detective movies, but he didn't. "Did you recognize the car?"

I could only shake my head; my lips clamped shut. I couldn't positively identify it as the one that had been parked outside the coffee shop where I spent half my waking moments. I mean there were probably thousands of BMW convertibles in Dallas.

"Would you like to press charges?"

"Press charges? The guy sped off."

With an unsatisfied sigh, he put the pad back in his front pocket. "Well, I'm going to have to fill out a report anyway, but since you're refusing an ambulance, can I at least give you a ride home?"

I looked down at the empty street, then at the dogs lined up just waiting for me to be alone again. "That would be great," I said with a pain-filled smile.

I'd never been in the back of a police car but I could see the odometer from there. As I gave the officer directions, I watched the numbers tick away. Seven miles. I'd run seven miles, saved a boy's life, and broken an ankle. That was a bit more than my standard afternoon. I longed for the days when I stayed in my office to write my little stories and only ran after ice cream trucks.

We stopped outside my townhouse and the officer rushed around the front of his patrol car to let me out. He offered a hand as I gingerly slid across the vinyl seats and stood on one leg. I looked down the quiet residential street. No dogs. No speeding sociopaths.

"Thank you again." He closed the door and walked back around to the driver side of the car. "We need more heroes like you."

I watched as he drove off. Wincing with every uneven step, the walk to my house felt like another mile in itself. As quickly as I could, I found my key, unlocked my door, hobbled inside, and slammed the door shut.

Exhausted, I leaned against the door and slid down to the floor. The sock was a lost cause. I'd forgotten my shoe at the scene of the crime. There was so much pain in my leg I didn't know if I would ever move from this spot.

Now I had a reason to never leave my house again.

I hate dogs. I hate lost shoes and I really hate exercise.

And thanks to what happened two weeks ago, I'd never enjoy another Cosmo again.

Chapter One

Two weeks earlier

That Friday in the middle of October was like all the other Fridays since I'd moved to Dallas: a swanky uptown bar with dark corners, expensive drinks, and less clothing than a beach cabana. Jessa had called the usual suspects together for a small celebration after landing a new client. Jessa, Carrie, Adrianna, and I were curled around a table at the back of the dance floor when goose bumps ran across my skin. Usually this is nothing; my hands have the ambient temperature of the polar icecaps and probably the number one reason I drink coffee like it's going out of style.

Straightening up to see around the bar, I caught a glimpse at the man who had lurked in our shadow for the last two months. A prickle ran down my spine as our eyes met.

"Stalker boy's here again," I said as I sipped my drink, looking over at Jessa.

"Who's Stalker boy?" asked Carrie, short blonde who had never had to worry about calories or paying for a drink,

Jessa rolled her eyes and flicked her gaze over her shoulder towards the man. She set her hands flat on the table, fingers spread wide. That was her drama pose. After two years of friendship, I was intimately familiar with the drama pose. In fact, everyone at our table stopped talking and leaned in, knowing it was time for a story.

"Like a dog with a bone," she started over the DJ's music. As she leaned forward, her black curtain of hair slipped down around her heart-shaped face. "So this guy came up to me in the bar and we get to talking and I don't think anything of it until he shows up at the same place I go to the next night and the next night. One conversation and it's like the guy is everywhere I go now."

Carrie frowned. "Why didn't you called the cops?"

Jessa smiled. "Because the boy is hot."

I shook my head but smiled as the other girls laughed. Classic Jessa. All about the looks, less about the details. Personally, I'd spent two months collecting the details. Stalker boy wasn't overly tall, blending into the twenty-something crowd with his black jacket and dark jeans, but an edge haunted his soap star looks. Even here in the smoky club with the dancing strobe lights, he was different from the other men who stared at our table.

Looking back at me steadily, he took a swig of his beer. The intensity of his gaze sent another bout of chills down my spine and the thought crossed my mind that maybe Jessa *should* have called the cops. Maybe this guy was trouble.

Jessa nudged my arm. I looked at her and followed her pointing finger to another man at the bar. He was skinny but hid it well with a corduroy jacket with patches on the elbow. "What's his story?"

I smiled at my best friend and sunk into the familiar story-telling game we played almost every Friday night. "He's a child prodigy, went to college at fourteen, and now teaches psychology as the youngest tenured professor in the university's history."

"And why aren't you asking for his number?"

"Chronically antisocial. He finds human companionship tedious and is waiting for the day he can clone himself to have a decent conversation."

Jessa laughed and playfully slapped my arm. "You are too hard on people Violet."

After two more hours of gabbing, dancing, and fending men off Jessa, I managed to herd the girls into a taxi and drop all of them off without any missing shoes, lost purses, or the maiming of clingy guys who didn't know "you leave with who you came with."

Applauding myself for remembering cash for the taxi, I paid the driver and trekked to the red front door of my little two-story townhouse. I was nearly to the door when a noise from the alleyway echoed between the two buildings.

"Not again. Stupid dogs."

Now normally, I'd have let my trash bags fend for themselves. But I had a few drinks in me and had managed to block a Dallas Cowboys linebacker from taking Jessa home, so I was feeling braver than usual. I was going to teach those stupid mutts a lesson: My trash is not a free buffet.

The broken safety light in the alley left me tiptoeing through darkness. Luckily, I knew my way around: four steps and a gutter; three and a dip to the left in the sidewalk.

Now, I write for a low-budget horror movie company whose creations are found only on the highest numbered cable channels. Even in cult circles, Cloak and Dagger Productions is well known for taking the imaginative leap a little too far. But nothing, even in my line of work, could have prepared me for what I saw, actually *saw*, as I stepped into the alley of garage doors.

A dark, solid shadow loomed over the pale fur of Happy, my neighbor's golden lab. The dog lay limp under the crouching form. By the snap of tendons and slow smacky chomping that echoed around in my ears, it was leisurely eating man's best friend.

I cupped my hand over my mouth from the stomach-churning sight. Part of me had known it was Happy eating my garbage. But this? I would never wish this on anything.

As I tried to stealthily back away from the gruesome sight, I bumped my garbage cans, sending them clattering loudly behind me, spilling my white bags all over the driveway. Crap.

I could make out only yellow eyes in the inky blackness as they snapped towards me. Double Crap.

Frozen in the eerie stare, I didn't move again until the shadow growled. The low, earthy sound echoed off the long corridor of metal garage doors.

Alone, in the darkness with a monster, I panicked. I had keys in one hand and a small purse with a credit card, cherry lip gloss, and loose powder in the other. None of that was going to do any good unless the black figure felt a little shiny.

The shadow began to move, its dark legs slowly stepping over Happy's golden fur. Its long body stalked towards me. I used the only weapon I could think of: my shoe. It was big enough to knock out anything.

My patent heel bounced off the black mass and clattered on the cracked driveway. The creature growled again unaffected by the barrage, keeping me in its sights.

One shoe off and three drinks to the wind, I darted back down the shadowy sidewalk between the buildings as fast as my tired size tens would carry me. Even with the adrenaline pumping through my veins, I couldn't push my legs fast enough.

Fire ripped through my body as the thing leapt and sharp, steely hooks pierced into the muscle of my shoulder and tore down my back.

Falling forward with its weight, I hit the sidewalk hard. My hands caught my fall, saving my face from the concrete, but losing a layer of skin in the process. My glasses flew off my face, landing just far enough away to be lost in the darkness.

The shadow ripped deeper into my shoulder. It shredded my shirt, snapped my bra straps, and tore through the tender flesh.

I must have cried out because, suddenly, help arrived in the form of black boots. The thing on top of me growled or screamed; I wasn't sure. The pain seeped into my ears making them useless, as spots filled my blurry vision.

There was a hollow click and I saw another sequence from the movies: the world fading to black. I could only hope that along with those big black boots came a white hat.

Chapter Two

"In the beginning, it was gray. Among those who wandered among the world, Guardians protected us. Not that there was anything to protect us from. We minded our own business, married our loves, had children, and lived peacefully.

"And then there were these new creatures called humans who lived among those who wandered among the world. They were small and frail and couldn't weave water, or see into trees, or change shapes. But they were passionate and artistic and curious. They were kind and cruel and humorous and sullen all in little mortal packages.

"As the humans evolved, so did those who wandered. Once gray, there were then light ones and dark ones, those who protected humanity and those who believed they were above it.

"A war raged in the dark silence around the fragile humans. Both sides had their soldiers. Once watching over us like angels, the Guardians now protected wanderers and humans from their darker counterparts, the Grifters. Guardians had speed and strength and inner fortitude to save those who needed to be saved. And hearts like lions and . . ."

"Mom, they didn't really have lion hearts, did they?"

Mom smoothed out my hair and whispered. "Some do, kitten. Just like lions."

I wasn't dead, but with the way my body hurt, I wished I was. Everything throbbed, including a telltale headache from too many drinks. I cracked my crusty eyes open and the first thing I saw was red-brown plaid sheets.

This was not my bed.

I didn't do plaid. And this was the manliest plaid I had ever had the misfortune of waking up on.

I lay on my stomach in an orange-lit room that didn't smell particularly clean. It had that musky male smell one can never quite get out of fabrics, no matter how much you Febreeze it.

A small lamp on a crooked nightstand next to the headboard lit the room softly. What I could see without my glasses matched what I could smell. Miscellaneous stuff was strewn around the guest room: baseball bats, old shoes, coats waiting for a winter that might never come, a kidnapped girl. You know, the usual for spare rooms.

When I pushed up off the mattress, my muscles felt like rippling lava down my back, a fire so hot it left white spots in my vision. My left side went numb and gave way beneath my weight, dropping me back to the springy mattress.

But the fear beating wild and willful in my chest completely overcame the pain in my back. I rolled over to my right side, only to discover I didn't have a shirt on. My hand flew to my waist and I was relieved to find underwear, if you could call these satin strings Jessa had given me from Victoria's Secret underwear. Why she cared about panty lines, I'll never know.

What I remembered was like a bad '80s movie montage. I remembered the club. I remembered Stalker boy and a linebacker. I remembered something dark in the alley. Then someone, or something, else there. Then there were spots and dreams of Bruce Campbell singing "Memories."

Using my right arm, the only thing willing to respond, I pushed up on the bed to sit and immediately knew I shouldn't have. The movement reignited the muscles in my shoulder into magma and my left hand, limp on my lap, twinged with pins and needles. Either I had nerve damage or my carpal tunnel was seriously acting up again.

My whole body tensed as I waited for the pain to ebb away and the starbursts behind my eyelids to fade. It took all my energy not to fall back to the bed in defeat.

Slowly, I strained to look over my shoulder. White gauze and surgical tape wound all the way up the side of my neck. Wherever I was, whoever had brought me here, had gone to great lengths to try to heal me. But why?

A commotion at the door drew my attention and I heard a chair pull away on a wooden floor. As a lock clicked and the antique handle turned, I pulled the plaid sheet over my bare chest just as the stranger walked in.

"Good to see you up," the man said as he stepped into the orange light of the lamp.

"Why am I locked in here?" I questioned quickly, pulling the sheet around me tightly, and tucking an edge into the top so it covered everything. My modesty intact even in crisis.

The man moved further into the room, his broad shoulders blocking most of a dancing light from a TV. It wasn't until he was standing over my near-sighted self I recognized who exactly held me captive.

"Stalker boy?" I asked and then wished I hadn't. I clamped my hand over my mouth like I had just cussed in front of my grandmother. This man had kidnapped me in a dark alley and tucked me away in a guest room. Maybe I should be on my company behavior for a while.

The man half-smiled as he sat down across from me on an old kitchen chair missing half the back spokes. He leaned forward, elbows on his knees, and I gulped as he came back into my field of vision. He was better looking this close, especially without my clothes on. That chiseled jaw was beyond soap star and straight to silver screen leading man.

As he looked me up and down with his chocolate brown eyes, fear slipped into something darker that forced my hand down to my legs to make sure I was covered. My heart pounded loudly in my ears and my stomach turned over on itself with tension.

"Guess I deserve that nickname."

I licked my suddenly very dry lips. I shook my head and squeezed the wad of plaid sheets wound tightly in my slightly quaking fist.

"Were you the boots in the alley?" managing to form words with my cotton ball tongue.

He nodded. "What do you remember?"

The memories flashed back again quicker, the montage faster, and with it, the pain came back as well. I tried not to arch my back but it burned, like every time I thought about it, the wounds were fresh again. I bit my lower lip and gripped the edge of the mattress, riding the wave of pain that was also quicker than the first.

I took in a slow breath and let it out when the pain faded. "I was in the alley behind my house and something attacked me."

"Get a good look at it?"

"Not really."

"Were you attacked before or after you lost your shoe?"

The embarrassment flushed in my cheeks as I vividly remembered my failed attempt at protecting myself. Humiliation drove the fear away for a brief moment.

"Why do I feel like I'm being grilled, Mr. . . . ." I searched for his name through my dense haze of a memory. I couldn't think of Jessa ever telling me his real name, if she even knew herself. That sounded like Jessa.

"Garrett, Charles Garrett," he said, watching me with a small furrow between his brow.

The gauze and tape began to itch like wool and I wanted to rake my nails across it. The irritation sharpened my senses and my tongue, even focused my eyes so the room was clearer.

"Well Mr. Garrett, is this an interrogation? Because if it is, I'd like my one phone call and at least a sweater."

Garrett looked down at his clasped hands then back up at me. "You're funny, Miss Jordan," he said with the twinkle in his eye.

"You've seen me in my birthday suit; I think you can call me Violet."

He smiled and I could feel the burning all over again. It was the injuries. Or the panic of being locked in with a man I only knew through stories and sideways glances. But he had rescued me or at least bandaged me up. He'd given me a decent name, not H-bomb or Axe. And he wasn't sporting a machete or a mask. So I pushed my luck.

"How long have I been here?" I asked as I tentatively stretched my back, testing the muscles, the skin, and my own strength. The pain was fierce but it felt like I needed to rub up against the corner of a brick wall. It itched like something healing.

"Two days."

"Two days! And you didn't take me to a hospital?" I shrieked, only to bring the pounding in my head to a roaring blur. I held my temples. If this was a two-day-old hangover, I was giving up on vodka entirely.

He seemed to wait until the rumble in my head subsided. "I didn't want to explain anything to them."

"Explain what? I got attacked by a dog or something."

He clenched his jaw and watched me through his long dark lashes.

I waited until the pain ebbed and watched that furrowed brow carefully. There was something different about him and I hoped I didn't know what it was.

"You don't think it was a dog, do you?" I finally asked, leading myself down the path I didn't want to follow.

"You're quick, Miss Jordan."

As the puzzle pieces fell into place, I shook my head. This wasn't happening. I wasn't going to let it happen. I wasn't going to be the victim of some crazy who watched too much bad cable TV. Bad cable TV that I wrote, and this was not in the dailies.

"No, Mr. Garrett. This is not one of my stupid scripts."

Outraged, I stood. The wounds covering my back screamed back to life. A claw of pain encircled my abdomen and squeezed, putting spots in my vision and weakening my knees. It drove the breath out of me and drove more fear in as I fell.

Garrett's strong arm curled around my waist in the blink of an eye. He rested my unresponsive body back on the bed and covered my shoulders with a thin blanket. He sat softly on the side of my bed and looked down at my paralyzed figure. My body twitched like electrified putty and all I could do was look up at him.

"As much as you might protest, Miss Jordan," he said with a hard edge to his smooth voice, "I'm going to keep you here until we know for sure."

He jumped up, jostling me roughly, and left, putting the chair back in its place.

I just tried to breathe, forcing air in and out, breathe through the burning at my back, the vice still around my chest. As the tear slid down my cheek, I knew he was wrong. I wasn't the buxom blonde who gets attacked in the woods by the beast the movie was named after. I was the sidekick, the one who survived. I was a Velma, the one who proved smart girls were cool, too.

It just wasn't fair. I had everything finally on track. My jobs were finally paying off. Jessa and I had carved out a few good friends and a decent social life. I'd found that cute little townhouse for a steal.

Six months down the drain because little Violet Jordan thought she could play tough guy and teach someone a lesson.

Maybe I cried myself to sleep. Maybe my brain wore itself out thinking of every horrible thing he could be doing on the other side of that old door. But sleep came, dreamless and fitful.

My eyes flew open when Garrett skulked into the room with a plate of food and a pile of clothing. "I thought you'd be hungry, with the healing and everything."

I sniffed but didn't bother to move, lying diagonally across the bed exactly where he had put me hours before. Face down on the flattened pillow, I didn't care if I looked like a pouting five year old, with sniffling nose and red eyes. Almost didn't care what he did to me. Figured this was par for the course for the life of Violet Jordan.

"Can I take a look at your back?" he asked softly, hovering over me.

"Have a blast," I muttered staring at his knees then up to the food in his hand.

His shoulders slumped a fraction of an inch, something most people would have missed but when you've watched from the sidelines your whole life, you catch the little things. I had hurt his feelings. And for an evil predator, or whatever he was, I couldn't imagine why. It caught my curiosity, which pushed my fears aside for a moment.

Setting the plate down on the nightstand and put the clothes on the broken chair, he moved slowly to the bed. I wanted to flinch, to pull away, but what was I going to do? Run three feet and fall down again? Run the risk of exposing everything he may have been gentlemen enough not to peek at already?

"You're extra timid."

"Figure I'd let you heal me before I made my escape."

Garrett chuckled as he touched my bare shoulder. The skin burned where his skin brushed mine and I couldn't figure out if it was the injury or if his hands were that hot.

He carefully peeled away the cloth tape and bandages and put them on the bed between us. The gauze was saturated with rusty brown, barely any white fibers. There was a lot of blood, my blood, absorbed into the bandages.

"Well those are . . . healing nicely."

"What do you mean?"

"Your . . . injuries are looking good," he repeated with a forced optimism.

"And what does that mean?" I said leaning up, moving without as much pain as before.

So he laid it out straight for me. He took a deep breath and said, "For being mortally wounded, you're doing fine. Stay there. I'm gonna get some new bandages."

He left the door open, and I could have escaped. A perfectly unprotected window hid just behind the headboard, but my curiosity got the better of me. Instead of going for the escape route now I had more than just a stitch of clothing, I reached back with my hand and felt around for injuries that floored me a day earlier.

I ran my fingers over something that felt like a scab but was hotter than a match head. Changing positions, I reached over my left shoulder where the bandages had come up higher. I could feel more there, like elephant skin, only searing. Three days and it was already scabbed over. That terrified me. Waking up in the strange bed of a strange man—I thought I was handling that fine. But finally feeling the healed marks on my back, having proof that something had actually happened terrified me all over again.

He strode into the room but stopped mid way as he saw my watery eyes.

"You're fine," he repeated.

"I got attacked," I said through gritted teeth as I curled my arms underneath the pillow. "Now I'm trapped in a stranger's house. Nothing about this is *fine*."

He sighed and sat down on the edge of the bed again. "At this rate, you'll be healed in about a day, maybe with no scars. And then I'll let you go home."

Putting the large plastic first aid kit on his lap, he picked out bottles and packages of gauze. I watched him open bandages and spread a white cream on a cotton ball. I gasped as he began to wipe the skin down with the cold cream.

"Sorry," he said.

"A kidnapper saying '*I'm sorry*.' That's gotta be a first," I grumbled.

"I'm not kidnapping you. I'm making sure that you are . . . safe."

"Safe from what?" I asked as I looked over at his knee.

He kept cleaning, kept dabbing on the cold cream with the soft cotton ball. It soothed the burning sensation but it did nothing for the aching muscles underneath and the scared girl underneath all that. "What exactly was in that alley?"

With pursed lips, he placed a large bandage across the clean wounds and ripped four strips of tape.

Giving up on getting any answers out of him, I buried my head in my pillow and let him finish taping the large bandage across my left shoulder.

He stood and collected the supplies, putting them meticulously back in their places in the large plastic first aid kit as if he had done it a million times before.

"You'd better eat and I'm sorry if the clothes don't fit."

Turning my head, I watched him go. He closed the door and put back the chair. My stomach growled with hunger and the burger next to me looked wonderful. Screw the diet. I needed to survive here.

After the caffeine and the clothes, I had enough energy to sit up in the bed and look around at my prison. As my mind raced through the clues in his room, I could only come up with three things that even remotely made sense.

1. He was a vampire hunter and I had been caught in the crossfire of his war against the dark arts. He was holding me here to make sure I hadn't been infected by whatever beastie he had been tracking. I had written it in a script that had been rejected but it had always been a favorite of mine.

2. He was plain psycho and since he couldn't have Jessa, he decided to take her friend to be his sex slave or his collateral when he bargained for Jessa's affection. Which wasn't going to work. He should have taken her Fendi purse instead.

3. In his TV-rotted mind, he had rescued me from an actual dog attack and was trying to do the right thing in very misguided sort of way. Which might explain why I was not as afraid of him as I should be.

When the fear crept away and I was sure I could stand, I tried the window, just for good measure. If something did happen and I ended up on the evening news, I didn't want some neighbor going, "Why didn't she just crawl out the window?"

It was unlocked. What kind of evil kidnapper doesn't secure a window? His loss, I thought as I quietly opened the window and peered out.

Huh. One story house with the neighbors only a few feet away. No alarms went off; there weren't bars on the windows. Just a short drop to the ground below. Something wasn't right about this.

I slid a leg out the window and stretched my leg down until my toes touched the cool grass. God bless a 34-inch inseam.

Careful of my left shoulder, I slid out the window with a little *umph*.

Take that, Stalker boy.

Running for the streetlights, my heart began to pound. Freedom. Where to go from here? I couldn't see downtown. Hell, I couldn't see three feet in front of my face. It was pitch black with no moon in the sky. Not that I could navigate home by it.

A hand clamped down on my injured shoulder and pain shot down through my torso. A boot nudged my knees out from under me and I fell hard. The jolt made me bite the end of my tongue and tears welled up in my eyes as I tasted blood.

"Really think it was going to be that easy?"

"Kinda."

He walked in front of me and looked down with a queer smile on his face. In one swift movement, he swept up my right hand, pulled me to my feet, and threw me over his shoulder.

Defeat didn't prevent me from struggling as much as I could. I kicked and pounded and screamed, but it didn't faze him, or the neighbors, as he walked us through the front door and locked it behind us.

He dropped me on the couch and my shoulder reared to life again. I clutched it tightly and glared up at him.

Garrett's head cocked and his hands rested on his hips. "How about you try a shower? Should make your shoulder feel better."

"Why?"

"Because you're getting a little ripe."

My cheeks flared with anger. "How about you let me go home and I'll take a shower there?"

He laughed. "Not yet, Miss Jordan."

I stood, holding my shoulder. It felt dislocated and my fingers now tingled.

As he guided me through the house, I looked around at the obvious bachelor pad with various stacks of things everywhere with accompanying smells. The french fry smell permeated the front of the house. The kitchen was spotless but the back hallway smelled of standing water. It didn't give me faith in the bathroom he was now pointing to.

I nodded and watched him close the door. It wasn't the cleanest place in the world but I didn't know if I had the option to be picky right now. As I turned to the shower, I saw a stack of clean towels on the toilet. I was pretty sure that serial killers didn't leave fresh towels.

"The window is nailed shut," he said through the door.

"Thanks for the heads up," I called back.

I really wasn't looking for an escape. Plus, I really didn't want him to catch me hanging half way out of the tiny window I was too chubby to fit through. I turned on the water full blast, as hot as I could stand it, and watched the bathroom steam up. I wiped the mirror and looked at my shadowed eyes, pale skin. I pulled off the maroon shirt and turned around.

I pulled off the large piece of gauze and there it was in all its glory. A full four slashes down my shoulder could have been fingernails, or a knife, or any number of weapons I could dream up.

After peeling off the rest of the clothes, I stepped into the hot water and immediately my muscles relaxed. I fell easily into the routine of showering. Washing my hair and face and finding a cloth to wash my body, I scrubbed the parts of my back I could, relieving some of the itch. The smoke from the bar still clung to my hair and I had dirt still encrusted on my knees from the fall in the alley.

From where that thing jumped me. Even in the hot water, I shivered at the images behind my eyes. I shook my head and tried to focus on one thing at a time. *Get out of this alive, Violet, and then we'll talk about never putting out the trash again.*

I dried off, wrapped the towel around me, and sat on the cold porcelain toilet for a moment. I figured I could play this two ways: (1) like a captive—be scared and terrified and not help myself at all or (2) be intelligent and witty, swallow my fear, and try to get some information out of this guy about why I was here and not in a hospital—and why wounds were now scabbed up on my back after only three days.

A tap on the door made me jump off the toilet seat.

"You okay?"

"Fine, just collecting my thoughts."

"Figured out if I'm a bad guy yet?" he said from the other side.

"Nope," I answered honestly.

"Cup of coffee?"

Coffee was my weakness, my kryptonite and the one thing that I could never turn down. Food, sex, and shelter were optional; coffee was not.

"Sure," I pepped up. "Add cinnamon and I'd think you're an angel."

He chuckled as he moved away from the door. I rested my head in my hands and prayed I would be okay. And I don't pray. Stopped praying about twelve years ago.

But something about him didn't feel evil, didn't make me quake in terror. Didn't make me cry any more than I already had. And he had spent two months following us without incident. He was there when I needed help and seemed handy with the medical tape. Maybe he was just weird. Weird I could deal with. Cannibalistic, not so much.

Sufficiently dry, I put the clothes back on. I ran my fingers through my wet locks and hoped his two-in-one shampoo would be enough to tame my kinky hair. In that motion, I was surprised to find my back didn't sting on the surface; it was more of a deeper hurt now, a muscle hurt. It still burned to the touch but the worn T-shirt felt good against the exposed scabs.

Shuffling out into the living room, careful to not step on anything in my bare feet, I immediately smelled coffee and cinnamon. It was much better than the french fry smell.

He handed me a chipped brown mug. "Have a seat," he said. It was more of a command than an invitation.

I stepped over a pile of clothes and sat on the lumpy couch where he had been watching TV. The place wasn't a fortress, just a living room. I didn't see any guns or knives, just a few baseball bats and a hockey stick, but nothing of real violence. The really odd thing about the scene was that nothing hung on the walls, no pictures or posters or anything. No clues of who he was. Probably kept it that way so his victims couldn't identify him later on. There was also a layer of dust an inch thick but I wasn't exactly the right person to be judging dusting habits. I could grow potatoes on my mantle.

Garrett sat at the other end of the couch, between me and the door, and watched as I sipped my steamy mug of caffeine. The hot liquid soothed everything, every muscle, every neuron. It was sweet and had just the right amount of sugar and milk in it.

"You must have been watching me."

"Like a hawk," he said as he took a sip of his own.

I finally caught the glimpse of the clock on the top of the TV playing a muted infomercial.

"Do you normally have coffee at 3 a.m.?" I took another long sip.

"Actually yeah," he said with a shrug.

"So when do I go home?" I asked bluntly, the warm cup in my hands restoring my witty edge.

"When I say," he responded. He sipped his coffee. "You're not like the others, Miss Jordan."

"How many others have you kidnapped?"

"I didn't kidnap you. I rescued you from a very large . . . thing," he corrected.

"What was it? What did you shoot it with?"

Garrett's eyes widened for a moment but snapped back to the unreadable face. "Didn't think you were awake at that point."

"I wasn't. I was guessing," I muttered into my coffee mug.

Garrett's jaw clenched as he breathed loudly out through his nose, scolding himself.

"You said you were waiting to see if I was safe. Am I safe?"

"I don't know," he said. "With the way you're healing, I can't be sure."

"Well, what do you think? Because I've had plenty of time to dream up thousands of theories with all the *Cloak and Dagger* stuff going on here."

Garrett looked deep into his coffee, avoiding my eyes. "Do you really want to know what I think?"

"Of course I want to know. I'm smart enough to know the thing in the alley was too big to be a dog but you took it down pretty quick. I know even in my younger days, I didn't heal this fast. I want to know why you brought me here and not a hospital."

Garrett pursed his lips and leaned back on his couch. His T-shirt stretched over his chest as he put his arm on the back of the couch. There was a dark mark there, some kind of tattoo on the inner side of his left upper arm. It was a small design, something in a circle. I tried not to stare at it but couldn't help myself.

He shifted position and kept his arm to his side from then on.

I curled my feet underneath me and waited, watching, as he decided what to tell me. I'd decided to give him the benefit of the doubt. He had healed me, fed me, and clothed me. And the addition of cinnamon was above the call of a normal kidnapper.

"You were attacked by a werewolf."

Laughter echoed in my head and I immediately knew number three of my scenarios was right: He was gorgeous but insane. I was about to be dinner. Only Violet Jordan could get herself into a situation like this. I smiled and was about to say something witty to that effect but the darkness in his eyes made my smile fade.

"I didn't get a good look but I shot it with silver. Works for most things if I'm wrong."

The penny taste of fear filled me. I gripped my coffee tighter as I worked through this in my brain. *He was insane*; it was the only thought that ran through my head. I mean sure, I wrote about this stuff on TV but it was *SCIFI*, hence, the *FI* part of it.

"Now, I'm waiting to see if you've been infected. It takes in some people but not in others."

"Why?"

"Depends on the person's blood."

"What about the blood?"

"Depends on if there is magic in it already."

Wasn't that some mythology he'd cooked up? But wasn't I healing too fast for it not to have infected me? The wounds were through muscle; wouldn't that be deep enough to infect someone with a mystical disease? God, I sounded like I was at work. Of course, I did do most of my work sitting on a couch with a cup of coffee. But not at three in the morning and not across the cushion from a mad man—or any other man for that matter. Maybe I was the one going crazy.

He must have read my thoughts, which at this point, I wasn't discounting. "I'm not sure if your healing is because you're a Perfect or if it's the disease."

The P word caught my attention more than the notion of lycanthropy or being filleted alive. "What exactly is perfect to you?"

Garrett just smiled that soap star smile. "It means you are perfect in every way."

My hysteric laughter echoed off the bare, wood-paneled walls. "You obviously didn't see me in high school with the zits and the braces and the frizzy, frizzy hair."

He waited to continue until after my fit of panicked giggles had subsided. "It means you were created for a specific purpose. There has been a prophecy. That's why I was sent to watch over you."

"But you asked out Jessa, you were following..." And then it hit me. I was always with Jessa when she spotted him and how else would he know how I took my coffee. "You were following me."

There was that look again, that dark look where he dropped his chin slightly and looked through his long lashes. It made me stop breathing and my skin grow hot. But maybe it was the coffee still steaming in my hands.

His voice was soothing as I dropped my gaze into the shaking liquid. "You're wandering through life. You live alone and nowhere for very long. No family, few close friends. Something is missing and you can't figure out."

"You've got it wrong," I protested. "I live alone because I want to live alone. I've got no family because they died in a car accident. I just moved here because I broke up with my boyfriend and I don't have millions of friends because I work seventy hours a week. Not because I was created. And nothing's missing. I've got my job, my house. And there is not an ounce of magic in my blood."

My overzealous rebuttal didn't stop his explanation. "Your potential is lying dormant until the time is right. It's all part of being fated for a specific purpose. Just like I have a specific purpose."

My jaw had clenched into a tight knot, but I managed out, "And what would that be?"

"To find people."

"And shoot things with guns?"

He shrugged. "Happens. Mostly it means I'm on the sidelines watching."

His sentence, though simple, was all too familiar. The life on the sidelines. Watching other peoples' adventures. Watching other people get the promotions and the happy endings. Watching as you're stuck in a holding pattern.

I took a moment to sip on my coffee and think. God, what's so wrong with me that I can't attract a normal stalker who wants to just have his way with me and leave me in little pieces for the city to pick up. I get a self-help guru with prophesies.

Why wasn't I running? Why wasn't I taking the hot coffee in my hands and throwing it in his face? Because the truth of it hummed through me. Vibrated along my skin and warmed me like a blanket. He spoke in familiar words of familiar worlds that I'd been surrounded with my whole life.

"So, if I choose to believe that I'm a . . . " I couldn't even say the word. It was too absurd. "Was getting attacked in the back alley part of the fated destiny or whatever?"

He looked down at his coffee and ran his fingers through his hair. "I don't know."

"Well if you were sent to watch over me, what were you watching for?"

"I don't know. They didn't tell me much."

"Well who sent you?"

"Can't tell you yet."

"What the hell? Give me something. This is my life we are talking about here."

Frustrated, I stood and he matched my position with a speed that blurred his form. It was just like the movies, like when vampires sped across the room to capture their victims. I froze in place as he stepped closer to me. My heart pounded, rattling my ribcage, as he looked down at me.

"I will never hurt you," he said softly, tenderly almost as he reached out to take the hot coffee from my hand. "I was just sent to keep you safe."

"Bang up job, Garrett. If I'm infected, won't you kill me like you killed that thing in the alley?"

He paused. It was a chilly pause that cooled the air in the room, cooled my fevered skin.

"If we get you help, no," he said in a low voice, looking away from me, taking a step back.

He didn't have to say the other part of the answer. If I didn't get help, he might not have a choice. I forced myself to swallow even though my mouth was bone dry.

"So there's help?" I squeaked.

He gave me a small smile and a nod. "There's a woman in Waxahachie, another shifter, who's already volunteered to help."

"Help how?" The vision of some creepy blood cleansing rite in the middle of a field under a full moon jumped into my head. I need to stop watching my own movies.

"She was the prima of the Pride here in Dallas but moved away to be a Shala to anyone who needs it."

I shook my head. "There were too many new words in the sentence to make it intelligible."

He chuckled. "You've got an interesting way of putting things, Miss Jordan."

"It's a gift."

Chapter Three

Garrett put his car in park across the street from my house. It was an older model Bronco, something made before both of us were born. The back was full of various and sundry things covered with a canvas tarp that rattled as we drove and the leather on the seats was cracked. It didn't even have a tape player in it, just one of those radios with the sliding, light up dial. But he looked like he belonged in it somehow. And it was more than just the dark jeans and flannel shirt he was wearing.

He turned in the seat to face me but I stared at my house, like it was a foreign country. "I'll check in everyday."

I nodded like a child, looking down at my hands folded on top of what was left of my shirt and skirt from the attack, dried blood stiffening the satin. I'd decided after he made me scrambled eggs that morning that he wasn't going to kill me. He wasn't necessarily giving me the whole story, but he wasn't going to kill me.

I wasn't sure I wanted to leave his car, though, and walk into my house. It looked so different from across the street. Or maybe it was me who was different.

"Here," he said softly as he handed me something. "Just in case."

I slowly took the piece of paper from his hand. On it was a phone number scrawled in black ink.

"Stalkers have business cards? Is there a union too?" I smiled weakly.

Garrett chuckled. "Jokes. You must be feeling better."

I looked at the paper in my hand and flipped it over. Nothing special, just a piece of cardstock with his number on it. It was fitting somehow. No frills.

"What happens next?"

"I'll keep looking, keep asking to try to find answers. You just need to keep an eye out. Call me if something goes wrong."

"What hasn't gone wrong already?" I finally looked up at him. Backlit by the morning sun, he looked like he should be shooting a GAP commercial and not walking me through a traumatic aftermath. The golden highlights in his hair danced with the sunlight and his eyes were more of a hazel this morning than the dark chocolate from last night.

With a deep breath, I opened the door and stepped out into the morning. The heavy metal door slammed shut with its own weight, shattering the silence of my perfect street. Tentatively, I scanned the street to see if anyone was anywhere. Nope, just me. I took in a deep breath amazed that there was no pain and took my first step to cross the street.

"Hey," I heard as I stepped up onto the sidewalk in front of my house.

I turned around and had to shield my eyes from the rising sun.

"It can be done," he said as he stood by the driver's side, looking over the hood of his car. "Lots of people do it."

I didn't have a witty comeback, so I kinda waved and walked up the sidewalk to my house. It felt like the walk of shame back in college, like everyone was watching me as I turned my key in the door, like everyone knew what happened to the poor single girl in 2G.

After my shower, which was clean and filled with my scented soaps, I was able to see my back. As of 8:30 on Tuesday morning, the four wounds that caused nerve damage and severe blood loss were nothing more than four dark shadows across my left shoulder. The bite marks and other small scrapes on my hands and knees were nothing more than a bad memory and writing fodder.

I dressed in a pair of comfortable lounge pants with a white tank top and sipped coffee out of my favorite mug, a ceramic turtle mug I had gotten at some aquarium with swimming Ridgley's on it. Something about the blues and greens usually calmed me. But not today.

As I stared at the perky curtains in my kitchen, my brain was filled with thousands of questions, racing around so fast I felt dizzy. What just happened? Was he telling the truth? Am I meant for something more? Have I been lying dormant? Am I destined to attract insane men for the rest of my life or is it just a phase?

I needed to do something. I couldn't just sit here. Idol hands and everything.

So I did the one thing I knew I did well, something that

would take my mind off all this supernatural stuff. I went upstairs to my office, flipped on my computer, and started returning messages.

"Yes, Sera. I know I missed the conference call on Monday but I really was just deathly ill," I tried to explain without too many details as I paced around my office on my cordless. "But if you'd check your e-mail, you'd see I've already sent the changes you guys needed."

The woman on the other end of the phone was quiet for a moment as I heard clicking and typing.

"Oh, these are good," she said, enthralled with the edits made that morning. My brain kicked into overtime to not think about what had happened to me and focused on what happened to Jada and Smith in *Everville*.

"That's why you pay me the measly bucks," I joked as I plopped down in my oversized desk chair and put my feet up on the little space of desk not cluttered with scripts and contracts and half-written 'zine articles and all the other projects I had taken on just to have an office to sit in.

"We wouldn't have this problem if you would move back to LA, Violet."

I pinched the bridge of my nose under my backup pair of glasses. I hadn't had the guts to go around the back yet to try to find my usual pair. Frankly, I was thinking I might never put my trash out again. "We've been through this a thousand times, Sera. I don't want to live in LA. Have no desire to be within ten feet of *him*. And things are working fine with me here in Dallas."

"But Dallas is so . . . Midwest. I don't understand how you can stand all the cows and spurs."

"You obviously haven't seen a good pair of Wranglers," I countered.

Sera laughed. She had the best laugh, a breathy sort of high-pitched giggle. She was another writer for Cloak and Dagger, my production company, producers of such cinematic feats as the *Beast of Briar Lake*, *Fear the Dawn*, and *Snake Mountain*. Quality film making. She connected me to the life I had left behind (read: *ran away from*).

"I don't know why I like it here, but I do," I tried to explain to her again. "And when the writers are happy . . ."

"The scripts are juicy," Sera finished. "I know."

"Besides, I don't want to fall into the ocean. I mean, what could happen to me here besides hitting an armadillo on the way home?"

Sera laughed again, but I didn't. I scratched my shoulder against the back of my chair and sighed. Finally giving up on the chair, I got up to scratch my back against the door frame.

"Fine. You're off the hook this time but we really need you in LA for the summer schedule meeting. Drew's not happy with the video conference call things. He's convinced someone's going to hack the feed."

"Lovely Drew. How is he?"

"Good. For Drew. I'm sending you the next project he's green-lighted. Kyle tried to draw up a plot but it's terrible."

I tried to keep from clenching my jaw so tight at the mention of *his* name so I wouldn't break teeth. "What's the general pitch?"

"Some werewolf thing," Sera said casually.

I choked on the air itself as she went on. Damn Kyle. Even in my hours of despair, he could push my buttons from across the country. And since we were together for two years, he unfortunately always knew exactly which buttons to push to turn me into a quaking mass of patheticness.

"Something about a newly turned werewolf trying to figure out if he's a good guy or a bad guy. You know, the moving of dark armies, seductive psychics, and such. Right up your alley."

I stopped breathing and my skin began to burn. Flashes of everything in the past four days, stories from my childhood, moments from old horror movies raced around my head. My knees went weak, and I fell to the floor. The phone slipped from my hand and I could feel the rip of the claw down my shoulder like it was happening again, like I was still in the darkness of my alley alone.

Sera's voice echoed out through my moment of insanity. "Violet? Are you okay?"

My eyes snapped open and I was on the plush carpet of my office. I scrambled for the phone. "Fine," I forced out, after gasping in a few breaths. "I have to go but I'll have something to you by the end of the day."

"Great. We need something ASAP. Call you at 5:00 your time."

I turned off the phone and dropped the handset to my side. I sat limp on the floor, staring wide eyed at my lavender wall.

The phone rang at one o'clock. It was Jessa. Could tell by the ring. This was the time of day she called to tell which fancy man took her to which fancy restaurant. Which made my usual lunch of green tasteless things seem even more tasteless.

"What's wrong?" Jessa asked midsentence about her morning.

"Nothing. How are you?" I asked trying not to sound too distracted, as I pushed peanut butter around in the jar with a celery stick and balanced my cell on my shoulder.

"The guy from CyberTalk just took me to lunch. He's really excited about the Silver Ball idea for his launch."

"That's great."

"So I thought drinks on Friday to celebrate."

It was always drinks on Friday to celebrate. But some weeks, if it wasn't for her celebrating, I wouldn't get out of the house. In the instant the phone rang, I had decided not to tell Jessa about what happened. Not even a modified version where there wasn't a werewolf in the back alley. Rehashing it wasn't going to do me any good right now and Jessa would only freak out and demand that I move in with her. And that was *so* not a good idea.

"Sure," I said with a shrug that I was sure she could hear in my monotone voice.

"What's your problem?"

"I'm in weird mood."

"It's because all you do is write. You need to get out, rub some elbows. Meet someone new, an actual person."

She meant I needed to meet a man. Jessa's big deal was that I lived in my head and not in the real world. She complained I made the men in my head better than any man I could meet in real life. If only she knew what had brought a new man into my life. If only she knew why I was in a weird mood.

"Did I mention Ben started calling again?"

"Uh-oh," I said and I knew she could also hear my rolled eyes.

"Nope. Not this time. I was strong and told him exactly what you told me to say."

This was a change. I perked up and listened carefully, putting the peanut butter down.

"I told him I didn't need his run-around anymore, and if he wanted me back, he was going to have to prove he was worth getting back with."

"Really? Wow, go Jessa. What did he say?"

"He said he understood and he would spend every day proving he was the one. So right now I'm looking at two tickets to *Carmen* and two dozen roses."

I would die if a man gave me tickets to *Carmen*. They sold out before I even knew they were on sale, not that I had anyone to go with.

"So you have a date for Saturday?" I asked.

"Where in *The Rules* does it say I have to take him to the opera?"

I shook my head. "I think that was the point, Jessa. For him and you to go together."

"But I don't know if I want to date Ben again. It was fun and all, but I'm glad he ended it."

I wanted to pound my head against my countertop; this was the same girl who nearly drowned herself in tequila shots when he broke up with her. I had to spend a whole day on the floor of her bathroom with her to make sure she didn't do anything stupid, like call him.

"So what are you going to do with the tickets?"

"I dunno. You want them?"

I choked on my celery stick. "Serious?"

"Sure. Meet me for lunch tomorrow and they're yours."

I wanted to jump at the chance but something held me back, something in the lilt of her voice. "Meet you *where* for lunch?" I asked suspiciously.

"Cafe Brazil?"

Seemed innocent enough. Cafe Brazil was our place. I'd been there a million times and the coffee was amazing. But then again, I'd been into my garage alley a million times as well. Maybe I was being paranoid. Can't think of a single reason I might be paranoid about leaving my house for the rest of my life.

"And maybe afterwards we can get manicures," she added in quickly.

I looked down at my toes. It wasn't like anyone besides me was going to see them and I really didn't have the cash for the places that she liked to go. But it got me out of the house and that was the one thing I knew I had to do. Get out, keep going. Worked before. Why wouldn't it work now?

Chapter Four

Once I finally talked myself out of the house for the first time, lunch at Cafe Brazil was normal for a lunch with Jessa. She talked, I listened. I got the whole sordid story behind Ben's midnight visit on Sunday. Her narration was as good as the real thing. It took her twenty minutes to rehash the whole ordeal but at the end of it, then she slid the tickets to the opera across the table.

"Who are you going to take?" she asked with a devilish look, no doubt hoping for some gossip in my answer.

"Well, if you *really* don't want to go?" I offered one last time.

She made a sour face and shook her head. She unfolded her napkin and laid it daintily in her lap.

"I thought I'd ask Devin," I shrugged.

"That dweeb from your book club?"

I sighed, "He's a doctor. Doesn't that earn him *any* points with you?"

"He's a dweeb, plus I think he's gay," she whispered the last part before taking a bite of her chicken salad.

I'd argue, but he actually was gay; Devin and I had discussed on several occasions how hard it was to find a decent guy in Dallas. Many a night, we commiserated over a bottle of wine. Too bad, because the guy was pretty perfect: tall, fairly handsome, and English. Let's face it, the accent counted for a lot.

"He's the only person in my life right now who will appreciate these tickets," I said as I safely tucked them into my bag.

"Well, while you are at the opera, I'll be at a charity event downtown. Some international children's organization is hosting a fashion show. Lots of big wigs to rub elbows with."

And by rub elbows with, Jessa meant flirt. Her father consorted with presidents and kings and now, his daughter flirted with them. She had met the president, two princes, and every eligible bachelor on the eastern seaboard before she joined me halfway across the country. Now the princes had spurs.

"Sounds like a lot of fun," I said with fake enthusiasm.

"So I need to go shopping tonight to find something suitable."

"Of course."

Jessa never really *needed* to find something suitable to wear. The girl had more clothes in her house than St. Mark's Square had pigeons. And more mirrors than Versailles. The entire second floor of my townhouse would fit in her closet. She'd probably faint if she saw the two racks of clothes sustaining my wardrobe.

My phone began to vibrate but I didn't recognize the number. The local area code danced across my screen but I couldn't remember any appointments or interviews I had made. But I had been slightly distracted the past few days.

"Hold on a sec?" I asked Jessa and I turned away from her to answer the call. "Hello?"

"Violet? It's Garrett."

I nearly dropped the phone. "How did you get this number?" I asked in a harsh whisper.

"I find people. It's what I do."

"Right. Well, what do you want?" I asked as I looked around, half expecting him to be lurking behind a fichus somewhere. I always felt like someone was watching me, pointing fingers, and whispering about the poor little girl who got attacked by a dog because of her own drunken stupidity.

"Where are you?" he asked.

"I'm at lunch. I am allowed to eat, right?"

He was silent for a moment. "How ya doing?"

"Peachy."

"No unusual symptoms? Unusual hungers?" he probed.

"Sorry to disappoint."

"You sure?" he asked again.

I paused. "Come to think of it. I do have the strange sensation of someone sticking his nose way too deep into my business. Oh wait, that's you."

He sighed into the phone. "That's not a nice thing to say to the person who saved your life."

Right. Stalker or not, he was the reason I wasn't a midnight snack. "I'm fine. I'm eating and sleeping and all healed up."

"That's better," he said, his voice sounding pleased.

"Can I go now, officer?"

"Goodbye, Violet."

I snapped my phone closed, half hoping Jessa had been listening in. Might be nice to have someone to talk to about being attacked in the back alley of my house, about being kidnapped for three days.

But as I turned back to her and saw her innocent eyes watching me, I still knew that someone couldn't be her. I just couldn't burden her with this.

Besides, I was fine. I was out, and making plans. She hadn't asked why I hadn't answered my cell in three days and I simply wasn't ready to say the words out loud yet.

"So Friday at the Ghostbar? Meet at my place?" she asked as she took another stab at her salad.

"Sounds great."

Devin, white coat and all, walked around the main desk of his office to give me a small kiss on the cheek. He smiled down at me and I heard a few of the mothers in the waiting room sigh. He was a catch at 6'3" with chestnut brown hair (always perfectly combed) and shiny brown shoes.

"Sorry to bother you at work, but it's important," I started as he guided me around the desk with his arm around my waist and back into his office.

"No worries. What can I do for you?" he smiled.

It had struck me after my lunch with Jessa that Devin was a doctor, wore a white coat and a stethoscope and everything. He could examine me to see if anything was wrong, if anything about me had changed. Answer some of these questions still racing around in their vicious game of duck-duck-goose.

"I need a physical," I said bluntly.

"I'm a pediatrician, Violet," he said confused.

"So, you're still a doctor. I just need a quick listen to my heart, take my temperature, just a quick once-over. There's opera tickets in it for you," I flashed the tickets from inside my purse, like a guy with hot watches in his coat.

"No," he said wide-eyed. "You got tickets for *Carmen*!" he said reaching for them.

I snatched my purse away from his fingers and smiled. "In a roundabout way, yeah and I'm inviting you."

He just looked at me with a raised eyebrow but I knew he couldn't resist free tickets to the opera. "So a physical? Is it for work?"

"No, I'm just a hypochondriac and I need proof I'm not going to wither up and die before I'm 30."

Devin laughed and I chuckled with him. It was a good lie. Something a normal girl in my situation might worry about: late twenties and no prospects. Plus I love to make Devin laugh. When he smiled, the whole room lit up and you seemed to forget all your problems because he had enough joy for two and would gladly share.

"I've about ten minutes between appointments. Shouldn't be a problem."

Devin guided me into a little exam room with little pink elephants on the walls and pink paper over the examination table. He patted the table and I sat down on the crinkly tissue. He went to wash his hands as I dangled my feet off the edge of the table.

"Have you been having any symptoms?" he asked as he rolled the stool over to me as I unbuttoned the top two buttons on my shirt.

"Not really."

Devin put the stethoscope in his ears and made sure to

warm the metal medallion before putting it on my chest. That's why I loved Devin, so considerate.

He closed his eyes as he listened for a moment. "That's a strong ticker you've got there. Like an athlete's."

"That's weird," I said as he moved the stethoscope to my back and he listened to my lungs. I flinched as he ran the medallion over the shadowy marks. I don't know if the tingle they still had to the touch was physical or mental. "Because the only time I run is to catch the ice cream man."

Devin laughed as he put the scope back around his neck.

"So are you really here for a checkup?" he asked as he felt my neck with his warm hands.

"Actually, I just wanted a man to touch me before I die."

Devin stopped what he was doing to recover from laughter as he stood and gestured for me to lay back on the pink paper.

"I thought the same thing until last week."

"What happened last week?" I asked as he thumped around on my stomach.

"Peter."

"Peter?" I leaned up on my elbows to look at him with a raise eyebrow.

"I met someone," he said little boy excitement in his voice. "His name is Peter and he's a lawyer."

"Wow, congrats."

"We've only been out a couple of times, but Violet, the man is perfect."

Uh-oh. The P word again. It was haunting me. I lay back down and stared at the Care Bear poster pinned up on the ceiling. Devin thumped around a few more times on my abdomen.

"I hope everything works out," I said, trying to mask the

sadness in my voice. Devin had been my fellow lonely hopeless romantic. Who was I supposed to commiserate with now?

Devin offered a hand and pulled me to a sitting position. With the triangular hammer, he began hitting around on my knees.

"Any news on the man front for you?" he asked as he made my legs flinch and kick.

"Nothing worth noting."

"Don't worry, luv. Someday someone will come and rescue you."

I had to force myself not to laugh so he could finish the exam. "And that's why I love you, Devin. Always the optimist."

"Glad I could be of service," he said, slightly confused at my response. "Well, I think you're fine. Seem to be in good health, but there is one concern."

"What?" I asked, growing very concerned very fast.

"You've got a fever," he said rolling over to get the thermometer.

He quickly stuck the plastic-wrapped stick under my tongue. We both waited for the gray probe to beep. When he removed it from under my tongue, the furrow in his brow only got deeper.

"What?" I asked trying to get the plastic taste out of my mouth.

"100. Perfect Score," he said showing me the read out.

I read it and my eye brows jumped. "Go me."

"Mild grade fevers can come with allergies, general tiredness, but you say you haven't had any symptoms?" he asked as he put everything back in its place.

"Not yet." I shrugged. It wasn't a lie.

"It's right here, Miss Jordan." Stan's voice cracked as he pointed to the lowest shelf in the aisle. "Here's the supernatural section."

"It's a bit small," I said disappointed in the public library's book selection.

"Oh, well," he said licking his lips and wringing his hands. "If you search the catalog and you find a book, we can always do an interlibrary loan to get anything you want, Miss Jordan."

I smiled down at the teenage kid. "Thanks, Stan. I'll start here."

He scurried away and left me with a shelf of books.

This portion of the library was just the place to do a little old-fashioned research about werewolves. Not for me, of course. For the script that jerk of an ex-boyfriend couldn't construct to save his flat ass.

I'd spent half the night locked up in my office looking on the Internet. It had some wicked stuff about werewolves, scary wicked stuff about demon worship, and satanic possession, and then there was the entire Furries community, which was slightly scarier than anything previously mentioned.

I settled in at a table in the 133 section with the whole shelf before me, opened to pages with snarling wolves and detailed diagrams about the metaphysical transformation of a human body into a wolf. Muscle by muscle. This was insane. Great for a movie though.

I started to jot down notes and then realized that, though I appreciated the tactical sensation of flipping pages, books had the same problem as the Internet only with a bibliography. Everyone contradicted everyone else. Some said the shift could be controlled. Some said it couldn't. Some said the person was still a person but in animal form. Some said the blood lust of the wolf took over and there was no person, just beast. Some ancient cultures said that it was a gift from the Earth Spirits to be that close with nature. Some said it was a curse from the heavens to descend into madness for three nights a month.

There was one notable exception in which a group of monks claimed that God had given them the strength of the wolf to fight his adversaries on Earth.

The only thing they did have in common was the moon. Whether it was what forced the change or just gave strength to the beast, the full moon was a part of it.

And the next full moon was only days away.

I couldn't help but look at the pictures and my heart beat a little faster.

No. The fever was just fall allergies and the ten pounds I'd lost was the severe lack of food in my fridge. The healing, well, I had started taking multivitamins recently. And I wasn't allergic to silver. Was wearing silver studs right now.

Take that, Stalker boy.

I slammed the book shut and leapt up in triumph. As I turned to go get a few more books from the section, I ran straight into the broad chest of Charles Garrett.

Stumbling back a step, I landed on the tabletop.

Garrett waited until I was settled on top of the *Encyclopedia Grimoire*. "Miss Jordan."

Mouth agape, I stared up at him and my entire body grew hot. The shadowy marks down my shoulder began to ache. "What are you doing here?"

Garrett looked down at the stacks of books on the table.

He pushed a few of them around and looked at the covers and smiled. "Working. You?"

Embarrassed, I pulled all the books into a stack and snatched one out of his hand. "I'm doing research for a project that I'm working on."

"Okay."

"This stuff is crazy." I rested my hand on top of the pile.

"Not from where I stand."

"No one knows anything about anything."

"If you'd just ask . . ."

"Listen, if I wanted stories, I'd make them up myself."

Garrett shrugged. "Then maybe I shouldn't give you this?" He pulled a small, soft covered book out of his jacket pocket and handed it to me. The cover just read *For Those Who Wander* in silver letters.

"What is this? You're Gideon Press too?"

"A brief history of our kind."

"What do you mean, *our kind*?" I snapped as I flipped the book over, expecting something more mystical looking.

"Wanderers, if you will. Read the book. It's got the answers you're looking for. Including what's in your blood that proves you're going to shift."

He turned to go and made it a few steps.

I couldn't just let him walk off, my curiosity completely unsatiated. "Why can I wear silver?"

Garrett paused.

"Why am I running a fever?"

Slowly, he turned and looked at me.

"I want answers. And I want them really soon."

"The Shala can give you real answers."

"I want proof."

He shrugged. "I can't give you proof. You'll just have to trust me."

I scowled. "About as far as I can throw you."

Something like a smile played on his lips as he slowly backed away. "See you later Violet Jordan."

Chapter Five

I flipped through my pathetic excuse for a wardrobe on Friday and took a chance on a black dress I had plumped out of three months earlier. I had gotten it on sale at one of the boutiques Jessa dragged me into and managed to wear it once before I started putting on my winter weight.

Wearing the appropriate underwear, I slid the dress over my head and down my torso. With contortions usually not possible, I zipped up the back of the dress without protest from the zipper. I stared at myself in the half mirror in the bathroom.

It fit. Perfectly. I spun around in the mirror in disbelief. But my celebration stopped when I saw the four dark marks down my shoulders. They were shadows of their former selves but they were there and visible to anyone who got close enough to really look.

Which meant I was fine. Standing next to Jessa, no one was going to really look at the Sasquatch by her side.

Jessa looked like something out of *Vogue* as she flipped her perfectly straight black hair over her shoulder. She checked her

Chanel lip gloss one more time in the mirror in her foyer before turning towards me. "Ready?"

"Sure," I shrugged.

"You okay?" she asked as she locked her front door and we started to the elevator.

"Fine. Work has just been rough this week."

"Typing your little fingers to the bone?" she said wiggling her fingers in front of her, mocking my daily activities.

"Yeah. And they want me to collaborate on this online thing they are cooking up."

"Uh-huh," Jessa said as she watched her reflection in the sliding metallic doors.

"So it's like double the work."

"That sucks," she said taking a deep breath and fogging up the place on the elevator doors that had caught her attention.

I stopped there. She had gotten that glazed look she sometimes got, which meant that she wasn't listening.

The other girls were already at the elevators that would take us up to the 33rd floor club, all looking straight out of the magazines with their little skirts and halter tops and perfect tans. And here I was, a head taller than everyone else, paler than everyone else, in a knee-length black dress with my hair in a ponytail because the curls just were not cooperating.

"You look really good, Violet."

The compliment caught me off guard and it took a second for me to respond. "Thanks, Carrie. I really like your new highlights."

"Really?" she squeaked. "I wasn't sure, it being so late in

the year, but I just saw this picture and I knew that I had to have them, she said spinning her finger around one of her curly locks.

"Good choice."

We filed out of the elevator of the Ghostbar and followed Jessa to the bar. Eyes followed her as she walked, swaying her hips to the rhythm of the music echoing through the blue-lit room.

And here is where the fun starts. Usually, within the first twenty minutes of entering anything that might be construed as a meat market, someone offers to buy Jessa a drink. Some nights, she can go the whole time without paying for a single cocktail. Sometimes, she can even swing getting drinks for the whole table. The guy comes over, maybe with a few friends that go for the shorter, cute girls, and then Jessa somehow gets them to go away to let another guy or guys come in and do the same thing.

It really is an art form. Something about the ebbing and flowing of testosterone really needs to be studied in a lab somewhere. There are strategic places and timing and hand movements and I have seen all of them so many times that maybe I should lead the study since I'm usually just watching anyway.

With the first set of guys, I was the odd woman out and decided to take my Baileys to the terrace to look out at the skyline. Dallas has one of the prettiest skylines I've ever seen. Maybe that's why I stayed here. Maybe it was the great weather. Maybe it was the fact there was a Starbucks on every corner. As I stood there looking out at the city below, I was content for the moment. Not feeling like a girl with a destiny, not feeling like a victim. Just feeling like Violet.

Jessa joined me.

"Is something wrong?" she asked, crossing her arms over her chest and looking up at me with a raised eyebrow.

"No, I'm fine. Just enjoying the view."

"You hate heights."

"I don't hate heights," I laughed as I looked down at the thirty-three floor drop below me.

"You sat on the floor of the Ferris wheel last year at the state fair."

I remembered. Terrified in the little cage, I was convinced it would snap off the huge wheel and we would all go tumbling down. But now, I could only shrug. "Doesn't bother me now."

Jessa looked out at the night with a huge sigh. "It is a gorgeous skyline, isn't it?"

"Sure is," I sighed as I sipped the last of my drink. Baileys wasn't my usual drink but something about the milky texture soothed me, and after what happened last week, I wouldn't be drinking anything heavier for a very, very long time.

"Do you ever regret it?" I asked.

"What?"

"Moving here from New York, starting your life over again."

"You mean to babysit you through a broken heart?" Jessa shrugged. "Never."

"Excuse me," a voice came from the interior of the bar.

Both of us turned to see a waitress in a white halter dress with a drink in her hand.

"There is a gentleman at the bar who sends his best wishes."

Jessa smiled and reached for the tumbler but the waitress pulled the drink away from her.

"It's for the tall brunette," the waitress nodded, handing the drink over to me.

Jessa looked like she had been smacked, but it was my cheeks that flushed and I was very glad I was on a darkened balcony.

I handed her my empty glass and took the new Baileys. No one had ever bought me a drink before. I stared down at the small crystal tumbler in my hand and couldn't help but smile.

"Which one is he?" I asked the waitress, excitement running up and down my arms like cool water.

She pointed discreetly at a man wearing a dark leather coat. I didn't need to squint to see who it was through the smoky bar. My excitement failed, but my manners didn't.

I lifted my glass to Mr. Garrett and thanked the waitress before I turned back to the window where a deep furrow had formed between Jessa's usually perfect brows.

"Are you okay?" I asked.

"Stalker boy just bought you a drink."

I pursed my lips. I had really been hoping that she hadn't seen him too. "Guess he's got a thing for Chewbacca now."

And Jessa did the one thing that reminded me why we were friends. She let out a Wookie trill that would have made George Lucas swoon.

I snorted with laughter as we moseyed our way back to the table, where I was sure another group of men would be waiting.

When a new bunch of boys came over, numbers uneven again, I snuck away to go stand at the terrace bar next to Garrett's hunched-over figure as he watched the plasma screen scream with psychedelic colors above the bartender's head.

"Didn't think I'd answer my phone?" I asked as I slid up next to him.

He looked over at me and nodded. He still had to lean in a little so I could hear him over the music. "Can't a guy just go to a bar and have a drink?"

"But of all the bars in all the world . . ." I quoted with a very bad Bogart impression.

He chuckled. I thought he was being generous.

As I watched him, I knew I should be feeling fear or confusion or something but I felt normal, good even. And it wasn't the Baileys talking. I took the seat next to him and crossed my legs, leaning on the bar.

"Read the book?" he asked.

"Cover to cover."

"Did it answer your question about silver and the fever?"

"Only heirloom silver is deadly and shapeshifters, the fancy word for werewolves, maintain a higher temperature around the full moon."

He chuckled. "Bet you were an A student."

"When I wasn't driving my teacher insane with questions. How have you been?" I asked.

He jerked back with a sharply raised eyebrow and sat up straighter.

"What?" I laughed at his reaction. "I'm not allowed to ask? Something in the stalker's union code? Conversations must be unidirectional and monosyllabic?"

"No," he said with a small smile as he settled back into his hunched position, elbows on the bar.

"Well then, how are you?"

"I'm okay."

"Just okay. What does it take, Mr. Garrett? I mean you *are* in the premier bar in downtown Dallas and you have a leggy girl by your side," I explained dramatically.

"That I had to lure with Baileys."

"Hey, whatever works," I shrugged with a smile.

He looked back at the TV for a moment with a grin, then back at the leggy brunette next to him. "Chaz," he said.

"What?" I had to lean in a little more to hear him.

"Call me Chaz."

"What about Chuck?"

"Never."

"Well, Chaz," I said. Just saying it made me want to giggle a little. I slid off the leather stool and smoothed down my skirt. "Since you can see I'm doing fine, I will take my leave."

"See you tomorrow, Violet Jordan."

"Joy."

"I'm sorry," I said over my glass of red wine.

"Why?" Devin asked taking a sip of his own drink.

We were pressed into a corner by the bar in Bass Hall. Everyone was paired off for the opening night and dressed in their finest, including me in a new dress I picked up two sizes smaller than I had worn a week ago. And a pashmina to cover my back. The marks still tingled when something brushed them.

"Because I should have offered you and Peter the tickets."

Devin smiled like a little boy when I mentioned Peter and looked down at his glass of wine.

"So the two of you must be hitting it off?"

Diaries of an Urban Panther

Devin only nodded. We had both agreed talking too much about something like this would surely jinx it. Yes or no questions were permitted, if nothing else, for the other to live vicariously through.

"Am I being selfish, keeping you to myself on a Saturday night?"

"I wouldn't want to be anywhere else."

I leaned in and rested my head on Devin's shoulder for a moment. He always smelled so clean and crisp. Not like the last man that I had been this close to. My mind drifted quickly to the dark man in the dark jacket and I clutched my purse to make sure my cell phone was still there.

The lights flickered in the old theatre and we paraded into the amazing box seats that Ben had scored for Jessa.

Half-way through the first act, Devin offered me his opera glasses but I shook my head. Then a little part of me chilled in fear, making my skin goose bump.

I didn't need the small binoculars because I could see everything in crystal clear detail. Startled, I sat up in my chair and looked around the dark theatre. I could see everything. In the dark. I could see the man in the front row who was already dozing off. I could see the young couple in the back already misty eyed. I could see the fake mole on the face of the prima donna.

Devin noticed my distraction.

"Are you okay?" he whispered, leaning in.

"Fine," I said back a little too quickly.

He reached over to touch my hand and jerked his back quickly. "You're hot."

"You look nice too," I said, hoping the joke would calm the extreme arch in his eyebrow.

"No, you've still got a fever."

"It's just the wine," I said as I turned back to the beautiful opera going on before us.

"I told you to go to a doctor," he persisted, drawing some dirty looks from those around us.

"I'm fine," I said back to him harshly. "Watch the opera."

He set back roughly in his seat, scowling at me with his arms crossed.

My hands were shaking and I hoped to God he didn't notice. I wasn't fine. As I thought about it, I hadn't worn my glasses in a week even though I was doing marathon sessions at my computer. As I looked around at all the extra details of the people I could see in the dark, I had the sudden realization it all might be real. People don't just grow out of their glasses; something had to have changed me to suddenly have perfect vision.

And that's when I panicked. A full-blown panic attack in the middle of one of the most beautiful operas ever written.

Besides the new vision and the slimmed down figure, I was on the umpteenth floor of a hotel last night looking down, not freaking out. This was real. I was changing, turning into something that ate dogs in back alleyways and attacked innocent bystanders.

Jumping out of my seat, I made a mad dash for the stairs. I needed fresh air. Needed to breathe. I clutched at my chest and flew past the ushers and the ticket takers and threw open the double doors, stumbling out into the night.

Leaning against the white stone front of the performance hall, I gulped down the cool air and tried to catch up with the thoughts racing around in my head. The copper taste of fear filled my mouth and ran like ice water through my veins. I could have sworn my shoulder began to burn against the cool stone. This was real.

And then I smelled it, smelled him. You don't forget the smell of a man, at least I don't. Sometimes a guy will walk past wearing the same cologne as my ex and I'm thrown back to all those unhappy days in LA.

So I knew this smell and looked up and down the darkened streets of downtown Fort Worth to find Chaz. I closed my eyes and took in a calmer breath and knew it was him, it was warm and musky and athletic and very close by.

I reached into my purse and scrolled through my received numbers to find his.

He answered on the first ring.

"Where are you?" I snapped, the panic replaced by paranoia.

I saw the slightest movement out of the corner of my eye. He was a block down, standing just out of the light of a street lamp. He stayed in the shadows but I could see his face from the glow of his cell phone.

"So is this what I'm going to be cursed with, a perverse sense of smell?"

"What?"

"I can smell you."

"I must be a block away," he said confused.

"Then maybe you need to take a shower."

"Are you okay?" But the question didn't come from the phone. It came from over my shoulder. Devin's hand slid around my waist, as if protecting me from unseen threat. He looked up and down the street with a viciously raised eye brow.

I watched as Chaz snapped his phone closed and slid back into the shadows down the street.

I turned towards Devin. "I'm sorry."

"You've been doing a lot of apologizing this evening," he said looking down at me with concerned brown eyes.

"I'm sorry."

"Do you want me to take you home?"

I shook my head and allowed myself to be guided back into the warm interior of the theatre. Even though the opera was beautiful and might have elicited a tear, I still couldn't shake the chill up my spine that this was real, and Chaz had followed me across a county to make sure that I was safe.

My stalker didn't call on Sunday, which was understandable. I wouldn't have called me back. I would have let me rot and gone on to my next holy mission or whatever he was on.

I was sitting in my favorite coffee shop Monday afternoon, reading the latest movie magazine without my glasses in the streaming sun of the front window. My feet were curled up under me as I sipped the cinnamon latté. It had taken me all night and a very hot shower the next morning to get warm again after the chill of last night's panic attack. But I got up, convinced myself I wasn't going to die today, a new daily ritual, and forced myself out of the house.

Suddenly, I was overcome with his scent again. I looked around and watched as he sauntered across the café and sat in the seat opposite of me. He was in a long-sleeved green buttoned-down shirt, the black leather jacket nowhere in sight. He looked almost naked without it.

I didn't exactly know what to say. He sat across the coffee table from me, very relaxed, looking very unsuspicious. Very "nothing to see here people, just a man talking to a girl. Move along."

"Was that your boyfriend?" he said, looking down at the table between us, strewn with the magazines I'd flipped through that morning.

"I thought you'd been watching me for the past two months."

He shrugged. "I've seen you have dinner with him, go to the opera."

He looked up at me with wide puppy dog eyes, searching for an answer.

I shook my head. "Devin's a good friend."

Something flashed across those warm eyes. "How are you doing?" he asked as if he had to, but didn't want to.

"Fine," I knew I'd said it too quickly the moment after it left my mouth.

He looked me over, top to toes, with a hard eye. "Where are your glasses?"

"Seems I don't need them anymore," I shrugged casually looking away from him, down at the magazine in my lap.

"Oh really. Any other recent advantages then?"

"Nope."

"Violet, look at me."

Like a guilty child, I moved my eyes slowly up to his face, keeping my chin low.

"What else?"

I sighed and shifted in my seat. "I'm not afraid of heights anymore," I said, thinking it was inconsequential and he couldn't read anything dark into it.

But he leaned forward with that ever increasing furrow between his brows. His hands clasped out in front of him, he asked, "What else?"

"I ran down the street to catch the ice cream man and didn't get winded."

"How far?"

"A hundred yards."

Chaz grunted and looked away. I didn't like it when he did that, it made me nervous, made me very aware of the four dark shadows still down my left shoulder.

He looked up from his hands, a determined jut to his soap star jaw. You have to see the Shala. She's the only one who can help you."

I just laughed. "Right."

"She is, Violet. She can guide you through this. We should go tonight; the full moon is less than a week away."

I stood and he mirrored my new position. "I can't just leave, Chaz. Some of us have responsibilities to actual people. Have commitments. Did you know that I have to work three jobs in order to pay my mortgage?"

"And keeping you safe isn't a full time job?" he snapped back. The muscles clenched in his jaw and my skin grew a hotter as my temper flared.

"Made it through the first twenty-seven years just fine."

Storming off, I threw my magazines back on the rack as I walked for the door. He caught my arm and spun me around harshly so we were practically nose to nose. I was awash in that scent that had haunted my dreams.

"You don't understand. You are changing, Violet," he said

in a low tone, almost a growl. "And if you don't get it under control, they will not hesitate to control it."

I tore my arm away from him and glared furiously until I fully understood what he was saying: If I couldn't get whatever was inside me, running through my blood, under control, he would shoot me, like he shot that thing in the alley.

I ran; the fight or flight response kicking in like it had never done before. My hand was on the door handle of my Miata when I saw a familiar sports car sitting across the street. The driver wasn't visible.

Chaz ran into my frozen figure. "What?"

His eyes followed mine to the car without the driver.

"I've seen it before. He's one of yours, right?"

Chaz grunted. "They don't pay us enough to have BMWs."

He moved around the front of my car, his eyes never moving from the car across the street. "Go home," he ordered.

Chaz was gone in the blink of an eye. Nothing figurative about it. Just gone, like The Flash minus the red tights. His scent lingered around me as I got into my car and quickly turned on the ignition. I heard the squealing of tires and the sports car was gone too.

I'd never driven that fast before. After what Chaz said, after seeing that other car following me around, there was no way that I was going home.

My car sort of steered itself to the only safe place that I could think of.

Chapter Six

Jessa opened the door with the phone attached to her ear. "I'll call you back," she said slowly as she dropped her cell phone from her cheek and the blood ran out of her face.

"Is it that bad?" I forced a smile.

Jessa stepped aside and I dragged my feet as I entered her perfect apartment.

"What's going on? You look terrible."

"Don't I always?"

Jessa ushered me into her flawless flat. She was the only person I knew who had actually hired a team of decorators to have her apartment match a picture in a magazine. And it did. Something out of the pages of *Single and Fabulous*. I ordered almost everything online from IKEA and Craigslist.

Jessa suggested a steak and cheesecake night. It was a bit of a tradition. Break up with boyfriend: steak and cheesecake. Have another script rejected before it even hit Drew's desk: steak and cheesecake. Lose your fiancé to another woman: steak and cheesecake.

I ordered a little fillet mignon with a side of potatoes and

Jessa ordered the thirty-five-dollar steak she would undoubtedly only eat half of. But that was Jessa.

"So what's eating you?" she asked as the waiter finally left, after offering Jessa every sort of appetizer and drink and even his phone number.

"Work's getting crazy and I needed to get out."

"You don't look too great, a little peaked."

Jessa knew the word *peaked*? "I'm fine."

I mean, doesn't every girl have a stalker who threatens her life when she refuses to buy into his little delirium? Isn't that part of the *Single and Fabulous* life style?

I looked down at my little steak and my mouth watered. It had been eight hours since toast. I was starving. I cut into my steak and took a huge bite. I closed my eyes and chewed on the juicy meat. It tasted wonderful, perfect, and as I swallowed, my mind flooded with the sensation of ripping the meat off of the bone.

My eyes snapped open and my pulse raced. What the hell was that? As I looked back down at my plate, all I could see was what my little steak used to be and how much better it would be if it was still connected to bone, still had blood racing through it as I sunk in my huge teeth and ripped the meat off it.

I jumped up out of my chair, much to the surprise of my dinner mate, stumbled away from the gorgeous meal, and ran to the bathroom.

Full visions of running, no, chasing something through the tall grass, filled my head. The wind in my ears, the need to pounce on the small furry creature, to sink large white teeth into the hot meat.

I threw up everything I had eaten that day and probably

a few days before. Stale toast with apricot jam was worse the second time around.

Jessa tentatively walked into the bathroom as I was splashing my face with water. I still had the vision of blood just behind my eyelids as I leaned over the white marble sink.

"You okay?" she asked with the concern written over every inch of her face.

"I'll be fine," I said through clenched teeth. Having to lie to another person almost made me sick again.

"Was it the steak?"

"Something like that." I patted my face dry and forced a smile. "I think I'll stick to the potatoes."

Jessa walked me out, her arm around my waist, and I was glad to see she had already ordered to-go boxes, and the waitstaff had taken away most of the meat at the table already.

"Is it the flu?"

"Must be something I caught along the way."

I'm pretty sure it won't surprise anyone that I don't exercise. So you can imagine my anger when the first, and decidedly only, time I decide to take a jog around my neighborhood, I get hunted down by a pack of big burly black dogs who want to play chase.

It had been an odd sensation. In the middle of an outline for a new script, I suddenly wanted to be outside. And more than that, I wanted to run. At first, I thought it was an instinctual retreat from the roadblock I had come across in this project Drew was trying to get off the ground. But it wasn't. My muscles wanted to move: my legs, not just my fingertips.

Standing outside, I tucked my spare key under a terra cotta pot without a flower and faked my way through the few stretches I remembered from the three scarring years of high school gym class before the school took pity on me and waived that class for an extra journalism course.

It was broad daylight. I was safe. Nothing happens in broad daylight. I started off down the sidewalk at a sedate jog. I figured I'd start out slow, maybe trick myself into actually exercising a block or two. It was nothing fancy, but immediately I felt better. Less restless. Dare we say invigorated? Can't say it was the weirdest moment in the past two weeks but it was up there in the top four.

Three blocks down, I was definitely running; I could hear the pulsing beat in my heart, a steady thrum, thrum, thrum, in my ears. My muscles stretched and pulled as I turned a corner. With each breath I took, I felt loosened, focused. I could feel oxygen flooding my body, coaxing my muscles to relax and move, encouraging the continuing patter of my feet on pavement.

For a brief moment, everything felt aligned and I felt alive. Maybe commercials constantly toting exercise and endorphin highs weren't total bunk after all.

And then I got the distinct smell of wet dog. When you hate dogs, you know the smell.

I stopped. Where was the smell coming from? As I glanced over my shoulder, five big black dogs stood on the sidewalk behind me. Crap.

Thanks to my recent encounter with a huge black animal, I froze. I could stay really still and hope a squirrel ran across the road to attract their attention, or I could make a run for it.

I looked down at my tennis shoes. My left one was untied. Great. I was toast all over again.

The leader, or at least the one in the front, barked a bark that shattered the silence of the street around us and started towards me.

My instincts took over. I turned swiftly and ran. All about the flight response.

Stride after stride, I didn't think. I just ran. Taking in deep breaths and pumping my arms. Even over the blood racing through my ears, I could hear the howling and snarling behind me.

They were keeping pace with me. I couldn't outrun a pack of dogs. What was I thinking?

I took a hard left down the main street into the neighborhood. There had to be people here somewhere. *God Dammit, Chaz, the one time I need you*, I cursed.

Heavy panting crept behind me and teeth ripped into my jersey pants. My heel caught the beast in jaw and I heard the familiar pop of teeth on teeth and little whimper. Take that, Fido.

The other four didn't break formation. They took turns snapping at the edge of my shirt, the side of my pants. I swatted them away the best I could.

I had the distinct feeling that they were enjoying this. Their barks were not of terror but of pure enjoyment.

I pushed the thoughts from my head. They were dogs, stupid, flea-ridden mongrels who could probably smell the peanut butter on my hands from my lunch of ants on a log.

Suddenly, a little girl rode into my path on her little pink bike with white streamers. At this speed, I couldn't stop.

Diaries of an Urban Panther

Instinct took hold. I leapt from the sidewalk and flew over the girl, size ten out before me, the other tucked up underneath me like an Olympic hurdler.

I didn't feel myself hit the pavement. I barely felt the impact of the concrete beneath my feet. I was moving. And it felt good.

The dog's heavy breathing faded away and all I felt was the wind in my face and smell of the outside air. It called to me. Called me to go faster. Called me to let go and run faster.

The greens of the grass blurred past, the cars on the street were streaks of reds and blues in my visions. I was the wind.

And then I was almost a pancake.

And then I saved a little boy's life.

And then I was Violet, Action girl, with a broken ankle.

Chapter Seven

My leg bounced a mile a minute. I bit my nails. And it wasn't the caffeine. I was only on my second mug that morning. I knew this feeling. I'd had it two days ago when I tried that exercise thing for the first time. Look how great that turned out.

When I finally got around to patching up my ankle with the little first aid kit I kept in my kitchen, there was a scratch above my ankle and it was bruised and swollen. By the time I got ibuprofen in my system, I was walking up the stairs, and by the time I went to bed, it was just another "Dear Diary" entry.

So for today's little craving, I tried running up and down my stairs. I tried popping in a yoga video I'd bought for some failed New Year's resolution, but it wasn't what I wanted. What I needed. This whole exercising thing was not previously on my list of needs; remember: coffee, food, shelter. No exercising.

Looking at the discarded tennis shoe by my front door, I sighed. "Fine," I snapped at the poor shoe. "But I'm going prepared this time."

After slipping on my Chuck Taylors, the only other things in my closet that resembled athletic wear, I shoved my keys, the can of mace, and a bottle of water in a small messenger bag. My hand trembled like I was coming off something. I shook it off and put the bag over my head.

Feeling more like Rambo than I cared to admit, I threw open the door and took in a deep breath of fresh air. There was a flutter in my chest, like, well, like nothing else that I'd ever felt before. It stirred just under my breastbone for a second and then was gone.

Again, I feigned through some stretches on the front porch and twirled my ankle around. There was no pain, no twinges. Good as new.

And then I started to run.

Heading back to the house, I slowed down when I saw the dark Bronco parked across from my house. He was watching me. Just sitting there, watching me in his side view mirror as he sipped out of a 7-Eleven cup.

I didn't want to deal with him right now. Right now I wanted a shower and a hot cup of coffee. And at some point I was going to have to e-mail Sera with the mad changes that I had been making to that werewolf script and e-mail the three articles I had cranked out that morning to the online magazine. Something about running, then subsequently mending a broken ankle, really cleared up the cobwebs in my head.

Chaz didn't give me a choice. He got out and leaned against the side of his car. Arms over his chest, he looked like an Abercrombie commercial.

Guess I had to talk to him. I took my time crossing the street, looking both ways as I tiptoed across. But I'm not paranoid about anything, right?

"I figured you would have fixed a pot of coffee before you finally moseyed out here."

"I can go back," I said hitching my thumb over my shoulder.

"Only if you bring some out here for me."

I smiled softly and crossed my arms over my chest to mirror him. My sweaty hair gave me chills, or was it the way he was looking down at me?

"How was your run?"

"Great," I shrugged. "Really hitting my stride."

I leaned against his car and faced my house. We were only inches apart, both staring at the little townhouse with the little red door and the empty flower pot. I could feel warmth radiating from his rigid bicep and forced myself to slip further down the side of his car.

"You have to see the Shala," he said softly, tenderly. "She can help with everything."

I just shook my head. "I just don't understand, Chaz. Why me?"

"I don't know," he answered honestly. "Couldn't tell you why any of us were chosen for this. It just the way it's written."

I looked up at him. It was the first time I'd heard an ounce of doubt in his voice.

"What was your deal again?" I asked. I vaguely remembered something about something but it was buried under all my own emotional baggage.

"Guardian. Heal fast, move fast. And I find people like a human compass."

"That doesn't sound like something you catch in a back alley."

He shook his head. "Born with it, just like my dad."

"So this stalker union is a family gig. That must be nice."

He took in a deep breath and his face hardened for a moment. His hands gripped tighter on his biceps as he studied his boots. It was regret and it didn't look good on those model features.

My chest hurt to see those kinds of memories flash under his hazel eyes. There was no family, at least not anymore. I had to do something that relieved the pain on his face and the pain in my heart. Screw the mystical stuff. In my world, laughter is always the best medicine.

"Well, I'd rather be able to find people than have the urge to rip apart a bunny."

The smallest curl of amusement played on his lips. "A bunny?"

"Full on rabbit action during lunch the other day," I assured.

He chuckled. Job done, I pushed away from his car to face him.

"I have so many questions," I said putting my hands on my hips.

"I gave you a book."

Ah, the book. I shook my head. "It wasn't exactly an *Idiot's Guide* to becoming a shapeshifter. Had some pretty wild stories in it. But nothing about the how, the why?"

"At least you're learning the language. And Iris, the shala, can explain our history better than I can."

I looked down my quiet little street in my quiet little suburb and sighed. Here was the big step. "I have a conference call until three p.m. tomorrow. Maybe after that?"

Chaz looked up from his boots. He didn't look overjoyed

but something else was there, something deeper than just relief. I didn't know what it was, but I was pretty sure that's what made my skin prickle.

"Why the sudden change of heart?"

I licked my lips. I had been saving this story. It was my story. But this was the man who had saved my life. And after what I had just seen, he could use a happy story right now. "I went running the other day and I saved a little boy from getting hit by a car."

"What?" he turned to face me, leaning against his car, looking even broader as his arm tightened across his chest.

"More accurately, I super-speeded across the street, picked the boy up, saving him from being hit by that sports car that's been following me, and broke my ankle."

Chaz's chin dropped and his lips parted. He looked down at my ankle and then back up at me. "But . . ."

"Yeah, something like that." I waited for the shock to subside as I looked at my house.

Chaz snorted and turned back to face the house. "Same car?"

I nodded. "I still couldn't see the driver though."

He took in a deep breath. "The plates aren't registered to a Texas address."

"So what does that mean?"

"It means that I don't know who's after you," he said before he turned towards me sharply with a finger in my face. "And that means you need to get someplace safe and fast."

It was my turn to furrow as I pushed his finger from my face. "Didn't I just say I'd go see your shala or whatever? Don't you think I know that something major is happening? I'm not an idiot, Mr. Garrett."

He backed away a little and the furrow softened.

"I know something's different now. I can feel it." I put my hand over where I'd felt the flutter earlier and looked at the cement next to us. "It feels like something stirring."

"It probably is."

My eyes snapped to his eyes and I glared, hard.

"What?" he smiled. "I'm being serious. And Iris . . ."

"Yeah, I know 'can guide me through all this.' You're like a broken record sometimes. I'll call you after 5 tomorrow. You can take me to your leader, or whatever."

Chaz nodded and got into his car. From the driver's seat, he looked up at me one last time and drove off, leaving me wondering what in the world I had just done.

Chapter Eight

I sat down in the soft hay of Iris's barn and couldn't believe this might actually happen.

Chaz knelt down next to me and I tried to manage a smile, but when your heart is knocking around in your stomach like a shoe in the dryer, it's hard even to fake a smile. He had followed me in from Dallas and sat through the big spiel Iris had given me. It was already nightfall by the time we'd gotten to her house and the moon was already out and proud by the time she finished her speech.

To be honest, I heard only about half of it. Between the pounding heart, the sweating palms, and Chaz's bouncing knee gently brushing mine under her kitchen table, I couldn't concentrate. All I remembered from the guru's little pep talk was that this was going to happen and Chaz had been wrong about something.

Iris followed us into the little cage that was about the size of my bathroom and offered me the sleeping draft in a small brown coffee mug. She had explained, very matter-of-factly, that I was not the first who had spent the night in the cage. She knew what she was doing and I needed to just drink it and stop with the questions.

"Just drink it and you'll sleep and not remember a thing," she said as if she had said it a thousand times before. "Sometimes the first time hurts because you're fighting it. You can't fight if you're asleep."

I nodded and took the old mug from the woman. She was a walking oxymoron. On the outside, she was this small white-haired old lady with wrinkles and a bun, but when she opened her mouth, she was bossy and just a little sassy. Most of all, she was wise; she reeked with it. I knew the second we shook hands that if all this was real, this was where I needed to be. Oh yeah, did I mention that she said she was a lioness, as in African Safari Lioness?

She shuffled out of the cage in her camel-colored SAS shoes and walked around the outside of the enclosure, leaving Chaz and I in the little cage.

"What if I was right all along and you really are just two complete nut cases and are planning on sacrificing me to some moon god?" I asked with an arched eyebrow.

"Just think of the material for all that writing you do," he joked.

"Ha, jokes. Just what I need."

Chaz rested his hands on his thighs. "Got another one for you."

"What?"

"When people ask you what you did for Halloween, you can say you went complete wild."

I laughed hard once. "Take you the entire trip to think that one up?"

He smiled up at me and watched steadily. It made my stomach flip over on itself.

"Are you going to stay?" I asked in a high, tight voice, suddenly nervous.

He nodded. "I'll be here when you wake up."

I looked down at the liquid in the little cup. It looked like milky tea.

"Bottoms up?" I said with a nervous smile.

Chaz watched as I drank the whole thing. When I was finished, he took the cup and set it aside by the entrance.

Fire ran down into my stomach and then warm little tendrils curled through my whole body. Like tequila, but chalky.

"Wow, stuff's quick." I lay down in the soft hay, my head already fuzzy and my body so warm I wouldn't need a blanket to sleep.

Chaz lay down next to me, mirroring my position. He reached out and brushed a curl from my eyes and tweaked my chin.

"Will you still be my stalker if it turns out I'm, like, a warthog or something?" I asked.

He chuckled and squeezed my hand that now seemed so far away from my body as my eyelids grew heavier.

"Yeah. I'll even build you a trough."

"Funny," I whispered.

It became hard not to close my eyes. I took one last look at Chaz and closed my eyes, still seeing his face behind my lids, the glint of his golden hair in the fading light.

"Hey," I whispered as I snuggled into the warm hay.

"What?" I heard him ask from far away.

"Do you think they have a Starbucks in Waxahachie?"

I fell asleep to his laughter as it danced around my brain and into my wild dreams.

Once, the lioness who ruled the pride had three daughters. They were always together and promised to rule the pride together one day. They planned to marry brothers and live in one big den together until their daughters took the pride from them. They were stronger and faster than the other cubs. They were fierce in the hunt. They helped their mother protect the pride that would one day be theirs.

Until one day, a hyena cub wandered wounded into the pack. The youngest of the sisters wanted to care for him until he was healed but their mother said "no," he wasn't one of their kind and he needed to go to his own pack. There was only so much food. The lioness turned her back on the outsider and ordered that no one help him: He was no good.

But the youngest took pity on the little cub and hid him in a cave. She brought him food and straw to sleep on. It took a while, but eventually the hyena healed.

Her two older sisters found out about the hyena cub. They scolded her and threatened to tell their mother, but the youngest sister cried and cried and told her older sisters that he didn't have a family to go to and that they could be his family.

At the tears of their younger sister, the two older sisters gave in and promised to keep her secret. The hyena cub grew strong and fast and was good company for the youngest lioness.

One night, the sisters could not find their little sibling. They looked in the fields and in the den and in the cave where the hyena slept. Nothing.

Then, a scream echoed through the fields and they knew it was their little sister. They ran as fast as the wind to get to her.

She was in the bottom of a pit, dug deeper than they could jump. As they were looking down into the pit, both were pushed in from behind. As the older sisters tumbled down, they heard a terrible laugh echo through the fields.

The three sisters looked up to see the hyena cub surrounded by others of his pack.

They growled up at the dogs who only laughed harder. With a yelp to the sky, the hyena pack took off in the direction of the lion's territory.

"What happened to them?"

"What do you think happened to them?" my mother said, as she brushed hair from my sleepy eyes.

I pursed my lips and thought for a moment. "They would jump on each other's back to get out and then rip down trees with their claws to help the other one out and they would go and beat up that stupid hyena for lying to them."

My mother leaned forward and kissed my forehead. "I wish that were true, little one."

I looked around when I woke up, half-blinded by the morning sun streaming through a high widow. As I rubbed the sleep from my eyes, I could see fingers and then toes and my ghastly pale skin that looked ill in the golden light. I was really naked, not even an embarrassing thong left this time.

As I pushed myself up, every muscle in my body screamed awake but the pain was gone in an instant, leaving a slight vibrating soreness in its wake. My head spun and I smacked my lips.

"Chaz left to preserve whatever modesty the two of you have," Iris said as I heard the clanking of the lock on the enclosure. She tossed a robe into the hay and turned her head.

I shook the rest of the fog from my head and slid the pink terry around me. "What happened to my clothes?"

"Destroyed," she pointed with her crooked hand.

I followed the finger and found the pile of jeans and T-shirt strewn throughout the hay, torn to shreds. "Wow, looks like I had fun last night."

"Not really," the old woman said. "Chaz stayed here as long as he could manage. Got a little picture of it on his phone thing."

There was a twinge in my stomach as I thought about him seeing me like that, whatever that turned out to be. No matter what he said, he had to look at me differently now.

We both had proof now. I wasn't just a quirky writer anymore. I wasn't just little Violet Jordan. The thought hit me in the lower stomach like a cheap punch. I leaned over, hands on knees and took in a deep breath. Crap. This is real.

"Why you dawdling?" Iris asked from the entrance to the cage.

I followed Iris out of the cage, picking off pieces of straw poking me in uncomfortable places, and then out into the morning. The sun felt miraculous. Energy danced across my exposed skin and I felt like I had never been in sunlight before. The crisp air brought the scent of the fields around her property to me and the faint scent of cows. That was not as miraculous as the feeling of the sun and definitely not what I wanted to smell first thing in the morning.

"It comes after the first change. You'll begin to notice more benefits of the shift," Iris narrated.

"Like what?" I stretched my neck and shoulders as we walked to the house and I tried to calm the hay-head that I was bound to have.

"Your senses will sharpen, your reflexes will quicken, lots of things."

I followed her into the house, holding the screen door. I could already tell Iris was not going to just burst forth with the details. This was going to be great. Like pulling teeth to get any real information.

Chaz sat at the kitchen table spinning a cup of coffee on the checkered tablecloth. His OU T-shirt had seen better days as it stretched across his hunched shoulders. He jumped up when we entered the room.

"How are you feeling?" he questioned, looking past Iris and directly at me.

"Like I slept on hay."

"I've got something for you."

He moved quickly to the microwave and clicked the "on" button. I looked over and saw the telltale white cup twirling around on the glass plate.

"Is that Starbucks?" I asked astounded.

He nodded and when the buzzer went off, he grabbed the cup and handed it over to me, not bothering with a real mug because he knew I didn't care.

I sipped the hot liquid greedily. It was perfect. A cinnamon dulce latte with two sugars and a sprinkle of cocoa. All the fuzziness from the chalky tequila was gone with the caffeinated warmth between my hands. I sat down at the little kitchen table, relaxed and centered.

"Okay, I've got my coffee. You can break the bad news to me."

Iris looked up at Chaz and then back at me. There was a silence between them that chilled me, like I hadn't just been in sunshine, like I wasn't holding hot coffee.

"What? Do I have a snout, fangs, what?"

Chaz pulled out the chair next to me and sat down. He reached across the table, taking my hand from around my coffee. I sat up straighter in my chair. My skin sizzled as his warm hands curled around my fingers; his soft hands squeezed mine. To be honest, the last person who did that was just about to tell me my parents died.

"Chaz?" My mouth went a little dry and my heart began to race.

There was a fear in his eyes that I hadn't seen there before. He licked his lips. "Panther."

I flinched in surprise. "Are you serious?" was my first reaction.

"Pretty serious."

"Why the face?"

Chaz was silent as he caressed my knuckles and he looked at me as if lost. I turned to Iris, needing answers, not looks of pity. I hated looks of pity.

"What's wrong?" I demanded, more power in my voice than I intended

Iris spoke slowly; it wasn't just the southern drawl. "So you know that the gift is passed on through a bite. There are only three families in the states that could pass on panther. Kye's line, Lura's line, and Haverty's. As far as I know, Kye has not bred any children and Lura's pard is in the northwest. But Haverty, we can't be sure of."

"So the thing that attacked me was from Haverty's line. What's wrong with that?" I asked, fighting to understand the hesitation hanging in the air.

Iris looked to Chaz to actually say it, and sighed when he said nothing. "Haverty is evil, like the damn lap cat to the leader of the Order," Iris said as she crossed her arms tightly over her light blue plaid housedress. "He cares about power and little else. Him and his son run Dallas and they have killed everyone to question their authority here."

I had read about the power struggle in the book Chaz had given me. The Order are the bad guys and the Cause are the good guys. The Order wanted to take over the world and subjugate humans and the Cause wanted everyone to live peacefully together. Seemed pretty black and white. "And?"

Iris snorted. "And when he finds out that you have been changed, he'll come after you and force you to choose."

"Choose what?"

"Him as your Primo or Death."

I gulped.

"And if he accepts you as an heir, well . . ." Iris trailed off, her eyes fading off into the distance.

Chaz finally entered the conversation, "The power corrupts and everyone in his line goes evil."

I pulled my hand away from his and put it back around the hot coffee in my hand, fighting off a clammy chill. It was the tone more than anything that scared me. Like a doctor telling you about terminal cancer. Like your aunt sitting you down to tell you that your parents wouldn't be coming home. Ever.

I looked down at the caramel-colored liquid, and then back up at Chaz. The heat had traveled up my arms and into my cheeks. "So you're telling me I die or I go evil? That wasn't the gallant effort I was expecting from a white hat."

I stood up and strode out of the kitchen, fighting tears. I wasn't a tearful person; ask Jessa, who still couldn't figure out why I wasn't bawling at the end of *Steel Magnolias*. Maybe I was evil.

I stormed up the stairs and went to my room. I began dressing and ran a brush through my hair, having to intermittently wipe moisture from my cheeks. I had gotten one shoe on before Chaz burst into my room.

"Where do you think you're going?"

"I'm going home."

"No."

"Are you going to kidnap me again?"

Chaz widened his stance to more fully block my door and crossed his arms over his chest. "You can't leave."

"Why not? Apparently I'm going to go evil anyway, so why don't we make this an epic showdown on the streets of downtown Dallas? Something to brag about to your white hat frat brothers? Or would you rather just take me out back and pull an *Old Yeller*?"

"Violet," he protested.

"Chaz," I mocked as I reached for my other shoe and started for the door.

He grabbed for my arm and I pushed him with all my might. Which was, unfortunately, more than I remembered having yesterday. Chaz went flying across the room, cracking the dry wall before he sunk to the baseboard.

I didn't care. I wasn't into this predestined shit and if I had gotten myself into this, I could get myself out. And if I couldn't get out, I could out run it. There was still one more coast I hadn't lived on yet and I'm sure Jessa would want to go home.

Iris was in the doorway as I scurried down the stairs. I stared her down and she moved out of the way pretty fast for an old girl.

I got to the car and was reaching for the door when Chaz caught my arm again, his fingers wrapped tightly around my forearm. He spun me around and slammed me against my car.

"Let me go," I demanded.

"I can't."

"Instructions from your mystical guru to chain the cat?"

Chaz jerked back a little like I had snapped at him. "You're mean when you're mad."

"Apparently I have a built-in dark side."

Chaz clenched his jaw and grabbed both of my arms, hard. And as much as I struggled, I couldn't break free. Kinda made me wonder if he hadn't tapped into another part of his supernatural something or other. He pressed me to the car with his hips and held me tight.

"We can't risk you turning against us. You don't understand the power, Violet. It's dark and . . ." His words trailed off.

I looked at him confused, angry; the heat in my face so blindingly hot it evaporated the tears from my cheeks.

"Have I ever done anything by the book, Chaz?" I said, fighting my quivering chin.

"No," he admitted, the furrow in his brow lessening.

"Then why are you so sure I'll do this by the book? Why are you so ready to give up on me?"

"I'm not," he sighed. "I'm cautious. There's just me and Iris left. We can't afford another attack."

"And I look the attacking type?"

"Threw me around a little."

I sighed. Crap. One day with a little power and I was already a bully. I dropped my shoulders in defeat. "I'm not weak, Chaz."

"I know. No one has taken to this like you."

He stepped back, releasing me from my car. Slowly, he released his grip on my arms. I looked down to see handprints on my skin. By the throbbing, bruises would form soon but be gone sooner.

"But you have to stay. You have to be able to control it before the Powers will leave you alone and hide yourself so he can't find you."

I clenched my jaw. "I'm already pretty tired of these Powers."

He cracked a small smile. "Wait until you work for them."

I shook my head vigorously. "No, sir. I already have a few jobs, providing that I don't keeping vanishing on them."

"Say you'll stay?"

I looked out at the fields around us. Looked like a pretty safe place, and they hadn't sacrificed me to a moon god yet. The soft rolling hills of the farm were peaceful and I hadn't taken a vacation in a long time. I could probably write a few articles while I was here and email them to the office, providing there was wifi in the boonies.

"Say you'll stay?" he repeated.

I just sighed and leaned against the car. Chaz took my chin and lifted my eyes to meet his.

"Going to bring me Starbucks every morning?" I asked with a raised eyebrow.

He dropped his hand to rest on his waist. "If that will keep you here."

As I looked out at the uncultured land, I felt it. Felt something with my chest, felt something I couldn't explain away stirring there. And it was more than just the memory of the long line of his body pressed against mine. The panther was fierce and fiery and it burned as I looked at the wide open space.

I sighed. "Let me make a couple of phone calls and I should be able to get a solid week off."

Chaz just nodded. "And I'll be here the whole time, if that's what you want."

I nodded. "So one week?"

"One week."

I pushed up off the car and stepped around him. "Better get back inside. I still have half a cup of coffee left and I think I need to apologize to Iris."

"Why?" he asked as he followed me back towards the house.

"I think I growled at her."

Chaz's laughter echoed across the fields as we went back into the farmhouse.

Chapter Nine

That evening, Iris and I were sitting on her back porch, sipping sweet tea, when Chaz came in from his grocery trip. Iris had not so subtly asked him to get out so us girls could have the afternoon to ourselves. He offered to pick up groceries and a few other things from the store.

"Wasn't sure if you wanted me to put them away," speaking to Iris, his hands jammed in his pockets.

"Nah, I'll get 'em, hon. You two, sit. Relax before tonight."

"What's happening tonight?" he asked, as the woman slowly pushed herself out of her chair and hobbled back towards the house.

"We're hunting tonight," I filled in with mock excitement, and then took a long sip of ice tea.

Chaz's gaze bounced from the old woman to me and then back to her. He didn't believe me.

"Have some tea before you hurt yourself," Iris said as she entered the house.

Chaz, still confused, sat in the vacated chair and poured himself a glass.

"Hunting?" he finally asked after he drank half the glass in one gulp.

"Working on the three primal urges," I said still uncomfortable with the idea as I stared at the drink in my lap. Something about intentionally provoking a metaphysical panther just didn't seem like a good idea, like poking a bear in a zoo wasn't a good idea.

His brow furrowed as he watched me. It was a look that I was getting used to.

"And hunting is one of them?"

"Yep."

"Gonna tell me what the others are?"

"Nope."

He sighed and leaned back in the chair as we both stared off at the broad landscape.

"What else did you do today?"

"Worked on brushing."

"Right," he nodded. "What's brushing?"

I looked up at him fighting a small smile. "You, the great hunter of paranormal and you don't know what brushing is?"

"I know a little about a lot of things. Just not that."

I put my drink down on the table and began my explanation, to the best of my abilities. "Brushing is something shapeshifters do to determine dominance. Since we can't tell how big or powerful the other person is in human form, the animal can all be picked up by other shapeshifters when you brush them."

"And can normal people feel it?"

"Humans can't, but we can." God, I really was buying into all this, wasn't I?

"So I could feel if you brushed me?"

"Yes," I nodded, feeling slightly ridiculous saying the words out loud. The entire day had been like that: finding out terms for things that I had written about in scripts. I'd learned that werewolves are just one breed of shapeshifter, heirloom silver is the only way to quickly kill a shapeshifter, and I was now part of a lineage of beings that predated humans.

"So do it," he said sitting up and putting his tea down as well.

"What?"

"Brush me."

"Why?"

He was silent for a moment, like he didn't have an answer, but I could see the second something clever come into his head. There was a little twinkle in his golden green eyes.

"Brush me, so if I ever meet another shapeshifter like you, I'll know what I'm dealing with."

I could only laugh. "I don't think you'll ever meet anyone else like me."

"Probably not," he said leaning back in his chair with a half smile.

I sighed. It was a simple enough request actually and I did need the practice. But part of me wanted him to still see me as a girl, as a nice nerdy girl. Then again, he had already seen me furry and he was still driving into town to get me Starbucks, so what was one more little display of abnormal?

Taking in a deep breath, I found my furry center. It was already easier to feel her in there after the lessons that day, to feel the other me curled up like a Siamese in the sun just under my breastbone. I surrounded myself with the thought of her, the energy prickling down my skin and making the hair on my arms rise. Then, I pushed it gently outwards with an exhaled breath.

Iris said since I was new to this whole thing, my effect would be minimal but when I opened my eyes, Chaz was sitting up straight and wide eyed, like I had physically hit him. His knuckles were white on the arms on the chair and his mouth was slightly open before he snapped it shut.

"Was that it?" he inquired.

I nodded.

He had the most peculiar look on his face as he looked out at the field.

"What is it?" I asked, slightly unnerved by his reaction.

"It felt," and his eyes dropped to the wooden slats of the porch between us to find the words. "It felt smooth, like silk, and smelled like flowers."

I nodded. That's what Iris had said it was like: magnolias. Irony abounds in all things. She had smelled of dusty books and cashmere and had nearly knocked me out of my chair, she was so powerful. She felt ancient, or what I thought what ancient would feel like, and her power hung around in the air long after she had brushed me. Me, I was still a gentle breeze that faded quickly.

"That was incredible," he breathed.

"Incredible? Really?" I asked as I scrunched my nose.

Chaz nodded and sat back in his chair and drank down the rest of his tea.

I sat there mildly pleased with myself as the two of us quietly watched the sun go down.

Iris came out and told us that dinner was ready. The two of us went inside like two little children, washed our hands, and helped her set the table.

It was a quiet dinner to say the least. I was nervous about tonight. I just had this horrible thought of waking up naked in the park like in the movies. Running naked through the town square of Waxahachie was not the way I wanted to spend my Monday morning.

I was so lost in thought that when Chaz's cell phone went off, I jumped, almost knocking my tea down. But I caught it just in time. Got to love those new cat-like reflexes.

"Calm down there," Iris scolded. "Nothing to be nervous about."

"I'm not nervous," I snapped as I watched him check his phone and frown deeply before he got up.

"Excuse me," Chaz said quickly exiting the room.

"You are as jumpy as a long tailed cat," Iris said, trying not to crack a smile.

"Ha. Seems fitting," I said back as I took a bite of the stew she had been preparing intermittently all day. It was cooking like I hadn't had in a long while—from scratch. It was the kind of thing you would make for a family after a long day apart—something to share with loved ones.

I stared down at the bowl sadly and sighed. I had the urge to call Jessa but I knew she probably had a date tonight and was in the midst of her date routine. I checked my watch. She was probably somewhere between putting her hair in rollers and putting on her makeup.

Chaz's entrance into the room brought me out of my melancholia for a moment. "I've got to go."

Iris just nodded solemnly.

"What?" I snapped.

He just grabbed his jacket from the back of his chair and walked out.

Startled, I looked up at Iris with questions.

She just shook her head, as if she knew exactly what I was thinking, and gestured that I should ask him about the thoughts that were flying through my head.

I caught him as he opened his car door.

"Where are you going?" I demanded, sounding angrier than I thought I was.

"They need me somewhere else," was all he responded as he tossed his jacket in the passenger seat.

"But what about me?" I asked, stifling the urge to stomp my foot. "You said you'd stay."

"The world doesn't revolve around you, Violet," he shouted back, quite unexpectedly to both of us.

It was like he had smacked me, a cold hard smack that chilled me down to my toes before my face turned to fire. I wasn't sure I deserved that. I turned quickly and started back to the house.

"Violet," he called out after me.

The tears burned in my eyes but I refused to let them fall. I turned back around to face him in the moonlight that flooded the front of the house.

I didn't have anything to say to him. So I just balled up everything in my chest right now and I threw it at him, the fear and the nervousness and this sudden betrayal that had worked its way in there as well and I flung it at him so hard that he stumbled back against his car.

Feeling less angry but not better, I went into the house and sat on the steps up on the second floor.

It was a few minutes before I heard his car start up and saw the headlights illuminate the living room as he drove off down the dirt road.

Iris shuffled into the foyer and looked down at me.

"Don't look at me in that tone of voice," I grumbled with a sniff.

Iris threw her hands up, complete with a white flag napkin from the dinner table. "You need to finish your dinner," she finally said.

I sighed and pushed myself up off the stairs.

"I'll give you one thing," Iris said as we sat back down at the table and I looked across at Chaz's empty spot with a clenched jaw.

"What?" I asked trying to be civil. She hadn't done anything wrong.

"I don't ever want to be on the receiving end of your fury. Ever."

"I'm sorry. I'm not usually like this. I'm usually the calm collected one, but lately . . ." I just shook my head and picked up my spoon.

"I know," Iris said softly. "Just eat your dinner and you'll feel better tomorrow."

We stood outside in the front yard bathed in the moon from high above. The chirp of the crickets and the soft swoosh of the wind through the tall grasses in the surrounding fields calmed me but the stirring in my chest was not abated.

"You just need to run, get it out of your system so when you're in the city, you won't have the urge."

"So are we actually going to be hunting?" I asked as my hands twisted at my waist, playing with the belt on the pink fuzzy robe she had loaned me to save my clothes from being shredded again.

"No, your cat just needs a safe place to stretch its legs, your legs."

I nodded. We had gone through the pronoun game this afternoon. It was not my cat, it was me. My other legs needed to be stretched out, needed to be set free to run and streak through the night air.

"But if you do grab a little snack, please don't leave it on my doormat," Iris joked.

And I laughed. It was what I needed right now to calm the jitters in my chest.

"And tomorrow we'll work on shielding."

"Going a little medieval tomorrow, are we?"

Iris pursed her lips. "Shielding is the opposite of brushing. It's putting up borders to protect yourself"

"Why?"

"People are going to begin to notice you walking into a room. And not the kind of noticing you want. Imagine if I just walked around like that, power out all willy-nilly, knocking people out of chairs all the time. So we'll work on it tomorrow, on how to put up borders to keep yourself hidden. Should protect you until we know what's happening and keep Haverty from finding you."

"Wait," I asked. "What about Chaz? Does he have borders up?"

Iris flashed quick smile. "Honey, that boy was born with his borders cemented in place. Never seen such impenetrable stuff. Known him for over ten years and I couldn't tell you what his insides are like."

She turned back to the fields, closing her eyes for a moment, the wind softly swishing the white wisps around her face. I was still looking at her when she opened her eyes.

"I'll work with you tomorrow," she repeated. "Otherwise, I have a feeling you could get yourself into trouble."

"Me? Trouble?"

Iris just raised an eyebrow.

"I might be able to stay out of trouble if I understood how it works," I said. The feline stretched in my chest, rolled around. The high moon called to her and she wanted to be free. "Still dealing with the whole magic is real thing."

Iris turned her golden eyes to me. She'd told me that she rarely shifted anymore, that the change was too hard on her old body, but she could still feel the pull of the moon. Tonight, you could see the pull of the moon in her eyes. "You a religious girl?"

"Used to be."

Iris looked long out across her land. "Well, I'm not an expert at the metaphysical stuff. I'm better at showing you how it works than telling you why is works. Our people sprung forth from the Earth and when they did, they kept the magic of their creation with them, practiced it and worshiped it. You'll feel it when you're older, how much potential everything has. The difference between us and regular folks is that we can tap into that potential and use it."

"This is going to sound contrite, but what else is out there?"

"Didn't Chaz give you the book?"

"Werewolves and demons and vampires, oh my."

"If you can think it, it was real at some point." Iris slowly looked over at me and raised her silver eyebrow above her sharp blue eyes. "You're stalling, aren't you?"

My chin hit my chest. "Maybe."

Iris smiled and put her hand on my arm. "It's time."

I took in a deep breath and slowly moved through the steps. We'd practiced all afternoon. Invoking the shift, rather than having it take me like it had the night before. Freaked me the hell out when I first felt it, what Iris told me was where my panther power slept. I think there may have been some unnecessary jumping and pacing. And a lot of deep breaths so I wouldn't pass out.

But tonight, I looked into Iris's eyes and everything told me that I could do this. A truth hummed through me: I was made to do this.

I looked out into the night and took the first of many calming breaths, hoping this wasn't anything like poking a bear in a zoo.

I closed my eyes. I could smell the night, the wind, the trees, the fields, smell Iris's rosy perfume. The crickets chirped on the warm October night. Nature was alive and well under the full moon.

I listened to my heart. Full of stories and wonder and still so very fragile.

I listened to my other heart. The one with power. The silent center hummed and throbbed and I could feel the potential waiting to be molded.

I felt the animal in the center. Fur and muscle and speed and veracity.

As I gently pulled at the panther in my center, it pounced, digging its claws into the golden center and tearing through my chest. White hot energy poured over me and I struggled against the inky blackness of its fur.

There was a flash of golden that pushed me into the abyss. As I fell, the panther took control.

Chapter Ten

I woke up bathed in sunlight and warm. I stretched and rolled my shoulders and wiggled my toes against the flannel sheets of my bed.

Bed? I thought quickly as I sat up. I was in the guest bed. How in the hell had Iris managed that? I grabbed the pink robe now thrown over the rocking chair and headed downstairs where I could make out the distinct smell of bacon.

"Good morning," Iris greeted as she poured a cup of coffee and handed it to me in the doorway. I was beginning to think that she might like me.

"Was everything okay last night?" I asked as I sat down at the little table.

It was a blurred dream. I was usually so good at remembering my dreams. Turned most of them into movies, actually. But this was different, this was hazy and just out of reach in the back corner of my memory.

"Were there any rabbits involved? I had this thing with rabbits a few weeks ago and it was awful."

Iris laughed. Iris's was three hardy laughs and then she hid her giggles underneath, like it was something that surprised her and she reeled back within herself. She shook her head as she cooked the eggs and flipped pancakes. "No. How do you feel?"

I thought for a moment. "Good. Really good."

Iris turned around with a big smile and a full plate of breakfast food. "Wonderful. Now eat up, we have a full day ahead of us."

I looked down at the plate and had a sickening thought. I wasn't hungry.

Later that morning, Iris and I were in the front yard and to an onlooker, probably looked like we were having one hell of an argument, standing roughly ten feet apart and both glaring in the morning sun. After loosening up with some brushing, Iris was trying to teach me shielding. *Trying* being the operative term.

"Brush me," Iris directed.

When I did, I didn't feel anything. No cashmere, no power, no nothing. Like she was human. Like she really was the innocent old lady she appeared to be.

"That's a shield. Think of it as a container for your energy. It keeps you in and others out."

"Why?" I asked.

"Without a shield, another wanderer could read your mind or take your energy or see your future or do a number of things, but shields can also protect other people from you."

"Like keep me from throwing boys against cars."

"Something like that. Try it."

"How?"

"Remember the examples that I gave you; it can be a brick wall, a steel door, a cape, whatever makes you feel safe."

Safe? Could anything make me feel safe anymore? "My townhouse. I feel safe in my house."

"Visualize your house around your heart then. Make it safe."

A house around my heart? My life was quickly going from the Syfy channel to the Lifetime Network.

I closed my eyes and relaxed. It was becoming easier and easier to find the gooey magical center. The warmth beat in time with my heart. I saw the golden ball in the darkness behind my eyelids and slowly visualized walls going up around it. But a birdsong distracted me.

"Concentrate."

I tried harder. Find the marshmallow center and put a roof on the top. But it wouldn't stay up.

An hour of this and my brain started to hurt. Iris went to sit on the porch but she made me stay out in the yard. "Keep concentrating," she would say at regular intervals.

"This isn't working, Iris." I was whining. It was true. Maybe my ADD was kicking in but it just wasn't working.

"Fine," Iris said as she slapped the arms of the rocking chair on the porch and got up. As she made her way down the steps of her house, I could not have predicted what she would do.

Iris ran at me like a line backer. Stunned, my feet froze on the ground and I stood there like a tree watching this little old lady lean forward and run at me head first.

But a force hit me before she did and it knocked me off my feet like a focused tunnel of wind. I flew backwards, but by the time I hit the ground it was gone. It knocked the wind out of me and I laid there for a moment trying to figure out what just happened.

Iris stood there her hands on her hips, looking innocent as always. "Check you center."

As I got up and brushed the grass off my jeans, I glared at Iris. "That was mean."

"Check your center."

I took in a deep breath and closed my eyes. The house was built. My two-story townhouse with the red door and the empty terra cotta pot on the porch. It was my house and the safest place in the world. I felt different too, the sun wasn't as warm. I couldn't smell the winds. It was like I was normal again.

"What was that?"

"Like you threw Chaz, powerful shifters can project their animal. Your instincts put up the shield to protect you when your brain was too busy to do so."

As I relaxed, the house faded away and the sun was warm again, the winds were fragrant and Iris was pissed. I tried to contain my giggles. "Can we do that again?"

"How are you doing?" Iris asked as she joined me on the porch that evening.

I squeezed my shoulder and rolled it to stretch out the muscles. "Still stiff."

"I really am sorry about that," Iris said, handing me a cup of hot tea before she sat in her rocker next to me. "I've been meaning to ask Chaz to check the floorboards in there."

I was quickly discovering this was the only thing to do in Waxahachie. Sit and rock, and I didn't mind it one bit. All the bustling around in Dallas made one's brain rush around at full speed; out here where the weather was the only concern, my brain had slowed to a nice intelligible pace, had a lot of time to think during the day, just *be* for a change.

I took the steaming liquid. "I should have been a little more careful."

Once I finally got the gist of shielding, we spent the afternoon working on drawing on my cat skills while in human form. Iris said that in her heyday, she could take down a grown man with one swoop of her paw. So she figured that I could probably jump, because that's what panthers can do. I wasn't even going for a real height as I found the cat's balance within me. Just jumping around, first from step to step, and then from the ground to the top of my car. Then from the first floor in the barn around and on top of things and off of things, like a pinball.

And it was really going well. I was like a gold medal gymnast. Until I landed on an old board that gave way underneath me and I fell from the second floor hay loft to the dirt on the first floor. Didn't land on my feet exactly, but I didn't break anything, just busted up my shoulder, which we quickly relocated and now I was fine. Well, maybe wary of going all Tarzan again.

After that little disaster, we just did housework, washed and folded laundry, and did dishes until our fingers got all pruny. And now we were on the porch, drinking chamomile tea as the night settled into its quiet.

"Who took you through this process?" I asked as we both leaned back and rocked.

"My sisters and I were all born to it. We all learned it together," Iris answered slowly.

I knew that voice though, had heard that tone in my own voice before, back when people cared enough to ask about the girl on her own for all major holidays. "Your sisters are gone then?"

Iris nodded.

"And you don't have any children?"

Iris shook her head. "I dedicated my life to the Cause, never had the time to find a mate, settle down. It always seemed there was just one more person to help, one more that needed training."

I didn't know whether to say I'm sorry or I appreciate your sacrifice. Instead, I just stared down at my tea and confessed.

"I'm all alone too," I finally said looking up. "Only child. Parents died in a car crash twelve years ago."

It was the first time I had told anyone here. I didn't even tell Jessa, but Jessa never asked. Maybe that's what I liked about her. She didn't ask many questions, didn't delve too deeply into the well that was Violet.

"You're not alone anymore," Iris said in the crisp darkness. "Now you know about the Cause, there will always be someone there for you. And you've got Chaz."

I had to laugh. "He'll be glad to be rid of me when I'm all trained up."

"Then I wonder why he called when you were in the shower this morning to make sure everything went okay last night."

I perked up a little. "Really?"

"He said that he would try to be back by Thursday."

"Where is he?"

Iris shook her head. "Didn't say. He's not much for details."

Wasn't that true. But he called. Which either meant that he didn't hate me, or he still felt bound to check up on me.

Thursday. I was headed back to Dallas on Friday morning. I kinda hoped we didn't miss each other.

"You need to be gentle with Chaz," she said as she rocked, watching the sun go down. "You're not the only person who's lost everyone."

"I'm learning that." I twisted in my seat to look at her. This was a story I wanted to hear.

"Well, he probably told you he was born to this life," she said as she rocked more vigorously, as if the story was drawn out that way. And if she was telling his, she wasn't telling hers. "His father was in the Cause, met his mother that way."

"He mentioned it."

Iris looked over at me and I felt the soft breeze of her power past me. She sighed and looked back out at the horizon. "His daddy was taken from him about six years ago. It was an epic battle, rang out through the . . . what do you call it?"

"White hat broadband?" I offered.

"Seth had figured out a way to take Haverty's power from him to release his hold on the pack here in Dallas."

"Haverty killed his father?"

My blood froze in my veins. The tea in my hands stopped steaming. I put the mug down before I dropped the stone cold contents on the porch. That's why he couldn't say anything the other morning; that's why he protested so violently when I wanted to leave. He couldn't risk another crazed panther on the streets.

Iris's knotted hands gripped her tea mug so hard her knuckles went white. "And Seth almost had him, but that damn son of his mucked everything up. Seth died before Chaz could get to him."

"Did Chaz try to go after him? After Haverty?"

"Hell, yes. Nearly got himself killed. Did some right stupid stuff before he gave up. I was expecting him to just drop you off and hightail it out of here. You being a Haverty."

My throat closed up, my mouth went dry, but my eyes began to water. Knowing that I was the one thing Chaz probably hated more than anything else in the world weighed heavy in my chest. "I suppose he's got his orders," I mumbled out from under the sumo wrestler on my sternum.

"I think it's you, Violet Jordan. He could have left but . . ."

I shook my head. "No, Iris. I'm just an assignment."

"I've seen the way you two watch each other."

I let out a nervous laugh. "You're dreaming Iris. I threw him into a wall. I'm the progeny of his mortal enemy. No amount of witty banter will ever overcome that."

Iris simply smiled, took a sip of her tea, and looked out across her backyard. "When you're older, you'll be able to see potential in everything."

Five nights and I was falling in love with the bed in the guest room. It was always warm and soft and felt like heaven after days of exhaustive learning and practicing and nights of doing whatever the panther's little heart desired. It was a routine that I fell into easily but knew would end too soon.

The previous night had been easier to draw the panther out. Less like a stumbling teenager with big feet. It was strong. And I was beginning to think that Iris wasn't being overprotective when she got onto me about shielding.

But I still didn't remember anything about the shift as I

ran. Iris promised it would come with time. She said that I had to completely assimilate myself with my cat half before I would be able to remember everything. What I could recall was like a dream, a dream where I was the night wind and everything sped past me so fast it was a blur.

I showered and dressed and hopped downstairs to see if I could beat Iris to making breakfast. But I didn't. She was already beating the eggs as I skipped into the room.

"You're up early," she remarked as she handed me a huge stack of bread to toast.

"Must be the country living," I said back as I put in the first of six pieces of bread. "You feeling the carbs this morning, Iris?"

She just looked up at me with a small smile and went back to her stirring of the eggs.

I wanted to clap. In the past few days I was beginning to decode her devious little looks. That one meant Chaz was going to be here for breakfast. The celebration stopped when I remembered how nasty I had been to him and what I had learned last night about his father.

"God, Iris. What do I say to him?" I said hopping up on the counter to watch her skillfully cook the eggs.

"I don't know," Iris shrugged. "Tell him you want to have his babies."

"Iris," I exclaimed and swatted her shoulder playfully. "It's not like that with us."

"I just say what I see."

"Well then, get a pair of glasses," I warned as my toast popped up and I moved across the kitchen to put in two more pieces.

Diaries of an Urban Panther

"Better come up with something soon, he's coming up the drive."

Stopping my breathing to listen, really Listen with a capital L, for what Iris could already hear. I jumped as I heard the telltale engine rattling down the dirt road. I ran my fingers through my hair and redid my ponytail in the front hall mirror. Something about losing yourself in the wind really put pink in your cheeks.

He knocked on the door, which I thought was strange but as I opened it, I saw why. His arms were full: a duffle bag of clothing, a large brown paper box, and, much to my ecstasy, a carrier of Starbucks coffee.

"Hey, Violet," he said as I opened the door so he could come in.

He offered the carrier of Starbucks. Eagerly, I took that and the brown paper package, leaving him with one whole arm free.

I just looked up at him, hoping something profound would work its way out, an apology from my reservoir of scripts would bubble to the top as I stared into his warm golden eyes. I realized I missed him.

Chaz looked down at me and opened his mouth but closed it again as Iris came into the room.

"You Garrett boys could always smell a free meal." She waved for him to set his bags down and come into the kitchen.

He moved slowly away from me and I closed the door, careful of the hot cups in my hand, and followed them both into the kitchen.

Chaz carefully took the package from me and handed it to Iris.

"It's from Balzac. He said it's in there."

Iris's eyebrows rose as she took the package. "Oh."

I desperately wanted to ask what it was, but neither of them were big on volunteering details. With the look that was passed between them, I could tell this was one of those topics "Violet didn't need to know about."

Iris took the package and went deeper into her house than I had ever ventured. Which left Chaz and me unchaperoned.

I set down the coffee and busied myself with checking to see which one was mine.

"They're all for you," he said in my ear, sliding down the table towards me so he only had to whisper.

"What?" I asked.

"I didn't know what you wanted this morning, so I got your three favorites."

I looked at the coffees and then up at him. "Is this an apology?"

"I shouldn't have yelled at you."

"I shouldn't have thrown you against your car."

"Yeah, you didn't need to throw me against the car."

"Well, it felt like you were dumping me here. But Iris and I had a long talk about the Cause and a few other things and I think I understand now."

"Really?" he asked.

I had to move away from him. I was getting hot with him so close, so I went to finish toasting the bread. "Iris explained the Cause is almost like taking holy orders. You dedicate everything to it, even marking yourself for life with that tattoo. I understand it takes priority over everything."

Chaz moved toward me like he was about to say something,

when Iris came back in the kitchen and his mouth snapped shut.

"Eggs are getting cold, people," she said sitting down at the table.

The huge volume Iris had drug out of her secret little back room made a heavy thud as it shook the kitchen table. She wiped her brow as she looked down at the volume. My mouth gaped at the dark leather with the darker symbol from Chaz's arm emblazoned on the cover. Every story of Necronomicons and Books of Shadows ran through my head. I love my job.

"What's that?" I asked as I slid across from her at the kitchen table.

"The Book of Prophesy." Iris pushed the chair aside as she stood by the table to maneuver the thick leather cover open. Dust wafted across the table and tickled my nose. It smelled like Iris, ancient and powerful. (And powerful smells like lightning, just in case you wondering.)

"Like the little book that Chaz gave me?" I propped up on my knees to see the stained, ripped pages.

"This would be the great grandfather of that book. Had a hell of a time getting it for you."

Corners were missing. Pages had been ripped out. Some had even been burned. I could smell the smoke as Iris flipped through the pages, daintily lifting and setting down each page.

Iris's eyes widened when she found the page she had been looking for. With light fingers, she lifted out a sheet of white parchment from between the sheets.

"What is this?"

"Chaz said you wanted proof. Seem to have the panther part down. A little too well, I think, but as for the other part, the Perfect part. This is all I got. This is the Book where the Powers found out about you." She turned the book around and pushed it towards me.

And I pushed away and scurried back until I hit the kitchen counter. I knew it wasn't going to bite me too, but I couldn't be too sure anymore. "What?"

"The people who sent Chaz to protect you. This is what they knew. This is why you were followed."

"This book was why I was attacked?"

"And don't you want to know why?"

Of course I wanted to know why. Why little Violet Jordan who never hurt a fly. Why Violet Jordan who just want to write about the supernatural, not actually live it. "Sure, play to the curiosity of the cat. Low blow, Iris."

Her brittle finger and ridged nail pointed out a section of script. There was a break in the text. It looked like someone has been making a diary entry, then stopped and started writing poetry.

"Who wrote this?"

"Someone a long time ago."

I licked my lips and took a few steps towards it. Even at this distance, I could feel it, like a hot stove burner it radiated life. I reached out to touch the paper but my hand stopped and hovered over it. I could feel it's power pushing against my palm. How can a book be powerful?

I tucked my hands back under my elbows as I studied the actual text. "I can't read it."

"It's the Old Language of our People," Iris said, pointing again. "You wanted proof. That verse about you."

A chill ran down my back as my eyes scanned the language. Somewhere in that swirly script was the reason I was plucked out of my life. Somewhere in that unknown language was why I was fated to get attacked in a back alley, turn furry, and be stalked by men in sports cars.

I jumped up from table and paced behind the kitchen chair. Guess I finally met a book I didn't like.

"Calm down. You're as nervous as a . . ."

"If you say long-tailed cat, I'll scream." I paced, looking down at her linoleum tile, pulling my hair back up into a ponytail. "I was written about, Iris. It's creepy."

"You were prophesied about. There's a difference."

"One makes me a character. One makes me a Perfect, right?"

Iris nodded as she watched me go back and forth. I scratched behind my ear and took in a deep breath. This was insane but hadn't I asked for proof? This was proof. "Okay. What's it say?"

Iris slid the white piece of paper across the table. "Figure it out."

"What?"

Iris sighed. "You're just going to make everything difficult, aren't you? Take the paper, figure it out."

"Do you have a dictionary or something?"

"You have to do this yourself."

I slid down into the chair and looked at the script. Staring at the pages didn't do anything. I flipped the book around and tried to read it backwards. "This is impossible."

"You'll get it," Iris said. "The powerful Wanderers can read the old language. Perfects can read their prophecy because it is connected to them."

This thing had my entire life written on it and it was in another freakin' language. Yep. That sounds about right.

I stared at that book for two hours. I wrote it, wrote it backwards. Even went all *Da Vinci Code* on it and got nothing but a flare in my carpal tunnel and a broken hair tie. All I knew for sure was it was the most beautiful language I'd ever seen.

"I can't do this," I finally said, giving up. The table skittered across the kitchen table as I pushed it away in frustration and jumped up.

Iris shuffled back into the kitchen. "Please let me know *before* you decide to redecorate." She pushed the table back into its place and went to the fridge.

"How the hell am I supposed to do this? I'm a writer, not a code breaker."

"Well, maybe if you would just realize that you're one of us now, it might come a little easier."

"I'm here, aren't I? I let you drug me. Isn't that enough?"

Iris only grunted. "Apparently not."

"I need some fresh air."

When I hit the front porch, I sucked in a deep breath of Texas air. What the hell? Friggin' A. I can't just be a shapeshifting freak, I have to be a shapeshifting freak with a prophecy.

"Hey Violet."

I jumped out of my skin and spun to see Chaz sitting on the railing of the porch. "What the hell, Chaz? Wear a bell!"

He just laughed. "How's it going in there?"

"You were right about the Perfect thing."

"Isn't that good news?"

"No." I cross my arms over my chest. "Maybe. When'd you get back?"

"About an hour ago."

"Why aren't you in there gloating?"

"Because if I go inside, she'll put me to work."

I wanted to smile, but I couldn't muster even a twinge in the corner of my lips. I sat on the other corner of the banister and stared at my feet.

"While I was in town, I researched dog attacks. Nothing in your area. Which tells me they are not dogs, if you catch my drift. And the car is still a wash."

"Yay," I said with a feigned celebration dance. "I've got a prophecy, a mysterious pack of dogs, and another stalker. This has really been a banner year for me."

"At least you have a prophecy. At least you have a direction."

I frowned. "How can it be a good thing? So far it's just made me a target."

Chaz looked over at me with his golden eyes and my entire body tightened and chilled. But I was going to blame it on the puddle of moonlight I was sitting in. "I'm not in the Book of Prophecy. No one in my family is. We're just a bunch of worker bees."

"What does that mean?"

"We're expendable."

"Chaz," I jumped up. "No. You've got an amazing gift. Creeps me out a little, but it's cooler than smelling people a block away."

"But you've got a purpose in the big scheme of things. A mission with an end. They sent people to protect you."

I crossed my arms over my chest. "You sound envious."

A dark shadow crossed his face as he looked back out across Iris's back property. It was that dark brooding look that made my heart sink into my stomach. God. I'd done it again. Why can't I just think for two seconds before I open my big mouth? The big Theys hadn't sent help to his father and look what happened there. That's what he meant.

"You must hate me."

He was silent. His jaw clenched as he kept his eyes as far away from me as possible.

"I mean, I'm a panther and a lousy one at that. And a city girl who was stupid enough to get herself bitten in a back alley, protecting herself with a shoe. A shoe."

There was a small twitch of something in the corner of his mouth as his jaw relaxed. That's what I was going for.

"I mean. They are pretty big shoes, but seriously, against a monster? See. Not the brightest bulb in the chandelier. Between me and you. I think that psychic might have picked the wrong girl."

"That's where you're wrong," he finally said.

Every fiber of my being vibrated as his golden eyes landed on me, like a plucked harp string.

"You're not a normal girl, Violet."

"Don't have to tell me twice," I snorted.

"Shut up and let me talk," he said as he slid off the banister and ran his hands though his hair. "I've been sent to find a few of these Perfects. Dad called them 'newbie runs' when a Perfect was awakened because their time had come, their epic deed was about to pass."

"Are there a lot in Dallas?" I interrupted.

Chaz sighed. "Not in years. There hasn't been much hope since, he took over."

"And by *he* you mean . . ."

"Haverty."

I don't know why I was surprised that he could say the word. Probably because I couldn't even think about it most days. Probably because if something besides an act of God had killed my parents, I'd have hunted them down to the ends of the earth. Still would.

"I've never seen anyone accept all this like you."

"Not smart enough to know better."

"The shifting. The brushing. I see you, Violet. You're the right girl. Now you've just got to step up to the plate."

"Step up to the plate? Are you giving me a motivational speech? Is this about to turn into *Hoosiers*?"

He grunted. "If you've been called, then it's here. Whatever They've got planned," he pointed to the sky. "And you're helpless to stop it."

"I'll see about that," I said. "They've never gotten on my bad side."

Chapter Eleven

There once was a little girl who was very lonely. All she had were her books. She read everything she could at the library, so she started to read everything at the local bookstores. She read adventure, and horror, and literature and how-to manuals and self-help books. By the time she was twelve, she had read every book in every store down her block.

Until one day there was a new store on the block. And when the girl found out it was a bookstore, nothing filled her with more joy. She threw open the door and relished the sound of the bell on the handle.

The owner, a small old man, pushed his glasses up his nose and looked over the counter.

"These books aren't for little girls," he said. "Get out."

"But your's are the only books I haven't read, sir," the girl pleaded.

"Go read Alice in Wonderland."

"I have. All of them."

"Go read Moby Dick. That's safe enough for a little girl."

"I have, sir."

The man grunted. "War and Peace?"

"Twice sir, once in Russian."

The man leaned down from his perch behind the counter to get a better look at the girl. "No. No Children."

I interrupted my mother's story. "Mom, this one is the Neverending Story, I've already read this one."

My mother frowned and stopped rubbing my back. "Don't you want a story? Isn't that what you begged for? 'Mom, I'm sick. Can you come tell me a story?'"

"Okay, but you're teaching me plagiarism."

My mother sighed and started back with her story.

So the little girl pleaded and pleaded, day after day until the man finally said yes. "Only the children's section."

"You won't even know I'm here."

She skipped back to the section under a small lattice archway that read 'Childrens.'

The section was colorful and chaotic and she loved it. It was like a garden of books. And they were all for her.

She decided that she needed to be organized about her approach. She would start at one end of the top shelf and work her way down to the stacks on the floor.

Everyday after school she would walk to the bookstore, sometimes bringing an apple or brownies left over from her lunch to the grumpy man behind the counter and she would read for two hours a day until it was time to go home for dinner.

One day she was sitting in the middle of the section, cross-legged on the floor, hunched over one of her books when something flashed in the corner of her eye. She looked up to find a floor-length mirror with only her reflection looking curiously back at her.

She went back to reading.

But the next time it happened she swore that the reflection was slower than hers.

The third time it happened she freaked out and was out the door before the book from her lap had even hit the floor.

The next day, she peeked into the section and only saw herself in the mirror. There was a book in the middle of the floor. It was the only one there, as if the section had been cleaned.

She approached the book with great apprehension. It was the book that she had been reading yesterday. The page was marked with a red ribbon.

She watched the mirror as she sat cross-legged in the middle of the section. Slowly she put the book on her lap and opened it. Her reflection in the mirror did the same.

She pulled the ribbon out and put it on the floor. She'd read about a page when she looked up at the mirror to see her own reflection playing with the ribbon. She sat frozen for a moment as she watched the girl of her reflection smile and wave and then lean forward to press her hand on what looked like her side of the mirror.

The girl slowly leaned forward to touch the surface of the mirror.

"Hi," the reflection her chirped. "I really like this one. Can you keep reading it?"

The girl just sat in awe. When she touched the mirror, her own voice echoed inside her head. "If you are reading it, then it appears on my side and I can read it."

"What are you?"

"A mirror."

"But you look like me."

"I look like lots of things."

The girl pulled her hand away from the mirror and thought for a moment. This was crazy. But she had read crazier things.

Her reflection smiled and patted the surface of the mirror again. The girl reluctantly put her hand back against the cool surface.

"Do you think that you could show me the pictures from your side?"

The girl pulled the book to her lap again and flipped the book around to show her the picture at the beginning of Chapter 12, where they were in the book.

As the girl watched the reflection clap silently, she saw that the picture was different in the mirror. On her side it was just a girl and a horse; in the mirror, it was a raging steed and a princess.

"Why? What?" the girl said as she kept looking between the two pictures.

"The truth of everything is reflected in a mirror," her reflection said.

I woke up in the middle of the field in back of Iris's property. Stark naked, I gasped and covered myself. It had to be close to morning, the moon was low in the sky and the birds had begun to sing.

"Iris!" I called out. Surely she would be here somewhere and it wasn't like my pale ass skin was hard to lose in this light.

"Hold your horses."

The woman shuffled through the high grass and launched my terry cloth robe at me. I quickly shoved my arms through the sleeves and tied the belt around me.

"Chaz hasn't taken the book back yet has he?"

"No, tomorrow."

"Good."

It was insane. I knew that it was insane. My mother wove

stories almost every night before I went to bed. Some were simple; some would take whole weeks to tell me and every night I would lay on my stomach while she rubbed my back and created the most beautiful worlds for me.

But me standing in front of a mirror with an ancient book was insane. But then again, so was what was in the book—and my current life. Maybe walking on the crazy side was just what I needed to do.

"When you say you dreamt the answer, was it like a prophetic dream?" Iris asked as she shuffled behind me in white slippers.

I chewed on my lower lip as I got everything into place. "It's just a story my mother told me."

"So, why do we need to do this at 5 a.m.?"

"Fine. Go to bed then. But you'll miss my descent into madness."

Iris put her hands on her hips and snorted. Just then, Chaz stuck his head in the doorway. His hair splayed out in all different directions and his lips were swollen with sleep. "What's the commotion?"

"In my world we call it 'Crossing the Threshold.' To everyone else, I've just officially gone insane."

Chaz rubbed his eyes and then ran his fingers through his hair. "I'm going back to sleep."

But he walked into the room and helped me with the full-size mirror in Iris's bedroom. I'd sat cross-legged on the floor and put the book in my lap. I flipped open to the page, my page, and took in a deep breath as I turned it around in the mirror.

I didn't realize that I had squeezed my eyes shut until I had to pry them open to look at my reflection in a mirror.

Nothing. There was nothing new about the text. Now it was just gobbledygook backwards. There was no Jabberwocky here, just an Alice on the floor looking like an idiot.

"Anything?" Chaz asked. He lifted up his too tight T-shirt and scratched at his hip, nudging his sleep pants a little too low on his hips.

I diverted my eyes quickly and rested my head on the binding of the book.

"I'm sorry, honey," Iris said with a warm hand on my shoulder. "Why don't we work on it tomorrow?"

My head stayed on the book. That was it. That was all I had. I finally looked up to see Chaz watching me in the mirror.

"I'll see what I can hunt down," Chaz said as he turned to go. There was a glint of moonlight off his watch that threw light onto the mirror.

I knew that I was tired, but not tired enough to hallucinate the quick flash of something across the pages of the book.

"Moonlight!" I jumped up and tossed the book on the bed. "Get the mirror into moonlight."

Chaz helped me pull the mirror in front of Iris' bedroom window. There was just enough light left to reflect back a puddle of light on the floor beneath the window.

I hoisted the book again, turned to the page and again sat cross legged on the floor.

This time when I opened the book and turned it around to be read in the mirror, it was an epiphany. Like when you're at the eye doctor and he clicks that last monocle down and everything suddenly comes into focus.

In the blink of an eye, the text went from unreadable to

clear as day. The English letters swirled beautifully and I was able to see my name in the middle of the verse.

> *"Daughter of Jourdaine,*
> *Oh Daughter of Mine*
> *Born of the ides will fall on two and rise on four*
> *And will protect crown and Veil*
> *from her dark reflection."*

The light faded and the last line went back to being unreadable again. I dropped my head back against the wall with a heavy thud. "The light's gone."

"Good thing moonlight is a renewable resource," Chaz said as he put the mirror back where it belonged.

Iris stood, her hand folded at her waist. "How do you feel?"

I shook my head. "I don't understand it."

"Some never do," Iris sighed. "But there you have your proof. You were able to read it when you accepted who you were."

"Because I was able to handle the shift?"

Iris simply shrugged.

"What gave you the mirror idea?" Chaz asked as he offered a hand to pull me up off the floor.

"A story my mother told me."

He pulled a little too roughly and I flew up and almost landed in his arms, the book acting as a padded shield between our bodies.

"Is it you?" he whispered.

My eyes began to water. Something in the back of my head had said that if I could prove to them that I was the wrong girl, all of this would just go away. But I wasn't the wrong girl. I knew it. Like I had written those words myself. The words seeped into my head, my heart and I knew. "My birthday is March fifteenth."

I let go of his hand and took a step back. I pushed my hair behind my ear and looked over at Iris.

"When my family came over from France, they changed our name to Jordan. It was originally Jourdaine."

"What about that second line?" Chaz asked. "The daughter of mine?"

I licked my lips. "Do we know who wrote the book?"

Iris shook her head. "It's ancient."

"I'll find out for you," Chaz offered quickly. "When I return the book to Balzac."

Slowly, I handed the book to Iris. "Never gonna sleep now. Thanks a bunch."

"Always here to please, your highness, now get out. I need my beauty sleep."

Packing is not my strong suit. Somehow I had managed to get all this stuff in here to begin with and was glad for my compulsive overpacking, but I just stared at the pile of clothes on the bed and the little bag in my hand. It just didn't seem physically possible. Could I just leave the stuff here? Seemed that I would be back in twenty-eight days.

Stuffing everything in the nylon bag, I decided to just wash everything when I got home. I was dallying and I knew it. I didn't want to leave here, to face the real world, because this was the first place that had felt like home in a long time.

Home.

I looked down at the bed and was almost sad to leave the soft flannel sheets with little duckies. My 500-count Egyptian cotton sheets at the town house had nothing on these.

Iris met me at the bottom of the stairs with a plastic container full of cinnamon chocolate chip cookies by the smell of them.

"These are for the ride back," she said, almost shoving the box into my hand.

I looked down at the older woman's lower lip and it seemed to be quivering.

"Aw, are you going to miss me?" I asked as I threw my open arm around her. "Don't worry. You're not getting rid of me that easy."

"Too bad," Iris joked as she squeezed back. "Because it's going to take me a year to get the smell of panther out of my sheets."

The two of us laughed and I rested my hand on her shoulder. "I don't know how to thank you, Iris."

"You don't have to. Just keep in touch and keep out of trouble."

"Me? Trouble?"

Iris's look turned dark and I knew that we weren't joking anymore. "They are out there, Violet. And if they sent Chaz to find you," she said in almost a whisper, "then it's for something big. Just be careful. Keep your shields up. And I *will* see you next full moon."

I nodded again. "And I'll bring you some of that lotion I was talking about."

I gave Iris another hug and she opened the door for me.

"Work on your shielding," she called out, waving as I went for the car. "Borders don't build themselves."

Chaz was leaning with his arms crossed over his chest, looking across the distance. Being the little tech-savvy girl that I am, I took out my cell phone and snapped a picture.

"Hey," he protested when he saw what I was doing.

"What? Am I going to need to call your agent?"

He just kicked at the dirt with his boot and looked up at me. "You're going straight home?"

"I'm surprised you're not going to tailgate me all the way to Dallas."

"Nah," he said putting his hands in his pockets. "Iris and I have a few things to talk about. And I have to return that book."

"And what advice are you going to get from the big guru?"

Chaz shook his head. "Nothing major."

"Be careful. She wants you to replace the floor of the loft in the barn."

I walked around to the other side of my car and opened it up. It still surprised me there were parts of the county where you could leave your car doors unlocked. Dumping my stuff in the passenger seat, I walked back to where I had been standing. "So this is good-bye?"

"Until I end up on your doorstep again because you didn't answer your phone."

"Still need to follow me that closely? I'm pretty trained up. Not feeling the call of evil yet. Got a little prophecy to keep me busy for at least a few hours."

"But there still is something out there, something big. And if Haverty ever found out there was another panther . . ."

I chilled at hearing the same words in a five-minute span. "You and Iris really are on the same frequency."

"White hate broadband," he joked with a full smile.

"I'll be careful, Chaz, and I will promise not to do anything stupid for at least a week," I said crossing my heart and holding up the Girl Scout fingers.

"Guess I'll have to take that."

I knew I had to go. I needed to be back in town for a conference call and I needed gas and a soda for the fifty-five-minute drive. But I wasn't sure how to say good-bye. "So do we shake like a business deal or hug like friends, or we could do that manly shake hug thing?"

Chaz laughed at me. "I don't know. Last time I touched you, I got thrown in to a wall."

"I promise to work on that too," I said apologetically.

He kinda lifted up his arms in a hug offer that I took. On my toes, my chin just slid over his shoulder and was reminded of the sweet scent of the plaid bed at his house. He squeezed briefly and I could hear him, feel him, take in a deep breath as he let go.

I stepped back and smiled. "See, didn't throw ya?"

"Better already," he said with a half smile.

"I'll be expecting my parole call around 9." I walked around to the driver's side of my car.

He nodded and gave me a half wave.

As I started up the car and started down the drive, I knew I shouldn't have hugged him. And it was more than just the fact I now knew that under all those loose button-up shirts, the boy was hard as a rock; it was more than the way he squeezed for just the right amount of time to make it a meaningful embrace. It was more than the fact he had just embraced a panther. It was the fact that I would now smell him for the entire ride home until that night when I finally took off the T-shirt to be washed.

Chapter Twelve

Jessa called to see what I was doing on Saturday night. She wanted to catch up, since she hadn't felt right bothering me while I was out of town on business. I let her believe that it was a writer's retreat and not a retraining of my mystical beast.

As I got out of the car Jessa was leasing this week and looked up at the neon lights of the club, I could smell people and life ebbing out from the building before me and it was invigorating.

I waited as she handed the keys to the valet and then handed the ticket to me, knowing I would keep better track of it than her.

Before we went in, I checked my phone to make sure it was on vibrate, just in case someone happened to call.

Jessa beat her own man-trap record, but as the night went on, I think it was a setup. We got into the bar and within five minutes, an entire table of men asked us to join them. Much to my chagrin, Jessa immediately introduced me to one of them. As I was pinned between her on my left and him on my right, I felt the distinctly trapped feeling of a caged animal. But he didn't set off the spidey sense, so I settled in with a Baileys and cream and made small talk.

My phone buzzed. I picked it up and Chaz's picture flashed across on the screen. He was going to hate that. It made me smile. But there was no way that I was going to be able to hear him unless I went outside and I was way too deep into the club to get out now.

So I sent him a text. *Checking up on me?*

It was a good three minutes before I got a response.

No. Where are you?

Tiger Room, celebrating Jessa

How r u?

Good, great, never been better.

Call you tomorrow?

How about lunch?

It was another five minutes before I got a response back on that one.

Returning book. Rain check?

Sure. Be safe

I set down the phone on the table before me, completely amused, and the man next to me turned and smiled. Deep dimples formed in his cheeks and the dancing colored lights reflected off his black-rimmed glasses. His name was Brian, I think, and he was an accountant from one of the firms Jessa worked with. Didn't catch too many more details over the loud music. I really wondered how Jessa managed to pick up so many guys in places like this. Oh wait, this was Jessa.

"You look happy," Brian said.

"I am," I smiled back and looked down at my very empty drink.

"Can I get you another?" he asked, his brown eyes twinkling behind glasses he pushed up nervously.

I paused for a moment at the surrealness of being asked that question. Old Violet would have said "No, thanks," and moved to another table—if she had ever been asked, that is. New Violet was in too good a mood to be thwarted by her independent ways, so she nodded.

"I'd like that," I answered as I slid my phone into my purse and crossed my legs and leaned forward to learn more about this man who smelled like old spice and Downy.

The Jeet Kun Do dojo was a traditional gym-looking place with mats on the floors and symbols painted in red on the wall, like Efficiency, Directness, and Simplicity, the three tenants of this particular practice.

After I got back from Iris's, outside of getting used to the smell of the city, I had to find something to do with all this energy I had now. It was like living in overdrive. Everything tasted different, felt different. When I woke up one morning with the urge to run, I knew I needed to get into some routine to keep the panther in check. Hence, the dojo. If I was part of some mystical line of what's-its, I was going to learn to protect myself. If anything ever happened again, I was at least going to muster a better defense than throwing shoes.

The sensei met me at the door.

"Good to see you, Miss Jordan," he greeted with a large toothy smile.

I cocked my head. "How did you know who I was?" I asked as he took my little gym bag and pointed to where I needed to slip off my shoes.

The older man just tapped his nose and gestured for me to follow him. He was shorter than me and wore a pair of red loose pants and a white T-shirt with the dojo's logo on it. Took away from the mysticism, but what did I know?

"We have a few clients like you, Miss Jordan," he said as we walked back into a separate area that was similarly matted and symboled but had a different feel to it. My skin chilled as I passed through the doorway and I looked back to see a silver ornament with a red tassel hanging above the door.

"To keep us safe back here," the man answered my unspoken question.

"What do you mean a few clients like me?" I asked as I set my bag in an out-of-the-way corner.

The sensei continued to move about the room, pulling out workout equipment and a few things I had no clue what a person would do with.

The man stopped what he was doing and looked at me with a smile. "How did you find out about this place, Miss Jordan?"

"Did some research about what kind of training I needed, and then looked you up online." The real answer was that yoga bored me to tears. I'd fallen asleep in two classes. The teacher hadn't appreciated that. "Why?" I asked.

The sensei laughed, finding my answer completely amusing. He waved his hands in the air as he chuckled. "You were directed here, Miss Jordan. Whether or not you choose to believe, that is your struggle, not mine."

I stood and watched as he came to the center of the mat.

Brought here, I thought. How could I have been brought here? It wasn't like the Powers could manipulate a Google search. Or could they? As I looked over the man before me, I caught a glimpse of something deeper, wiser and ancient in his black eyes.

"Are you Cause?"

He pulled up the sleeve of his T-shirt and a faint scar was carved into his bicep. It wasn't the Cause tattoo that Chaz had. "Former Order."

I gasped. "Former?"

"A few of us broke free from Haverty."

"How are you alive? They said he killed everyone."

"We hide and hide well. The Cause won't have us because we are tainted by the mark. But I do believe that you were guided here. You've got some higher powers moving around you, Miss Jordan, higher than both the Cause and the Order answer to, more than just a little Guardian."

Frightened, my skin goose-bumped all over, just like when I had passed through the doorway. Part of me wished that little Guardian was here with me. But I shook my head. No. I could do this on my own. It was my power, my panther. And I was going to do this.

"I will teach you how to hone your power. How to hide until it is like breathing for you."

My head swam with questions and I'm sure he could see it in my wide eyes.

"Shall we begin?" he offered with a small smile.

Chapter Thirteen

I had written about people getting into fights at bars; some picked on purpose for some cathartic reason, some engaged for the purpose of defending someone's honor, and some just because a good bar fight is what a dried up plot needed. But never could I have imagined actually engaging in one myself.

The group of us, Jessa, Adrianna, Carrie, and I were in a nice bar uptown minding our own business when Jessa had the urge to take out her compact and check her makeup. Again. We were all sitting around our table laughing about something that had happened on Monday when this woman came up to Jessa and yanked on her hair, jerking Jessa's head back sharply.

Quickly, I caught the compact as it dropped out of Jessa's hands and vaguely heard something about "looking at my man."

The hairs on the back of my neck bristled as I slowly put the compact back on the table. Even through my shields, I could feel a Wanderer here and they were charged. It was the same feeling I got when Iris was frustrated, and when Chaz was just about to yell at me.

Jessa whipped her head around holding the sore spot that

was now missing a patch of hair. "What the hell!" she yelled with a glare that could have melted metal.

The woman, short and chunky, stood behind her with her hands on her hips. Her black hair was almost blue in the smoky light and her mascara was smeared, like she had already been in one altercation that evening.

As I stood slowly and turned to back up Jessa, I knew it was not this woman I was sensing. She was nothing, just some woman who didn't have enough sense to not take on a table of four women in stilettos.

"You've been eyeing my boo all night and I want you to take your trashy ass out of here before I kick it out," the woman demanded with some fierce head movements and an even more fiercely pointed finger, complete with four-inch airbrushed nails.

"Trashy? This is Prada, bi—" Jessa started, but I quickly put a hand on her shoulder and Jessa stopped before she went too far. But she clenched her jaw and mumbled the rest of what she was thinking to herself.

"I can assure you she was not looking at your boo," I said calmly.

"Whatever! She's been looking in that mirror all night at him," the woman retorted with more head swiveling.

"I wouldn't take two looks at that," Jessa snapped.

I winced. This was not going to be good.

The woman reeled her four-inch fingernailed hand and prepared to slap Jessa with her tiny little might, but my hand shot out almost of its own accord to catch the woman's arm as I smoothly slid in front of Jessa.

I held the woman's wrists firmly and looked down at her with a raised eyebrow. The woman didn't even reach my shoulder. "Are you sure that you want to do this?" I asked softly, my panther beginning to stir at the raised adrenaline running through my system. It was like a knot in my stomach that was fuzzy and spun.

The woman, glaring at me with a hatred that had never been glared in my direction before, drew back her other hand as if trying to strike again.

It was instinctual, I guess. Wasn't like I had been at Jeet Kun Do for long, but I hit her hard, with the palm of my hand, square in the chest and she flew backwards, over a table and through three chairs. She landed legs up in the air, exposing everything to God and anyone else who was watching.

I froze. I wasn't used to violence. Especially coming from me. I thought I heard someone yell and clap but all I could do was stare.

Jessa's cold hand clamped down on my arm and I turned away from the wreckage. Could have been the adrenaline, the sudden rush of power, but I could have sworn that her eyes flashed lilac for a moment. "We need to go. Now."

I nodded and the four of us ran for the door, scurrying through the crowd who was still watching the woman being pulled up by her boo.

It wasn't until we were in the car that I thought about that other presence in the bar. What had it wanted? Had it had anything to do with the fight? And why did my hairs stand on end even now when I thought about it?

The ringer on my cell phone sounded deep into the night. I fumbled around on the nightstand to find the dancing square.

"Hello?" I mumbled, rubbing my eyes as I rolled onto my back.

"Violet? Are you asleep?" Chaz sounded almost confused.

"It *is* two in the morning," I sighed, pulling the blankets straight on my bed.

"But you guys are usually out late."

"We had to end the night a little early," I said before I remembered who I was talking to.

"Why? What happened?" he asked with his detective edge.

I sighed. Why had I opened my big mouth? "We had a little altercation at a bar tonight."

"What happened?" A slight note of panic lifted his voice into a higher octave.

"Nothing. Some girl thought Jessa was eyeing her boo and she got a little angry."

"And," he persisted.

"And I pushed her down and we left."

"Was there anyone else there?"

By the intonation of his voice, I knew exactly what he was referring to. I sat up in my bed and tried to focus, remembering the feeling I had that was so quickly forgotten with the whole running for our lives thing. "Yeah, actually. But it wasn't her, wasn't the girl who tried to start something."

"Did she take anything from her? Did she get anything from Jessa?"

"Maybe a few hairs?" I tried to recall.

"That may be enough," he mumbled into the phone.

"Why? What are you thinking?"

"Nothing," he said quickly, too quickly.

"Liar," I exclaimed. "You can't keep me out of the loop on things that involve Jessa."

I heard the sigh on the phone, the way his pulse raced a little when I yelled at him.

"Magic is real, Violet. Spells can be cast using something as small as a piece of hair."

"But, this woman wasn't anything special."

"Then, unless Jessa is one of us, it was probably just a cat fight. Get it?"

I rolled my eyes. "Ha, ha. Don't give up your day job."

His words weren't comforting enough and now I wasn't going to sleep anytime soon.

"Why are you up at two in the morning?" I asked, not liking the creeping feeling down my back as I thought about this evening. I could still see the slight lilac flash in Jessa's eyes and that gave me the willies almost as much as the essence in the bar.

"I just got in."

"What were you doing?" I asked casually as I lay back down in bed.

"Why?"

"Hey, you're not the only one in this relationship that gets to ask questions."

He chuckled softly over the phone. It made me smile.

"I was watching a movie," he finally confessed.

"That's nice. Life shouldn't be all work and no play. As long as you weren't following someone else."

The line was silent.

"Were you following someone else? Because I might get

jealous if you're stalking two people at once," I said playfully as I stood and went into the bathroom.

"No. You're the only one," he said, keeping with the playful mode.

I filled up a glass of water and looked at the mirror as I took a long gulp.

"Good," I said dumping the rest of the water out and going back into the bedroom. "Because I have a feeling the new me doesn't share well."

"The new you?" he asked, as he ran some water himself. I could just see him ambling around his little messy house in one of his university T-shirts, maybe Duke this time, and his dusty jeans, leaning against his kitchen counter with a questionably clean mug of water.

"The one who seems to be emerging through all this, the catty one," I tried to explain.

"I think the catty one was always there. You just didn't let it show."

I laughed. "Maybe."

He was quiet for a moment. I thought I heard the rustle of sheets along the line. "I'd better get to bed. Long day tomorrow," he said with a soft sigh following.

I sat back on my bed and curled up underneath the covers. "Whatcha got planned?"

"You know me. A little stalking, some lunch, hunt down a banshee at the library, some coffee, and then some more stalking."

I smiled as I lay back on my soft pillows. "I'm wearing off on you."

He laughed and I heard a door close on his side of the line.

"Maybe you are," he said softly, as if he was settling down for the night too.

"Well, enjoy your day tomorrow."

"Talk to you later, Violet."

"Night, Chaz."

I closed my cell phone and laid it on my night stand, suddenly overcome with this warm sensation and as I fell asleep, I could have sworn I heard purring.

Chapter Fourteen

Of all the places in all the world, Chaz Garrett decided to go grocery shopping at my Kroger. Nearly fifteen miles from where he lived, he decided to pick up milk and eggs and bread? Right.

I was staring at the canned vegetables, trying to make the most depressing decision, as if grocery shopping isn't depressing enough on a Friday night: Do I give in and buy the single-serving size or do I buy the regular size and end up throwing over half of it out? An age-old dilemma.

"Hello," came softly over my shoulder.

I turned quickly, too quickly, my heart racing in my throat. Chaz was standing right there, very close. So close, I could feel the warmth off his flannelled chest.

"You're following me to the grocery store now?" I said, pulling a small can of peas off the shelf. "Is no place sacred?"

He thumbed over his shoulder to a cart that was a third filled with a random amalgamation of bags of chips, frozen dinners for one, twelve packs of soda. It too closely resembled my own. "I need to eat, too," he shrugged. "Nice shields by the way, took me a few minutes to get a fix on you."

"Is that how yours works? Finding a person's energy trail."

"Sometimes. With you, it is even easier than that."

"Why? Because I'm so boringly predictable?"

Chaz laughed. "You are anything but boring, Violet."

"Well, just be careful. This could be considered an outing," I warned, pushing my cart slowly down the aisles. "Don't want to be accused of mixing business with pleasure."

Chaz followed, throwing things, seeming haphazardly into his cart as we wove through the store.

"Is that bad?" he finally asked in the middle of the pasta section. "This being an outing?"

I let the question hang there as I we passed through boxed dinners, and I didn't answer until we were in front of the meat section. "No."

"Oh, this should be interesting," he muttered from behind me.

I shot him a dirty look as I perused the meat section. Made me a little hungry, actually. I had become somewhat of a connoisseur, researching all the cuts and the different types of high protein sources. I picked up two steaks, a package of frozen chicken breasts, and boneless pork chops. I'm not a cook, but frankly, steaks were on the simple side of the culinary world. Cook. Flip. Repeat.

"Gee whiz," he said as he looked down at my collection.

"Whatever keeps *her* happy," I shrugged and I pushed on to the household goods with him following.

"What else keeps her happy?" he asked with a low, intimate tone.

I was just about to not justify his question with a response when I ran into Devin. As in ran into him with my cart. I hit him full on in the side of the leg as I was distracted by Chaz's devious smile.

"Holy..." Devin cried out before he saw who it was.

I froze, suddenly aware that I had my two very separate lives crashing together in the household goods aisle.

"Violet," Devin greeted with a pain-filled smile. He slightly limped around my cart and gave me a hug and a peck on the cheek. "How are you?"

"Great. You? Besides the leg?" I hoped beyond all hope he wouldn't notice the man behind me. But then again, my life couldn't be that simple.

Devin did notice the man behind me with a full head to toe once-over, and a raised eyebrow back at me. "And who's this?" he asked softly to me.

I took in a deep breath. Nothing was going to happen here. We were in public. There would be no fireworks, explosions, or depth charges if my friend met my, uh, other friend.

"Devin, this is Chaz. Chaz, this is my friend Devin."

The two men shook hands and I was pretty sure the world was not collapsing. But it was still early at this point. There was always calm before the storm.

I distractedly grabbed a box of dish-washing detergent off the shelf behind me to hide behind until the flames died from my face.

"So, what have you been up to lately?" I asked, casually tossing the soap into my basket and turning back to Devin.

"Nothing much, taking a painting class at nights. Trying not to think about... anything particular," he said.

I reached out and squeezed his arm in consolement. Boy problems. Didn't we all have them.

"And you? How do you like the Jeet Kun Do classes?" Devin asked, trying to keep focused on me, but sneaking looks at Chaz who was reading the back of a Swiffer Dusting wands, like he'd use them.

"I love it. I'm sore half the time, but it really is better than therapy."

"Wonderful," he said with a wide smile. "I always thought that you might like a physical sport. I bet it gives you a lot to write about."

Devin crossed his arms and leaned against my cart, still trying to hide his study of Chaz.

"It does. I've worked in quite a bit actually."

Devin smiled up at Chaz and then back at me. "I'll let you two continue shopping. Pleasure to finally meet you," he nodded to Chaz, then headed off to the dairy section.

I stood there and watched him walk off, practically skipping. I was so going to hear about this later. I could write the conversation now.

"Nice guy," was all Chaz said before he pushed forward to the shampoo section.

I was stunned. "Nothing?" I asked as I scurried behind him. "I was expecting a lecture. The value of a solitary life, the dangers I could put my friends in . . ."

Chaz stopped. "There is one thing," he said turning to me, that dark golden glint in his eyes. The unhappy glint.

"What?" I asked softly, stopping besides him, still preparing for the "you need to be more careful" rant.

"Why did you tell him about the Jeet Kun Do, but not me? I had to follow you to the dojo."

I opened my mouth and then shut it again. Why hadn't I told Chaz? "Devin asked."

Chaz had to think, review. "Oh," he said his shoulders dropping.

"It's what friends do. They ask questions about the other person's life, even the mundane stuff."

"I ask you about stuff," Chaz protested.

"Your questions are more geared towards whether or not I feel like pouncing on anything that day."

Chaz tried to maintain his straight face. But I was too good. The furrow melted between his brows and he cracked a smile.

"Friends care about the silly stuff and know what you do for a living and . . ."

"And they don't throw you against walls?" he finished.

I sighed and just arched an eye brow at him. "It was one time."

Chaz continued down the aisle a bit further as I searched out shampoo.

"So what is this?" he sprang on me as I was picking up a bottle of my orchid and coconut milk shampoo.

"What?" I asked out of shock, more than misinterpretation.

He pushed his cart so that it was next to mine facing the opposite direction. Cart spooning. "If we're not friends, then what are we?"

I slowly put the shampoo in the cart, sure that I was going to drop it on the ground along with my metaphoric jaw.

"Well, um . . ." I grasped at things. Wasn't it usually guys who were okay with not defining things? I think at this point I knew Chaz was not a normal guy, but this cemented it. "I thought I was an assignment of some sort."

That was not the right answer. I read it in his whole body. Not only did his jaw tense up but his whole body turned rock solid and his knuckles grew white as he gripping the blue cart handle.

"It's a working relationship. You watch my back and I work your nerves," I said with a weak smile.

He relaxed a little.

"You lead me down the straight and narrow and I drive you completely insane. We're like Will and Grace, really."

"You think I'm gay?" he asked, trying to keep up.

"No. But you're the good one and I'm the mess."

He lowered his chin and shook his head. "You're not a mess."

I whispered. "You haven't seen my house."

Chaz just looked at me, like he wanted to say something. He had a look in his eye like he had at Iris's house that morning before breakfast. Like there was something just on the tip of his tongue that couldn't quite struggle free. His eyes turned a slightly warmer brown as he looked at me.

"I know what you do, but I don't know who you are. I don't know your favorite color. I don't know if you played sports in high school. I don't know about your family," I explained. "I know that you are a guardian. And I know without you, I would have been a meal in my driveway or evil incarnate. But that isn't everything."

He finally looked away and I could feel myself breathe again. Didn't even know that I had been holding my breath.

It was time to tell him. It was time for me to let someone in a little closer. Why not Stalker boy? Why not in the middle of the hair care products? Seemed par for the course these days. "I'm a big girl, Chaz. But I need to learn to take care of myself all over again. New questions to ask myself, new moral lines to draw. It's been me for so long with no regards to anyone and now I've got this prophecy that puts other people in danger and a crazy man possibly after me. I won't let myself rely on you guys."

He shook his head. "It's what I'm here for, what I was sent for."

"Doesn't mean I don't like having you around."

"Why? Can't talk to your friends about the new you?"

I nodded. It was true. He was the only person who wouldn't think I was certifiable, not that we did that much talking, but he knew and he still stayed around. "But hello. Kettle black. I'm not the only one shopping on a Friday night all alone. How many other guys do you know who carry shotguns full of silver in the back of their trucks?"

"This is Texas. Everyone has a shotgun."

I laughed. "Right, still getting used to that."

I watched his warm brown eyes for a moment and took a deep breath. With the confession of words I'd had building up for a while, I was impressively in one piece. The world wasn't ending yet, and maybe I wanted to add a handsome guy to my speed dial list. Jessa's number had been there all by itself for a very long time.

"What's your favorite color?" he asked as he turned his cart around and we began shopping again.

"Green. Yours?"

"Black."

"Figures."

Curled up in my office chair cradling a cup of coffee, I stared at the blank Word document staring back at me. Three weeks ago, I'd logged into the database to grab a freelance article and, now, I had to turn it in this week or not get paid.

Despite what Jessa thought, I did get out, but it was more in an undercover reporter kind of way. If this article was about the best places to get sushi, I'd go the restaurant, eat a plate, read the menu, and have the entire article done by the time it took to scarf down a California roll.

But this was about dogs. And I hate dogs. Need I replay the scene?

So the Internet was the only way I was going to finish this article. Maybe the Internet had an answer. This article was the only way I was going to make the mortgage this month and still have a little to eat off of. And unfortunately, eating had become less underrated than it had been two months ago.

As I was looking through maps of White Rock Lake, I knew I needed to research something else. Sure I had a prophecy, but it didn't pay the bills

When an advertisement for Ansestry.com popped up on my screen, I looked at the ceiling. "Seriously? That was subtle."

Maybe *they* with a capital T had manipulated my search for martial arts training.

If the Internet could bring me enough information about dog parks to make me sound like an expert on canine exercise, maybe, just maybe, it could bring me a little more info about my family. Not that there was anything special about the Jordans that I could remember.

The genealogy websites were flooded with Jordans. It's not the most unique name ever. As I scrolled through the lists of people who came up in my search, I did find my great grandmother. In 1910, Violette Jordan was registered at Ellis Island with the vast crowds who came over from France. My mother had told me stories of her in her big house in France, running across the fields. Always made me wonder why she had moved halfway across the world to live in a Chicago walk-up. Maybe I had more in common with her than I thought.

I didn't make it a habit of lugging around stuff when I moved, but there was a silver picture frame from my mother's side of the family. I brought it to school once for show and tell. It was an heirloom. And now, heirlooms were deadly. Might be good to pinpoint exactly where the only things on the planet that could kill me were.

The chair in my office was left spinning as I darted through the upstairs and slid on the floor next to my bed.

I had a box, a small violet box where I kept everything sacred. The papier-mâché box was in the safest place I could think to stow it. No one ever came into my house, and certainly never ever came into my bedroom, let alone got anywhere near the bed.

The box was covered in dust and enough hair to look like four people lived there, and maybe a few animals. I blew the dust off the top and set the box on my bed.

Undoing the purple ribbon, I lifted the lid carefully. It was given to my mother by the hospital staff where I was born, which should have told the logic part of my brain that there were several people out there with little violet boxes, but as I pulled away the tissue, I got a tingle in my palm that told me that maybe there was something else in that little violet box that I just hadn't been able to pick up on before.

There were five things in my little box. I pulled out the scroll with my first story on it, a ghost story about a ghost who fell in love with a boy and made a deal with Hades to have a body for one night just to tell him that she loved him and then she would be a reaper for the rest of eternity.

Yeah, I know, Little Violet needed therapy.

The second thing was my dad's business pen, a golden Cartier with his initials on the clip. I was fascinated by the way he'd have to refill the ink cartridges and I used to sit in his desk chair spinning as I twisted the point up and down.

I picked up the coffee mug next. I'd made it for my mom when we went to this paint your own pottery shop. It was purple with red flowers on one side and had "Mother" written on it with a crown painted on the M. It was the ugliest thing but she used it every morning after that weekend.

Folded in tissue paper, there was *the* picture frame. It was a silver ivy picture frame that currently held the last picture of my mother and me. My eyes watered immediately as any thought of a mystical scavenger hunt disappeared from my head. My mother was gorgeous. Long legs, long dark smooth hair, and the clearest light-green eyes. She deserved to be on the cover of magazines, not kneeling next to a thirteen-year-old me who was thirty pounds overweight with zits and Coke bottle-bottom glasses.

An echo of her laugh brushed across my memory. It was clear like bells and would make anyone who heard it smile as well. And my father would make her laugh to hard she couldn't breathe some times.

We were happy.

And then one day in October, she left me with my Aunt Glory and never came back.

But there was more to the task at hand instead of just a painful trip through memory lane. I flipped the picture frame over in my hand. Nothing special. No inscriptions. I opened the back and nothing mysterious fell out. No secret note from an ancestor saying that *Sure enough, Violet Jordan Junior was the chosen one.*

With a heavy sigh, I put the frame back together and was just about to put the picture frame back when it hit the last thing in the box. It was a small black velvet box. With a shaky hand, I picked up the rectangular hinged box. I sucked in a deep breath as I flipped open the lid.

Three rings waited patiently inside. A man's silver band, a woman's silver band, and the most perfect little quarter carat diamond solitaire. Now there was a story.

Without trying them on like usually did, I snapped the box closed and sucked in a deep breath. I didn't know that I had stopped breathing.

Leaving the picture frame out, I packed up all the other contents of the box and shoved it under the bed again to be protected by the evil dust bunnies that protected it.

Shivering at the thought of bunnies under my bed, I grabbed the photo frame and headed downstairs. This was my past, I thought. And that's a part of me. And if I can accept that I'm going to turn into a panther once a month, maybe twice, then I'm grown up enough to keep a picture of my own mother on the mantle.

She looked a little out of place all by herself in the undecorated room. But a smile like that was an accoutrement to any décor.

Chapter Fifteen

Chaz caught me at an odd moment. I was talking on my house phone to Sera discussing the script changes and the new story web thing Drew decided we were going with, brewing my first pot of coffee for the day, and trying to find where I had put that script she had faxed me yesterday.

"Hold on Sera, I have a call on my cell."

"Sure, hon."

I had to search under every piece of paper on my dining room table before I found the stupid chiming thing under my morning paper and flipped it open.

"Hello?" I answered, balancing the little cell phone on my left shoulder as I grabbed the paper to bring it in to the kitchen.

"Violet?"

"Chaz?" I questioned back as I still held the cell phone with my shoulder, held the cordless with my right hand, and sifted through the morning paper for my script. "It's a little early for my daily parole call."

"Who's Chaz?" I heard Sera question from the other phone.

I shook my head and ignored her question as I continued

to search. I had just seen the stupid script. Was I losing my marbles?

"I was wondering what your plans were for tonight," he asked, kind of rushed.

"Why? Still got a week till the full moon or do you just miss me?"

"Maybe," he answered honestly.

My cheeks grew hot for no reason. "I've got some work to finish up but nothing exciting. Why?"

"Thought I could join you instead of skulking around."

"What exactly do you have in mind?" I asked suspiciously. I had never taken the time to consider what a man like Chaz might do in his spare time; besides his one movie outing, I hadn't really heard him talk of anything else but work. And most men don't say the word *skulk*.

"How about dinner, maybe a movie?"

I froze. It was so normal, so within the box. I froze until my coffee pot began to steam wildly, hissing and spewing out hot water and coffee grounds all over my counter. I dropped the cordless phone on the ground and reached for the paper towels to mop up the mess.

"Violet?" he questioned. "Are you there?"

"Okay," I said quickly, throwing away the soppy paper towels only to find the script I had been looking for on the top of my trash, now covered in coffee grounds.

"Around eight then?"

"Okay," I sighed, anything to just get him off the phone at this point.

"See you then."

"Okay." And I heard a click from his line.

Unbelieving, I slowly closed my phone and set it on the kitchen counter, like it might bite me or rain down some more confusion in my life.

"Violet, Violet!" I heard coming from the phone on the floor. I quickly snatched it up.

"Yeah, I'm here," I said as I still distracted watched the cell phone on my counter.

"Who's Chaz?" Sera asked with a devilish lilt to her tone.

"No one."

"A no one who you have a date with tonight."

"It's not a date," I said defensively, still wiping down my counter before the coffee stained the grout.

"Chaz is a male, I'm presuming, who just asked you out for an evening away from home. That's a date," Sera defined for me.

I sighed and looked at the phone. How was I going to explain this to her without explaining it to her? "You know Adderall?"

"The loner from *White Heat*?"

God that was a horrible movie. Can't believe my name was attached to it. "Chaz is an Adderall only with model good looks."

Sera paused for a moment, rerunning through the scripts that we had written together when I was still in LA. "But hot?" she clarified thoughtfully.

"As in red."

"So what if a semi-psycho, massively armed, demon hunter asked you out? It's a date. With a boy. You haven't had one of those in ages."

"You should be really glad I'm half way across the country," I threatened.

"Love you too, Vi. Now go get ready for your date."

"It's not a . . ." but I couldn't finish my sentence before she hung up.

I really wasn't sure what to expect when I opened the door that evening. I had changed three times trying to find something fitting for the occasion. But what do you wear to go out with a guy who's already seen you naked?

I settled on a little black dress. That was noncommittal enough. Didn't say *hey we might as well be bowling* but it didn't scream *take me, I'm yours*. I'd already decided on the light cashmere coat I'd picked up last year that still had the tags. The shoes were the real outfit: red Stuart Weitzman peep-toe pumps I had never worn before, except walking around in my living room. Chaz probably wouldn't even notice.

But as I opened my door, I really, really didn't expect to see a fashion photo from GQ standing on my porch. The moon silhouetted his charcoal gray suit and crisp white shirt. And I thought there actually might be gel in his hair.

His golden eyes started at my flat ironed hair and progressed down to the shoes. "Hey," he finally greeted, jamming his hands into his tailored pockets.

"Hi," I finally mustered. I must have looked like a framed picture, completely frozen in my doorway.

"Ready?" he asked as he scratched the back of his head and looked down at my feet.

"Sure." It came out sounding smooth enough, despite the pulse pounding in my throat coaxed by the scent of his cologne and the starch from the new shirt on the breeze.

I quickly grabbed my little black purse from the foyer table and stepped outside to be met with another surprise.

A new car. It was black and shiny and was surely going to be the envy of everyone we drove passed this evening. The long line of the two-door sports car gleamed under the waxing moonlight.

I locked my front door and thought as we walked down the sidewalk towards his car, that this was a beautiful night. I paused and took a deep breath of crisp cold air and looked up at the twinkling stars.

"You alright?" he asked looking back at me.

"I really wish people would stop asking me that," I smiled as I continued down the walk.

He opened the door and I slid perfectly into the leather seats that reeked of novelty. As he walked around the front of the car, I peeked at the odometer. Twenty miles. He's just bought this. Like this afternoon.

I watched amused as he got in. He took a deep breath and let it out slowly before he turned the key in the ignition and drove slowly away from my house.

Awkward silence does not begin to articulate the car ride to the restaurant. In fact my hands began to twitch nervously because I didn't know where we were going or what I was supposed to say to him. Shop talk didn't seem appropriate in this attire.

When we suddenly stopped in a downtown parking lot, I swallowed because I didn't see any restaurants around here.

He paid the attendant the fifty bucks and gestured I should follow him. I knew we were somewhere downtown and it's easy to get your bearings once you can see the skyline but I was still a little confused as I had to trot to keep up with his pace.

"Slow down. Three-inch heels back here," I said when I finally caught up with him at a stoplight.

"I don't want to forfeit our reservation," he said as he began to cross the street.

I paused on the corner for a moment. Reservations?

He opened up the front door to Nine Steakhouse and I just looked at him. This place had valet and I had just hiked a half mile in heels.

"I could have sprung for valet," I whispered bitterly as I passed.

"And have some punk drive my new baby? Never." He stepped around me and to the hostess podium.

The hostess's eyes dilated and her pulse warmed her cheeks as she looked up at him, pink lips slightly parted for a moment before she shook her head and looked down at her reservation list. Chaz smiled patiently and waited, unaffected by the girl's obvious attraction.

I looked away from the scene. *Don't think about his tapered waist and how the cut of the suit perfectly outlined his frame. Focus on the interior.* I read about this place in the Dallas guides and listened to Jessa talk about how some of her boys took her here. But never had I imagined coming here. With him.

We were seated at our reserved table when he finally said something of worth over his menu. It jolted me out of my study of the place. You never know when you might need a small piece of information for writing and I was getting a volume from the décor and the people here, especially the women who were watching Chaz with a sharp eye.

"So what exactly do you do again? Besides drink coffee."

It was the third question of friendship, paired with a joke. I could do jokes. "I'm a writer for Cloak and Dagger Productions."

"What's that?"

"We specialize in cheap horror movies."

He smiled. "Seriously?"

"Yeah. Why?"

"Those things are so wrong about everything," he said as he looked down at the menu and smiled.

"Well, maybe I can change that."

"What? Write the truth? People couldn't handle the truth."

I eyed him over the menu. "Okay, Jack. But you did just give me a guide to living furry in the big city."

The waiter came over and Chaz left me speechless. Again. "The lady and I will have the ten-ounce top sirloin cooked medium well for me and medium rare for her. Two potatoes and Caesar salad with the house Shiraz and water," he ordered flawlessly.

"Yes, sir," the waiter said with smile and a nod as he took the menus.

I waited to speak until he was gone. "Okay. Spill. You and Iris are all *evil is everywhere* so I've been cooped up in the house for three weeks. But the second you get the munchies, I get a hall pass?"

"Wow." He smiled.

"I'm serious. I want answers. Like is the suit new or just the shirt?" I asked.

He looked down at the table with a small smile. "How'd you catch me?"

I tapped my nose. "Can't miss that new shirt smell."

Chaz shook his head. "That's incredible."

"Not really. Jessa swears that she can smell the difference between real Fendi and fake."

Chaz laughed. "So how did you and Jessa meet? You two don't look like you even belong in the same room together."

"Thanks," I said with mocked offense.

"You know what I mean."

I did. Looking at the little pixie next to the wookie always made me scratch my head too. But it was a funny story. And being funny was what Violet did best.

"Fine, but I'm not forgetting you owe me an answer. I was still living in LA and her company flew her out there for a fashion thing and we both ended up at a party. I was standing next to the bar and she gave me her drink order because I was dressed like the waitresses.

"When I explained to her that I didn't work here, she apologized and we started talking. But this jerk she'd come with walked up to us and said he was ready to go home. It was obvious she didn't want to go, especially with him, so I kinda stepped in and made him go away."

"What did you do?" Chaz asked leaning across the table, an amused look on his face.

"I threw two drinks at him in rapid succession and yelled something like *'No we will not have a threesome with you'* and grabbed Jessa's hand and stormed out of the room."

"Seriously?" he laughed.

A real laugh. It made my skin hum. It was warm and golden but it faded like a sun slipping beyond the horizon, quickly and leaving me cool.

I nodded as I studied him. "Turned out that this guy was some bigwig at his company and he ended up getting fired soon afterwards. Apparently, he actually *had* propositioned someone at the party and she went to the top and reported him for sexual harassment."

Chaz just shook his head with laughter. "You're fearless."

"Just not smart enough to know better," I shrugged.

He leaned back in his chair as the waiter came with our wine, water, and salads.

"So how did you get to Dallas?"

I looked down at my salad and knew that my cheeks were turning red just thinking about what had actually caused me to flee across the country. Even though it happened a little under a year ago, it was still a touchy subject.

"Oh," Chaz said, putting the napkin on his lap, something I couldn't imagine him doing with his bagged burgers and fries. "I know that look."

"Pretty trite, I know."

"Boyfriend or husband?"

"Fiancé. You'd think that since I'm so creative, my life wouldn't be so predictable. First, my fiancé cheats on me and I catch him. Then I get attacked in a dark alley under a full moon. I'm kinda expecting to get on a bus one day with a bomb under it."

"I'm sorry," he said. "On behalf of all men."

"I'm fine now," I said with a shrug, stabbing my salad that

didn't really look appetizing compared to the lure of future steak. "But I wasn't then. So I packed up everything in LA and moved halfway across the country."

"And Jessa?"

"Silly thing picked up everything and met me in the middle. Been together ever since. She was great during the whole grieving thing, prevented me from doing some stupid stuff."

"Like what?"

"Like giving him the ring back. It was the gaudy three-carat thing I never liked," I said remembering the distasteful ring and the way it used to weigh down my finger.

"So what did you do with it? Because I'm imagining you throwing it in the Trinity," he offered as he took a huge bit of his salad.

"Turned them into these," I said brushing my hair back behind my ear to show off my sparklies. "The most perfect pair of diamond earrings I could find. I was all for the Trinity thing, but Jessa is much more practical."

Chaz chuckled and continued on his salad.

I just pushed the leaves around the plate and sighed. "She is the only family I have. Taking care of Jessa is the only thing I know I do well. But enough about me, I know all about me. I want to hear much more about Mr. Garrett who stalks around in a redesigned muscle car," I leaned back and took a sip of my wine, which was wonderfully earthy and dry at the same time.

"Not much to tell," he said as he finished with his salad, putting the fork on the plate.

"Right, because all the men I know answer to an actual higher Power and carry around guns with silver bullets," I whispered the last part.

Chaz leaned forward on the table and clasped his hands. His eyes took on a steady look but I matched it easily. Very little was scaring me these days and there was no way I was going to be intimidated by a deep stare from a handsome man.

"I was born here actually. And raised by my dad..."

I leaned forward and listened as he dropped his voice a little.

"Like I told you before, it turned out I had the same gift and he taught me the trade, got me involved with the Cause, and by 17, I was working my own missions for them".

"And do all of them involve stalking single woman?" I asked.

"No. Some are more dangerous. Some are as simple as delivering a package."

We were silent as the waiter brought out the meals. My mouth immediately began to water as I looked down at the pink meat. At least I could eat this without guilt. I needed the protein to keep me grounded until I went to Iris's next full moon. She had promised a quiet place to work and shift because she was certain I was not going to be able to stop it this early in the game.

The steak was heaven on a plate. Hot and thick and juicy and not a bunny in sight. I closed my eyes on the first bite and just sorted out the spices that had been used and savored the flame-grilled taste.

"Good?"

I opened my eyes to find him watching my little display. "Perfect. Thank you."

He just smiled and looked back down at his meal.

We really didn't start talking again until we were both finished. Steak isn't a really conversation meal, with all the chewing. Pasta was more of a date food. One dainty ziti at a time, with a toss of the hair and a flirty smile.

But this was not a date, I kept telling myself. It was just two people, enjoying a meal on a Thursday night together. Dressed in heels and a suit and complete with awkward silences, but this was not a date.

As the waiter cleared away the plates, Chaz drank the last of his wine. "You said something the other day."

"I say a lot of things, mostly with my foot in my mouth."

He licked his lips. "You said that the job wasn't who I was, just what I did."

"I do remember something like that."

He leaned forward, clasping his hands together. "I've worked my tail off for the Powers for six years now and I can't remember the last time I did something I wanted to do."

"Sounds like one hell of a revelation but you could have eaten steak alone."

He shook his head. "I eat too many meals alone. Out of paper bags. I wanted some decent company for once and silverware."

"And the car? Was that something that you wanted?"

Chaz laughed and again, I was surrounded by that golden wamrth. "God yes. Dad's Bronco is great for lugging things around, but I've been eyeing the new design of the Challenger for ages."

I laughed and drew the jealous glance of everyone around us. Something had changed. This wasn't the Chaz that had previously been stalking me behind plastic house plants. He was different, despite the same half smile he was giving me now.

And here I was, well fed, well dressed, and willing to suspend my disbelief for at least one evening to also be sitting across from a man having a nice meal that I had no intention of paying for.

"So where to next?" I asked. "Drinks might be nice but nowhere too packed."

"Something wrong?" he asked, arched eyebrow.

"Can't I just want a quiet place to talk?" I countered as I leaned back.

Chaz chuckled. "And I just wanted a place to listen to music."

I looked hard at him. "You wanted a place where you can avoid questions."

"Guilty," he held his hands up in defense. "Well, that, and there's live jazz at this place down the street."

"Jazz?"

"Got a problem with jazz?"

I shook my head. "You just don't seem like the jazz type."

"What type am I?" he asked, a smile curling up only one side of his mouth.

"More Motley Crüe than Miles Davis."

The waiter stealthily put the bill on the table and he paid. I didn't protest.

"Let's get out of here," he said as he stood.

The hostess held the door for us and we exited into the cool night air. It refreshed me immediately and I took in a deep breath of the downtown air. Smelled like people and coffee and rain. Didn't remember bad weather on the forecast but the nose knows.

Chaz smiled and stretched on the corner as we waited for the pedestrian right of way. He swept back his jacket and put his hands in his pockets. Looked like a Versace ad with a small hand gun tucked into the side of his pants by the strange lump there. Knowing Chaz, there was a knife somewhere under that flawless suit.

Filled with steak and bravery because of the rising moon, I just had to ask. "Did you ever do any modeling?"

Something shimmered over Chaz's brown eyes for a split second as he looked down the street and I knew I was right. It was like the cherry on the top of the meal. "You were a model."

His jaw clenched. "I have to make money somehow," he shrugged as he motioned that we needed to cross the street while the light was good.

I jogged along next to him in the high heels, still giggling to myself.

"What?" he grumbled.

"You *are* a model," I repeated with a sing-songy voice.

"What about it?"

"Nothing. Just never imagined the guys on the billboards with shotguns in their cars saving damsels in distress."

He stopped walking in the middle of the sidewalk and turned to me, chin lowered and eyes dark.

I froze. Who would have known that of all the other things I egged him on about, this would be the touchy subject?

"Like I said. It's a job. Pays the bills and keeps my schedule free for things like this."

"Dates or sacred destinies?" I asked quickly.

Chaz just lifted his left shoulder briefly and the glare faded into an odd grin. "Both."

He turned quickly and started up the street.

But I was still frozen. Damn it. He might have just admitted this was a date. My cheeks flushed and so did my senses as I caught a tendril of his scent on the wind, that starchy musk that had come over me earlier. I wanted to close my eyes and curl up in a little ball surrounded by that warmth.

He was half a block down when he realized that I wasn't next to him. He stopped and turned around confused. "What?" he called out.

Suddenly, there was a shift in the wind and I was no longer caught up in his smell and the idea of a first date. I was surrounded by dogs, the smell of wet dog, mildewed and sewage-soaked, coming from up wind. Made part of my steak dinner come up a little. A shiver racked my spine and I moved quickly for Chaz, as quick as I could in three-inch heels.

He knew what I knew in the moment he caught my elbow.

"Lose the shoes," he said in a low growl as he pulled me quickly down the street, gracefully guiding us through the growing night crowds.

As smoothly as I could between our long strides, I slipped off the red pumps and carried them in my free hand.

I could still smell them, the way they felt in my head. Iris had always said you could tell the good guys from the bad in an instant. I chilled, finally knowing the bad guys felt like thick, sticky fear that crept down my back.

The boot steps quickened behind us and Chaz pulled me into a run, my bare feet slapping against the cold sidewalk.

"Run," he said, dropping my arm, stopping in our flight. "Go someplace safe."

"Are you insane?" I snapped.

"Go!" he repeated and I caught a light in his eyes, a glint of something more powerful than I had ever given him credit for.

I simply nodded and took off down the street at panther speed.

I didn't hear anything beyond the wind in my ears as I cleared two blocks in three seconds. I stopped and stood flush against a building to look back down the street. No one was following me, Chaz was gone, and the passer-bys didn't even look twice at the woman breathing heavily against a building corner. I was nicely dressed and therefore not a threat to their normal Thursday night.

It was dark and quiet and there was no dog smell on the wind, no Chaz smell either. I sucked in the cool safe air.

What the hell was I doing? I asked myself. Who were they? Haverty's men come to collect? And why the hell had I run? I'd just left him there, to fight my battles. Just left Chaz to deal with the beasties because they were his thing; they were part of his world.

Screw that. When the last time Violet Jordan let someone else fight her battles?

Oh, that's right, until I met Chaz, there were no battles to fight. And if there was anything that invaded my little fortress, I ran. It's what I had always done. Run, move, and start all over with a fresh slate when things got hairy.

Wasn't getting any hairier than this.

I looked up at the waxing moon and felt the stir of the cat in my chest. I wasn't the Violet Jordan who ran anymore. I was the Violet Jordan who threw drinks in men's faces and threw sensei's across the room. I was the Violet Jordan who dated male models.

And those jerks had just ruined the first good date I'd had in years.

Without a plan, I went back. Half-way to where I'd lost Chaz, I jumped as I heard a cry carried on the wind. It was him. I looked around at the other people who walked around unknowingly of the battle going on down the street, looked at their happy faces and listened to the echoing laughter.

Chaz. I couldn't leave him there, despite the mixed signals, despite the threats, despite his completely butting into every aspect of my life.

I could hear grunts and caught a whiff of Chaz's starch.

It only fueled my blood as I walked past an alleyway where I could feel them again. I stepped around a garbage bin that was blocking most of the alleyway from view of the sidewalk.

I gulped and had a very vivid flashback. Two months ago, me in an alleyway, trash cans, my shoes in my hand. And we all know how wonderfully that went.

My resolve faltered and I slid behind the dumpster. What the hell was I doing again? Right: saving the boy. Me against three grown "men." Banner idea, Violet.

Closing my eyes, I tried to swallow the steak-tasting fear rising in my throat. I should run, call Iris. She surely knew someone who was burlier than me. Hell, Iris herself could probably take these guys down with one flick of her little finger.

The distinct crack of bone echoed through the alleyway and I could taste blood like copper in the air.

He would do this for me, had done this for me. And, hell, I healed pretty fast the last time. Without Chaz, I'd be dead in an alley. Look like things were about to come full circle.

"Here kitty, kitty," one of the men called out from the alley.

"Crap." I had been made. Though part of me doubted they could smell my magnolia over their sewer stench.

With one last deep breath and the passing thought that I really wished I had finished the last edit on that script I'd been working on, I slid around the corner.

Chaz was on his knees. In the faint light, blood glistened as it poured from a cut in his forehead. Two men held him by the elbows as the third punched away at his ribs.

I dropped the heels and they made a wonderfully hollow echo as the sound bounced up into the night sky. I also dropped any pretense of my shields as I opened the door to my town house and let my power dance excitedly along my skin.

The pummeler, the one doing a number on Chaz's torso, looked over at me with a grimace and I flinched. It wasn't that he was ugly, but his animal was right on the surface, seemingly right under his skin, and the canine features were pushing against his lean face.

I vowed I would never look like that as I stepped fully into the alley.

"Violet," Chaz breathed, trying to threaten me again.

"Sorry. Terrible with instructions," I apologized.

He shook his head and left it down. His fight was gone. Mine wasn't. These were the bastards that chased me. These were the mutts that had me on house lock down. As I watched them, smelled them, watched as they licked their lips, every muscle in my body tensed and then I relaxed. I could hear Iris, *"Embrace your beast and it will set you free."*

"You're the one we wanted anyway," the closest one said as the wall of a man turned slowly towards me.

The magic he invoked danced in the small space of the dark alley as he reached for his animal.

I remember him coming at me with lightning speed I knew I could beat.

I remembered catching him mid-step, mid-leap, mid-shift as my nails dug into the flesh around his throat and into his abdomen.

I don't remember screaming into the night as I slid down into the darkness in my chest and let the panther take hold.

Chapter Sixteen

Once there was a very lonely fairy princess who couldn't sleep. For when she slept she had dreams of great adventures, but when she woke, there was no one to go on an adventure with. So she sulked around her castle looking for playmates. She asked her mother for a little sister, she asked her father for a little brother, she even asked her maid for a dog. But no one could give her what she needed.

So she ran away. As most princesses do at some point.

She walked as far as she could and when her feet were tired she took a rest on a stone by a lake.

"Why don't you have a drink?"

The fairy princess looked around and finally looked down to the surface of the lake to see a young face in the ripples of the water.

"Who are you?"

"Just a boy in the water. You look tired. Take a drink."

The water looked cool and refreshing. She looked back at the long road that she had taken and the long road ahead of her.

She reached her hand out and dunked it under the surface of the pond. Just then a cat came out of the reeds and, teetering on the rock next to her, the cat scratched her hand.

"Ouch," the fairy princess cried as she clutched her hand to her chest. Little drops of blood fell into the water.

The water rippled fiercely and the face of the boy pressed against the surface. The cat scratched at the face. Bubbles poured out of the mouth in a silent scream and the face sunk into the darkness.

The cat sat pleased on the rock next to her. "He tried to pull you in."

"What?"

"If you went in, he could come out."

"I've never heard of that."

The cat sighed. "I supposed that you have never heard of a hagfin or a liger, either?"

"What's a liger?"

The cat shook its head. "I suppose that I'll just have to protect you then."

The princess jumped off the rock and looked down at her hand. The scratches were just small pink lines now. The sting was gone.

"I don't need a silly cat to protect me!" The princess balled her hands up into little fists and stomped away.

"That's the way you came," the cat said casually as she licked a paw.

The princess huffed and turned around sharply to head in the correct direction.

The cat lazily jumped off the rock and began to follow the princess.

"Stop following me," the princess yelled.

The cat simply followed the girl down the road.

When she settled in to sleep, her body exhausted from the adventure of that day, she said "I don't want a cat. I want a real friend."

"But who will protect you from water dragons and reedwasps?"

"You're making them up," the princess said as she curled tighter into her pillow of grass and weeds.

The cat curled up in the folds of the princess's dress and slept. As she had never been this close to a cat, her mother and the cook had always shooed them away as foul beasts, she looked down at its sleeping form and smiled. The princess fell into a peaceful sleep, lulled by the soft sound of purring.

I sat up quickly, naked as usual. Surprisingly enough, I was okay that. The mongrels were all face down on the blacktop of the alley. I could make out the shreds of the black dress that had only been worn once. Does it still count as one hell of a date when you wake up naked surrounded by burly men?

Quickly, I drug the nearest body closer and pulled off his long trench coat. Ignoring the offensive smell, I wrapped it around my bare shoulders. I reeked but I couldn't be picky.

I stood and looked around. There wasn't much blood, couldn't smell any, which was good. I cinched the black trench coat tightly around my waist and stepped over the bodies and the shreds of my new cashmere coat. Damn it.

Tidbits of what happened floated behind my eyes, feelings of it ran up and down my skin. I remembered Chaz cornered and then I shifted. I remembered grabbing someone's throat and backing someone against a wall and something about a brick but it was still fuzzy. I remembered only three, but as I counted, there were five bodies on the asphalt. Go Chaz.

When I found Chaz, I ran over to him, my bare feet splashing through the puddles in the alleyway. I had been out long enough for it to have rained.

He was unconscious as well. I knelt down by him and curled my fingers underneath his head. It was wet and warm, and when I drew my hand back, it was covered with blood.

I gulped. Blood meant a concussion and concussions usually meant hospitals and I wasn't sure I wanted to walk into a hospital wearing only a trench coat.

I reached down with my clean hand and touched his skin, ran my fingers across his bruising cheek bones. I could see the model features in the shadows of the alleyway.

His long lashes began to flutter and I pulled my hands away quickly, folding them together on my lap.

Chaz opened his brown eyes and looked up at me.

"You're naked," he whispered, in sing-song voice.

"You're funny," I said as I helped him to a sitting position.

He reached up the back of the head and came away with blood on his fingers as well. "Not good," he muttered.

"Do we need to go to a hospital?"

"Nah," he countered quickly as he began to stand.

His knees nearly gave underneath him, but I was able to catch him. Extra strength really came in handy sometimes. And I felt extra strong. Nose was on overtime as I caught a full whiff of Chaz's sweat and blood.

"What'd you do to them?" he asked, looking around at the three guys on the ground.

I had to focus on walking, on the rocks in my foot, anything that wasn't the hard line of his body pressed up against mine, to get an answer out. "I dunno. But they're still alive. And I seem to be scratch-free."

"Wow," he breathed. "Remind me to send a thank you to the sensei."

Slowly, we wove through the alleyway, looking very suspicious as a girl in obviously nothing but a man's trench coat and an injured companion emerged from a darkened alley onto the night street arm in arm.

Chaz's finger shot out and I nearly missed what he was pointing at. My shoes. I did take them off. I made sure he was stable for a moment, leaning him up against the brick wall and went to retrieve them, having to pick gravel out of the soft flesh of my foot before I slid the shoes on. I immediately felt human again.

I also took a moment to make sure that my borders were back. I easily slipped back behind the protection and went back to Chaz. Protected behind my walls, his body wasn't as hot against mine.

"Why did they attack us?" I asked in a low voice as we walked out onto the sidewalk to seamlessly join a crowd of people. They shouted jokes to each other and their merriment only increased the shadow of our recent struggle as they covered our exit.

"Maybe Haverty was ready to bring you home," Chaz whispered as they passed.

"What?"

Chaz just shook his head, which surely made it throb. His face winced in pain as we made our way back to the parking lot.

"Let's go to my place," I suggested. There I knew would be a first aid kit and a place clean enough to use it.

He didn't protest and even handed me the keys to his precious car.

"This is a big step," I said jingling the keys. "Are you sure?"

"Shut up and drive," he grumbled, but I saw a small smile play on his lips before the pain in his ribs made him crumple again.

He was quiet in the car, looking out at the night's skyline. I just drove. After having my first official attack and first official offense, I wasn't sure if I was ready to talk. It's something else when you realize that you are the power out on the streets, after so long of just being a nobody. That you are a force to be reckoned with, with your fists and not just your words.

He was still a little shaky as we got through the front door and the oddest thought crossed my mind, which made me chuckle as I threw my keys on the foyer table.

"What's so funny?" Chaz said as I shuffled him into the living room.

"You're not going to believe me," I smiled as I went to the kitchen to get my first aid kit and wash my hands.

"Try me," he responded, plopping down on the couch.

I came back out into the living room and sat gently on the edge of the couch next to him, making sure that the trench coat hadn't exposed anything. Being this close to him made my hands shake and my skin warm. But maybe it was just the adrenaline in my system.

"You're the first man I've had in my house," I confessed.

Chaz chuckled softly.

"What?" I prodded playfully as I opened up the gauze and the peroxide.

"I don't believe you."

"Why not?" I asked hoping that if we kept talking about my painful love life, he wouldn't pay attention to the fact that

I was about to put peroxide on a very deep gash on the back of his head.

"Because you're funny, and tall, and smart."

"But my friends are pretty," I countered.

He winced loudly as I dabbed the wound with the white gauze. I winced with him and tried to blow on it. Talking must have helped with the sting as he continued on with the conversation.

"Why should that matter?"

"I don't know. But when we are at a bar, guys are buying drinks for everyone but me. You did. Technically you bought a drink for Jessa first."

"Do you go anywhere else to meet . . . new people?"

"Didn't you know? That's why I was in the alley way that night I was attacked."

Chaz laughed and I finished wiping off the dirt and gravel embedded into his scalp. It had to hurt but he was taking it pretty well. I could see his fists clench on his lap when I hit a particularly sore spot.

I continued talking as I still had some work to do. "And now what am I supposed to say to Mr. Right. *Hi, I'm Violet, I'm an Aries, and I go wild once a month.*"

"Try. *Hi, I'm never going to be able to finish a conversation with you because I've got six million people that go before me.*"

"You win."

I couldn't tape the stupid gash because it was in his hair and I didn't want to wrap cloth around his head. The only thing I could think of was a cap to keep the wad of bandages in place, which I excused myself to go get.

Half an hour later, he was resting on my couch after a few Advil and a cold beer, which I had forgotten I even had in my fridge. I was showered and dressed in lounge pants and a zippered sweater and curled so tightly in my favorite chair I thought I might actually break something.

He looked comfortable lying on my couch in his suit pants and a light gray North Carolina undershirt. "So are we going to talk about what happened tonight or not?" he asked before he took a long sip of his beer.

"I'd rather not." I wrapped my arms around my knees. "I'd rather discuss your obsession with college T-shirts."

He looked down at his shirt. There were a few blood spots down the front I tried to ignore. "Some people collect shot glasses from the places they visit, I collect T-shirts."

"You've been all these places?" I remember Harvard, Stanford, and now North Carolina. "You get around."

He just looked over at me with a raised eyebrow. "Just like you get around what really needs to be talked about."

I bounced out of the chair and started cleaning up after my horrible patch-up job. Nervous feet don't stay still.

Chaz fought a smile and licked his lips. "I was referring to the fact that you were able to shift when you needed to."

I had, without the meditated breathing or Iris watching over my shoulder. I picked up the last of the white bits from the coffee table and jammed them into the plastic bag I'd grabbed earlier. "I guess I did."

"Told ya you were the right girl," he smarted as he took another sip.

I rolled my eyes at his assuredness and headed for the

kitchen. I grabbed the horrible smelling trench coat. I already had plans to burn it in some cleansing ritual I was sure Chaz could get his hands on. But I noticed a weight I hadn't before in my desperate attempt to get out of it and into something that smelled like it had been washed this century.

Putting the trash on the table, I held the coat at arm's length and carefully patted down the sides. Who knows what I might find in the pockets? Doggie treats? What was left of a tennis shoe? Because a wallet with an address would be just too easy.

"Whatcha got there?"

"Something's in the pocket."

Chaz looked over the top of the couch with a deep furrow between his brows.

Grimacing with the thoughts of the sludge that might be in the pocket of this coat, I slid my hand down into the left side pocket and my fingers brushed a moist paperback.

Dropping the smelly coat to the ground, I looked at the book. It was an almanac. A wet soggy almanac. Nothing special. I thumbed through the pages and found one dog-eared page towards the end. I tried to ignore the obvious pun.

As I opened to the page, a picture of me slid out. It was a candid Polaroid in the front of my coffee shop. I shivered. That opened up a whole other can of weird.

Chaz's warmth chased away the slimy fear crawling up my arm as he stood just over my shoulder. "What..." His question dropped off as he pulled the Polaroid from my fingers. "Well, I guess it's official."

"What? They can't afford digital." I looked up at him. I needed some of stalwart strength by proxy.

"You're on his radar."

"I'm guessing that beating up a pack of wild dogs probably wasn't exactly under the radar."

"I'm guessing those mutts were Haverty's. He's testing you, Violet. He's finding your weak spots."

"I'm guessing that there is way too much guessing going on right now and not enough sleeping."

Chaz's eyebrow rose sharply.

"Whoa there boy. You're on the couch."

Chapter Seventeen

I shuffled into the kitchen, rubbing my eyes, and went straight for the coffee already brewing. It was the good French roast with a stick of cinnamon in the filter. The smell of coffee and pancakes had pulled me from my restless sleep.

"Good morning," Chaz greeted as he flipped pancakes on the grill.

Finger up between us to stop any further notion of human speech, I poured myself a cup of coffee, put in my two sugars, and a splash of milk from the jug in the fridge. Then I took a long warm sip and leaned against the counter. "Morning," I managed.

Slightly amazed or slightly still asleep, I watched mesmerized as he flipped the most perfectly round pancakes. Did I even have pancake mix in my cabinet? There didn't seem to be a box anywhere. In fact, the kitchen looked cleaner than it looked last night. Oh God, could he be a morning person?

Bandages gone, the only remnant of the wound itself was the funky way his hair stuck out in the morning light. Still in the undershirt, he'd traded the suit pants for an old pair of sweatpants I'd dug out of the back of my dresser.

"Did you know this is the first meal I have fixed in probably three months?" He gave me a wide smile as he flipped another perfect golden circle without even looking.

"Show off," I whispered. "Those look good."

"I thought you were a coffee-only girl." He kept his voice low, pointing the spatula to my usual morning breakfast held tightly in my hands

"Turns out a girl can't live on caffeine alone."

Chaz chuckled and put a heaping pile of pancakes on the breakfast bistro set in the sunny corner. I slowly moseyed around the small kitchen space and got the syrup, again, that I didn't know I had. Even managed to pour a cup of coffee for him.

"Thanks," he said as he sat down in the puddle of morning light.

Chaz didn't waste any time, pulling two pancakes off the top and drenching them with syrup.

Slowly, I sat across from him and watched him eat. He had an amazing amount of gold in his hair in the morning sun. Guess I hadn't noticed since we had more of a sundown relationship. A relationship where I knocked people unconscious to protect him. And vice versa.

Eventually, he looked up at me with a guilty look. "What? Did you want me to wait?"

I shook my head. "No. Your head looks a lot better this morning."

"Feels better," he smiled before he completely filled his mouth with a forkful.

I still wasn't a breakfast person but I managed to cut up a few of the perfectly fluffy pancakes and push them around my plate with puddles of syrup running trails around the Corningware.

"So what's the plan for today?" he asked.

"Work. I'm two days late with my part of a script rewrite. And I've got three blurbs due yesterday."

"What about last night?"

I shook my head. My brain hadn't shut off after I'd tucked him in on the couch and I went up stairs. Even the second hot shower that rinsed away the residual smell of sewer water didn't calm my brain. I spent most of the night thinking up what to do next. Hence, the desperate need for coffee this morning. "Ever think running is what they are expecting? They are going to be looking for two scared people running out of town. They're not going to be looking for a screenwriter and the gardener?"

Chaz stopped chewing and just looked at me.

"Well, I don't want you to get too far away if I'm wrong and you seem like you'd be handy with a weed whacker for protection and lawn care?"

"How do you know that?" he protested.

I just raised an eyebrow. "Are you?"

His shoulders slumped, his eyes dropped to his plate. "I might have something to do," he grumbled before he swallowed his cheek-full of pancake.

"I'm sure you do," I said as I playfully took a sip of coffee. "But what would those Powers of yours think if you let me get kidnapped."

"Fine." His response was simple and casual. "On one condition."

And here was the catch.

"I want a story."

"It's a little early. Maybe after coffee."

He shoved another forkful of pancakes in his mouth and then asked, "The picture on the mantle. I'll mow your lawn for the story of the woman on the mantle."

My mouth fell open and I felt the blood rush from my face. I shook my head.

Chaz finished chewing and took a swig of coffee. "I'm ready when you are."

I shook my head again. I wasn't ready for this; I wasn't ready to tell anyone really. My skin goose-bumped with fear.

He leaned across the table and the golden in his eyes danced. "Just tell me who she is."

Watching him, I knew that this was a test. Some sort of cosmic test. Like what happened last night was some sort of a test to see if little Violet Jordan was strong enough for something.

"She's my mother."

The churning sensation in my midsection lessened when Chaz leaned back in his seat and smiled. "You look just like her."

He stood up and put his plate in the sink.

"Seriously?" I asked as I turned around in my chair as he put the rest of his cooking utensils in the sink.

"Could be twins. Mower in the garage?" he asked as he headed out the back sliding glass door to the garage.

I sat there for a moment, slightly confused. There wasn't any crying. No painful backlash, not that I really knew what I expected. But he now knew more about me than anyone.

I shook my head. Stop postulating, Violet, and get to work.

My second floor office overlooked the lovely street I lived on. I could sit there and type all day and be happy as a kitten. And watching Chaz mow the front yard of the fourplex without a shirt on wasn't hurting my mood any. So I'd just gotten myself a yard man. Unless there was some sort of underwear modeling emergency.

Staring out the window, lost in all the other types of emergencies the modeling field might have, I nearly missed Jessa's BMW pull up in front of my house.

I jumped up and watched as she sauntered past Chaz as he took a long swig of water from the bottle, ignoring the woman trying to be noticed.

I ran downstairs and opened the door before she even had a chance to ring the bell. "Jessa, what are you doing here?"

"Now I see why you work from home so often," she said taking one long glance back at the new gardener.

"Yeah, guilty," I said with a quick smile as I stepped behind her, shuffling her into the house quickly and closing the door.

"What are you doing here?" I repeated,

"A client gave me these, thought you might like them," she said as she handed me an unopened bag of Godiva chocolate-covered espresso beans.

"Thanks Jess. Why don't you have a seat?"

I sat down opposite her on the couch in my living room. Had to be a record for me to have two houseguests in one twenty-four-hour period. "So how have you been?"

Jessa kept looking around the place, inspecting it. "Great. You've been pretty hard to find lately."

"Working on this new project." I lied. Didn't like the taste it left in my mouth. I'd never lied to Jessa about anything. Never had a reason to until that stupid thing in the stupid alley.

"What's it about?" she asked, seeming interested. But she was more interested in the reflection of the glass surface of the coffee table.

I just shrugged. "Have to wait and see."

Jessa waved it off with her hand. "By the way, you look great. A glow in your cheek. Did you finally find a diet that worked?"

"I've been running." It wasn't really a lie. Wasn't like I could tell her that when I run, it fulfills one of my primal urges and helps me keep control of the panther that sleeps within my chest. But I thought that may be too much information for such a causal visit.

Jessa stood up and looked around with a little nod, her long ponytail swinging around her shoulders.

I thought she was going to move for the door. I thought she was going to leave and go back to her side of the world, back into her niche on the non-weird side of my life. I really didn't want to explain the insanely hot gardener mowing the lawn outside. Hadn't had enough coffee yet today.

"What's that?" Jessa asked innocently as she walked in front of me and to the other side of the couch.

Her manicured hand reached under the corner of the couch and pulled out a white button-up shirt.

My heart immediately stopped in my chest as I watched frozen as she unfolded Chaz's shirt from the night before and held it up before her. The blood spatter was dark across the crisp shirt and I could see the shadow of it from the other side.

"What's this, Violet?"

"Nothing. Just an accident."

Jessa dropped the shirt to her waist, from the air between us, keeping it clenched in her little hands. "When did you start wearing Calvin Klein?"

It was the most confused I'd ever seen Jessa's face. Her lips drew into a tight line and her perfectly shaped eyebrows almost touched with a firm wrinkle between them.

The little do-gooder in the back of my head leapt up and screamed I needed to tell her, I needed someone to talk to. People could actually explode by keeping stuff like this inside. Spontaneous combustion is real.

The buzz of the lawnmower stopped, creating a sudden chilly silence in the room between us. I couldn't bring myself to say the words out loud.

"Did you get hurt?"

I stood. I needed to be on my feet for this, for what I felt brewing in the air around us. "It was nothing."

"A nothing like the nothing in the bar?"

"No. We got mugged."

"We?" her voice was high and tight as she clamped down harder on the white cotton.

"I had a date last night." I thought I'd had a date last night. Jury was still out on that one.

"With who?" Jessa asked. "Was it Brian? Did he ask you out?"

My answer was meant to come out casual. It was meant to be just a small little answer that might prompt her to leave but it came out harsh. "No one you know."

"Where was the heads up?" She dropped one of the corners

of her shirt and her hand went to her hip. "Come on. It's the first date I've heard of since you moved here," Jessa said with a faint smile.

"Wasn't that big of a deal." Another lie. I was two for two now.

"We could have gone shopping."

I frowned. "I don't need you to pick out my clothes."

"I didn't mean that," Jessa tried to backpedal. "I just meant that we could have done your hair, or something."

And there she was, toting the *Let's change Violet* banner again. This is wasn't what I wanted to hear right now. For the first time in my life, I didn't feel like there was anything that needed changing. And I thought I looked good last night, pre-panther, that is.

My face was beginning to ache with the frown now etched upon it. "I managed."

Jessa crossed her arms, keeping the white shirt clutched in her fist. "Why didn't you tell me, Violet?" There was a hard edge to her voice, a seriousness in her looks I had never seen in Jessa.

"You didn't ask." That bit of truth flew in from left field. It actually felt kind of good to say, like running endorphins but better. Felt much better than lying. So I continued. "Come to think of it, lately it's been all about Jessa."

"So tell me now."

"Why?"

"Because I'm asking."

"Doesn't work like that Jessa. Can't just pick and choose the scandalous parts of my life to suddenly be interested in." I felt better, getting some things off my chest, and the frown had slowly melted away.

Her jaw was clenched tight and I could have sworn her skin glowed. "But nothing happens to you. You locked yourself up in your tower, barely interacting with the world. I'm surprised you have anything to write about at all for your . . . movies."

"Missing an adjective there, Jess?" I snapped with a raised eyebrow. I didn't know where she was trying to go with this little visit. Except to insult me, and frankly, only I got to do that.

Jessa struggled for words. The word was there; she just didn't want to release it.

"Stupid? Maybe. Lame," I offered.

"Well, yeah."

My blood began to boil. "They are not stupid movies," I growled.

"*White Snake Ridge*, *Shadow Stalker*, oh and my personal favorite *Goblin Rock*. Yeah, not exactly winning Oscars there, Vi."

I felt the skin prickle between my shoulders, couldn't help my head from sinking down as my weight shifted uneasily between both feet. "We all can't be rich, princess. Some of us have to work. So don't you judge what I do. Mommy didn't buy me a penthouse downtown."

"I work hard too," she demanded, pointing her tiny finger into her no doubt designer blouse, perfectly tailored to fit her small frame.

"Lunching your way across the Metroplex, one wealthy Y-chromosome at a time.'

Jessa gasped and then glared. Her arms went straight down at her side and her little hands were clenched into tight little fists.

The hanger on the decorative mirror next to us snapped. The mirror slid down the wall and crashed onto the table below it. Half my turtle collection was pulverized and the other half launched towards us like shelled artillery.

My hand flew to my face to block the glass. Little cuts grazed my forearms and neck. After the shards fell around us, my eyes snapped from the decapitated tortoise heads, beady eyes staring up at me, at Jessa. She hadn't moved, hadn't even flinched as the glass flew around the two of us.

"I came here to invite you to a party, to get you out of whatever's been up with you lately. But you obviously don't need me with your perfect little life here," she huffed as she threw the white shirt at me and turned towards the door. "Maybe my family was right about you."

"That's right, just leave. You'll never have to lower yourself to middle class again."

"Thank God."

When Jessa slammed the front door, the mirror above the foyer table flew off the wall and shattered into a million pieces. Great, another mess.

I stood there fuming. Jessa better inherit that fourteen years of bad luck.

When Chaz came in the front door, I hadn't moved. Not really. I was sitting cross-legged in the middle of the silver rain of glass, headless turtles lined up in front of me. And the Godiva espresso beans were half gone.

"Violet, what the hell happened?" he asked as he carefully

stepped around the first disaster area with long stride and made his way over to me.

I offered up the bag of chocolate. "Want one?"

"No. Are you okay?"

I gulped. "Jessa's never going to speak to me again."

My face heated and the anger, fear, and newly forming anguish all came rushing back. Groaning, I put my head in my empty hand, not relinquishing the bag of chocolate.

"Get up, Violet."

I offered a hand but didn't look up at him. I'd been crying and I was sure my eyes were a lovely shade of salmon.

With one strong pull, he lifted me up off the floor. My head fell forward against his shoulder. His heartbeat calmed my racing thoughts. He rubbed my back as I sucked in a stuttered breath of his sweaty, earthy smell.

"It's not the end of the world," he whispered.

"You got a heads up on that, do ya?"

He chuckled and pushed me away from him. He wiped the few tears that had fallen already. "What happened?"

"She asked me about your bloody shirt. And I called her selfish and she stormed out."

Chaz looked as confused as I was. We just stayed there for a few moments, silent and awkward, not quite knowing what to say next. Not that I expected much verbal consolation from Chaz.

I sniffed and wiped my eyes.

"I'd offer coffee but after those," he said, his eyes glancing down at the bag in my hand. "You're not going to sleep for a week. So how about some lunch?"

He took a thirty-five minute shower in my shower. I think it was a record, but I did have the best shower head in the world. I sat in the kitchen waiting for the dryer to finish. It still had twenty minutes. I'd actually done his laundry. Willingly. I'd offered somewhere in the verbal confession in the kitchen after he'd fixed ham and cheese sandwiches for the both of us. He'd listened like a true professional and I was reminded that he was the professional at this; chasing and violence was a normal workday for him.

Something was brewing in the ether, dancing along my skin as my leg bounced with anxiety. Yet, I felt numb, battered senseless. Like none of it had really settled in yet. These were things that happened to people in my head not to me, not to little Violet Jordan who really had locked herself in a tower.

Chaz tromped down the stairs and finally ended up in the kitchen, dragging me painfully from my pity party. "What's going on up there?" he asked as he flopped in the chair across from me.

"What?"

"You're bouncing like a rubber ball," he said pointing to my leg.

"Jessa, on top of this thing last night," I finally said.

"Took you long enough," he grumbled.

"Well forgive me," I snapped. "Been a while since I've had to deal with traumatic aftermaths."

I took in a deep breath. Now was not the time to be snippy or mad, or weak. Look where it had just gotten me, what it might have just cost me. I exhaled slowly and he looked up at me. I needed someone in my corner right now.

He moved around the place like he owned it, as he opening cabinets and drawers to find the making for a bowl of Cocoa Puffs. He looked good in my kitchen as he moved around, already knowing where everything was from his Julia Child routine this morning. He sat back down across from me and began to shove huge spoonfuls into his mouth.

"Do you always get hungry when you're talking about mortal danger?"

"No, I get hungry after I'm used for slave labor."

I tried to fight a smile. "You seriously could have said no."

He just shrugged. "I wanted to be here."

I watched him eat for a moment. Did he have any idea what he was saying in between the shovels of sugar? "So what do we do?"

He shrugged as he rose to rinse out the bowl and put it in the sink.

I had nothing. I looked at the bare wall where my mirror had been and then out at the clear sky of the November day. The clouds moved carelessly across the sky, free, and, at least to my knowledge, without the threat of mortal danger looming over them.

"Come on, I've got an idea."

Chapter Eighteen

"Tell me why we are here again?" I whispered as I felt the stare from the line of men behind the glass gun counter. I gulped; all of them were openly carrying guns. Welcome to Texas.

I held my coffee tightly and looked around. The writer in me thought this was great material: the guns, the accents, all wonderful little accoutrements for a future scripts. The animal in me didn't like being around so much ammunition. And really didn't like the mounted animals head above the row of shotguns on the far wall.

I also had the creepy feeling I was the only female who had visited these premise in a very long time. There was a hungry look to the men's eyes as they watched me cross the room. I stayed just behind Chaz's shoulder as we walked through the aisles of ammunition and practice targets. There was a distinctly grimy feel to the beige-stained colored walls and the smell of spent gunpowder was everywhere.

"I come here when I'm having a rough day," Chaz said simply as he slapped his gun range pass down on the counter next to the register. "And you need to learn to protect yourself."

The white-haired man in a flannel shirt with a rocket launcher strapped to his thigh took it and began hitting the keys on an antique cash machine, running the station fees, looking up intermittently at Chaz and then at me.

"I thought the dojo was enough," I whispered to him.

"Last night, it was. But you have to be prepared for every possible scenario."

I glanced at him. I suppose thanks to his fancy shotgun, I wasn't dinner. "Fine."

"I need your driver's license."

I dug through my huge purse groping for my wallet. Found a book, a notepad, my cell phone. Finally, I found it and pulled it out for him.

With a slightly bemused look, he took the license and handed it to the man. As he was signing the receipt, I took a moment to peruse the merchandise.

The guns were intense. Different brands, different sizes. I knew a little from the research I had to do. Frankly, I was more a proponent of the Louisville slugger kind of self-defense than a Colt 45.

"Can I show you somethin', miss?" the salesmen asked.

"Can I see this one?" I pointed to a shiny silver revolver. Very classic, very old time detective.

The man smiled and pulled his keys out from a pocket on his holster and unlocked the cabinet.

He opened the chamber before he handed it to me.

"It's heavier than I thought."

My finger curled around the pearl handle and I spun the chamber. Something about the solidity of the silver in my hand felt good.

"Your girl's got a good eye," the man said.

Chaz pulled up alongside me. "Yeah, she's a quick learner."

I laughed at the comment and flipped the chamber into the gun. Even after I handed the gun back to the man, I felt the residual weight of it in my hand.

The men began to discuss calibers and ammunition and my attention drifted over the man's shoulder to see their "Perfect Score" board, as announced by the black Sharpie letters scrawled on a white piece of spiral-bound paper. It was blue poster with Polaroids stapled to it. More proof there was not a female touch around this place. The pictures displayed men proudly holding up their targets. My eyes glanced from face to face but one jumped out of the flannelled crowd.

It was a young Chaz with a taller man's arm slung across his shoulders. The man had sandy brown hair and golden green eyes, just like Chaz. Both were smiling, dressed almost identical, both holding up bull's-eyes.

I leaned across the glass counter as far as I could to get a better look at his father. The scribble in the white space of the photo was dated March 1995.

Chaz leaned over to see what I was looking at.

I straightened up quickly, coming practically nose to nose with him. "You and your dad used to come here."

Chaz's eyes dropped when he saw the picture. He took a small step away. "Yeah."

"So you're really good at this?"

"Kinda," Chaz mumbled, as he put his credit card back in his wallet and the wallet in the pocket.

The man behind the counter hacked out a laugh as he slid two boxes across the counter. "Don't be shy, Charles. This 'en won the state sharpshooter championship at fourteen."

I looked back at him. He looked young as he fiddled with the zipper on his tote.

"His dad was a helluva shot too," the man continued. "God rest 'im."

"Thanks for the ammo, Buck," he said, his eyes locked on the two boxes.

The man nodded and walked over to another customer.

Chaz stepped around me and gestured to the back of the shop towards the inside ranges. As we cleared the earshot of the other men, he stopped and turned towards me. He couldn't look at me as he spoke. "Dad wanted to make sure I was good; that I could protect those who needed protecting. We came out here a couple times a month to practice."

Brushing past me, he headed for the back of the building. I took one last look at the board and slowly headed towards the brown signs that read "Lanes 1–7."

Chaz hoisted the olive drab duffle from the back of his car onto the ledge behind the shooting alley. I just watched him. I'd never seen him this focused. As he began to set the guns and boxes of bullets on the wooden ledge, he didn't have the furrow he usually had.

Three different handguns and a shotgun. I was pretty sure I had seen a "no shotgun" sign in the front room. But this was Chaz, he probably got special privileges.

He reached into his bag and pulled out a pair of headphones. They were huge and orange.

"Got an eight track to go with those?"

He handed them over. "They're monkey ears. They'll block the noise."

"Monkey ears?" I looked at the awkward, heavy things. My pride prevented me from putting them on. I wasn't much for the Princess Leia look, but hey, maybe he was.

"Just put them on," he griped with a small smile curling at the corner of this mouth as he readied a pistol.

I put my coffee down on the ledge and pried the headphones open and put them around my neck. They weighed heavy on my clavicle. "There. On."

Chaz shook his head. Picking up the nearest gun and clip, he strode to the lane, jammed the loaded magazine into the gun and fired off four shots.

The boom of the rounds not only startled me but the smell of gunpowder assaulted my nose as the crack ripped through my eardrums.

"Crap," I yelled, covering my ears.

"I warned you." Chaz said innocently as he left the gun on the ledge of the lane and walked back to where I was still holding my ringing ears.

"Super sensitive hearing, you jerk!" I dropped my hands from my ears and punched him in the arm.

He shrugged as he lined up the weapons for the day's lesson.

The headset was heavy and it took a while for me to get them on comfortably. But with it came a newfound respect for Carrie Fisher and a little bone to pick with him later, maybe when there wasn't live ammunition around.

He motioned for me to join him at the lane. Through the headset, it sounded like he was yelling at me underwater, but I got the gist of his speech.

"Here's the trigger, the slide, the clip releases and the shell will fly out here," he pointed in quick succession. "There's two triggers so you'll need to pull them both back evenly."

He put the warm gun in my inexperienced hand.

"That's it?"

He nodded and backed away.

"So I point and shoot?"

He nodded again. "That way," he pointed down the range.

I turned towards the paper silhouette about ten feet away. He really didn't expect much.

"Are you going to hate me if I'm some sort of prodigy?" I called back over my shoulder

"I'd probably marry you."

My cheeks flushed and my hands went slick with sweat. He just had to say that now.

I took in a deep breath. I had seen guns fired tens of thousands of times on TV. It couldn't be that hard. Of course, all the actors on TV were shooting blanks and hadn't just been proposed to by a supermodel.

Okay. Hold my arms straight out before me. Line up the sights, I thought. Relax. Exhale to focus; this was beginning to sound like shifting.

I didn't even have to close an eye to focus. God bless hunter's vision.

I widened my stance, just like he had done, held my breath, and pulled the trigger.

The power of the shot jerked my arms back and the fire rung in my ears even with the mufflers on. But there was a hole in the target. Right lower quadrant. In the circle. Crap. Maybe I was a prodigy.

I heard a rumble from behind.

Suddenly, his heat was at my back. Goose bumps blazed a trail across my skin, and the panther stirred a little. I gulped. Damn him for smelling so freakin' wonderful even over the sting of powder in my nose.

The little stall left us a mere foot of personal space. I held my breath as he reached out as if to stroke my cheek. With a cocky grin he leaned in, and flicked the switch directly behind me, sending the target sailing out to twenty feet.

"You really shouldn't creep up on a girl with a gun," I said to him, my voice muffled by the monkey ears.

He looked down at me and smiled with one side of his mouth. I watched his perfect lips as he spoke. "I like to live dangerously."

Moving back to the shelf, he crossed his arms and watched as I turned back towards the alley.

I mumbled curses under my breath as I squared up to shoot the hell out of this target. Let's see if you really can resolve sexual tension with gunfire.

Five rounds into this set, he crept up behind me again, but I didn't jump, just pulled the headphones down. All amped up and nowhere to go, I could feel his heat before he slid his arm down mine.

"See how your shots are to the right? Your finger isn't on the trigger properly, so when you fire, it's pulling right."

He wrapped his hand around mine on the hot metal of the gun and pulled my finger out a little from the trigger guard, so the pad of my finger was on the trigger better.

"There you go. Try that," he whispered into my ear.

He had to know that his breath sent shivers down my neck and tingled all the way down my back. Damn him.

"Are you sure you want to be that close?"

He drew his hand back down my arm and stepped away slowly. I pulled the monkey ears back on and let that poor little paper target pay for his sins.

Ten shots later, the heat had barely begun to fade from my skin as the slide locked back empty.

"My turn."

I released the clip from the gun and left it on the ledge for him.

"Show me how it's done, sensei."

I moved back to where he had been standing and watched his wide shoulders as he snapped in a fresh magazine into the 45. He rocked his feet into a comfortable shoulder width apart and let seven rounds loose, all perfectly in the center circle.

"Let's see how you do with some distraction." I called out.

He looked over his shoulder with his little furrow back between his brows. "Violet. I've got a gun. Now's not the time to play."

I held my hands up in surrender. "I'm not going to move an inch."

He turned and focused back on the mutilated circle.

I took in a deep breath and felt my furry center. With a small push, I bathed him in my magnolia scent.

The first shot went wild, hitting the target of the lane over from us, sending it dancing wildly.

I smiled. *That'll teach ya.*

Chaz looked over his shoulder with a raised eye brow. "You want to play that way?"

"Yes please."

"Fine."

He took in another deep breath. And steadied his arms. Chaz squeezed off the rest of the magazine. Perfect. He ejected it and turned around with a look of satisfaction. "Are we done?"

"Not even close."

Pulling off his ear plugs, he walked back to the shelf with all his supplies and picked up another full clip. "Feel about ten times better than you did this morning, don't ya?"

I did. I hadn't thought about Jessa since we hit the door. But as I looked up at him, I honestly didn't know if it was the mutilation of the fluorescent targets that was making me feel better or if it was his relaxed frame as he showed me part of his world.

"Let me fire off a few more rounds and we'll see."

Chapter Nineteen

My sensei at the dojo leaned over, his hands on his knees, as he took in large breaths.

"Didn't think you could knock the wind out of a wind elemental?" I joked as I walked to the edge of the room to get my bottle of water.

"Neither did I," he said as he straightened slowly. "You are a very quick learner, Miss Jordan."

"Thank you." I took a long swig of water. Outside of shooting guns, kicking ass Bruce Lee style also helped with the inner turmoil. We'd been at it all morning, locked up in his back room with the door shut so his regular students couldn't see him throw me into mirrors and me jump kick off the walls. On the outside, I was a ninja master. On the inside, I still felt like a pile of melted cheese and dirty socks all mixed into together with a sprinkling of confusion and extreme guilt. But at this moment, I was too exhausted to care.

"Too quick, I think."

I frowned and turned towards him. "Iris said something like that."

Sensai shook his head. "I've never had a better student. Your ability to harness your cat is incredible."

"You'll still teach me though, right? I need my biweekly ass kicking so my confidence doesn't get too high. Except for next week. I'm going out of town."

"Are you finally leaving his forsaken town?"

"Not quite. I'm leaving tomorrow for LA for work. But I'll be back."

"Don't know why." He rubbed his hand over his bare head and the dark mark on his arm stared at me. He'd said it tainted him to the point that he could never be part of the Cause, but all I saw before was a strong man who cared for his students and could create a hurricane in the dojo but not harm a hair on my head.

"Tell me about Haverty."

The old man grumbled a "no."

"I've got no one else to tell me where it comes from, the fear, the way things work."

"It is no surprise that Prima Iris cannot speak of it."

I gulped. "Prima Iris?"

"Well, yes. But that is her story to tell, not mine."

"So tell me yours."

Sensei shook his head as he too went for bottle of water after our exhaustive exercise. "I was young and weak. Haverty promised power and protection and when Haverty overtook Iris . . ."

"He overthrew her?"

"With our help, I am forever ashamed to say. She did not have his power and he didn't have the morals to prevent him from using his. It was like a golden age for a while, until we saw the real him. Until he started marking all of us with the Order."

He walked over to me and saw it again. I had to stop myself from reaching out to run my fingers over the paper thin–looking skin. "It's not a tattoo."

"He burned the mark into us and with it, took our power to bind us to him, which made him stronger still."

My stomach began to churn with the story and my eyes filled with tears. "Please stop."

"There is no crying at the dojo."

I laughed and sniffed.

"The Garretts stayed. All other Cause fled or were killed, but they stayed. I do not know why. Seth Garrett freed me, helped me get rid of the mark, took a chuck of my soul with it, but the mark was gone. He left us soon after that."

A tear trickled down my check and he swiftly reached up with his rough thumb and brushed it away.

I sniffed again as he carefully held my chin.

"Know Violet Jordan that you, your power, is nothing like his. I see you take it to a good place, where his is blood and ash. You are breath of fresh air."

I smiled as he dropped his hand.

"And I think you're ready for a flying arm bar now."

The word *what* barely escaped my lips as he yanked my arm toward him. His body weight dropped as he climbed up my torso with his feet. With the awkward weight, I tumbled forward as his legs wrapped around my arm and his legs seemed to throw me down so hard on the mat all the air in my lungs leapt out.

Twisted up in his short legs, my arm hyperextended painfully and I tapped out, still gasping for air.

He released me quickly and left me trying to recapture my breath. "Crap" was the first thing I managed out.

Sensei was on his feet in an instant.

It took me a few more instances before I was up on my feet, doubled over, panting. I shook out the pain in my arm that was quickly fading.

I smiled up at him, the beast within me playful and challenged. "You gotta teach me that."

The flight to LA was the best I'd had. There was no motion sickness, no fear of looking out the windows. My ears didn't even plug up. I felt great. At least on the outside.

A guy in a chauffer's hat with a little white sign reading "Ms. Jordan" picked me up at the airport and drove me to straight to the secret meeting location. Drew was constantly paranoid another production company was going to steal his writers. Always made for an interesting trip; it was always small rooms in the highest hotels or the back rooms of some restaurant. This time, it was a conference room in a for-lease office building. As I scrolled through the script I had opened on my laptop, trying to get in as much work as possible, my cell phone rang.

"Yes?" I answered, distracted by the notes in my lap. Drew wanted us to be prepared, especially me. And frankly, my brain had been on other supernatural things rather than on the despair and desperation of Jada and Smith in *Everville*.

"Where are you?" Chaz snarled. "You're not at your house or the coffee shop."

I froze and my cheeks flushed like a child caught in a lie or with her hand in a cookie jar. I hadn't told him that I was leaving. I'd had this on my calendar since, well, before the night in the alley.

"I'm not in town."

"Where the hell are you?" he yelled.

I flinched and my skin chilled. "I'm in LA for a writer's meeting."

"LA? Violet!" he exclaimed so loudly I had to jerk the phone from my ear. My driver looked back in the rearview mirror and I forced a smile, giving him the okay sign

Chaz didn't say anything but I could hear the way his heart sped up.

"I'm going to be fine. I'll stay in my hotel room and I'm going to be back in Dallas on Thursday morning," I said as the car pulled up to the building.

I was getting nervous. I wasn't sure if he was going to yell at me or just sigh again. I didn't know if I could take any more of either. So I asked him.

"Are you going to yell at me some more or what? 'Cuz I'm just about to go into an all-day meeting and Drew is going to take my phone."

I could have sworn that I could hear his teeth grinding.

"Watch yourself. See you on Thursday," he said before he snapped his phone closed.

With all the other things floating around in my head, the script, the flight home, the possibility Jessa might never talk to me again, being attacked at any moment by a panther hungry for more power, I had completely forgotten that I would be face to face with Kyle.

Ah Kyle, beautiful, handsome, way too good to be true Kyle.

Every woman, I've come to find out after several bottles of red wine, has a Kyle: the charmer who made them feel they were the only woman in the world. The He's in question are usually a first in something: first college love, first working world love, first lover. For me, he was the first to notice I had the makings of a real writer. Behind the frizzy hair, thick glasses, and the stacks of scripts Drew had me collating and stapling, Kyle saw potential. In the beginning, he made me feel like I was the most beautiful, the funniest, the smartest woman in the world. I was happy. Really happy.

I wised up real quick when I found him in my bed with another woman, making her feel just as special.

Three years and a sleep number bed down the drain.

I straightened my shirt and flipped my hair behind my shoulder as I stared at the door to the meeting room. It was a new shirt and I had taken the time that morning as I waited in the airport to straighten my hair with a Chi flat iron Jessa had gotten me for my last birthday. Just using it had made my eyes watery. Part of my heart still ached and the other part was still furious. *They were not stupid movies.*

I could do this. I could face down Kyle. Bitter banter was my specialty and I was feeling a little more catty lately. I strode into the conference room with a big smile and three-inch heels.

Sera gave me a huge hug and quickly ushered me into the saved chair next to her.

"You look fantastic," she whispered.

"Thanks. Like the blonde."

Sera tousled her newly platinum-blonde curls. "Felt a little Marilyn last week."

Drew began to hand out the secret agenda he had no doubt been at Kinko's copying at two this morning with sunglasses and a low-slung hat.

I looked down the table at the familiar faces. Sometimes I thought this was what home felt like until I saw Kyle at the end of the table next to Drew, always the suck-up.

I just flashed him a quick smile and a wink and looked down at my notes. This might actually be fun.

We took our first coffee break at 10 a.m. Drew had Starbucks delivered by his poor assistant, the only fresh face in the room, if you could call the dark circles under her eyes and the messy ponytail a fresh face. That had been me five years ago. Working my tail off to get Drew to notice that I was a writer, and a good writer. He gave me my first job out of college and solidified my caffeine addiction.

Sera left my side for the first time all morning and I was joined almost immediately by a distinct warm body and a distinctive scent more pungent than ever before.

"Hey there, Lettie."

A chill ran down my spine and the cool rivets of residual anger trickled out from there. "Do not call me Lettie," I said through clenched teeth.

Kyle fixed his coffee; still black with three sugars. He liked things extra sweet. I remembered he always had a fetish for candy, always had his pockets full of jelly beans and M&M's. By the smell of it, today was jelly beans.

"How ya been?" he asked, leaning casually against the catering table, stirring his coffee as he watched me meticulously fix mine with two creamers and two sugars.

"Great. You?" I asked turning to face him.

He looked old. There were distinct lines forming on his forehead, ones that I hadn't put there. His dark roots were growing in under his beach-blonde hair. He was tanner than me, but so was everyone in the room. And he smelled different. I remembered Downy. This incarnation was more Old Spice and mildewed sock. He was just older, less glossy that the me in love remembered and dare I say stressed. Six months ago, I would have run from the coffee table just to avoid him. Today, I told him he looked like crap.

"You look like crap."

His usually smiling visage rippled for a moment. Something was wrong. In the past year, his life had always been perfect, or at least Sera's reports made them seem so. That in turn usually made my life even worse. I couldn't have asked for his downfall at a better time. This was going to be fun.

"Just a lot of work, you know." He looked down in his coffee.

"I do. I work here too."

He snorted and raised his eyes and an eyebrow. "You work from home."

"I headed four scripts this year from home and the online blog and seventeen magazine articles. Last count you were only at two and nothing else. So what's so stressful? Flavor of the week not working out so well?"

Another ripple and he shifted his weight from one leg to

the other. Oh joy! I wasn't being petty. This is poetic justice; this is just desserts. This is also the same dance we've been doing since the breakup only this time, I was going to lead.

"Did she find out that you couldn't get her onto the newest reality show?"

He lowered his chin and glowered. I had struck a nerve and it rang sweetly in my ears.

"That was low."

"I know."

"Lettie," he started something in that same sweet tone I associated with falling into my sleep number bed. "At least I'm getting some."

"And how exactly would you know that I'm not?"

"Come on, Lettie, you were never the type to sleep around."

"You did enough of that for the both of us."

"Lettie," he chided, his tone condescending and bile-inducing.

"Listen mister," I hissed. "You gave up the right to that information and tone when you decided to take 'Blondie' into our bed. I figure I've got another two years of unabashedly deserved hatred to work through. So you just need to grow a pair and live with the fact you were too stupid to see what you had."

I spun around quickly and headed out of the room. Once out of view, I flattened against the cool wall outside the conference room and took in sharp deep breaths. Blood pounded through my ears and my head spun a little in my victory. Holy crap. I really just did that. I really *finally* said that to Kyle.

God, it felt good. Where the hell did I get the balls to say that? Write it, sure, but to actually say it.

Wow, I felt like I deserved a cape, or a shot of tequila. Or both.

Sera joined me soon after, when the roaring in my ears had gone down but my head was still a little giddy.

"You all right?"

"Yeah, fine. Just a little disaster a la Kyle."

Sera put her hand on my shoulder. "I'm sorry. I didn't think he'd pounce so soon."

I smiled at her words. "I'm fine, but he might need a Band-Aid."

A smile swept across Sera's fuchsia lips. "Go you."

Go me.

I wanted to call Jessa. I wanted to tell her how ruthless I had been and she would love it and applaud me from across the country. But I couldn't. Because I had told her she never really cared about me.

I needed to tell Jessa everything. As I thought about all the writers and producers in the room, I knew they weren't my family. I may have spent the past five years working with them, having dinners at their house, buying presents for their kids, but they weren't my family.

Jessa was my family and I had to tell her. I had to make things right. After the meeting. When I got back into town. And then there was that whole full moon thing. So I'd call her on the way back home, and then spend the weekend at Iris's and then be able to make things right after that.

Drew started up the meeting talking a mile a minute, as Drew tended to do. To be honest, I was only listening to every other word. I caught production cost, budget cuts, and lemonade somewhere in all that. Mostly I was just thinking about Jessa. Not the jerk sitting across from me. And even if I focused on the jerk across the table from me, I didn't have anyone to rage to about it. I supposed I could impose on Sera a bit more, but she had to work with this ass here in LA. Jessa was the only person I even had on speed dial. Her and Stalker boy. And frankly Chaz didn't seem like the tub of Hagan Das type.

Somewhere in the middle of the pity party for one, I heard my name.

"Yeah," I perked up, sitting up straighter in my chair, looking around at all the eyes looking back at me.

"*Moon Blood: The Waxing*. We're going with that one for the summer shoot."

"Seriously?" It was the first word out of my mouth. Summer shoots were the big ones with the multiple locations, where we actually auditioned people and worked with some of the bigger houses with actual budgets.

"Yeah, Violet," Drew said. "It was great. Pithy and touching and exactly what is going to boost our little company into Blockbuster's view."

I gulped. Drew was just about to give the green light on my cat therapy, the script that was me unabashedly displacing all my fear and anxiety onto someone else. Drew was about to green light the *truth* about shapeshifters. "Are you sure?"

"It's great," Sera said as she hit my arm. "Everyone loves it."

I looked around, mouth agape at the other faces. They were all nods and smiles, but Chaz was going to kill me.

"Sera's going to executive produce this one and we'd like to start sending the scripts out as soon as possible, with a few rewrites."

"Seriously?" I whispered to Sera.

"Shut up and take your moment."

I looked around the room, the familiar faces who I'd known forever. Even Kyle nodded his head in approval.

"Great," I shrugged.

"Okay," Drew said as she clapped his hands together. "I'll give you the rewrites at the next break. And this means we know what you're doing this summer."

The entire table laughed at the bad joke and I smiled along with them, but who knew if I was going to be available this summer. Who knew if I was going to even be around then?

Chapter Twenty

I had thrown my bag on the bed in my bedroom on the second floor of Iris's house. I'd come there straight from the airport, ready for my monthly visit. After hair and teeth brushing, I hopped down the stairs to the kitchen where she was no doubt preparing a feast.

"Can I help with something?" I asked as she cut up potatoes and threw them into a pot of boiling water.

"Biscuits," she said, pointing her knife to a tube of Pillsbury biscuits.

I bounced around the kitchen, remembering where everything was from last month's visit. There may have been humming involved as I placed the sticky biscuits on the tray one by one.

"Why are you so happy?" Iris asked as she slid the rest of the potatoes in the pot.

"I don't know. I got some good news at work. And I've been asked to collaborate for a comic book by a few guys back in LA."

"Nothing to do with Chaz coming to dinner?"

I swear my mouth smiled at its own accord. "You need to get over your obsession with Chaz and I hooking up."

Iris huffed and threw a handful of salt into the boiling potatoes. I finished arranging the gooey biscuits on the cookie sheet.

"Well, I do have a few more things to tell you. Didn't seem right over the phone."

I sat down at the table and listened as she busied around, opening cans of French cut green beans and cream of mushroom soup. I hadn't had green bean casserole in, well, a very, very long time. I watched carefully as she added all the ingredients and started mixing.

She was having a hard time trying to formulate her words as she stirred away. Her lips were pursed and she would open them and then close them every now and then as the spoon went faster and faster in the bowl.

"There is one more thing that we are going to have to work on with you. And quick."

"What?"

"You're stronger than you were just last month."

"I've mastered my shields. Don't even have to think about it most days. Just leave the house and when I lock the door, I lock them into place." I offered, turning to follow her small figure around the kitchen. "Sensei is helping me focus and concentrate. And kick some major ass."

Iris shuffled to a cabinet where she grabbed a glass dish. As she pulled it from the high shelf, the glass slipped from her fingers. Her body was faster than even I could see as she caught the dish six inches from the floor.

"Damn pan," she muttered to herself as she went back to her bowl. As I watched her, slack jawed, she just continued with her spiel. "Remember how when I brushed you, you nearly fell out of your chair?"

"Yes, ma'am."

"Well Rea . . ." she licked her lips and started over. "The Havertys have been known to use that energy as a weapon."

I gulped. "Like when I threw Chaz into a wall?" I really wasn't ever going to live that down.

Iris nodded. "Most shapeshifters can't do that, Violet. Most shapeshifters can shift and that's it."

My entire body shivered and I stared at her. "I did that after my first full moon, Iris. Without even thinking."

"Imagine if it had been an actual fight. He could have been in Ellis County." Iris making a joke at a time like this unnerved me more than the information she was giving me. "Each person has his or her own strengths. In my day, I could lift a car if I needed to."

I frowned. "And how often did you have to lift cars?"

Iris looked over her shoulder with a silencing eyebrow arch. I zipped my lip.

"The Havertys can use their power to physically harm others." Iris took in a deep breath and she dumped the green beans into the pan. "I've seen them take another Wanderer's power. Rip it clean out of their chests until there's nothing left. Which means that you might be able to as well."

I shook my head adamantly, tears beginning to form as I remembered Sensei's story. "I don't want to practice that, Iris. I don't even want to think about that."

Iris turned quickly and wiped her hands on her apron. She walked over to me and wrapped her arm around my shaking shoulder. "No, honey. I'm not going to make you."

She rubbed my arm until the chill went away, leaving the smell of cream of mushroom on my shirt. "I just need you to know the Havertys are strong and you're going to have some unique challenges along the way I can't prepare you for. You're just going to have to use that big imagination of yours to figure it out."

As I took in a long steadying breath, she released my shoulder and went back to her fixings. I stared down at the checkered table cloth and picked at a small hole in the vinyl. It was the size of a dime before I stopped. "You mean being single in the big city isn't enough of a unique challenge?"

Her shoulder shook with a chuckle. "If you'd just let Chaz . . ."

"Please Iris, it's not going to work. I'm cute for about ten minutes and then it's all a little too much to handle."

"It's not going to work because you've already made up that stubborn head of yours."

I rolled my eyes. "God, Iris you sound like my . . ."

I couldn't finish the sentence. The word knotted up in my throat. All these years and I could still barely say the word. I could talk about demons and monsters and other vicious things that go bump in the night but I could say one simple loving word out loud.

She turned around slowly with the red can of fried onions in her hand. "We know loss here, Violet. It's why we fight so hard for the ones we love."

My voice sounded small, childlike, but the words came out.

Diaries of an Urban Panther

"I run. Did that quite well before the attack. Something hurt and I was gone. I've never stayed and fought for anything."

"Maybe you just haven't had anything to fight for yet."

A few things jumped to mind as I heard the telltale rumble of Chaz's old Bronco grumble down the dirt road.

Iris smiled. "Go see if he needs any help."

I didn't exactly jump up to meet him at the door. But I made it to the porch before him, my hands in my back pockets.

"Hey there, stranger," Chaz greeted, throwing his bag over his shoulder.

"Hey yourself," I smiled. "We're having turkey for dinner."

"Well it is Thanksgiving," he smiled.

I froze on the porch. "Seriously?"

I'd remembered a lot of bustle at the airport that morning. And I guess it was the end of November. "Huh?"

He held the door open for me. "You really do live in your own world, don't you?"

As we both walked into the house, Iris was waiting for us in the doorway to the kitchen.

"I have a game for the two of you while you're waiting for dinner," she said with her hands clasped before her, like a true schoolmarm, hair bun and everything.

"But I'm hungry, Iris," Chaz said setting down his bag in the hallway where we stood.

"It can wait," she said quickly.

I had to laugh at the scolded puppy look on his face.

"Chaz is going to run around the house and hide, and Violet, you are going to find him."

"You want us to play hide-and-seek?" I asked.

"With your nose," she nodded. "Blindfolded."

"Blindfolded!" I protested.

"You need to learn to track things with your sense of smell. It comes in mighty handy sometimes," she said handing Chaz an old necktie. "Cat noses aren't as good as canine so you have to practice."

Chaz tried to keep down a smile as I stood there unbelieving.

"And I suggest that you get it done with before the turkey cooks much more."

I looked over at Chaz. "This is weird."

"This is nothing," he said as he walked around me. "Try learning how to hone psychic GPS."

"So that is the fancy term for what you do? Gonna have to write that one down."

Carefully, he put the blindfold over my eyes and tied it gently. My skin chilled at him being close enough I could make out what kind of soap he used that morning and that he had tacos for lunch.

He tapped my shoulder and whispered. "Tag, you're it."

Chaz walked away quickly.

"You may want to take your boots off," Iris hollered.

"Do I have to count to 30 or something?" I asked, getting a little excited by the game. It was a new challenge, a new superhero talent that needed to be developed. It was like when Peter Parker first figured out that he could shoot webs.

"Might be nice to give him a head start," Iris said and she padded into the kitchen.

So I counted to 30 like a good little girl and then took in a deep breath. *Remember his scent*, I told myself, the soap, the taco, and the musky smell that was always around him. I didn't need to be reminded of that.

I knew the layout of the house as I stalked through the downstairs. He had walked through the living area; the smell was cold but there. I can't explain it more than that. It was cold like sniffing something out of the fridge. I followed it through the back of the house and then up the stairs. I hadn't heard him walk up the stairs.

The smell was getting warmer, more alive. *This is strange*, part of my brain said as I followed the soap through the upstairs into the dusty storage room. Even through the smell of old books and the rising smell of the cooking meat downstairs, I could tell that his scent changed here, it was suddenly stronger and sharper. I stopped to listen and I could hear a heartbeat just to my right.

This was so freakin' cool.

"Marco?" I whispered as I reached for the blindfold.

"Polo," he responded.

He slid out of his hiding spot next to a huge armoire as I pulled the tie off my eyes.

"Well that was just too easy," I smiled.

"Maybe you're just too good."

"Maybe you just need to avoid having tacos for lunch."

He gave me a funny smile and gestured for us to go downstairs for dinner. "You're going to be an amazing hunter someday."

We went down stairs to find a feast waiting for us.

"So the game went well?" Iris asked as she put the turkey on the table. The smell made my mouth water.

"Found him in record time."

"Well, we will do it again tonight, outside," she said as she handed Chaz a knife to carve our Thanksgiving meal.

The outside chase was a little harder. Out in the night air, the smell of the wild all around, I wanted to shift but I held it in check. It was something that I *had* to learn to do. No matter how strong the pull of a full moon was. No matter how much I felt the panther circle and pace within my chest. No matter how hard, I had to resist it.

The scent of Chaz was cold everywhere I went, the night spread the scent around with its light breeze. But near the barn, the scent warmed up. I stood as still as I could in the door and opened my eyes wide. The darkness in here was almost palpable, soft, welcoming.

Slowly, I moved through the darkness with my other eyes, with the widened pupil of the cat. Taking quickly little sniffs, I found him in the cage where I'd had my first shift.

"Marco."

"Polo," he responded as he stepped out into the center of the cage.

There was barely any light in here and I wondered how he had made it through the maze of Iris's barn. I came to stand before him in the middle of the confining space.

"I'm not going to be here in the morning," Chaz said softly.

"Okay."

"You're not going to throw me against anything?" he asked. His voice was as soft as the darkness around us.

I laughed, "No. Go, live your sacred destiny."

I watched him in the little moonlight infiltrating the cracks between the beams of the barn's roof. He was stunning. The gold in his hair was shining silver and the outline of his face was something from a Frank Miller comic book, all contrasts and lines. Simply beautiful.

"Be safe," I said.

"You too."

I watched as he walked away, respecting my need not to have him see me shift more than he had to. But this was the only space I could ask this question. There was something safe about the darkness, something like a confessional.

"Chaz?"

"Yeah," he turned around quickly in the doorway of the cage.

"Can I ask you something?"

"Sure," he said leaning against the door frame.

"Did Haverty kill Iris's sisters?"

"What gave you that idea?"

I licked my lips. I was ready to tell him this. I wanted to tell him this. "I had this dream or a memory of a story my mother told me."

"Like with the mirror?"

I nodded. "I know it's probably nothing but..."

"Yes."

His word hung in the darkness and over me like a smothering blanket.

Chaz sighed and moved back into the little space. His scent was all around me now, his body warmed by the pounding heart in his chest. "I've only got bits of the story. Found a picture when I was a kid, but I think they were friends at one point. I think he helped her run the city."

I shivered at the information. Chaz moved closer. "I don't know what happened."

"He promised power to the others in the Pride and they overthrew her."

The familiar story flew around in my head. Iris, younger, full of power with her two sisters, kicking ass and taking names, and then in swaggers a handsome face with as much power as they had, maybe wounded. And then one of them fell in love with him, maybe, divided the group. And this handsome stranger was able to pick them off one by one. Divided they fell.

I felt tears streaming down my face, hot stinging tears as my chin quivered.

"Violet?" He reached out to touch my face.

I ducked and moved quickly around him. "I need to call Jessa."

I didn't make it to the phone, didn't even make it to the foyer to get my purse.

There was a rumble in the ground, like an earthquake. I rushed to the porch and as I had my hand on the door handle, the world was pulled out from under me.

I was thrown back and landed on the four porch stairs. My head cracked against the edge of the bottom stair. I could feel the blood pour out of the gash at the base of my skull, feel my ribs crack against the old wood.

But that was nothing compared to invisible anvil on my chest. I couldn't breathe, couldn't suck in any air. I pushed against the stairs and managed to crawl down onto the cold grass.

The pressure pushed and pushed and I squeezed my eyes shut as I tried to push back, tried to gulp down air.

"Violet?"

Iris's voice sounded so far away. I opened my eyes only to see spots and a flash of her silver hair in the moonlight.

"Violet!"

Chaz's heavy boot steps vibrated the dirt beneath my ribs before he fell to his knees beside me.

Two heads hovered over me and I could only see spots. I felt like a fish gasping for air. And then I was harpooned through the chest like a marlin. A deep dark stabbing pain shot through my chest, just under the breast bone.

I don't know if I had enough air left in me to scream out but everything burned, everything sizzled as the pain twisted slowly in my chest as I writhed on the ground.

I felt the panther scream out, her claws digging into the ground beneath her.

The pain began to slowly retreat, the metallic hook pulled out centimeter by centimeter. The pressure slowly lifted and I was able to suck in air, the chilly night air filling my lungs. I took shallow quick breaths, the broken ribs shooting fire through my sides.

My hand flew up to my chest, expecting there to be a wound, a gash, a hole the size of my fist, but there was nothing. Not even blood.

"Don't touch her," Iris hissed.

My vision cleared and I saw Chaz back off.

"What the hell," I managed out.

"I don't know, honey," Iris shook her head with more worry in her eyes than I had ever wanted to put there. "But it was powerful."

"Yeah me."

"Darling, you need to shift. Take hold of your cat. You'll heal faster that way, especially under the full moon."

The inky blackness of the cat was just behind my eyelids. Nodding was proving too painful, so I licked my lips. "See you in the morning."

Chapter Twenty-One

There once was a prince who had everything he could want. If he wanted a horse, he got a horse; if he wanted a new dog for his pack, he got a new dog for his pack. If he wanted a new castle built for him, his father would call the royal architect right away.

But it was never enough. And the king knew it. Knew that his son was going to ask for the kingdom one day, and he knew that his son would ruin everything that he had built. So he wanted to teach his son that to rule is to sacrifice, that to rule is to be alone with the thoughts of many.

He pulled his son out into a field by the castle. "Son, I know that you have wanted a new horse in the stable. But there isn't enough room with the horses you already have."

"So build a new stable," his son said simply.

"No. If you want a new horse, you have to give away one of your own. If there are too many in the barn, there will not be enough food and they will die."

"The weaker ones will die, leaving the stronger ones for me."

His father was disgusted with his son's cruel outlook. "I will not buy you a new horse."

So the son disobeyed his father and went into town to buy a horse and brought it back to the stable. He placed the magnificent beast in a stable with a colt that his father had bred from many generations of the best horses in the kingdom. Proud of himself, he strutted back to the castle and went to bed, forgetting that he had left a lamp burning as he gazed at his purchase.

"Wait mom," I said as I leaned up from the bed. "This isn't going to be a happy tale, is it?"

"No honey," she said as she rubbed my back. "Not all stories have a happy ending."

"Jessa!" I called out as I beat on her door. "Jessa, we need to talk."

I kept knocking. Red welts were forming on my knuckles but I didn't care. "I know you're there."

I could smell her perfume. She was home. About fifteen feet away from the door eating chocolate chip cookies.

When I brought my knuckles back, there was a red smear on the door. Crap.

"We are going to talk," I said through the door. "Even if I have to tie your perky ass to a chair."

I stormed back through the long posh hallway and wiped my knuckles on my black sweater. By the end of the hallway, the cuts were gone. As I reached my car, the redness had faded.

What the hell, I fumed as I screeched my tires outside of her complex and headed back to the highway. I was trying to make amends here. I was trying to be the bigger person here.

I dragged my many bags into the laundry and then took in a deep calming breath. It had been almost a week and a half since I'd been home.

Place was still there, untouched, still smelled like Violet, which still ironically smelled like magnolias now all the time. I started a pot of coffee that would be waiting and wonderful after the hot, hot shower I was planning to take.

I slid off my shoes and walked across the plush carpet, ran my hands over the edge of the couch. Just being home relaxed me. Being back in my precious lair.

I would have smiled at the little joke, but there was a dark car parked outside my house. Pushing the drapes aside, I saw Chaz sitting outside in his sports car, reading.

I unlocked the front door and stepped out.

His head snapped up at the crack of the door. He had his windows open and some music playing in the car. Quickly, he got out of the car and walked across the street.

"Got some info for you. You're not going to like it," he said quickly as he brushed past me in the doorway and went straight for the couch.

"I'm doing great, Chaz. Broken ribs all better. Thanks for asking," I sassed as I closed and bolted the door.

He turned to face me with a frown before he flopped on the couch. "Been up for two days."

"Whadaya know? Me too."

And I would have gone on a little further but he turned to look into the kitchen where the coffee was beginning to brew and I saw a dark shadow across his face. A pretty little bruise was healing fast.

"Rough nights for both of us then," I said as I pointed to my cheek.

"Yeah," he reached up to run his fingers through his hair. His knuckles were freshly scabbed.

"I'll shut up now and get the coffee."

I curled up on the far side of the couch from him, careful of the hot coffee in my hand. The milk had curdled ages ago and I had to drink mine black like Chaz did. Wasn't bad. The three packets of sugar helped.

"Bad news or bad news first," he started.

"Got an inkling about what happened that night?"

"Yeah," he shook his head. "The baddies I could find said Haverty Junior got disowned by his father."

"So?"

Chaz shook his head and put his cup on the coffee table by his knee. "This was more than just disinherited, Violet. He banished him from the pack, which means Haverty ripped out any power that he had gained from the pack."

"Ripped?" I gulped. A brief hint of pain returned to my chest as I distinctly remembered the filet-of-fish feeling.

"Apparently the only thing left is his panther. He's like a newborn."

"He's me a month ago."

Chaz nodded.

"What's it got to do with what happened last night?"

"Iris said the link is always strongest to your first heir. Which means that Spencer is your sire."

I licked my lips. "So it was Spencer in the alley?"

"Makes sense. Haverty hunts on his own private ground. He'd never go out in the city."

"Then isn't it sort of good news if I was his only."

"It means the link between you is strong. Strong enough to control both of you."

Gulp number 2.

"And that's the better of the bad news?"

I watched as Chaz struggled through the words, watched as he clasped his hand to tightly together to hide the shaking. "It would be better if Haverty were after you. He's methodical. Old school. He'd send his Rottweilers after you, bring you in, torture you."

"What about that is the better part?" I struggled to follow his logic through visions of me strapped to a chair under a bright flood lamp.

"I can't predict Junior. Can't say what he'll do. Can't even imagine what his next move might be."

I can't protect you. He didn't have to say it. I read it in every muscle of his body, in the tension across his shoulders, the white of his knuckles.

"I bet you know someone who can."

He looked up from his tightly wound hands. "Huh?"

"You really need to get some sleep. You're running a little slow," I said as I took a sip of coffee. "All these white hats and you don't have a psychic in your back pocket."

The blood drained from his face as he stared up at me. "Sort of."

"Where is she?"

"Here."

"Well then, drink up, Chuck. And take a shower," I said as I got up from the couch.

After the array of emotion I had just been through, having a plan made me feel ten times better. The coffee maybe another three times better.

But Chaz didn't move from the couch.

"What's wrong?"

"Nothing, nothing. I'll take you to see . . . Cristina."

There was a pause in that sentence. And where there was a pause, there was a story. "What's the sitch?"

"Nothing, nothing," he repeated as he headed up the stairs to the shower. "Just my funeral," he muttered as he hit the second floor.

"Super hearing, remember," I called up the stairwell.

An expletive was mumbled as he went into the bedroom to take a shower.

"How good is a psychic who advertises 2 for 1 deals in the front window?" I asked.

"Just my funeral," he whispered again as he got out of the car.

As I got out of the car, I studied the storefront. As we were driving to Irving, I'd imagined what a powerful psychic's place would look like. Frankly, I was expecting something a little more gothic, with spooky windows and at the very least a small black cat creeping along a yard of dead grass. I really didn't expect it to be nestled between Rick's Tropical Fish and The UPS Store. The plain storefront had a hand-painted sign reading "Culandera" above the plain glass door with a cracked OPEN sign swinging from its hook.

Chaz took a deep breath before he walked up to the front door, his hand pausing over the metal door handle before he swung it open.

The foyer was dark and cool, the curtains over the window sill rustled in an invisible breeze and the beads that separated this waiting area from the back swung back and forth. The white tile floor needed to be mopped and two tired couches waited for a steam cleaner. It smelled intensely of nag champa and tamales. Framed drawings of chakra points and zodiac wheels hung on the walls. I stifled a laugh when I saw the infamous palm charm I'd actually used to write a fortune teller's scene two scripts back.

It was a joke until a slightly built woman in a long red dress swung the curtain across and looked out at us with her dark eyes. She was *real*. Her power poured out around her and it lapped against me like a cold New England tide. This was real power. The smile faded from my face and I licked my lips.

Well, if a panther could have a townhouse in north Dallas, then a real Seer could have a shop on Beltline Road in Irving.

"You are late," the woman grumbled with a Spanish accent. Her gold bangles jangled as they slid down her slender arm as she brushed a short curl out of her dark chocolate eyes.

Chaz's gaze hit the white tile beneath our feet.

The woman stepped through the curtain, letting the strings of beads drop back into place. Her dark eyes studied Chaz just over my shoulder, her perfect skin wrinkling slightly between her perfect brows.

"Pleasure to meet you," I said as I stepped between them and stuck out my hand in a friendly greeting.

Cristina looked at me and then at my awkwardly outstretched hand and then over at Chaz. "This is her?"

"Cristina, this is Violet Jordan," Chaz introduced.

I dropped my hand and rested both on my bag. I was suddenly getting a very, very bad vibe from all this.

Cristina looked me up and then down. "She was shorter in my vision."

She extended her hand in another rush of jingling and gracefully swept back the beaded curtain. "We should talk more privately."

As I moved towards the door, I had the distinct feeling of pressure down my shoulders. I looked around the empty backroom, expecting to see someone. Even took a little sniff, but there was nothing over the incense. Still a little paranoid. So sue me.

"Huh."

We both looked back at Chaz who was looking around the ceilings. "Your wards. What happened to them?"

I looked at the spot on the wall that he was looking at. There was a distinct stencil of something that had been on the wall for a very long time.

"You haven't been here in a *very* long time." There was a distinctive low growl in Cristina's voice.

Chaz looked at me with a slight crease in his forehead. Something was wrong. His arms crossed over his chest as he looked around. His unease made my unease greater.

I turned back to the dark room and took a deep breath. I

could do this. We needed this. I needed to do this for both of us to see what we were up against. "You coming?"

"Not exactly welcome," he said. "I'll just wait out here for you."

My eyes darted between Cristina's glare, to her hand as her fingers dug into her hip and Chaz's clenched jaw. Looking between the two people who were glaring at each other, I gulped. Ex-lovers? I looked at Cristina. She was stunning. A solid ten. Well, he was a supermodel; guess he was allowed to date the hottest psychic I'd certainly ever met.

I followed her into a room where red and purple abounded. Everything was in heavy velvets and satins, draped in gold adornments. The Persian rug beneath our feet was thick and plush as she led me to a large table in the center. The atmosphere was so different in here. The air even smelled heavier, more intense. This was why she didn't need to adorn the outside. The real magic was in here.

"It is not magic," Cristina snapped as she arranged herself in her chair.

"Sorry," I said adjusting the bag on my shoulder.

"Sit," she ordered.

I slowly slid into the high-backed chair across from her. As sly as possible, I clicked on the tape recorder in my purse and placed it on the top of the junk in there, nestling it beside me in the chair.

Cristina reached out, placing her hands out on the table between us. She tapped her knuckles on the table impatiently, insisting that I take her outstretched hands.

"I'm warning you, I have no idea what you're going to see

up there," I joked as I reached across the table with sweaty palms.

"Like I want to rummage around your head."

I rested my warm hands in her clammy ones. My skin goose-bumped as our circle completed. Her power rippled around me and she smelled like her incense and hot red wax.

Cristina closed her eyes and began chanting in a meditative whisper to herself. She took in a deep breath and let it out slowly across the table. I was beginning to see that shifting was a lot like a lot of things: shooting guns, yoga, summoning ancient spirits to enlighten the future.

This wasn't so bad, I was about to say before liquid lightening shot up my right arm, across my heart, and then down my left arm.

I let out a small yelp because Cristina clenched my hand tighter, in camaraderie or shared pain I wasn't sure, but I was glad for her cool embrace to focus on. When I could breathe again through the tenderness in my chest, I heard Cristina's voice softly waft across the table. Her eyes half-closed and her head slightly tilted back, she was speaking to no one.

"Ripped veil. Magnolia death. Mirrors broken."

Just as I thought maybe that was the end of the show, white hot images flashed across my eyelids, like a thousand photos flashes going off.

Jessa's reflection in a mirror

Blood on cement.

Chaz crouched in the darkness

The sinister glint off a cat-like eye.

Suddenly, Cristina gasped and her head dropped down to her chest. All the energy rushed from the room, stirring my hair as it went. The scent of hot wax and incense was lost as her hands went limp in mine.

I ripped my hands from her and covered my eyes, still able to see the brightness of the images burning in my retinas. The actual images faded quickly. I struggled to remember them and forget them at the same time. The searing blue spots were left as I dropped my hands and fluttered my eyes open to look at the dimly lit room.

"Dios mio," she whispered.

"What?"

"Water," she ordered.

Slowly I stood, bracing myself against the table and moved to the back of the room where another curtained doorway led into a brightly lit break room. The glasses were easy enough to find and on the way back to the table, I snuck a glance at a few family pictures on a bookcase full of doodads.

"Are you okay?" I asked when I returned, tall cold glass of water in my hot hand.

Her head rose slowly and her red watery eyes met mine.

"Cannot say you did not warn me." Her breaths were rugged and her words poorly formed. "But some of that was you."

"I'm sorry."

"No," she shook her head. "It's like this every time."

I gulped. "Every time?"

She nodded slowly. "Every time. It is the sacrifice I have to make for my gift." Her breaths were normal again; her words fluid again and perfectly exotic.

"Is it true?" I didn't want to push her, but this was what we had been searching for.

"Clear as day. Protector of the Veil," Cristina nodded and

put her water back on the table. "A reincarnated warrior sent to guard the princess."

I frowned. "Princess? When did this turn into Mario Brothers?"

Cristina looked up at me. "You don't know?"

She muttered a long line of something in Spanish under her breath as I flopped down in the chair across from her and stared down at the carpet.

I could see Cristina struggle with words. She rose slowly from the chair, bracing herself for a moment before crossing the dark room. She pulled a wooden box from a shelf and worked her way slowly back to the table.

With a reverence I've only see in church and when Chaz handled his guns, she opened the box and carefully unfolded a deck of tarot from a green satin scarf.

She closed her eyes and flipped the first card over. When she opened her eyes, she jerked her head in surprise and put the car back in the shuffle. She licked her lips.

"Your friend. Jessa Feychild. She's the key to the Veil."

Jessa? The key to all of this was *Jessa*? How could an affluent New York socialite have anything to do with this? Her family was influential in the business market.

As I thought about her, the pieces snapped into place like another picture in my brain. My shoulders slumped. "Crap. Her last name is Fey Child."

Seemed par for the course. Seemed like something I would do to one of my characters, frankly. When the situation is as worse as it could be, twist it to make it worse. So, I couldn't just be a panther dealing with a dark legacy. I had to be a reincarnated panther with a prophecy to protect the Veil between the worlds and the key to that was an actual fairy princess currently not taking my calls.

"Do you know what the Veil is?" Cristina asked.

I nodded. "It's a wall between this realm and a purely magical realm."

Cristina flipped over the next card in her desk and she shivered. She quickly laid out five cards in the shape of an X between us. She sucked in a shuttered breath as her hand hovered over the Tower card.

"What does it mean?"

"This isn't for you." She snapped, as she reshuffled all the cards quickly and laid out another X with the Tower card in the center. Again.

A chill spread throughout the room.

Cristina wrapped her cards in their scarf and put the cards in the box and the lid on the box.

She spoke quickly, softly. Even with the super hearing, I could barely make out what she was saying. It was a hurried confession in the darkness of her sanctuary. "He's been trying to find a spell to open a doorway. To rip the Veil. On the darkest of the darkest night. There is a beast on the other side who has offered him power to defeat his father. You keep Jessa safe, protected, it can't happen."

Jessa. Then this was more than just a little friendly feud. This was actually life or death. "What does the mirror have to do with it?"

As soon as the words left my mouth, I knew the answer. The mirror was how the Veil ripped. Give the mirror an offering, it would give you something. Send something one way, something else come back. Break the mirror, break the spell.

I shivered with the realization I hadn't read that in the little book Chaz had given me, never written that into a movie. It was just a fairy tale my mother told me and it was about to come true.

"You can have Wonder boy explain it to you," she said with a flick of her hand towards the door.

As the mood changed, I watched as she brushed a curl from her eye and licked her lips. "So you and Chaz *do* have history."

Cristina's eyes snapped up to me.

"Didn't have to be psychic to pick up on the *ex* vibe."

"Charles and I were long ago and far away," Cristina said as she leaned back in her chair. Her eyes went distant for a moment before she looked back at me. "He's a very pretty, very damaged boy. Like playing with shiny broken glass."

"Good thing my kind prefers string."

She didn't smile. She didn't even fight a smile. This woman was stone. "You have many lives before you, Violet Jordan. They will not be easy."

"Hey, means I'm going to get through this one."

"The future is never certain. You of all people should know how quickly lives can change."

We both stood, knowing she was not going to give me more information.

I showed myself out of her little back room. Chaz leapt off the couch and attacked me with questions. "What did she say?"

"You should ask her," the voice startled both of us.

I turned around to see Cristina leaning in the door frame, looking tired and smaller than she had before. Her arms were locked across her chest as she looked over at Chaz.

I really tried not to smile as I watched Chaz pale and his Adam's apple bob slowly in his throat.

"We need to go to Jessa's," I said. "As close to now as possible."

With small nod and a thank you, I went outside to bask in the sunlight. I leaned against his car and rested. Even the December sun helped chase away the cool chill from her back room.

"What did Cris tell you?"

"Oh, it's Cris?" I asked innocently. "That's very familiar of you."

We were on the highway before he spoke again. Chaz licked his lips as he changed lanes, driving faster than I would have preferred. But when you've got a car like this with an engine like this one and the world as we know it is at stake, why drive slowly? "We were sort of together for a while."

"I know, *Charles*."

His knuckles grew white on the steering wheel. "You were in there for ten minutes and you swapped life stories. What about the answers we actually came here for?"

"Actually I guessed. About you and her," I slunk down in his passenger seat and crossed my arms over my chest. "And I did get answers."

"And," he prompted.

"And I need to talk to Jessa."

Someone had wiped off the red smear I'd left last time. Chaz kept looking around the place like a little kid. His hands tucked into his jean pockets as if to ensure he wouldn't touch anything.

"Do you know how much she pays in rent?" he asked as we stood outside.

"End of the world and you're thinking real estate?"

Chaz shrugged. "Been thinking of selling my dad's place."

"Seriously?"

"Yeah," he said as he leaned against the wall, facing Jessa's door. "Too big for just me."

Well that was an odd piece of news. Not that his dad's place was a palace but it was weird. First the car, and now this. "How bout we get to saving the princess and then we can play Monopoly?"

He sighed and gestured for me to get on with why we were here.

I looked at the cream door and sighed. Three knocks. "Jessa? It's Violet."

"What do you want?" she snapped from the other side of the door.

I closed my eyes and leaned against the elegant door. I could feel her there, her energy on the other side of the door. Why hadn't I see it before? That's right. Too absorbed in my own little drama. Who was the selfish one now?

"I need to talk to you about . . . stuff."

"Talk to your little boyfriend there."

"He's not my boyfriend, Jessa. And if you'll let me in, I can explain."

"Never."

"Isn't that a little dramatic, Jessa?"

"Apparently all I am is a selfish drama queen, so I'm just being true to form."

I pounded on the door. "Damn it, Jessa. This isn't a game anymore."

"And it was before?"

With a thud of my forehead on the door, I turned to face Chaz. "Got anything?"

He shrugged. "You could always throw her against a wall."

"Would you get off of that already?"

My hands were in fists at my side and I had to take in a long cool breath to unclench my jaw enough to even speak. I turned back to the creamy door. "Jessa," I said softly. "I've got information about the Veil."

There was a cool ripple of something from the other side of the door. "No one's getting married in here."

"That's it. I'm not playing anymore."

I took two steps back and sucked in a deep breath.

"Violet, what are you doing?" Chaz asked.

"Going to throw her against a wall."

There was a small yelp from the other side of the door as I dropped my shields and gathered a little more power. Wasn't any time like the present to see if I really could control my power like a true Haverty should.

"Vi?"

But I was already moving forward, throwing my power forward and into the wooden door. Barreling towards it, the panther hit it before I did and my shoulder took barely any impact as the door splintered into a million pieces.

I found myself in one piece in her foyer. I rolled my shoulders and put the cat back where she needed to be. Brushing off chunks of door, I looked around her place. Her living room windows were open, letting in a cool breeze.

"Jessa?" I called out looking around.

Chaz followed me in slowly. "Shit Violet."

"Built-in dark side."

"They are going to call the cops."

I took in a deep breath as I looked out her ninth-story penthouse apartment. "It's okay. We can go. She's not here."

"What do you mean?"

I turned on him quickly, lightning quick, still a little jazzed from the adrenaline. He jumped back. "As in she's not here anymore."

"Where did she go?"

I looked into the mirror at my left. "Don't know."

We walked out of her apartment building just as the cops were pulling up. Chaz's souped up engine once again aided in our escape.

"What do you want to do?" he asked as we sped back to my place.

In the car, I had found a piece of her door that had jumped into a pocket of my coat. I spun it around and around. "Will you watch her tonight?"

"You gonna be okay by yourself?"

I was quiet. I didn't really have the heart to lie to him right now.

Chapter Twenty-Two

As we drove up to my house, the two police cars waiting outside made the hairs on my arm stand up straight. Two uniforms were standing outside like dark blue lawn sculptures.

Chaz pulled up to the curb on the other side of the street and I jumped out. No fire. No flood. Locusts maybe?

Slowly, I walked across the street. People had gathered outside the other units and were gossiping. Their whispers carried on the wind. *Poor single girl in 2G.*

An officer approached me quickly as I crossed the yard. "Hold on a moment, ma'am."

"This is my house. What happened?"

The man turned over his shoulder. "Get Briggs."

The other officer walked through my front door and disappeared into my living room. My living room. Without my permission.

"Tell me what happened." My fists were little balls at my side.

Chaz put his hand on the center of my back and the adrenaline and fear pooled in my chest dissipated for a moment.

"Everything okay?" he asked.

The officer nodded. "We got a call from a fellow officer about a break-in."

"Break-in?" An immediate inventory of everything worth anything ran through my head. My computer, my laptop, my binders full of research material, my French press, my violet box.

The man who exited my front door looked familiar as he walked across my front yard. "Miss Jordan. I'm Officer Briggs."

His face finally clicked when I saw the tennis shoe in his hand. "You're the one from the hit and run."

The man smiled a soft sympathetic smile. "I'm afraid I have some disturbing news."

"Apparently my house was broken into."

He nodded and handed me my shoe, which I immediately began to twist mercilessly with anxiety.

"I stopped by to return your sneaker from that day. I'd thrown it in the back of my squad car and I kept meaning to return it, but you know how life goes." He motioned that we should follow him to the threshold. "I rang the doorbell and heard a crash in the back. When no one answered, I tried the handle and it was open."

"We've taken pictures and we think we know what happened. But we need to ask you a few questions. I have to warn you. It looks pretty bad."

I gulped and my knees went a little weak. I leaned back into Chaz whose solid form braced mine for a moment.

With a deep breath, we followed Officer Briggs into my living room. I slipped a little in the tiled foyer. Chaz caught my elbow.

When I looked down, cotton stuffing covered the floor. The

pool of white wisps drew my eyes into the living room to my gutted couch. Pillows lay disemboweled all over the floor. Picture frames were smashed. A canvas painting above the couch was shredded on the wall. Books were ripped in two.

I stepped into the middle of the storm and took in a deep breath. The oxygen-filled lungful was supposed to keep me from breaking down into a puddley mess but I was met with the pungent odor of wet dog. It stung my nose and I winced.

"Sonovabitch," I heard Chaz whisper behind me.

I nodded as my jaw clenched. Those damn dogs. They were dead. The next time they came within five feet of me, they were toast and I was in for a mutt-shaped rug in front of my fireplace.

The wisps of cotton began to stir around my feet.

"Calm down there, kitten," Chaz whispered.

I hadn't even noticed my borders were out of place, let alone flailing out in all directions. As I tried to reel it in, putting up the brick walls in my head, I swore I could still feel the energy of the dogs bouncing around the room, shaking their vicious little heads as they ripped apart my decorative pillows.

I put my sleeve to my nose and took in a long deep calming breath only to find that my sleeve smelled like Chaz's new car. It didn't suck.

"When were you home last?" Officer Briggs asked as he drew a notebook out of his front pocket.

"This morning," I answered as I moved slowly though the first floor.

"What time did you leave?"

"Noon." The toppled over clock on my wet bar had stopped at 4:15. When we were with Cristina.

The surface of the coffee table had been busted out; sparkly glass covered the destruction of the couch. It was like sparkling snow. I hate snow.

"Did you lock the doors?"

"Yes. I remember flipping the lock before we left."

"We?"

I hitched my thumb over at Chaz who was standing still in the middle of the living room, watching me work my way through the wreckage.

"And you are?"

"Charles Garrett."

"And what is your relationship to Miss Jordan?"

My eyes snapped to Chaz's golden ones. *This should be an interesting answer.* He was looking straight at me when he answered. "I'm a close friend."

There was a little shiver down my spine that I blamed on the slimy feeling now permeating the place. The Violet warmth was gone, replaced by something cold and exotic. It drove me deeper into the wreckage of my first floor.

I stopped before the turtle table. The few remaining survivors from the disaster with Jessa had been ground into bits of porcelain and stone and left in perfect little piles of dust. That was just cruel.

"Does anyone else have keys to your house?"

"Yeah, my friend Jessa, but I saw her today."

"Did you give anyone permission to be here? Workmen? Electrician?"

"No."

I turned to walk into the kitchen when I saw something that was almost more disturbing than the blizzard that I called my living room.

There was a crystal vase, something dug out of the back of my kitchen, filled with two dozen lavender roses. The bouquet stood as tall as I did and the scent of the fresh flowers almost overpowered the fragrance of wet fur.

"Chaz," I whispered.

He was at my side in an instant.

"Please God tell me those aren't from him," I whispered. The pit of my stomach began to tremble and I reached out to grasp the top of my dining room chair. The only one that hadn't been turned into match sticks littering the floor.

Chaz leaned in. He shook his head stealthily.

There was another officer taking pictures of the shattered back glass door. The glass reflected the flash of his camera everywhere around us like a disco ball.

I released the top of the chair only to find my hands covered in black powder.

"Fingerprint powder. The tech came through here a few minutes before you arrived. We might need your prints."

I nodded as I wiped the black powder on my jeans, which in turn now had black streaks across the thighs.

"And you, Mr. Garrett?"

"They're on file."

"Oh, that's a story you can distract me with later," I muttered as I turned towards the kitchen.

Not that I had much food at any given moment anyway, and practically nothing after being gone for a week. But what I had was spilled across the kitchen floor. Cereal boxes had been ripped in half. Coffee beans were thrown around like sprinkles on top of the floured floor.

I put my face in my hands. That was a twenty dollar a

pound Hawaiian blend. Those dogs were not just going to die but going to die a painful horrible death.

Chaz put his hand on my shoulder and squeezed.

Officer Briggs's voice broke my moment of canine contemplation. "If you're up to it, I'd like you to look around to see if anything was taken."

I ran my fingers through my hair and nodded. Chaz followed me back through the first floor. The TV was still there, the DVD player, the DVDs, even the rentals from Blockbuster that I'd forgotten to return before I left to LA.

"Violet," Chaz whispered.

I followed his pointing finger to the mantle. The very empty mantle.

"Oh god. Seriously?"

The absence of the silver frame with the picture of my mother felt like a knife wound. I held my stomach in place as it turned over on itself.

"Miss Jordan?" the officer walked up beside me.

"A picture of my mother and me in a silver frame."

"Is it of any worth?" he asked as he scribbled notes.

"It's an heirloom from my mother's side."

The officer nodded as he scratched down notes. "Would you like to go upstairs?"

Chaz and I slowly walked upstairs. I was imagining the same fate for my bed as the couch had suffered. The doorframe was covered in the same black powder from down stairs so I nudged the door open with my foot.

The bedroom hadn't been touched. The bed was still half made. The vanity, which was usually disorganized anyway, hadn't been re-disorganized. My small closet door was still standing half open just as I'd left it. Nothing had been touched.

There was a smell there, though. Glad that the officers weren't around, I sniffed at the air. It was something sharp, like exotic flowers. There wasn't any wet dog here at all. A single stemmed purple rose rested gently on my pillow. Another shiver ran down my spine.

The bastard had been in my bedroom.

Chaz gasped when I dropped to my knees by the edge of the bed. I reached under the edge and scooted the violet box towards me.

Kneeling, I opened the box and counted all the items inside. I took in a deep breath and felt a small bit better. At least they didn't touch this. I got to my feet and clutched the box to my chest as I walked to my office. I was going to burn those sheets.

I think I wrote a poltergeist scene once, set in a library. It was an angry little girl who was trying to kill the little girl in the house so she would have a playmate. She had levitated all the books off the shelves and then dropped them all to the floor.

Someone did this to my office. Books lay on the ground ankle deep. The computer monitor was on the floor, but the tower was still there. My lap top bag was upside down, but my lap top was sitting on the chair. The software binders were still there, the phone, the fax machine had been knocked off but was still there and there was another strong odor of dog.

"Is that urine?"

Chaz nodded as he nudged a few of the books over with his boot.

"But nothing's gone," I said still looking around.

"Don't think they were after your stuff, Violet," Chaz said as he lead us downstairs.

I kept the box tightly to my chest. Officer Briggs came to stand with us at the base of the stairs. "What's missing?" he asked, his note pad ready.

"Nothing. Nothing except that picture."

A deep crease formed between the man's brows. "Nothing?"

"Computer's still there, laptop, everything's here, just upside down."

Briggs closed his note pad. "Can you think of anyone who might want to do this to you?"

I looked at Chaz who shook his head. "No," I said. "I'm no one. I'm a writer for a Dallas blog."

"Professional enemies?"

I dropped my chin in disbelief. "I'm a writer. We don't interact with people. We don't like you, a character dies a horrible death. Most of us rarely leave the house."

"What about you, Mr. Garrett? Do you have enemies?"

Chaz shook his head. "None that I can think of, sir." Note to self, not only is Chaz good looking enough to be on TV, he's got the acting chops to back it up.

Office Briggs sighed and scratched underneath his hat behind his ear. I remembered him doing that after the hit and run. Those hats must be uncomfortable.

"It does sound personal, Miss Jordan. Very rarely do people just break in to ransack the place. Unless this is some sort of gang prank. But I doubt it. There's been nothing like this in the neighborhood."

"What do I do?"

Officer Briggs nodded as the other men packed up and gestured that they were going to be outside. "If you've got someplace to stay, I suggest you go there. Maybe stay with Mr. Garrett or that friend of yours?"

I nodded. "Thank you, Officer Briggs."

"You're welcome, Miss Jordan. I'll be in touch with any information that might come off the prints or if anything new arises."

I stood there quietly as the men paraded out of my house. I counted to ten after the door closed, box clutched tightly to my chest, before the tirade began.

"What the hell?" I screamed. "This is my house. The bastards broke into my house."

I wanted to pick up the vase of roses and throw them across my already destroyed house. Instead I put my box down on the table next to it and searched for a card.

"No card," Chaz said calmly. "But I think the message is clear."

"What?" I snapped. *"I'm a crazy lunatic."*

"More like he knows where you live and he can do whatever he wants."

Volcanic didn't quite describe my anger. It sizzled down my back as I leaned forward and gripped the edge of my table. I completely understood the phrase of seeing red as my nails dug into the wooden edge.

The ribbon on my violet box started to flutter.

"Violet." Chaz backed off a few steps.

"Don't Violet me. I'm angry. Just let me feel violated for a moment." I took in deep breaths that were tainted by the sweet scent of the flowers. "This is my house, Chaz. My House."

"I know, Violet."

"No, you don't," I said as I turned around and leaned on

the edge of the table. I wiped the moisture from my cheeks and crossed my arms tightly around my chest.

"It's been a long time since I felt at home anywhere, and I was finally finding some happiness. Boring pathetic writer happiness but it was a start. And it was like as soon as it happened, as soon as I found a little place to call my own, I get mauled in the back alley, almost hit by a car, attacked on my first date in years, and now my house got broken into. It's like, why bother? Shit happens, and nine times out of ten it's going to happen to me."

"Come on, if you hadn't been a Perfect, you'd have never met me."

I sniffed and wiped the tears from my face.

"Hey," Chaz said as he stepped between me and the wreckage. "Why don't you get out of here? I'll clean up as best I can."

I shook my head. "Why don't I just leave? Period. If I'm not here, the dogs have nothing to chase. I still have one coast I can live on."

Chaz's jaw clenched. "Violet. If you're not here to stop this, we can't predict how bad it's going to be."

"Maybe if I'm not here, it doesn't happen at all. Cristina said it was about me and Jessa. If there is no me and Jessa, there might not be an apocalypse."

"Are you listening to yourself? Mights. You're putting the fate of the world against a might." Chaz grabbed my upper arms and shook me. "He messed up your house Violet. That's nothing. The Havertys killed my father."

His words slapped me out of my pity party. "I'm sorry."

"You are going to get through this and then kick some major ass."

I nodded. "Okay."

Chaz's hands fell away from my arms. He took a step back and leaned against the wall. "What's in the box?"

I looked back at the little box on the table. "Not quite yet, Chuck. Maybe someday, but not yet." I drew the box to my chest again and hugged it tightly.

"You are something else, Miss Jordan," Chaz pushed himself off the wall and slapped this thigh. "Okay. I want you to go pack a bag for three nights, take your laptop and anything you think you need to figure out what the hell Cristina told you. And then you're going to Iris's."

"I won't run, Chaz. Not anymore."

Chaz deflated. His plan was foiled. By me. Again. But his eyes twinkled when his new plan formed in his head. "Devin!"

"What?"

"Stay with Devin. He's safe, practically untraceable."

I frowned. "Why are you trying to get rid of me?"

"Never," Chaz shook his head. "You need to rest. You need to figure out that prophecy. I'll clean the place up. Keep an eye out for looters."

I knew he was right. The emotional roller coaster that was today had made my skin hurt with its ups and downs. Or really mostly the downs. "You just want to play hero if they come back."

Chaz shrugged. "I did get a new shotgun and a box of silver buckshot."

"Boys and their toys," I said as I started climbing the stairs.

Twenty minutes later there was a ring at the doorbell. I froze in place. Were they back? I shook my head and shook the fear from my skin. Don't be an idiot, Violet. Would they really ring the doorbell if they were back?

Bag over my shoulder, I went down the stairwell silently. Until I heard the familiar voice.

"Devin!" I dropped the bag on the floor and went to him quickly.

He opened his arms wide for me and I squeezed him tightly. "Are you all right?"

I nodded against his chest. I looked up at him. "He called you, didn't he?"

Devin nodded. "Doctor Devin to the rescue."

Stepping away from him, Chaz came up behind me and handed Devin the bag I had gleefully left on the floor. Figured I'd just take what I took to LA. It was one of the few things I knew that they hadn't touched. Guess they drew the line at dirty laundry.

"Stay inside," Chaz said. He looked down at me with stern eyes. "Work on that script that you've been putting off."

Geez. Note to self: We need to work on Chaz's subtle. "I've got my laptop and the tape recorder from our notes earlier."

Chaz handed me my violet box. "Keep it safe until we can find a place for it."

I nodded and took it, immediately holding it like a protective teddy bear.

"Ready, sweetheart?" Devin offered as he gestured for the door.

"When you are," I smiled and followed Devin out.

Chaz's hand caught my shoulder. I turned around and looked at him as we straddled the threshold of what use to be the safest place in the world. His hand slid up to the side of my neck and the pit of my stomach flipped as I looked up at him.

"Be safe, Violet."

I nodded.

His hand trailed down my arm and then fell away. "Go. Get inside as soon as you can."

"So, no barhopping then?"

He rolled his eyes and pushed me gently to where Devin was waiting with my door open.

"If I liquor you up, will you explain why you haven't called in ages?" Devin said waving a bottle of wine between me and my computer screen.

"God. Devin. I'm sorry."

"Don't be sorry. Just start talking. Not that I didn't enjoy Stalker boy's little chat on the phone," Devin marched back to the kitchen and began to rummage loudly around in the drawers for a bottle opener. "Ah-hah," he cried out as he found the corkscrew. "Oh, is he the reason you haven't call? God. I need details. Really steamy details."

Pushing up from the table, I turned around to watch him pour two very full glasses of red wine. He gestured for us to go into the living room, but paused as he looked at the research strewn over his dining room table.

"Oh god, Vi. Please tell me that's just research for a script," he gulped, his eyebrows steeply arched above his worried brown eyes.

"Yeah, of course," I said as I quickly closed the top of my laptop, hiding the picture of the demon that I had brought up, trying to comprehend just what kind of wickedness could be conjured with a mirror.

"You and your imagination," Devin shook his head as he walked into the front room.

"Wish this was in my head," I whispered.

He sat down on the couch and patted the cushion next to him. I really didn't have time for this. I needed to be saving the world. But as I looked into his brown caring eyes, I couldn't deny that I needed a friend right now.

I stayed standing as I looked down at him, his long figure on my couch, his slender arm along the back of the cushion. He really was a friend. No weird destinies. No mystical weaving of fates. He was just Devin.

He frowned. "Something wrong?"

"No."

He patted the cushion next to him again. "So what's going on in your world, Violet Jordan?"

"So she hasn't talk to you in a week?"

"Yep," I nodded as I reached across to put my empty glass on the coffee table.

"Jessa'll come around."

"Can't wait for that, Devin. Need to make things right."

"Why push her?"

"Because," I said as I leaned back on the couch and looked over at him. "Because she's my family Devin, and I can't keep losing people that I love."

"Oh, dear heart," he said as he wrapped his arms around me. "It's going to be okay. We'll get her back."

I nodded against his chest as he stroked my hair. Stupid hot tears ran down my cheeks and I tried to wipe them away before they smeared his perfectly fitted Armani shirt.

"But don't ever think that you're alone, little Violet Jordan. You've at least got me."

"Thank you, Devin. For everything."

"And you've got Stalker boy."

"Not really."

Devin pulled me in against his chest and scooted down into the couch. "When he called me tonight, he was scared. He said, 'Devin, I need you to take care of our girl.' I thought it was just him being all macho, but when I saw the two of you tonight, in the door way," Devin shook his head. He let out a soft whistle. "Wow."

"I'm just a project for him. He'll fix me up and then be on his way. It's his modus operandi."

Devin made a play shiver. "You know I like it when you use those big words."

We settled back on the couch, his arm still around my shoulder. I rested my head on him and all the information of the last hours danced around in my head. Something was brewing in the back of my brain, like a French press just ready to be pressed.

"Is your birthday this month or something?"

"Nope. April tenth."

"Oh."

"Jessa's Silver Ball is in two days," he said casually.

We both gasped and sat up straight on the couch.

"The Silver Ball. I'd forgotten."

"Certainly she invited you before the fight."

I ran my fingers through my hair to get it out of my face. "I was so mad, I tossed it."

A devious smile crossed Devin's face. "Want to be my plus one?"

"You've already RSVPed?"

"It's perfect," he smiled as he pulled me back to him. "Like it was written in the stars or something. Doctor Devin to the rescue."

The brief thought crossed my mind that maybe it was. Maybe someone up there liked me. Or just liked jerking me around. Currently, I was thinking the second option.

"You'll wear something fab, and I'll look handsome as ever. We'll go shopping tomorrow, after work. She'll have to be civil to you. It's her party."

"Aren't you a little schemer?"

It felt like a weight was lifted off my chest. I had a plan. There was a light at the end of the tunnel, even if it was the train.

"Mirrors break. Magnolias bleed. At the darkest of the darkest night."

It was the umpteenth time I'd listen to the chilling words emanating from the tape recorder. Cristina's cadence was creepy in real life, but every time I heard it I could see her eyes staring into the void, her white-knuckled hands as they clenched mine. My skin was permanently goose-bumped and my eyes were wide as I began piecing together the chilling puzzle strewn across Devin's dining room table.

After he'd left for work, I'd hooked my laptop up to the recorder and it transcribed the words into English, well, mostly English. Cristina's mother tongue swirled in between the ominous English phrases. Depending on which side of the freaked out pendulum I was on, her accent either made the words softer and almost acceptable, or added the extra fear of the unknown. I couldn't seem to stop shivering. And that was before I started fixing words here and there, giving the string of gibberish meaning. Then the gripping truth relieved itself on the glowing screen.

"Mirrors break." God bless Google. A simple search brought up a news article describing the burglary of several antique shops across the Metroplex over the past two weeks. Among the looted materials were three ancient mirrors. The article also mentioned a suit of armor, a chair that belonged to some king, and some ancient dagger thing. I knew that mirrors were used in all kinds of wicked little deeds. Guess Snow White's queen had the right idea with her "Mirror Mirror" routine.

"Magnolias bleed." I didn't really want to dig too deeply into that one. I was toast.

"At the darkest on the darkest night." This still had me stumped.

Pushing away from the table with shaking arms, I got up, fixed another pot of coffee, and put some laundry in the dryer. I was being chased after by god knows what and I still had five loads of laundry from my one week of being gone. A girl can't win.

As I was sorting whites and colors, I came across the bloodstained shirt from the Worst Date Ever. How in the hell did this get in my suitcase? Before I could contemplate the divine hand it would have taken to get Chaz's shirt from my hamper in the bathroom to my suitcase, it hit me. As I was measuring out the lilac-scented fabric softener, all the pieces fell together in my head. That night in the alley. The trench coat. Hadn't we found a book of some sort in the brute's coat pocket? Where the hell was that?

I tore through my purse to get my cell phone. God I needed to get a smaller purse.

Chaz answered on the third ring. There was music blaring in the background, angry boy music.

"What are you doing?" I winced as I brought the phone away from my ear for a moment until the music subsided.

"Cleaning."

"Which is closer? The gun or the vacuum?"

Chaz chuckled. "What are you doing?"

"I'm saving the world. Guess the tables have turned."

"There's my girl."

My skin chilled as I remembered what Devin had said the night before. "Right, well, I need to know what page was marked in the book that we found on the mutt, the night of . . . The night that we . . ."

"Book . . . got it," he saved me from myself.

I could hear him stomp up the stairs of my place and closed my eyes. He was in my office right now, kicking books around to find the black trench coat on the floor. His tight T-shirt was probably stretched over his chest as he put his hand on his hip, looking around the mess, his . . .

"Got it," he exclaimed.

I jumped up and snapped out of my revelry. "Check the dog-eared page."

"Um. The New Moon, the darkest night of the month. December sixteenth."

"Crap," I muttered. I stood up and began to pace. "From what Cristina said, I think they are planning some mirror magic on the longest night. Think that's what Jessa pulled on us the other day."

"I could have told you that."

"Well, don't you just get a gold star." None of this enlightened me as to exactly why they would need Jessa or how either of us was going to be involved in all this. But it seemed that I just had to keep her safe for a little more than a week while she continued to completely hate my guts. It was going to be great. Just awesome, really.

"What's the plan?"

"Devin and I worked out a way to get Jessa to talk to me that doesn't involve tying her to a chair."

"Really, what's that?"

"We're going a party. Wanna come?"

"Seriously?"

"As a heart attack. I just need to have you watch her until Friday night."

The line was silent for a moment and I closed my eyes. My shoulders relaxed and I leaned against Devin's wall and just listened to him breathe. How pathetic was that?

"If that's was you need, Violet."

"That's what I need. By the way, did that guy tell you who wrote the Book of Prophecy?" Since I was knee deep in one vision, I'd been thinking about the bigger one now I know that the Crown and Veil meant.

The line was silent. His heart beat sped up.

"Chaz?"

"He wouldn't tell me who wrote it."

"Did you not say please?"

"He simply wouldn't tell me. He took the book and kicked me out of his place."

I frowned so hard that my brow hurt. "I thought he was a good guy."

"He is."

"Why wouldn't he help?"

I was focused so hard on his words that I could hear him lick his lips.

"I don't know, Violet."

I took in a deep breath and exhaled. "Right, we will handle that when it comes. Well, get some sleep because this is Thursday, which means happy hour at Gloria's probably and then whatever date she's got lined up."

"Will there be coffee involved?"

"There's a coffee shop in every direction from my house. I'll be expecting your call around nine."

"Yes, ma'am."

I smiled and snapped the phone closed. That boy was going to be trouble.

"You need to look fabulous. Beyond fabulous," Devin said as he flipped frantically through rack after rack of dresses, intermittently taking one out and throwing it on the pile in my arms. "Is Stalker boy coming?"

"Don't think fancy parties are really his scene."

"Oh," Devin said, his shoulders falling for a moment. "Oh, well. You're going to look great anyway."

The instant Devin came home, he'd dragged me out shopping. I fought him at first. I was perfectly content spending the rest of my life in a row house in the most fabulous part of town. I'd already planned that I could have his office and really all I needed was a couch to sleep on for the rest of my life. But Devin wouldn't hear of it. "It's just stuff, Violet. Don't let them win."

I'd laughed. If only he knew what would happen if they did win. But damn it, he was right. If I didn't want them to win, I had to get Jessa talking to me again. In order to get Jessa to talk to me again, I had to go to this party. And in order to go to this party, I had to have *the* dress. Who knew that the fate of the world relied on the fashionable cut of a dress?

Devin distracted my train of thought by tossing another green dress on the top of the pile. "Okay. I think my work here is done."

We were in the dressing rooms when I my spidey sense kicked in. I was contorting into all of these short little things Devin had picked out, thankful that I'd remembered to shave this morning. I swear, some of these dresses were a little too complicated for me with straps and zippers in the weirdest place.

I thought I'd just twinged a muscle in my neck when the cool chill of magic ran like a feather down my exposed spine. Quickly getting the dress situated, I stood perfectly still in the dressing room, back to mirror. I quieted everything in my body: my heartbeat, my breathing, and just listened. I heard the whirr of the air-conditioning, the movement of a security camera, someone sliding a credit card through the reader, but nothing that felt like harm.

Turning the handle as silently as I could, I stepped out of the dressing room. Could there be someone in the stalls with us? Could those bastards have followed me here? I hadn't heard anything. And these days, the senses were on overdrive, if I wanted them to be or not. Could there have *been* someone in here with us? I sniffed the air and didn't smell any recent scents, just Devin's cologne.

I stalked down the aisle of the dressing room soundlessly. I pressed my ears against the door of his dressing room and could only make out Devin's breath as he pulled on a shirt. He was safe, and by the steady beat of his heart, blissfully unaware of my panic.

Then, it wasn't here anymore; the feeling, the heaviness in the air running down my back was gone. But the goose bumps still covered my arms, like a visual cue from my subconscious that I shouldn't be out shopping. There were darker stakes at hand. Still spooked, I started back to my own dressing room.

Halfway back, Devin popped out of his room.

"This is the dress," he exclaimed as he grabbed my hand and spun me around. "You look fantastic."

He maneuvered me in front of the full-length mirror at the end of the row of dressing rooms. In the fit of panic, I'd missed the obvious: It was a stunning dress and more leg than I had shown since preschool. Devin's hands rested at my hips, so he could turn me whichever way he wanted to get a better view of certain parts.

"It's official," he smiled.

"What?"

"You've turned me; I'm not gay anymore. Your legs, this dress. It's sinful, Violet."

"I don't want to look sinful. I want to look apologetic."

I looked at him in the mirror. His smile lit up the dressing room as he rested his head on my shoulder like a Cheshire guardian angel.

"She's going to forgive you, Violet. You're the only family she's got. Hell. You're the only family I've got."

I leaned my head against his and his arms slid around my waist. "Right back at you, kid."

He squeezed briefly and then let me go. I was suddenly cold for the loss of him.

And on that thought, I turned to him. "It's going to be forty tomorrow night. What do I wear over this?"

"Ughh," he said as he pushed me towards my dressing room. "Do I have to do everything for you?"

Chapter Twenty-Three

The bouncer at the door (who was about as wide as the door itself) checked Devin's invite and, with a head to toe look at me, lifted the velvet rope. We proceeded past the rest of the people waiting in the cold winter night. I'll admit, most of the time I felt bad bypassing all the others to get in the door. This was the first time I was not willing to wait out in the cold. The dress I had picked met Jessa's two favorite criteria: a need for special underwear and way too skimpy to be out in 45-degree weather.

As I walked inside, appreciative of the inspection by the huge man outside, my eyes quickly adjusted. The space was incredible, silver everywhere. Everything sparkled and threw light merrily across the bar. It was exquisite and very Jessa. I knew she was good at her job, despite my previous sentiments, but this place was a work of art. My feet paused in the doorway as I gaped. If she didn't want to see me, I was going to ruin all of this for her.

Devin grabbed my hand and pulled me forward into the fray. "You look amazing," he smiled over his shoulder, as he eyed a few of the other attendants. "You're wearing her favorite designer. There's no way she's not going to talk to you."

I spotted the table where Carrie and Adrianna had set up, right next to the dance floor. I squeezed Devin's hand and pointed.

"Good eye," he said as he lead the way again, guiding me through the already growing crowd.

As we slid into the empty seats, Carrie filled us in. "Jessa is running a little late. She's got extra primping to do. Word is she's bringing a boy."

"Really? Have you met him?" I missed being in the loop of such things. It felt wrong, Carrie knowing this before I did.

"Not yet. Tonight is the test run."

"Where did she meet him?" I asked, looking around the place, feeling like I was in some sort of a wonderland.

"Don't know," Carrie shrugged. "At least one of us will have a partner for the dance floor."

"You won't be alone," I responded back automatically.

Devin shook his head as he scanned the crowd. He was on the prowl more than I was lately. "I don't know. In that dress, you might have to beat them off with a stick."

I laughed. "Right. Because it's happened so many times before."

"Tonight's different. You're radiant."

I looked over at him. "Were you drinking before we left?"

"Not yet. Want something?"

"God please."

Jessa sauntered in an hour after her own invite said the party was supposed to start. But it was worth it. She was dressed to the nines in a gold halter dress and the highest, strappiest gold heels ever made. Her hair was a curtain of black silk that she tossed effortlessly over her shoulder as the photographer at the door snapped a few shots.

Only Jessa would wear a gold dress to her own Silver Ball.

She took her time getting over to her circle of friends, mingling with every male in her path. She greeted Devin cordially and then looked down at me still in my seat. Her brown gaze was stony and, in the dancing lights, I saw a flash of lavender cross her eyes.

"Hello, Violet," she greeted flatly.

"Hello, Jessa."

She glared at Devin. "Guess this was you're doing?"

"Guilty as charged," he said as he lifted his hands in surrender as he slid out of the seat next to me. "I'll leave you to it," Devin whispered before he made a beeline to the bar.

Jessa crossed her arms and began to tap her foot. She was being bitchy, but I deserved it.

I waited until Devin was out of ear shot. "Listen, I know that I said some pretty wicked things. I lashed out at you. I just feel," I said, stressing the *feeling* words. It's what the conflict resolution people online said to do. "I just felt like you were leaving me out of some major stuff."

"And you weren't?"

"I'm not denying that."

"And?"

What else did she expect? That was more of an apology than I had ever given. Usually didn't care this much to even muster an apology. Usually I was half way across the country. I licked my lips. "And I know you're fey."

She shifted to her other foot. "And I know you're a shapeshifter."

I gulped, the blood rushing from my face. There it was; no more secrets now. Fear chilled my skin and the fluttering in my stomach that had been squelched by the three drinks was now back in full force. "How?"

"Local psychic. How'd you know?"

I shook my head, looking down at the black table for a moment. I could just see Cristina laughing at the two of us. "Local psychic." I said. "Well, that and you disappeared from a nine-story penthouse."

"You owe me for the door by the way. Pissed off panthers aren't covered by insurance."

It was weird to hear her say *panther* so casually. But how long had she been familiar with this? Her whole life? Two months and counting like me? Would I ever know?

But she'd made a joke. At this point, I would take a joke at my expense to patch up this mess.

Her arms dropped down to her waist to hold her gold clutch. She looked hard at me, her little jaw tight. "Is that dress Ralph Lauren?"

I shrugged. "Had a friend who taught me about the finer things in life."

Jessa took a long look around the place and then up at me.

I couldn't tell what she was thinking. I didn't know if I ever would again. "So we're good?"

"I don't hate your guts."

I smiled. "You couldn't hate my guts if you tried."

Jessa's cool exterior faded and she fought a smile on her perfectly glossed lips.

"Heard you met a guy." I said as I gestured to the seats next to me.

"He should be here tonight," she said calmly, but her cheeks blushed as she sat down. The long line of her smooth leg reflected the lights and I was pretty sure that was part of her craft. I really needed to learn that trick.

"Do I get to meet him?"

She looked around and her entire face lit up, literally. "He's here."

After being secluded in a corner for forty minutes, Jessa and her date walked up to the four of us. Well, Jessa sauntered because that's what Jessa did, just enough of a sway in her hips that the short golden dress flipped up dangerous high. Her date stalked. Shoulders down, his long arms gracefully swayed by his sides, his eyes focused forward as the crowd parted before them. He was taller than her with blonde hair and a sharply tailored suit. What caught me off guard were his incredibly blue eyes, the color discernible even in this dimly lit room.

Devin and I stood from our seats to meet the anticipated date.

"Haydn, this is Devin."

He shook Devin's hand with two strong pumps. "Pleased to meet you."

"Any friend of Jessa's . . ." Devin trailed off into a debonair smile.

"And this is my best friend, Violet."

I couldn't deny that my skin warmed when I heard her say that. Couldn't say it was still warm a second later as her date turned his gaze to me. There was a sharpness to his blue eyes that sent a shiver down my spine.

"Jessa has told me so much about you," he said.

Haydn offered his hand and I took it carefully. When our hands touched, it was like cold lightning sizzling up my arm.

I ripped my hand away from his and he smiled. *What the hell?*

Jessa frowned.

I kept my eyes on him. Caught in the depth of his blue eyes, my skin crawled. I watched as he slid his arm around Jessa, whose frown faded quickly at the attention.

My gut instinct told me to rip Jessa from his arm and throw two drinks in his face. But I was still on thin ice with her. Maybe I was just picking up his skeeziness with my preternatural senses. Maybe it was the two drinks putting stories in my head.

Just so I couldn't again be accused of being a bad friend, I carefully cracked my shields open and brushed him stealthily.

Nothing. Like a cement wall. Like nothing was even standing before me.

Jessa's eyes bounced between me and lover boy. "Well, you must be thirsty," Jessa said, patting his chest.

"We just had a drink at the bar," he laughed with a charming smile.

As Jessa drew him away, I sucked in a deep breath. Didn't know I hadn't been breathing.

"I can see what Jessa sees in him." Devin broke my glare into the back of the man's head.

"What?" I grumbled.

"Boy's got a butt that you could bounce a quarter off of."

I turned to Devin. "I don't like him."

"Neither do I," he echoed. "Guy's a prick. Jessa deserves better."

We slid back into our seats and I watched as Jessa crossed the ballroom. I wasn't going to take my eyes off him all night. Sure, he reeked of wealth and he was good looking, but I still wasn't buying it. I, of anyone here, knew what could lie beneath a normal exterior.

As Haydn was regaling the tale of how he and Jessa met, I sat with my legs crossed, still feeling on edge. Everyone fawned over the little playboy, asking questions and listening as if hypnotized by his stories.

The lights dimmed slightly and a spotlight directed our eyes to an MC by the DJ booth. "Ladies and Gentlemen, Welcome to the First Annual Silver Ball Hosted by Cinetech."

The crowd clapped politely.

"And the president a Cinetech would like to thank Jessa Feychild for her efforts in putting together this extraordinary event."

A spotlight hit our table and Jessa rose, graciously waving to the crowd.

"As our evening now progresses, our hosts would like to suggest you make your way down to the dance floor to enjoy the excellent DJ and to the bar while the drinks are still free."

The crowd applauded wildly and Jessa turned to me. "Come on, we need to dance."

I shook my head. "You know I don't dance."

Her face turned hard as she glared down at me. "You will dance."

"Okay. Okay," I rose, smoothing my very short skirt down with my palms. Anything the fairy princess wanted.

Diaries of an Urban Panther

The entire table joined us on the dance floor. Who doesn't like dancing to the fifties music medley with 40-year-old investors? The three Bailey and creams made it a bit more palatable.

About 15 minutes later, Jessa gave me the signal she was going to the bathroom, no doubt to check her flawless makeup. I didn't like the idea of leaving her alone.

"I'll come with," I said.

Jessa pushed me towards Haydn. "Dance. Talk." It meant that she wanted me to find out if he liked her. We'd dance this dance before. If she was entrusting me to do this, maybe our friendship was on the mend.

"I'll go," Carrie said as she smiled.

Jessa curled her arm through Carrie's as they headed off the dance floor before I could lodge a protest.

It left me on the dance floor with *him*. So at least I knew where *he* would be and she'd be safe.

I turned my side to Haydn, keeping him in my periphery. I still didn't know what it was that made my hairs stand on end. He was too perfect. And I really didn't like the way he looked at Jessa. There was hunger there I knew intimately.

"Why the cold shoulder?" he asked with a smile.

"Nothing," I shrugged and I kept on twisting and mashing potatoes.

"Then come here," he demanded. His hand shot out and his fingers curled around my waist, digging in as he pulled me to him. Any pretenses of him being any shade of decent melted away.

I pushed him away with all my might but he held me flush against his front. I wasn't budging. The man was stronger than he looked. Too strong.

"Let go of me," I screamed, still pushing against his broad chest with my fists.

He just tilted his head back and laughed. "Calm down, little sister."

"I'm not your . . ." but I stopped when I saw his eyes.

Deep golden irises reflected the sporadic flash of the disco lights. I gulped and suddenly felt him surround me, enveloping me within his borders. He was panther. He smelled like stormy night air and a sharp plant scent so exotic I couldn't name it. Bile rose in my throat when I realized where I knew that smell from: my bedroom.

"But you are," he purred with a raised human eyebrow over his inhuman eyes.

"Spencer," I whispered and my fight was renewed, the adrenaline adding to my strength as I pushed and kicked for freedom.

He held me too tightly, both arms around my waist. I couldn't get out of it, could barely breathe. Couldn't kick, could only wriggle.

"Let me go," I cried out. Desperate, I looked around at the computer engineers and investors who all kept dancing to the "Shout" throwing their hands up madly in the air.

"But I want you." Sincerity sounded sinful in his smooth voice. "I've wanted you since you threw that hussy across the bar."

"It was you!" I gasped. "You and your mutts have been stalking me."

He smiled and, for the briefest moment, I glimpsed the malevolence behind the perfectly crafted façade.

Spencer lunged forward and pressed his mouth hard against

mine. The kiss was more bruising than breath-taking and more possessive than passionate. The panther stirred in my chest as he grabbed the back of my head and forced his tongue past my lips. He tasted like the Scotch he had been nursing at the table, and something else. Something dark and heady.

For all that I wanted to fight back, the part of me that was pure animal didn't. His power felt natural against mine, one in the same. My panther arched into his energy as though it was a welcome caress. A deep purr rumbled in my ears. It made me feel sick when I realized it had come from me.

Desperate for air, I bit down his lower lip; the metallic taste of blood was instantaneous. A small part of me was satisfied at having drawn *his* blood for a change of pace.

He jerked back, dropping his hand from my head. Blood pooled at the corner of his mouth, which curled up into a smile, but he didn't release his hold on me. He leaned in again to repeat his sin, his arms tightening around me but I arched away from him. To everyone else on the dance floor, it probably looked like a dip to the Latin rhythms now mashed together over the loud speakers.

He jerked me back to our previous position, and our eyes locked. "We should be together."

My mouth felt bruised from the trauma and I desperately wanted to wipe the taste of him from them. "No."

"I need you Violet. With you, god, the two of us could destroy my father and revel in the chaos." He ducked his head beside mine and nuzzled his nose behind my ear, taking in a lungful. My entire body tensed up and then a wave of cool goose bumps ran down my skin. "The two of us together. You can feel it too, can't you?"

"No," I growled the lie. I could feel it, how easily it would be to open up to him and run his panther past mine. But this was the bastard who attacked me in a back alley. This was the bastard who had trashed my lair. This was the bastard who asked out my best friend to get to me.

He ran his hand down the side of my face, then grabbed my chin, fingers digging into the bone. "You look just like your mother," he smiled. A flash of white pressed down on his bloody lip. "I could have never imagined that Saturday night leftovers could be such a blessing."

"Flatter all you want, I'll never be yours."

His jaw clenched and the feel, the smell of him, grew so intense it permeated the air around us. Surely the people around us had to feel it? But they danced on not seeing anything abnormal here. Many other couples had paired up to salsa to *Suavamente*.

Arm still around my waist, he hit me with a wall of energy that beat anything I had ever done to Chaz. It flared out around us quickly outward as he readied his power. Thick as cement, it crept over my skin, the cool gritty feeling touching my skin through my clothes. Then it drove into me, like a spear through my midsection. He blasted through the paper thin protection I held around me like a cannon ball through dry wall.

My cat screamed out at the sudden attack as his power rammed through me. I'd felt this a week ago at the barn. Like he was trying to rip out the cat within me. I felt nails digging into flesh. I didn't know if it was my cat digging in her claws to stay where she was or if it was my own claws piercing his perfect pectorals.

"I made you, Violet Jordan. You're mine. Willingly or not," he growled and his eyes blinked back to normal.

The pain was everywhere, blinding and hot, like daggers and needles all over my skin. Then, there was nothing. His power retreated, leaving a slimy chill in its wake as his cat went back behind his rock-solid borders he hid so easily behind.

I went limp for a moment, not strong enough to use my knees. I hung loosely on his arm before I could feel my feet, let alone stand on the two of them.

Dropping his arm, he pushed me away and left the dance floor. I stumbled into a few other dancers, who laughingly set me upright again and then returned to their reverie, leaving me wobbling on my feet. The first wave of nausea hit in the middle of the strobing lights and dancing bodies. I bounced between the dancers, brushing up against them as I drunkenly worked my way to the edge of the dance floor.

I flew to the bathroom, passing Jessa on the way in.

As I locked the bathroom stall door, I leaned against the cool metal. The vice in my stomach twisted, right in the center, like cramps from hell that pulled at my diaphragm and made it hard to breathe.

It was her, the panther. She was clawing around, injured, angry, and looking to get a piece of him.

My borders shot, I couldn't keep her in. I couldn't stop her. Didn't want to. But there were people out there and some of them I loved and could never hurt.

Fumbling at small purse clasped around my wrist, my cell phone fell out and clattered on the white-and-black tiled floor. I stared down at my hand. It was covered in blood. His blood.

"Violet," Jessa said from the other side of the thin stall door.

I could feel her energy for the first time, her light sprinkles across my hot panther. Her scent filled my nostrils, not her perfume, her *real* scent. Roses and raindrops.

Dropping to my knees, I reached out for my cell phone. My hand shook and I could swear it was darker than usual.

Jessa's hand reached under the door and grabbed my hand. "Violet, what's wrong?"

I ripped my fingers out of hers. "Get out," I hissed.

Jessa's pale hand disappeared with my cell phone. I heard a click echoed through the black tiled bathroom. She'd locked herself in. Stupid, stupid girl.

"Three, speed dial three," I managed out.

Jessa must have done what I asked.

I stood back up, needing to use my legs, my human legs. I pressed my back against the wall. The metal was startling cool on my flesh. I took in sharp shallow breaths. I couldn't inhale, like my panther was trying to climb up my throat and suffocate me in silky fur.

"Violet?"

I heard the faint echo of Chaz's voice. I closed my eyes and imagined him sitting in his car somewhere, probably closer than I'd like, watching.

"Something's wrong," Jessa answered.

"Who's this?"

"She's all over the place. I think she's going to shift."

Those were all the words I heard. The panther pushed against my chest, wanting to slide up, slide out. She was angry and the taste of blood still on my lips came back into sharp focus.

What the hell? I forced my eyes open. I could see the blurry reflection of myself in the dull metal stall. Stay Violet. Stay Violet, I kept repeating to myself. Keep it together.

"He's coming," Jessa said from the other side of the door. "Whoever he is?"

The panther raged again, more powerful this time. She slammed my head against the wall behind me and stretched her leg. Four red long fiery welts appear down my thigh. My foot contorted and my right hind paw tore through my new heel.

There was a small yelp on the other side of the door. I heard her heels scurry away from the stall door.

The fear in Jessa's cry snapped me back for a moment. It took everything I had to keep the damn cat in. She clawed down my arm this time and four long marks appeared down my bicep.

"Violet?" Jessa whimpered. "What's happening?"

I couldn't talk, couldn't answer. I pressed myself in the back of the stall. I focused on the cold tiles. The smell of the air freshener than covered the harsh cleanser. Sucked in any air that the panther would let me.

"Violet, honey, I'm sorry. I'm sorry if I did this to you."

My chest hurt. I pressed my hand against the invisible wound. The pain of his penetration flared again, the feel of his energy sliding over my skin, touching me in places no one had ever before.

The panther flared again, raging against our violation. She was angry, she wanted revenge, and she was so much stronger than me. And he was so much stronger than us.

Suddenly, I was surrounded by roses. Cool feathers of

energy brushed lightly over my exposed skin and the panther stopped, suspended in the cool floral energy. My thoughts cleared as I sucked in a shuttered breath. "Jessa?"

I could feel her on the other side of the metal door, could almost see where her hand and head pressed against the door. "Just a few minutes more, Vi."

A furious series of bangs on the door echoed through the silent bathroom at the door. I jumped then and pressed myself back harder against the stall wall.

"No," I cried out. *He was back. He was coming to finish the job.*

"Stalker boy!" Jessa gasped.

"Where is she?"

The door to the stall slammed open, the weak metal lock clattering to the ground.

Chaz was standing there, outlined by the lights behind him. "We're getting you home," he said.

"I can't," I whimpered.

"My ass," he growled.

As he took off his coat, his scent surrounded me. He was all man and musk. My eyes focused on his wildly beating pulse at his throat and I licked my lips.

The panther sprung forward, ripping me from where I had pressed myself against the tile. I stumbled forward with one heel on and Chaz caught me quickly. He wrapped me tightly in his jacket. I couldn't move. He pulled me out of the stall and scooped me up into his arms. I buried my nose into his neck and took in the deepest breath of him as I could.

"Stay with me, Violet," he whispered into my ear.

He laid me on the couch and Jessa tucked my favorite blanket tightly around me. She squeezed my shoulder hard.

"I'll take it from here," Chaz said softly.

Jessa knelt by my head. Her eyes were watery as she brushed my hair behind my ear. Her cool fingers felt like petals as she stroked my face.

I tried to say I was sorry. I wanted to tell her that she was my family. But as I opened my mouth, the panther tried to rise again. My entire body tensed up as I held on for everything.

Jessa smiled and kissed my forehead, the most intimate thing she had ever done in our two year friendship. "If you need anything . . . ever . . ."

She moved away from me, her rose scent fading fast as she crossed the room

Every muscle was clenched tightly. It held the panther in. In the back of Chaz's Bronco, I'd discovered that if every one of my muscles was tensed, alert, the panther couldn't climb through. But I was getting tired. She still managed to send me into convulsions and I was quickly running out of strength.

Chaz locked the front door behind Jessa and took out his cell phone.

I focused on his voice as he began to walk the whole length of my first floor. Listening to him, smelling him calmed the panther, calmed me.

Turning my head to watch him, he looked very worried. He ran his fingers through is hair. "But she's convulsing. Okay. No, I wasn't with her. Because she's a big girl."

A wave of nausea hit me and I rolled off the couch, finally breaking through my leather straight jacket. I landed hard on my knees and waited. I'd never gotten nauseous before with my shifts. Never been this out of control before.

"Okay. I think we do. Yeah. You want me to what?" he protested as he went into the kitchen.

The conversation faded away as another seizure took my body. It was taking longer to get her under control each time. I was losing this fight. My hand dug into the carpet, claws rippling just under the surface before I could tense back up again.

The notion hit me that I needed fresh air. Fresh air always helped when I was sick before. With all my might, I pulled myself up off the plush carpet and pin-balled my way across the back of the room to where the glass door used to be. A sheet of plywood was leaning up against the frame.

I used all my weight to slide the wood away from the frame and the cool night air hit me like a wall of crisp energy. Leaning against the wall just inside the door, I took in deep breaths of the night air, but the wild scented night air called to me to run like the streak of black fur that I really was.

I stumbled out the door and stood drunkenly out in the night air, swimming in the scents around me. The dogs next door. The flowers in Mrs. Henderson's garden. Someone having sex with the window open. I could just let her go. I wasn't in a crowded room. I could just streak away in the night and I wouldn't have to fight anymore.

An arm circled around my waist and pulled me back into the house. A whimper escaped when the makeshift door closed, cutting me off from all those wonderful smells.

Chaz leaned me against the wall, keeping me there by pressing his lower half against mine and turning my face to his with his hand. He flooded my senses. The sight of him, the smell of him, the feel of him. The panther stilled for the moment as we watched him, watched his hazel eyes.

"You've been poisoned. We need to find the wound and clean it out."

"What?" I managed to get out. It wasn't just Spencer's power? Cheater.

"Iris said you need to stay grounded to your human form because, otherwise, you could be lost to the panther forever if you shift."

My jaw was sore from being clenched. The words came out slow. "I'm better as a panther."

"Don't be smug, Violet," he snapped.

I looked back at those concerned eyes, the deep furrow between his brow and how much deeper it had gotten since we'd know each other. "I'm telling the truth," I said. "I'm a wreck of a girl."

He sighed and the furrow got even deeper. He slid his hand up my cheek and around my jaw. "You are a spectacular woman, Vi."

Chaz kissed me. His deep kiss brought a heat to my body, warming every inch of both of us. The warmth started below my breastbone and worked its way up and down, making my toes tingle and the breath get caught in my throat. I felt the whole line of him. As he suckled at my lower lip, massaged my tongue, I could feel just as much of the kiss in the taut line of his stomach, the line of his leg that held me to the wall.

He pulled away breathless and I could see the pink of his swollen lips.

I leaned my head back against the wall and took in a long slow breath. I relaxed against him. The panther didn't lunge forward, didn't try to fight him.

He pulled my head forward again, his warm hand still on my jaw.

"I think I'm grounded. For the moment."

He flashed a half smile and leaned his forehead against mine. I took in another exhausted breath and felt the sizzle of energy between us.

"We should look for the poison," he finally said, looking up at me.

"Poison, right. Dying. Check."

He let me up from the wall but stayed inches away until we were both sure I could stand. He led me into the kitchen around the corner.

I was sore, weak, and unsure that I'd be able to battle with the cat any longer. As he searched for something, I leaned back against the fridge and let him find it. The cool fridge felt scandalous against my bare back.

In that one instant, as I closed my eyes while he was away, the cat made another spastic attempt to be freed. I felt her claws down my neck and cried out as my knees gave way under me.

Chaz was there to catch me against his strong chest.

"Whoa there," he cooed as he leaned me against the counter. He wrapped his arms around me and we just stayed like that for a few more minutes. I inhaled his warm scent, focused on the way he stroked my hair and the panther calmed.

"Better?" he asked as he lifted my chin up to his eyes.

I nodded.

He carefully pulled me away from the counter. Keeping

me only an arm's length away, he looked slowly down my neck, palpating it gentle with his cool fingers, and then my arms. His fingertips brushed lightly over the tender red welts and I watched him lick his lips.

Slowly, he turned me around and looked down my back. Chaz ran his fingertips down the edge of the halter topped dress and I winced when he reached a spot just inside the thin fabric covering my waist.

Carefully, he pushed the fabric aside as I leaned forward, putting my palms on the counter, curling my fingers underneath the ceramic ledge.

"Sure enough," he whispered "Still poison in there too."

The hot breath from his words seemed to travel up my back and right around my neck, soothing the fresh wounds as he wiped away whatever was there.

The moment he moved away though, the panther made her final attempt to get her way. The edge of the counter crumbled to dust in my grip as I tensed every muscle I could to rein her in.

It wasn't enough. I'd fought too long and hard and didn't have the strength to stop it. I felt myself falling down into the inky blackness.

"I gotcha," I heard above me. "You're safe."

Swimming in the darkness, I felt him. Not his arms; they were far, far away. I felt his power, a deep golden warmth that wrapped around me. My panther relaxed against it, wounded from this evening, exhausted from our battle. There was a twinge in my chest, just under my sternum, but the panther retreated. I fluttered my eyes open and found Chaz. He was holding me close again.

"I think we need to get you to bed," he said softly.

Effortlessly, he lifted me into his arms. He carried me through my house and up the stairs. He pushed the door open with his foot and carefully laid me down on my unmade bed, pulling the covers up to my chin.

Chaz moved away to close the door and a wave of nausea hit me again that curled me up into a quivering mass on the mattress.

"Hey, there," he said as he closed the door. "I'm coming back."

He slipped his boots off and then his button up. And then his under shirt.

I rolled to my back to watch him walk around the foot of the bed and lift up the edge of the covers. He slid into bed next to me.

"What if . . ." I whispered.

"Shh." He pulled me closed to him.

I felt his hot skin against my back, his strong arm curled under my head as he leaned me against him. His breath trickled down my neck as he bent his legs to fit against mine.

I was still shaking from the last wave of whatever it was.

"Come on now. Breathe."

At his provocation, I took in a deep, shuttering breath. There wasn't any pain, no vice around my chest.

"There now," he whispered. His fingers began to unfasten the buttons at the back of my neck that kept my dress up.

I didn't protest as he slid the satin down and pushed it past my hips.

Chaz adjusted our position. I rested on my stomach, one arm under my head and one at my side. With his forefinger, he drew a long line down my spine.

"How's that?" he asked.

Finally relaxed, finally feeling safe, the events of the evening rushed back into my conscious mind. My chin began to quiver and tears ran freely down my face. "Everything hurts," I whispered.

"Just don't think," he said softly, as he began to stroke the space between my shoulders. "Just sleep . . ."

I closed my eyes and took another shaky breath. I felt his chest rise and fall against my side. I felt his jeaned leg as he bent his knee slightly to cover the back of mine, felt his socked foot tuck under my ankle. His fingers traced shapes along my spine, up my neck.

He leaned forward and kissed the back of my neck before he pulled me to him tightly and nestled his nose into my hair.

I took in one last smooth breath. Exhausted but safe, the world melted away.

The sun was warm and blinding as it streamed in my bedroom window. I shifted to pull the covers over my head as I rolled away from the perky morning and straight into a body.

Startled, I sat up quickly. My body protested violently and I fell back onto the pillows. My head began to throb at the sudden movement. As I lay there, parts of me quivering and everything sore, I wondered if this is what being dragged through a knot hole backwards really felt like.

"Hey," Chaz yawned as he rubbed his eyes and looked over at me.

"Morning," I frowned.

"What's wrong?" he asked as he leaned up on an elbow.

"I need drugs."

He nodded. "I can arrange that."

I stared at the ceiling. I took a long hard inventory. Ten human toes. Ten human fingers. Two long legs, two arms, one belly button. All very naked underneath this thin white sheet. I tested my boundaries and even my paper thin protections were eerily fine. Dare I say stronger?

"Everything okay?"

"I think so."

He smiled, and looked like he wanted to say something, but his eyes flicked to the corner of the bed and his smile faded quickly. He moved suddenly, jostling me roughly, and threw his legs over the edge of the bed. I tensed for a moment in pain, which just brought out the immense soreness in every muscle in my body. I held my breath until it stopped. It was a long breath.

"I need to get home," he said quickly, reaching for his shirt on the floor. "Check on Jessa."

My whole body chilled at not having his warmth so near. I was startled at his back suddenly dropped to the farthest edge of the bed to put on his boots. I pushed myself to a sitting position and held the covers to my chest.

Standing, he pulled his flannel shirt back on and then checked his jean pocket for his wallet.

I watched him walk out of my bedroom. Like a scene in one of my movies, I rewound it in my head back to the part where I had woken up and realized that I hadn't done anything wrong. There was no foot-in-mouth scene. I was actually not in the wrong here.

Which lit a fire under me so quickly, I barely had time to rip the sheet off the bed and stumbled after him down the stairs where he was grabbing his keys from the foyer table.

"What the hell, Chaz?" I said resting exhausted against the door frame, blocking his exit.

"Violet, don't play games," he scolded, taking a step forward as if I would move.

I didn't even flinch. "Not until you tell me where the fire is?"

The little furrow between his brow appeared and he clenched his jaw. He radiated danger but I didn't budge. He huffed and stared down at me.

"Why are you running?" I repeated in a very civil tone.

"I have things to do."

"At eight in the morning. On a Saturday. Without your socks."

"Yeah."

"So it doesn't have anything to do with your father being killed by a panther?"

He didn't answer but a dangerous glint flashed golden in his eye. He probably never would have imagined that I would bring it up at a time like this.

"Why did you kiss me last night, Chaz?"

He looked away from me and glared into the living room. "Iris said you needed to be grounded," he said through clenched teeth. "I got caught up. Now let me go."

Chaz grabbed my arm and lifted me out of the way of the door, turning the handle with the other one.

He strode down the front sidewalk, passing Jessa as he ran away. Jessa scurried out of his way, her hands filled with a bag labeled doughnuts and carrier with three coffees.

"What's wrong with him?" she asked confused as she joined me on the porch.

I was standing, feeling lost, wrapped in a sheet as the man who had just saved my life gunned his engine and slammed on the gas, tires screeching down the quiet street.

Chapter Twenty-Four

Jessa threw her arms around my neck and began to chant. "It's all going to be okay."

And I couldn't keep it in. I don't know what happened to me. It just all fell out of my head and down into my mouth. I told her about the first night that Chaz and I met, when I was attacked in the alleyway and when I went to Iris's for a week to learn about being a were-panther and how he was great there and supportive and brought me Starbucks and how we had survived an attack by a gang of mongrels. And how her boyfriend had poisoned me at the club and Chaz had taken care of me and he had kissed me, really kissed me. And how I had woken up with Chaz, and everything was perfect and he looked so good in the morning light and he had bolted just like that, without any explanation. And now I felt so alone in all this.

I looked up, suddenly exhausted, my mouth dry after the verbal diarrhea, my eyes red and a little blurry. Expecting some sort of horrified look.

Instead, I saw wide brown eyes with a look of understanding, a faint smile on her lips as her head shook slightly.

"But you're not alone, Violet," was all she said afterwards.

"What?"

"Granted, I couldn't tell that you and Chaz were dating," she said as she twisted a strand of hair that had fallen in my face. "But you'll never be alone in this, Violet."

A disbelieving laugh choked out. I was caught somewhere between disbelief and delirium. "You knew. The whole time, didn't you," I asked disbelieving.

Jessa nodded. "I also know you've been sent to protect me."

"Why not talk to me for two weeks if you knew the risks?"

Jessa sighed. "I figured that if I ignored what happened to you, I could ignore this huge responsibility that I have. Got some heavy stuff dumped on me about two weeks ago, didn't want to deal with it."

That was right before the fight. Right before LA and right before everything hit the fan. The situation echoed with a familiar twang, like a bad country song. I sniffed and wiped my face. "Why do you need to be protected?"

Jessa sighed and a little furrow formed between her perfect brows. "Why don't you go, take a shower, put on something a little more than just a sheet, and we'll talk?"

"When'd you get all mentor-y?"

Jessa swatted my arm and pointed up the stairs.

Halfway up the stairs, Jessa called out after me. "So Haydn's a bad guy?"

I turned around and went back down the stairs, leaning against the railing. "His name is Spencer. He's the one who attacked me in the back alley."

Jessa's hand clenched into hard tight fists. "That bastard. I'm going to kill him."

"Get in line."

Without the weight of impending doom hanging over my head for at least a few minutes, I slowly went up the stairs. Shower first. Mysteries about the universe later. We must have a plan and this time I was pretty sure it didn't involve swapping zip codes.

I turned into my bedroom to shower but froze at the door. All was not right with the world.

I'd taken the white flat sheet with me but not the fitted sheet. The fitted sheet was hanging onto the corner of my bed by threads. All but the top corner. The top corner lay in shreds. As if a large cat had been using it as a kneading pad.

That's what Chaz saw.

That's why he ran.

He'd been in bed with a panther.

Weak-kneed, I fell back against the door frame and the second wave of many tears began to fall.

Jessa was standing in the middle of the living room when I came downstairs, showered and dressed with one thing crossed off the "How to save the world" checklist forming in my head.

"Your house is a wreck," she said, with her hands on her hips.

"Spencer and his mutts tossed the place." I pick up a re-stuffed pillow from the blanket covered couch only to see its insides being kept in with a strip of silver duct tape. It was a manly touch that made my stomach turn over a little. "Haven't had a chance to reorganize."

A little crease formed between her brows. "Didn't Chaz tell you to call the cleaners?"

A sharp quick pain ran across my heart and I immediately headed for the kitchen. Hadn't she brought a carrier of coffee this morning? I needed coffee and quick.

"Sorry, I said the C word."

"I'm fine. I'll be fine." By the way, my arms crossed tightly over my chest, I knew I wasn't fine.

"You're not, but I'm not going to push. We've got bigger things to talk about." She handed me the coffee she had brought in from the carrier, sitting on the counter next to me. It was a caramel macchiato.

I looked up at her and again had the feeling that I had overlooked so much in the last two years. "Like what?"

"Well, you and Stalker boy had a moment last night, but so did we, and I need to explain what happened."

"That sounds a little *L word*." As the smell of the coffee filled the room, my brain cleared out from the emotional swamp I was currently wading through. "The smell of roses. I smelled roses and rain last night."

Jessa nodded. "You're going to need a cup of coffee for this. And then maybe a stiff drink."

We sat next to each other on the couch amidst the ruins of my town house. The poof of air that came up from the unstuffed couch still smelled like dogs and Chaz. It was a stomach-churning smell that didn't faze Jessa.

"While we are in confessional mode, get it out on the table mode, first I need to tell you why we are in Dallas."

I frowned. I'd replayed nearly every scene of our friendship in my head since I knew what she really was, but I couldn't fathom that the conspiracy went back that far. "You suggested that we meet in the middle to start a new life. Try our hand in another zip code that I could afford."

Jessa leaned forward on her elbows. "I was sent here by my family. Haverty was getting too powerful and they needed someone to watch over the Veil. And then Kyle happened and it was perfect. I had no idea any of this would happen."

I chuckled. "And here I thought it was just being an awesome friend."

"You were the amazing one. I only said yes, because I knew that you would be here with me, be my rock against this crazy calling. Ready for the rest?"

I nodded, slowly. I was sinking in, slowly.

"Remember when I went to the Hamptons for the weekend?"

I sipped my coffee.

"And remember that huge fight that we had?"

"Not exactly forgetting that any time soon. And neither is my turtle collection."

Jessa rubbed her arms, little goose bumps forming on them. "They aren't entirely unrelated. My mother laid some news on me and most of it had to do with you."

"Me?"

Jessa nodded and pulled a blanket from the edge of the couch. It revealed the torn insides of what once was the prettiest couch I'd seen at IKEA. "How much do you know about what's happen to you?"

"Just what the books told me. Been through Shapeshifter 101."

"So you know about the Veil?" her hands had begun to shake and she set the coffee on floor by her feet.

"Nothing really specific. It sounds like a thin barrier that keeps the beasties in another dimension."

Jessa nodded. "Exactly. After the First War of the Wanderers, the Powers set up a corner dimension where the prisoners of war were put, those deemed too powerful for their own good. But as time goes on, it gets thinner. Easier to poke through." she licked her lips and took in a deep breath. "Our magic isn't what it used to be."

"So your family are wardens?"

Her dark brows knitted together. With a deep breath, she looked me the square in the eyes and I knew I wasn't hallucinating when I saw a flash of lavender cross her irises. "I'm the new key to the Neveranth dimension."

"What? How?" I wasn't freaking. This wasn't me freaking. Freaking would be me storming off and throwing my coffee in all directions. Coffee strongly in hand, I was as cool as an iceberg.

"One person in each generation of my family holds the key. It's not an actual key, though we like everyone to think it is. We've got physical objects hidden all over the world so that the bad guys think they are looking for something, not someone." Jessa reached out and took my hand. I was unprepared for the sudden show of intimacy. Jessa didn't touch, didn't hug. It wasn't a Jessa thing to do. "You have to understand I was terrified you were going to shift. I still don't know exactly what happened, but I opened up to you. I was trying to make you calm down, at least, that's what it does to men. But with you, it bonded us together."

"As what? Exactly."

"As a Key holder and its Guardian."

"What?!"

"It means that the universe knows that we are strong enough together to protect the Veil. We are like a two-part key. Which means that only our blood can open a portal."

Jessa squeezed my hand and I suddenly felt much better, like the world wasn't crumbling down. It made me pull my arm back quickly. It was magic. I knew just enough to know it when it was used on me.

"Pretty strong stuff you've got there," I said on edge now.

"And if you were sent to protect me, then you're not a weakling either."

I just shook my head and looked down at my hands in my lap. "Power, yes. Not so much on the control part."

"It's what my mother warned me about. It's an old story that she tried to tell me about key holders and guardians. But I was too naive to take it seriously. You were Violet. Funny writer Violet. You couldn't be a Guardian. People are born as guardians."

"You're about as surprised as I was. *'And will protect crown and Veil from her dark reflection.'* Which means that I get to protect you from Spencer Haverty," I sighed and leaned back on the couch as Jessa sat with her mouth agape. "My mother told me a story and I think I have inkling about what will happen if the portals are opened. Guess that means we just jumped up the mystical food chain about six steps."

Jessa's eyes went a little glassy as she stared at my fireplace. "My mother was right to warn me about you. I just thought she was being overprotective."

"I've heard that mothers can be that way."

A sharp knock at the door made both of us jump off the couch.

Without the spidey sense alarm, I tip-toed over to the door and looked out the peep hole. Nothing seemed out of place about the four men who stood outside. But they smelled funny, like aloe and Burberry's Beat.

"Who it is?" Jessa whispered, suddenly just behind me, holding my arm as she tried to look over my shoulder.

"Don't know. One of them has a lamp shade."

Jessa squealed and bumped me away from the door with a sharp hip check and threw open the door. "Kurt."

"Princess," the man squealed back.

A parade of four men, all looking like something out of a fashion magazine, went through my living room and settled into the corners. These were Jessa people; there was an excited energy about them and all their suits were tailored sharp enough to cut firewood.

"Someone's got some 'splaining to do." I looked at Jessa who was smiling.

"Violet, meet the Cleaners. Cleaners, meet Violet, your project for the day."

The one she had called Kurt looked at me head to toe with a sharply arched blonde eyebrow, his lips pursed.

"It's just the house. I'm going to take care of her."

"Oh, thank god. I was just about to say I'm a Cleaner, not a miracle worker."

The foursome laughed simultaneously and stopped just as in synch. It was creepy. Their perfection was creepy. And then it struck me. Glamour. Can't fairies do glamour?

Jessa turned to me, which was good because the arch in my eyebrow was beginning to ache. "These are the Cleaners. They get called in after a disaster, like your break-in. They are going to clean the place, clear the space of any negative vibes, and then set up defenses so it doesn't happen again. They are also the ones who decorated my place and put the ward up there."

I looked at the fearsome foursome and then back at her, "I'm thinking queer eye for the Fey kind?"

Jessa nodded. "One for each element. And while they are working their magic, we are going shopping."

"No, Jessa. It's dangerous out there. He knows about both of us. His dogs know where I live."

Jessa put her little hands on her hips and set her jaw. "After the night we've had, we need a little retail therapy. And after these guys are done, he won't be able to set foot in this place."

I looked around the living room. It was bare boned. Chaz had done all that he could, but it was pathetic and the faint smell of dog still permeated the air.

I nodded. "Okay."

"Just one question," Kurt asked. "Who are we protecting her from?"

Jessa looked at me. I licked my lips and looked squarely at the slender man. "Haverty."

A small gasp echoed around the room.

"Welcome to my life."

Chapter Twenty-Five

Even though I had told her time and time again that they hadn't been in my bedroom, she still insisted that we buy all new bras and underwear and socks and pajamas. It took a few stores for me to realize that she was *actually* putting together a new wardrobe for me. Which, I discovered between the third and fourth pairs of jeans I was forced to try on, I was completely okay with. New Violet, New Clothes. Where was the flaw in that logic?

But a new house? Jessa got the call around five that the house was done. We sat outside in her car and I stared at my house. This was very déjà vu. Me coming home, sitting outside, changed. There were too many parallels in this picture.

"It's going to be okay," Jessa said as she watched me.

"If you say that people can live through it, I think I might scream."

Jessa got out of the car. She wasn't going to allow this pity party. She wasn't a pity party person. She opened the truck and grabbed an armload of bags. I followed and stared at the bags that went from one side to the other of her trunk.

"Are you ready for this?" Jessa asked before she knocked on the door.

I just took in a deep breath and nodded. "Sure, why not? It has to be better than it was."

Jessa opened the door and the smell of crisp rain flooded my sense. "Honey, we're home," she called out as she entered the foyer.

I stayed out at the doorstep and looked at the fully flowering pot of green things out front. The empty terra-cotta pot was no longer empty. It actually looked like someone lived here.

"Violet, get your tail in here. It's gorgeous."

When I stepped inside, a chill danced down my back and I looked up to see a silver charm hanging above the doorway.

"The strongest barrier we could muster," Kurt said as he joined me in the foyer. "There's one here, and in the back and smaller ones woven into the curtains."

"Holy Moses," I breathed.

Kurt took the bags from my hands and set them down in the foyer under the new foyer table and the new mirror that hung there with a vase of lavender. "Lavender will ward off evil doers as well."

I nodded as he put his arm over my shoulder and tossed a curl away from my face. "Fabulous highlights, BTW."

"Thanks," Jessa smiled as she flopped down on the new sofa.

The room wasn't out of a magazine; it was out of my head. The soft gray couch, the silvery curtains, the mantle, everything was just as I had imagined and then tried to desperately recreate at IKEA.

"Seriously, guys?" I said as I pointed to the painting of a magnolia above the fireplace.

"It was the right color," Kurt said as he pulled me through the front room and into the dining area. We stopped in front of a new turtle collection that was encased in a glass china cabinet.

"Unbreakable glass to protect your precious things," he said and then pointed to a small mirror that hung in a collage of small paintings on the wall. "Break this one and Jessa will know something is wrong."

"Providing I ever let her leave my sight again." Jessa joined us on the tour with her hands stuck in her back pocket with a look of complete satisfaction on her face.

"Jessa will have one just like it at her place. Same thing, hers breaks, yours breaks."

The other guys were in the kitchen burning a small cluster of herbs in a bowl. "Just finishing up," they smiled as they tossed the herbs down the sink and rinsed them down the drain. "That should do it."

"Protecting my pipes? That's serious detail work."

They all laughed and then stopped. It was still creepy. "No, just getting rid of the waste."

A bright sparkly thing on the counter caught my eye. "Is that . . ." but the words failed me as I walked over to the brand new cappuccino machine with steamer. "It's gorgeous."

"My idea," Jessa beamed as she leaned in the door frame. "Knew that you needed to be caffeinated to save the world."

I playfully punched Jessa in the arm. "Aw shucks."

In unison, the men lined up and marched to the front door. Jessa and I quickly followed.

"Thank you guys, so much."

"Just don't let the world fall around our ears. They are very handsome ears," Kurt said before he gave us both quick air kisses on both cheeks and then the parade was out the door and gone.

I turned around to look at my new place. I walked slowly around the edge of the room, running my hands across the mantle, picking up pillows and squeezing them tightly.

"I've got one more little thing for you."

Jessa went to one of the bags that she had pulled out of the car and pulled out a white box.

"What's this?"

"Just take it already," she said as she held it out between us, looking at the carpet (the new light gray carpet).

Flipped open the lid of the shiny box, I pulled out a small silver frame. It was a picture of us, a candid shot from some party we had been to ages ago, before the fight, before the panther, when it was just me and Jessa.

"It's not a picture of your mom, I know. But I figure it would be a good placeholder until we get it back."

I didn't have words. Little Violet Jordan was struck dumb for the first time in her life. Maybe second.

My arms seemed to wrap around her of their own accord and I rested my head on hers. And between us, as she hugged me back, there was a warmth I felt in my chest and I didn't think it had anything to do with any panther or fey mumbo jumbo.

"Are we done with the chick moment?"

"Shut up," I said as I let her go and strode over to the mantle to put up a picture of me and my best friend.

I had a picture in my house. In my new house, in my new lair, and so help me god if anyone took this away from me they were going to be toast.

Chapter Twenty-Six

Jessa went upstairs to tell her family about what had happened. I wasn't going to ask if she even needed to use a cell phone for something like that. For all I knew, she was using my bathroom mirror to phone long distance. We were going to need back up. Time to call in the cavalry.

As Jessa called her family, I called the only man who could kick my butt, my Sensei. It was later afternoon, between the daytime appointments and the evening sessions.

He answered on the first ring. "Violet."

"That's creepy."

"Are you okay? You missed your session."

"It's happening. The thing. The reason They threw me in your path."

"I've taught you everything I can."

I frowned and leaned against the wall. "That doesn't sound good."

"You are going to ask me to help you."

"Well yeah. You're kick ass and one of the only other white hats that I know of. We are going to need people, information."

"I have taught you everything that I can." His voice was faint and strained.

His parrot act sent fear sliding down my spine that ended in a full body shiver. "But I need..."

His voice was suddenly strong and stern. "I can't, Violet."

I closed my eyes and listened to him, less with my ears and more with my heart. His pulse beat hard and his breath stuttered as he took in air. There was great pain in his words.

"I am an old man, Violet. I am weak and flawed. He took me once and I can't risk that again. I have a family, grandchildren. I can't be a liability."

I clenched my hand into a tight fist, digging my nails into my palm to keep from crying. "I feel like I'm being broken up with."

"Even though I can't be with you now, in this, know that I am yours, Daughter of Jourdaine."

Goose bumps rose all over my arms. It sounded like he was choosing a side in the battle to come and he was choosing me.

"I will see you on Tuesday?"

"If I'm not toast, that's the plan."

"Good-bye, Violet Jordan."

The line went dead and I dropped the phone to my side. A sense of utter loneliness consumed me for a moment and I leaned my head against the wall. I couldn't do this. I was just a writer.

The floorboards in my bathroom squeaked and I remembered I wasn't alone. I had Jessa and a lioness I could call. She needed to know what her little protégé had gotten herself into this time. So much for staying out of trouble.

"Hello?" the fragile voice came over the phone.

"Hey there, Iris."

"Hi Violet," she said but then I heard muffled whispering of a man's voice.

"Iris? Do you have male company?" I asked, a hint of scandal in my voice. Iris was old but maybe she still had it going on.

"No, just the TV, darling. What can I do for you?"

Iris never called me darling. It was mostly *pain in the tail* and *hairball*.

"What's going on, Iris? What's wrong?" The space between my shoulders twinged and my entire body felt on edge.

I could hear her orthopedic shoes shuffle across her laminate flooring, possibly into the hallway. "Chaz is here," she whispered.

"Oh. Good guy talk?"

"Not exactly," Iris sighed.

"I can hear you," he hollered from the other room.

It was him. I hadn't heard his voice in almost two days and it still made my skin sizzle. God, I was pathetic.

"Did you call for Chaz?"

"No."

"Why not?"

"Defeats the purpose of not speaking to him."

"I swear," Iris railed. "You are the two most annoying people I have ever met."

And she slammed the phone down in my ear.

Jessa's footsteps skipped down the stairs and I met her at the bottom. Her face was pale, her lips slightly parted. "We have a problem."

All the strength I had gathered with the new house and

the new highlights teetered on the edge of completely losing it again.

"Mom and Dad can't come."

"Why? Another apocalypse that they have to avert?"

"No, like they tried and they *can't* come."

"Blanking on this one, Jess."

Jessa walked into the living room and began to pace across the new area rug. "So part of the gig is that we can jump into mirrors, ride the Veil to where we need to be. And they tried and they couldn't."

"What does that mean?"

"Either they've gone rusty, or Haverty's put up wards that we can't cross."

"So we are trapped?"

"Or he's officially on Apocalypse countdown. I just know that whatever heavy hitters we might call on probably won't be able to make it."

Crap. Big Crap. "What about the Cause?"

Jessa shook her head. "We don't play well with them."

"You guys are the keepers of the Veil. How can you not be on the good guy side?"

Jessa licked her lips. "We keep the Veil. We keep people from crossing over on both sides."

"Oh," I said as I nodded. And then it hit me. "Oh crap."

"Neveranth isn't just for the bad guys, Vi. It's anyone who has abused their power, including the witch who created it. And sometimes we butt heads when the Cause tries to bring an ancient across. A hole is a hole."

So I had to get Chaz back to get back up, if he could even

make it across whatever borders had been put in place. Destiny sucks.

Iris called back as I was folding laundry. Too bad the Cleaners couldn't install some sort of magical device that just took care of laundry by itself. It wasn't the lugging it downstairs; it was the folding. The standing there and not moving allowed dark thoughts to race through my head. Like what was coming, like all the stories my mother told me about the other side of a mirror and whether I wanted Chaz back in my life.

"I'm sorry about earlier," she said right off the bat.

"It's okay, but I've got some pretty major news. Are you sitting?"

"Oh god."

I told Iris everything I knew. All about Spencer and the dance floor and what Jessa and I had done. She was quiet. Too quiet for Iris. I was half expecting a huge lecture. I needed her to yell at me for being careless, but nothing. The only proof of life on the other side of the line was her slow and steady breath.

"So how's Chaz doing?" I asked carefully.

"Good as he could be I guess. They've got him on hiatus right now. So he's floating without purpose, which doesn't suit him much."

"Did he do something wrong?"

"No. They just stopped talking to him."

Not being part of the good fight would kill him. He needed to be fighting; he needed to be out there rescuing the damsels. It was who he was. It literally ran in his blood.

"So I'm guessing he took off?"

"Yeah, just stopped by for a visit. Unlike you who only comes around when you need something."

I had to chuckle. "Yeah. I'm such a taker."

"Well, you do leave plenty of hair for me to clean up."

"Hah, hah." This was the Iris that I knew. There was a click in my head as another puzzle piece of the story fit into place. "Wait. Chaz was able to go to your house and then come back?"

"As far as I know. Why?"

"Jessa's parents tried to come here and they couldn't make it through some kind of ward that Haverty's put up. Heard anything on the broadband lately?"

Iris was quiet on the other end of the line. "They've stopped talking to me as well."

"Why?" I snapped.

"I don't know. I tried to call Balzac and nothing. He wouldn't answer."

"Have you guys been blackballed or something?"

The line was silent.

"Iris?"

The line was quiet for a beat more. I could almost hear her face wrinkling more with concern. "You need to fix this thing with Chaz."

I pouted instantly. This was not the kind of advice I wanted from Iris right now. "Trying to prevent the end of the world as we know it, Iris."

"He's really sorry for what he did."

"Doesn't mean anything unless he says it."

"But he knows now why he did it. He wants..."

I cut her off. "No buts, Iris. If it doesn't come from him, it really means nothing."

"You're too hard on people," Iris snapped.

"I've heard that before. Anything new to lecture me about?"

Iris huffed. "I'm not going to continue to lecture two grown adults who should be able to take care of their own business."

There was a deep sigh on the other end of the line and my frustration was fading fast.

"I care for you, Violet. You're like the daughter I would have grounded until she was thirty. And it hurts to see two people I care about gridlocked in this game of wills. You're going to learn very quickly how precious life really is."

Her words were foreboding. It had been almost three hours since I had been reminded something big was here, that Haverty was still around. That Jessa needed to be protected. That even though Chaz and I were on the outs, we still had a common mission.

"I know, Iris." I sighed playing with the fringe on the leg of my jeans.

"As long as you realize that."

Jessa and I were crashed out on the couch of her apartment, keeping in behind our charmed doors and windows. Nothing to be paranoid about. If we couldn't go to the party, we'd bring the party to us, steak and cheesecake style. I think I had already finished two slices.

"So why'd he really leave, Jessa," I demanded as I shoved another forkful of turtle cheesecake. "He's seen me in panther chic before."

"Well," Jessa said as she finished off her second slice. "I think he was scared."

"Scared?"

"You can be a little intimidating."

"What are you talking about?"

Jessa licked the caramel off her lips and put together her sentence carefully. "I'm saying, and this is not the cheesecake talking, that you have changed in the past six months since we moved here. After Kyle. It's more than just the panther thing, Vi. You've gotten stronger and, now you're gorgeous? Giving me a run for my money."

I laughed. "Right."

"He's scared because you are amazing and if he screws up, he'll lose you. Not to mention the whole end of existence as we know it."

I sighed and looked across the cream suede at my friend. "So what do I do?"

"Nothing. He's got to figure this out on his own. You just need to be your fabulous self, but give him the chance to apologize. If you want him to apologize."

"What's that mean?"

"Well, do you? Do you want little Stalker boy to come back and play the hero?"

Sighing, I stood and went to the kitchen to refill our plates. My lovely increased metabolism was burning through the calories on the first two slices of cheesecake I was trying to drown my sorrows in. I needed one night of just quiet, just peace and quiet, but there was a burning under my sternum at the mention of his name and my gut knew the answer.

"God, help me I do," I sighed as I cut an even bigger slice than before.

I crossed her plush carpet and flopped pathetically on the couch.

Jessa laughed and held out her fork. "A toast. To powerful women and the loneliness that ensues."

We clinked silverware and both took another huge bite.

Absorbed in a book on ritual mirror magic that too closely echoed what I already knew about mirrors, I neglected to check the number flashing across my cell phone when I flipped it open.

"Hello," I greeted as I flipped through the section on protection spells. I did a celebratory spin in my desk chair as I found the one Jessa mentioned. I could finally stop looking. Been at it all morning and my eyeballs hurt.

"Violet. It's Chaz."

All the celebration melted away and suddenly I was awash in the pity party I had been throwing myself. My chair slowed to a sad stop.

"What do you want, Chaz?"

"We need to talk."

"You need to talk," I corrected harshly.

"I've got information on why else you were an assignment."

"So tell me."

"I'd rather talk to you in person."

"Why? So you can just up and leave me again?"

The line was silent for a long while but I didn't hang up. I hadn't realized until now I missed listening to his breath over the phone.

"Please, Violet."

Every bad thought about him flashed through my head but they were quickly outweighed by the good things he had done: saving my life, buying me coffee. And maybe the minor facts that he was an excellent kisser and had abs you could do your laundry with.

"I need a coffee, which means you'll have twenty minutes to plead your case."

"I'm going to need more than twenty minutes, Vi."

"You're getting fifteen and it's Violet."

He snapped his phone shut and I slowly set mine on the desk. I knew halfway across town he was cursing up a storm in his living room.

How many times had I talked Jessa through this? And here I was, falling into the same trap men used on her time and time again. Just that one last meeting. Just that one last chance to wiggle back into my life. But what had we talked about just last night? Give him a chance to apologize. Fifteen minutes was enough to apologize if he had been rehearsing like I had.

Crap, I thought as I got up to go to my closet, which had expanded significantly. Shopping really was as therapeutic as Jessa espoused and apparently I had been in desperate need of therapy. If I was going to play this in true form, I was going to have to look amazing, which, luckily, was getting easier and easier these days.

Chaz was already waiting for me when I walked in the door. He stood at the pair of chairs in the far corner of the busy shop as if I was going to miss him somehow, as if I couldn't smell him the moment I opened the door.

With measured precision in my pace, I went to the counter, ordered my coffee and waited patiently as they made it before I even acknowledged he was there. Being friends with Jessa did teach you a thing or two regarding how to make men wait for it.

I sat down across from him and he followed suit. I crossed my legs and sipped by coffee. "Fifteen minutes, Chaz."

He looked terrible. Iris hadn't been exaggerating when she said idleness was not a good thing for him. Dark circles ringed his eyes and his hair was flat. And even the gold that used to dance like a halo around him seemed dull.

"They've had me on hiatus since you were attacked."

"Iris told me."

"So I asked a few questions, cracked a few books on my own and found out a few things they've been keeping from us."

"Like what?" I asked as I sipped my coffee, the perfect calming agent for the way my nerves were jumping around like five-year-olds on a sugar high in a bounce house.

Chaz leaned forward and I was awash in his smell for a moment, bringing back the memory of the night in bed, the way his hand trailed down my back, his hot lips on my neck. I closed my eyes and thought of barbed wire and puppy dogs and burnt tongues and anything that wasn't him.

He clasped his hands in front of him and began the narration. "A long time ago, before your prophecy was ever written, there was one about the resurrection of a demon. I think its Jovan. They've done everything they can to keep him in the Neveranth."

"Who's Jovan?"

"Think Keistral from *Black Magic Mountain*."

My jaw dropped. "You've been watching my movies?"

"Needed my daily jolt of sarcasm," he shrugged. "Jovan can't be corporeal on this realm, he needs a host. The prophecy says that the Veil will be broken and he will cross over and possess a prideless panther to bring on the Great War."

"What's the Great War?"

Chaz gulped. "The final war of Those who Wander. It's what determines the future of our kind as saviors or monsters."

I had to put my coffee down so he wouldn't see my hand shaking. Plus this top was silk and I didn't want to stain it right off the hanger. "But I was followed because of the prophesy I read."

Chaz nodded. "I think they knew you'd be bitten."

I looked down at my white knuckles in fists on my lap. Rage flooded through me and the pages of the magazines on the table before me fluttered as my energy swirled wildly around me. I had to force words through my clenched jaw. "But when they found out it was Haverty, they naturally assumed I would go evil and become this prideless panther?"

Chaz nodded again, his brown eyes watching me steadily. "They don't have the inside intel that we have about Spencer being disowned."

"Well, this is just another thing I'm not doing by the book."

"It's more than that, Violet. They are letting it happen. They've cut me off, Iris. I think they are responsible for the wards that are set up around the city. Being a worker bee, they didn't affect me but I felt them."

"Letting it happen!" I shrieked. The customers in the coffee shop all turned to me and I glared back at them. They were the ones who dropped their eyes.

Frustrated, I needed to move. I needed to be outside. I jumped up, grabbed my coffee and headed for the door.

He followed me out of the cafe and to my car. He grabbed my arm and spun me around.

My coffee flew from my hand and landed elegantly upside down on my front windshield. The steaming liquid poured down the dusty glass making a caffeinated paste on the front of my car.

I didn't know if the ice water in my veins was from the loss of sixteen ounces of perfectly good caramel macchiato or if it was his need of me. But I was scared because he was scared. It radiated around him.

"We're a good team, Violet. What did you say? I watch your back and you work my nerves."

"What's really going on here, Chaz?" I asked softly.

His jaw clenched as he dropped his hand from my arm. He licked his lips and looked out at the unknowing city surrounding us. "The Powers aren't doing anything about it. I think they want to use it as a cleansing. Jovan comes over, wipes out everyone who brought him here. The power vacuum lets them get a strong hold in Dallas, where they haven't had one since Iris and kick his ass for good."

"But they risk starting the Great War. What kind of ace to they think they have up their sleeve?"

He leaned against my car and jammed his hands in his coat pockets. "As much as I want Haverty in pieces, it can't be like this. Jovan will decimate him, but how many others with him?"

The answer echoed through me. Like someone had struck a pitch fork and put it to the top of my head, the vibration humming all the way down to my toes. "So screw them. We take care of it ourselves."

Chaz's eyes snapped to mine.

I gulped. The wild look in his eyes was overwhelming and the butterflies rammed into my stomach walls. I just wanted to reach out and caress his stubbled chin and lean against that broad chest, whisper in his ear that everything will be all right. But I restrained my hand to my chest.

"We are going to need more info than Jessa and I can pull together. In case you haven't noticed, we're a little new to this saving the world thing."

He pushed off from the car and stood before me.

"We work together until whatever happens, happens."

Chaz nodded.

"So back to the phone calls. I'll keep you in the loop as to what Jessa and I are doing."

"What about Haverty?"

"We've put up protective spells against him at my house and her apartment. Even managed one at the coffee shop," I narrated as I pointed to the new charm hanging above the doorway. "We are trying to keep our shields up and heads down until the darkest night."

Chaz nodded impressed.

"Hey, we're not small time anymore, buddy. You're dealing with a Fairy Princess and a Guardian now, capital G."

Chaz smiled a small smile and his shoulders relaxed a fraction of an inch. But then the smile faded and he jammed his hands into his pockets. "So it's a working relationship then?"

"You walked out on any chance of their being another kind of us."

Chaz's eyes hit the pavement between us.

It sounded practiced as it came out and it was. I had been working on that line forever. Felt good to finally say it to a person and not the mirror, but saying it to him didn't make me feel any better.

He ducked his head further. That just made my stomach sink.

"So what do we do next, fearless leader?"

"Meeting Jessa for dinner in West Village."

"Isn't that a little public?"

"Precisely. Luckily, I'm best friends with a gorgeous woman and people tend to stare at her. It's like a million extra eyes keeping us safe."

Chaz finally dared looking up. "See, you are good at this, Violet Jordan."

"I'm getting by on instincts and witty banter."

I turned back and opened the car door. "Meet me there."

With one last look at him, I got in and turned on the engine. He walked away and I watched him in the rearview mirror get to his black Challenger.

Jessa was waiting in the window of the restaurant talking on the phone. I quickly slipped up beside her.

"Yes, mom. I know ... We have ... Listen. I'm with Violet right now ... No, you can't talk to her."

And Jessa got the palest fear-stricken look on her face that

I had ever seen. She gulped and handed me the phone. "My mother wants to talk to you."

I took in a deep breath as I took the foreign phone. "Hello, Mrs. Feychild."

"Violet, darling, how are you?" the woman asked. I knew she had to be at least in her fifties but she didn't sound, or act, or dress a day older than Jessa. I had seen her in a few of the pictures Jessa had in her apartment. They looked exactly alike, dark hair, dark eyes, not fey like at all. And, knowing Jessa, she'd be just as fiery when she didn't get her way.

"Doing great, grabbing dinner. Then back to the fort."

"Don't either of you girls cook?" There was the classic mom tone that I'd been saved from.

"But the professionals do it so much better."

Her mother laughed. It was like the twinkling of a wind chime, soft and sweet. But then her laughter stopped and there was this chilly silence on the phone and I knew the conversation was just about to turn to business.

"I want you to know you're family now, Violet. Anything you need, just ask and you'll get it. We are doing everything we can to break the barrier but those Cause idiots always think they are doing the right thing. Makes my head hurt."

Goose bumps ran up and down my arms. "Thank you, Mrs. Feychild."

"Just take care of my little buttercup."

"I will."

"Good night, dear."

Her mother hung up and I handed the phone back to Jessa. "What did she say?" she asked eagerly.

"I think she just adopted me."

Jessa smacked my arm. "I'm being serious Violet."

"I am too. She said that if I ever needed anything, just ask."

"Wow. Well, sis, then you're buying dinner."

"Why?"

"Isn't that was *older* sisters do?"

"Shut up, buttercup," I looked at her with a smile and drove us to dinner.

Jessa glared back at her nickname. This really was like being sisters, almost too close for comfort.

"So I have a surprise for you," Jessa said.

"What kind of surprise?" I asked wearily.

"You and Chaz are good again, right?"

"We talked. I don't hate him and he's on his way over." I leaned across the little table. "Why?"

Her smile reached from ear to ear. "You're going to love this."

She reached into her beach bag–sized purse that was all the rage now and pulled out one of her hundred-page fashion magazines. "Found this this morning."

She opened the magazine to a marked page and handed it over.

It was an underwear ad. Calvin Klein, by the logo on the bottom left. And it was Chaz, standing in a brightly lit window in nothing but a pair of tighty whities. Very arty in its black-and-white contrast, but very revealing, down to the perfect curve of his belly button.

My gut reaction was to laugh, and then to hide it away. It was him though. The highlights were a little more golden and his skin was a little more tan than it was now. And clean shaven, don't think I'd ever seen him really clean shaven except for the date that wasn't a date and more of a horrible memory of what could have been before it wasn't.

I was trying my damndest to not let my eyes really study his chest. But they did and I wish they hadn't. Perfection. Abs chest, legs, everything perfection.

"*That* was under all those leather jackets and oversized button-ups?" Jessa laughed, feigning a hot spell and fanning herself. "Did you know he did this?"

"He mentioned it," I had to force thought to the language part of my brain and out of the gutter it was currently splashing around in. "He can get a lot of money in a short period of time, freeing him up for more paranormal endeavors."

"But the boy is hot!" Jessa exclaimed.

"I know."

"And you kissed that."

"And he left me after I scared him to death."

After a brief glance over my shoulder, Jessa snatched the magazine back and I stared down at the black bar, still seeing the picture in my head.

"Well, I hope I wasn't wrong in thinking you would enjoy that," she said as she folded the magazine back up and put it in her purse.

"Enjoy what?" came from behind me.

I jumped and spun around at the male voice.

"Nothing," I snapped as I gaped up at Chaz.

I just stared at him. The vision of what was underneath that baggie black sweater made my mouth dry. Not that I hadn't felt what was under them on a few occasional but to have the visual keep flashing before my eyes . . .

"Catching flies," Jessa whispered.

I snapped my mouth shut.

"What's going on?" Chaz asked, his furrow in full force as his eyes bounced between the two of us.

"Nothing," Jessa repeated, fighting giggles. I couldn't figure out if they were aimed at me or the previous discussion. "What's the scoop?"

"Chaz has been fighting the good fight." I filled in.

We turned to him, ready for a story.

"I talked to this guy who thought he might know of a man who's been looking for a guy to find him a key to the Neveranth."

Both of us girls gulped.

"Really?" Jessa asked, looking over at me. "Anything else?"

"Not really. Info gathering is usually a long hard business."

I wasn't paying attention as they went into detail as to where Chaz had found the information or when. I was just trying to keep my cheeks from flaring red as the picture flashed before my eyes. Unfortunately, my tasty thoughts of Chaz's chest were destroyed by the sudden smell of dog. God, I hated that smell.

I flinched and my brain went into hypersensitive mode. That's all it was now, like flexing a muscle. Perked ears and focused eyes, I took in a deep breath and looked slowly around. I didn't see anyone suspicious, but then again, we had a guardian, a panther, and a fairy princess at our table and we weren't turning any heads.

Chaz's hand came to cover mine. "What's going on?"

"Dogs," I whispered. "Not the ones from before. These are cleaner?"

He squeezed my hand and stood up. My speeding heart

pumped blood even faster through my veins and I caught a whiff of his wonderful smell, which made my panther stir a little in my chest.

He motioned with his hand for us to stand. Jessa's eyes were filled with panic. She hadn't looked this scared, well, since the night at the party when I was attacked and Chaz came to the rescue. So it had been, what, four days since mortal terror and a near dead experience? Wondered if that was a record in one of those mystical books somewhere?

I nodded to Jessa who slowly stood and grabbed her purse. I followed, keeping the senses perked.

As Chaz led the way to the front of the diner, I could see the moment they both felt the beasts that I had smelled earlier. From behind, I watched as the feeling crept down their necks and they shivered in sync.

Chaz held the door open for us and kept his eyes peeled on the crowd that had gathered on this Friday night in West Village.

"Car's this way," he said as I passed him and he went to take my hand and lead me to the street.

"My car's in the lot," I said back to him, making sure that both hands were casually in my pockets.

"They know what you drive."

"Your tank can be heard for miles."

Chaz paused for a moment and his hazel eyes met mine. Something passed underneath them as his hand was held out between us empty. It dropped slowly to his side.

Poor Jessa was stuck between us.

"Let's just go," she said, pushing both of us towards the parking structure.

Chaz and I both stumbled in that direction with her harsh shove but eventually moved to keep her between us on the sidewalk.

As we slowly walked to my car, me in the front of the line, I couldn't help but feel that this was the way things would be from now on. If this was what I was made to do, then I was determined to do it well. I wasn't a writer anymore; I was a Guardian.

As determined as I was, I still wasn't fast enough. A large black dog came flying out from the corner of a stairwell, not ten feet from my car. Mouth open, teeth bared, it chomped down on my arm and sent me flying across their path. I twisted to land on my back, the dog on top of me, teeth sinking quickly through my jacket and into my forearm.

Jessa screamed and out of the corner of my eye, I saw another.

"Behind you," I called out and Chaz moved quicker than I had, missing the pounce of the second attacker.

I stared down the Rottweiler's muzzle as it tore my jacket. When the dog's teeth finally sunk into skin, the panther leapt in my chest, like she was clawing up my throat to get out.

Angry heat sizzling down my body, I sucked in a deep breath and gulped her down. I was not going to shift in front of the crowd of people who had gathered to see wild dogs attack this nice little threesome. I was not going to become the monster I knew raged inside.

The dog ripped its head away from my arm, taking flesh and cotton with it. I didn't feel it, the adrenaline and panther both running hot through my veins. The dog lifted his head enough that I reached under with my uninjured hand and grabbed its throat.

That was the only thing I let the panther do. No escape, but defense. The inky power slid down my arm and claws easily wrapped around the beast's neck, nails piercing its soft dark fur.

The dog began to stomp on my midsection as he tried to pull away. His wind gone, he stopped attacking and tried to tear his airway from my grasp. Blood began to run down my hand and I was about to let him go. No need for dead. I could see in his eyes, in the laid back position of his ears, that he was defeated.

But a gunshot tore his body away from me. The dog flew a few feet and landed limply on the ground.

I sat up and clenched my arm to my chest. Surely Chaz hadn't opened fire. I turned around to see a police officer with a rifle. Wow, authorities came through on this one. I took in a deep breath as I saw the other dogs back away quickly and then hightail it out of there. The panther calmed herself and went back to her little lair for the moment.

Jessa peeled herself away from the wall and rushed to my side.

"Are you okay?" she asked as she helped me up.

"Peachy," I grunted as the fire flew down my injured arm, not enough adrenaline to drive the pain away now.

Chaz joined us with the two police officers.

"Ambulance is on its way," the officer said. "You may want to sit down, ma'am."

Jessa didn't let me protest. Wasn't like I could say, "Don't worry, it will be healed be tonight." She escorted me over to the stairwell where the dogs had been hiding.

One police officer stayed with me and the other took Chaz off to answer some questions.

"You handled yourself pretty well back there," the officer said.

I looked up at his name tag and then his warm brown eyes. "Thanks. Can't say I practice much."

"Are you in self-defense?"

I nodded. He was good; his soft voice drew my attention away from my throbbing arm.

"Jeet Kun Do."

His eye brows arched. "No wonder you took that fall so well."

"You saw it?"

"You were pretty amazing." The officer immediately looked down at his feet when he realized what he said. "I mean, I'm a black belt in judo and you don't find a lot of people who can move like that so instinctually."

If you only knew, I thought to myself.

The flashing lights of the ambulance guided me away from his comment. The officer offered a hand to help me up from the stair, which I didn't take, but he walked me over to the back end of the ambulance before joining the other officer interrogating Chaz.

Jessa stayed quiet as the tech double wrapped his latex gloves and pulled out the scissors to cut off my very ruined jacket.

The tech asked some fairly basic questions which I answered in a fairly basic way. The arm looked worse than it felt and as I looked up at the tech, there was a spark there. Something silver in his light blue eyes and in the cool flutters of his fingers over my wounded arm. Something not quite human.

I looked at Jessa and she nodded, confirming my suspicions. Wanderer. So much for being one of the few, the proud. Stories filled my head as to how he'd escaped Haverty's wrath, but I couldn't bring myself to ask. He knew what I was and I knew what he was. It was enough of an exchange for right now.

"Wow, you're good," I said to the tech.

"Thanks," he said with a small smile.

Jessa slipped up closer to us and ran her finger along the edge of his ambulance. "So what is it? About a quarter witch blood?" Jessa asked him in a hushed tone.

The EMT looked at her and I could see that there were going to be digits exchanged later. He had that doe-eyed look that all men got when they looked at Jessa. All men except Chaz.

I strained around to find him. He was still talking to the officers. He glanced over his shoulder and looked at me steadily. I winced but didn't break eye contact as the tech poured something over the wounds that stung like mad. He winced with me and then smiled slightly when it was over.

Any girlish thought of Chaz without a shirt was gone and all I saw was the man who was trying to protect me. I looked away, back down at my arm already feeling better. It wouldn't need any more than the glue the EMT was putting on it now.

Twenty minutes and a boatload of questions later, the police, ambulance, and animal control drove off, leaving the three of us standing there in silence.

"So what do you think that was all about?" Jessa asked.

"The universe not wanting me to wear a fitted jacket," I said as I turned for the car. Chaz had returned my purse to me and now I fished for my keys.

"You're going to drive home?" Chaz asked.

"And you're going to follow me."

"Just like old times."

Jessa grabbed the keys from my hand and I didn't protest. Everything would be fine in a few hours but right now my arm throbbed under its tight bandages.

"They're out to get us, whether they know the truth or not," I explained to them. "We need to stay together. At least for tonight."

Chaz nodded. Jessa was a little harder to persuade. "Are you suggesting your place?"

"I am. Farther away from the incident and more exit routes. Not everyone can jump nine flights."

"They know where you live, Violet."

"I need my shower, Chaz. And my house doesn't smell like French fries."

"It's safer," Jessa said. "We've made sure of it. They might tear up the yard, but we're good there."

Chapter Twenty-Seven

The three of us circled around my new dining table and just stared at each other. I had made coffee, as I do in time of crisis.

"Aren't you the expert at these things?" Jessa asked Chaz, who was sitting quietly, staring down at his cup of coffee. She rubbed her arms covered in goose bumps despite the hot mug that steamed before her.

"Never actually been the huntee before, usually the hunter."

Jessa's shoulder slumped. "Well, what are we going to do?"

If this was my movie, and I had the three main characters together in a crisis, what would I do? "We need to know how much they know. That's got to be the primary thing."

Both looked at me. "When did you become the strategist?"

I shrugged. "I'm a writer, I see the big picture."

"How's the new movie going, by the way," Jessa asked as she leaned her head on her hand, casually sliding into girl talk mode.

"Going great actually. Got the first scripts done and off to Sera whose editing them right now."

"You got a movie?" Chaz asked confused.

"Yeah, based on a character I created. Well, technically, Kyle created, but I brought to life."

"That's great," he said with a perky smile that faded into a scowl. "Can we get to the life and death stuff now?"

"Fine," I snapped. "Since you're the only one who knows the whosits and whatsits, Got any suggestions as to where to look?"

"Already been searching. Nothing's panned out yet." His hands had clasped in front of him and his knuckles were turning white.

"Well, you're obviously not searching in the right places."

His scowl did not improve.

"All we need is a hint of what they know before we try to high tail it out of here."

"I'm not going anywhere," Jessa protested.

My eyes snapped to her. "They are after you."

"They are after us," she corrected.

Damn, I hated when she was right. It threw my worldview when the little princess came up with something good.

"But they all went after you first," Chaz said.

My cheeks flushed as I remembered our night out when things were still cute and light and flirty. I looked at him and he looked back at me. His hazel gaze met mine and I knew he was thinking the same thing. Things were never going to be like that again. No more games of hide and seek. It was going to be Defcon 5 from now on, until we stopped whichever Haverty was after us. No rest for us wicked.

"Let's spy on him."

Chaz and I broke our little staring contest and looked over at Jessa. Her hands were spread wide on the table, but this wasn't her drama pose. This was something deeper. This was a resolution pose, knowing that she had the answer. "Get me a mirror," she ordered. "Jerk gave me a card. Should be enough to make a connection."

There was an edge in her tone that made me jump up and run to my bathroom. The handheld mirror was plastic and purple but it would do.

"Is this toothpaste?" she scrunched her nose and handed the mirror back to me.

"You suck," I muttered as I went into the kitchen to wash the mirror of its white spots.

As I was washing off the remnants of my dental hygiene, I heard the front door open and close. Chaz and his jacket were gone when I came back.

"Where'd he go?"

"All I got was a glare."

I handed her the mirror.

"Better?" she said with a raised eyebrow.

"Not all of us can have a cleaning service."

"Think I just found your next birthday present."

"Providing I get to my next birthday."

Jessa jumped up from the table, making me take a quick step back and she confronted me, her little frame puffed and her hands on her hips. "Don't say that." Her dark eyes teared up. "You can't say that. We are going to survive this and I'm going to be the pain in your side for a long while."

Jessa had never said anything like that to me, ever. My eyes watered up just looking down at her little figure.

"Looking forward to it."

She hugged me. A tight, trying to squeeze all the air out of me hug and I couldn't help but return the gesture. She let out a little humph at my enhanced strength and when we let go, she was laughing.

"Okay. Let's spy on Spencer, shall we?"

"It's not working," Jessa said as she slammed her hands on both sides of the travel mirror.

"Why not?"

She jumped up and began pacing next to the living room table. I'd seen that a lot lately and suddenly knew how she kept so skinny. "I need a bigger mirror."

"Thanks to the Cleaners, I've got lots. Take your pick."

Jessa sucked in a deep breath and put her hair into a ponytail. I'd never seen her like this before. So determined and capable. "I need a needle."

"Why?"

"Do you have to question everything, Violet?"

"Yes," I said as I walked to the wet bar, which had a sewing kit still in its original package. "I'm curious," I said as I ripped open the package and pulled out the package of needles. "Apparently it's built in."

I handed her the needle and stood behind her. I could see over her head in the mirror and the reflection was comical. But by the look on her face, the hard determination, I knew this wasn't time for a joke.

With a small wince from both of us, she jabbed the needle in her forefinger and smeared it across the silvery surface.

Just as I was about to say "eww," the surface of the mirror rippled.

My skin chilled as the room filled with Jessa's power and the overwhelming scent of roses and raindrops.

She began to whisper to the mirror. It didn't sound like another language but what did I know about any of this stuff? A smoky figure began to form.

"He's too hidden."

I put my hand on her shoulder as an act of sympathy, but a jolt of lightning ran down my arm. As our powers joined, Jessa jumped and the image in the mirror became crystal clear. The Wonder-Twins had nothing on us.

"Holy Crap," I whispered as I watched Spencer.

"Guess you're a better connection than a business card."

He was in an office talking to two straggly men I recognized from the alley.

"We can't hear them," Jessa sighed.

"Yes, you can. Put your hand on the mirror." I said it before I realized what I was saying.

"Thought I was the fairy princess."

I took her hand and put it on the lower corner of the mirror, mine covered hers to keep the connection.

His crisp voice racked through our skulls. *"Idiots! It was a simple grab."*

"She is stronger than we thought."

They were talking about me. Little old me.

"She is one girl," Spencer raged.

"I think she's more than just a girl."

The echo of knuckles on chin resonated perfectly through our link to the mirror.

"This is creepy," Jessa whispered.

"Uh-huh."

Spencer pulled a revolver out of the desk drawer and looked at it, measuring the weight in his hands. The other men gulped and shifted uneasily on their feet.

"This isn't for you," he snapped as he opened the chamber and spun it. "I've got a guest in the other room. I'm returning a gift to him."

He reached under the collar his shirt and pulled something off a chain around his neck. He rolled the silver bullet around in his fingers.

"We knew that she was strong, got that from your brilliant routine in the alley. But now, she's got a little family. She's got something to fight for. He says that little stunt they pulled at the club is exactly what we needed. He says that the night we need is coming soon and we'll need the fairy for that."

"So why don't we just grab the fairy?"

"Don't question me," Spencer roared.

Jessa and I brought our hands away from the mirror, like putting the conversation on mute. Her body was rigid and I put my other hand on her shoulder as I took her hand and put it back to the mirror.

"I want her there. I want her by my side. It will be sweeter with my sister there."

Spencer dropped the bullet in his fingers into the chamber of the revolver. He snapped it closed with a flick of his wrist and pointed it at the man on the right. The man whimpered and ducked his head. He looked up at the men and smiled. "You have no idea what it's going to be like when he's here with us. It will be fire and chaos and power and I want to watch it burn in her green eyes."

"Watch her and when I tell you, I want them both."

The men nodded.

"Out!"

The grown men scurried out like mice.

Spencer leaned forward on his desk and shook his head. With a deep breath he straightened up, grabbed a knife on his desk, and strode out of the room.

Jessa pulled our hands away from the mirror and backed away from the fading image on the mirror quickly. "I've never done that before."

"Welcome to being six steps up the apocalyptic food chain and having a Guardian with a big G."

Jessa walked to the other side of the table. I got the sense that she needed to be as far away from the mirror as she could. Not a magic thing, just a creeped-out thing.

I took one of the wipes from the first aid kit and wiped her smear of blood off the mirror. My mother's pale green eyes stared back at me. Her fair skin. Something itched in the back of my brain. Something about what he'd said.

I went into the kitchen to toss the wipe but emerged with a frown on my face.

"What's wrong? Outside of the fact that we've just learned that I'm toast."

"We're toast," I corrected as I leaned forward on one of my chairs.

Something was there, aching in the back of my head to get out. It wasn't the cat. It was a memory, I thought. Something I couldn't remember.

"How are you with memories?"

Jessa shrugged. "Why?"

"I need to remember the day my mother died."

Jessa grimaced. "Violet, why would you want to see that?"

"Because I don't remember it."

Jessa frowned. Well, really, she frowned more, if that was possible. The crease in her forehead ran almost all the way up to her hairline.

"Not a single thing. Like it's been blocked. The only thing I feel I have are these stories that I dream."

Jessa slowly shook her head. "I don't think we need to drudge up such traumatic events."

"No," I said as I looked back at the mirror. "Spencer said something. Something about sister."

"Metaphysically, he would be your sire."

"I know but . . ." I sighed and dropped my head. The words just weren't there to explain the feeling in my gut. "Please Jessa."

"Fine," she shrugged as she grabbed the needle off the table. "Never been this juiced before. Probably take you back to your conception."

"Eww, that's gross."

A small smile curled up at the corner of Jessa's mouth.

She turned me around to face the mirror. "God, Sasquatch. I can barely see around you."

"Shut up."

Jessa jabbed and pinched the end of her finger and a red drop bubbled up. "Here goes."

She drew a circle around the edge of the mirror, having to stand on her tiptoes to get there and put her other hand at the base of my neck. My skin chilled immediately and I was surrounded by roses.

"Think about the closest thing that you remember afterwards."

I did exactly as she asked me. I thought of the moment that my Aunt Glory said that they were dead.

Jessa began to slowly draw her finger counterclockwise. An image formed in the mirror, smoky figures walked about, and I saw a woman standing before me.

"Here," I whispered.

Jessa drew her hand away from the mirror as the picture cleared. It was from my perspective, through my thirteen-year-old eyes.

My twenty-seven-year-old eyes watered as my mother came into focus. She was in her green dress. I remembered that green dress with little pink flowers on it.

"You look just like her," Jessa whispered in my ear.

I clutched my hand to my chest. As confident as I was about all this, I still wasn't sure that I wanted to hear what she had to say when I saw her again.

Jessa nudged my elbow from behind.

"I know."

Slowly, I reached out to touch the edge of the corner of the mirror.

"But I don't want to stay with Aunt Glory. Her house smells funny."

My mother smiled and brushed a curl behind my ear. "She doesn't smell funny."

"No, but Waylon does."

"Your cousin doesn't smell funny either. You're being immature, Violet."

"Why can't I go with you and Dad? We've always been the fearless threesome."

She took in a deep shuttering breath but forced that perfect smile. "You need to stay here with your aunt." She kissed my forehead and put her hand on my chin. "They are your family, Violet."

""No, you and Dad are my family. I just happen to be unfortunately related to Waylon."

My mother shook her head. "You are so headstrong, Violet. Always fighting me. Always questioning. You're going to need to keep that."

I frowned. "What are you talking about?"

She just wrapped me up in a big hug. When she let me go, she straightened my T-shirt and jacket. Her eyes were teary, but she smiled all the same, and her eyes were clearer for the water.

Dad honked the horn as he waited out on the street. I looked around Mom to see his wide grin as he waved at me. I waved back.

"I love you Violet. Remember that. Remember what I've told you. Take care of your real family. You'll know them when you meet them."

"Mom, you're being weird."

"Takes one to know one," she smiled, that lovely smile that brightened the rainy day. "You can't do everything by yourself. You'll need help. And your help will be needed."

I nodded. "But I'm not helping with the housework. I hate laundry."

She ran her fingers through my long, frizzy hair. "What are we going to do with you, Violet?"

"Love me unconditionally?"

She tweaked my chin as she walked down the slick sidewalk to the car.

I took my hand off the mirror and backed away. Jessa's hand dropped from my neck.

"Vi..."

I held up a finger to halt any sort of human interaction. My face was wet with tears and Mr. Sumo Wrestler squatted heavily on my chest so I could barely get the words out. "She knew," I whispered. "She knew it was going to happen."

"Violet. We don't know that," Jessa said shaking her head.

"How could I have not realized that? She knew it was all going to happen."

I fell backward and hit a wall. I sunk down to the floor under the 500 pound weight on my chest. She knew. It was all clicking together. The pieces were falling brilliantly together around in my broken head.

The stories.

My nickname.

"Vi, I need you to talk to me," Jessa said as she knelt down beside me.

"My mother told me stories," I started. "These crazy fantasies about a princess and the cat who kept saving her life. I lived and breathed these stories my whole childhood."

Jessa cocked her head. "Are you trying to tell me that..."

"I think she saw our death and saved me. She knew about my prophecy. That I had to live to protect the world. She would have never left me there with Aunt Glory otherwise. The two barely spoke."

Jessa's jaw dropped.

"I thought the stories were just her trying to stoke my imagination. But she was preparing me," I dropped my head in my hands and worked my fingers into my long smooth hair. "She was preparing me for life without her."

I heard Jessa scurry back on the carpet and smelled roses. Borders? What borders? My shield in shambles around my broken heart.

"Holy cow, Violet. Your mother was a psychic." Jessa sat on the floor next to me and reached out for my hand. When I didn't give it willingly, she took it and set it in her lap.

My whole life, everything, the schools, the deaths, the bad ex-boyfriends, were all leading me here, to be this. Wonder what the fates had to do to get me in the alley that night?

Jessa broke the pain-filled silence. "If your mother did what you're saying she did, she was an incredible woman. And her daughter is an incredible woman who is going to kick some major panther ass and stop whatever that blonde-headed prick is planning."

My red eyes snapped to Jessa. "That was a very un-Jessa thing to say."

"Maybe you're finally rubbing off on me."

I rested my head on the top of her head. "What do I do now?"

"Take some time. I'm going to make a few phone calls."

"We don't have time," I sniffed as I wiped my face. "We've got to . . ."

Jessa pinched my lips together. "We've got time. You come to terms with this. This is your heritage, Violet. As sad as it is, it's made you what you need to be to save the world. Can't argue with that kind of cosmic direction."

"Cosmic direction, my ass," I grumbled as I sat back up and stared at the wall.

Jessa got up and sucked on her pointer finger as she retreated to the kitchen to do god knows what. Three second later, there was a huge crash in the kitchen.

I jumped up and ran in to see Jessa holding a silver lever in her hand and the espresso machine hissing wildly. I zipped around her and unplugged the contraption.

"Thought a coffee might make you feel better," she said apologetically as she handed me the steamer handle.

"Thanks, Jessa."

"I'm going to order some food. What do you feel like?"

"Sushi, actually."

"Check, the cat wants fish."

I shot her a dirty look but she just beamed back. "Do you realize how many cat jokes I've been thinking up in the past two weeks? I've got loads."

"Joy. Why do I get the sidekick who thinks she's funny?"

"Who said that I was the sidekick, sidekick?"

I shooed her away with my hand. "Go call someone."

She sauntered out to the living room to get her cell phone and I stayed in the kitchen to study my perky curtain windows.

My mother knew. I remembered the flash from The Book. My mother knew, and so did Violette Jourdaine. I'd bet my Stuart Weitzman's that she was the psychic who wrote the book. I think I knew that before now, just didn't want to think about it. As if the panther wasn't enough, I had a psychic bloodline.

Could that be why the change came so easily? Could that be why Iris thought I was too powerful too quickly? Could that be why . . . Aw, screw it. I could think myself dizzy with the coulds and woulds and ifs.

This is who I am now. This is Violet Jordan's life and come hell or high water, I was surviving this.

Chapter Twenty-Eight

We were five days and counting until Cristina's deadline of the new moon. I was in my coffee shop waiting for Jessa to call me after her meeting. A crazy panther was gunning for our blood, but she still had to lunch with some investor. I still couldn't convince her that we should at least try to get out of the city. Go to Iris's for a weekend; just get away from anything that Spencer could think up. But she wouldn't have it. She wouldn't run. Which meant I was here, waiting for her to call me from across the street to go get her.

When Devin called that morning offering to bring me back my stuff from the few days at his house, I relished the idea of being just Violet for a few moments. I needed to see Devin to remind me that there was more to this world than my destiny and magic mirrors. Remind me there were 6 billion reasons we couldn't let a demon run loose on the streets.

Devin's warm smile brightened up the coffee shop as he entered, duffle bag in hand. He strode across the shop and sat next to me on the loveseat. "I want details. Hot steamy details of what's happening with Stalker boy."

I laughed. "We had a huge fight and are currently on rocky terms."

"You know what that means," he smiled.

"What?"

"Steamy makeup sex."

I laughed louder and stood to get a refill on my coffee. The kid behind the counter refilled my cup and I turned back to Devin on the loveseat.

It was like someone cued the porn music in my head. The lights softened and when my eyes met Devin's, there was a sizzling heat in the space between us that suddenly seemed like a thousand miles.

He licked his lips, soft luscious things, and ran his fingers through his hair.

There was a pull in my chest and I slowly sauntered back to the seat, unable to control the swing in my hips. I sat close to him. I could feel his breath on my hand.

My senses flooded with him, his baby powder scent, the red of his chestnut hair, the quick beating of his heart under his gray T-shirt and the slight perspiration on his brow. It tightened the space between my shoulders and warmed places a little lower down.

My hand reached out to touch him. I ran my fingers down the sweet hollow of his throat. Something stirred beneath my breastbone and I desperately wanted to see if he tasted as good as he smelled.

Devin shifted in the love seat and drew his arm up the back of the couch and turned towards me, displaying his broad chest. His pupils were dilated and his lips fuller. "Violet?" he breathed.

The sharp jingle of the entry bells ripped me from my study of him. I shook my head and scurried to the other side of the couch. What the hell?

This had to be a spell or something cooked up by the baddies. In my coffee? In the air? I grabbed my bag and darted out of there before I jumped him, right there in the front window for all to see.

The fresh air of the afternoon didn't help any at all. There seemed to be men all around and they all looked delicious. Runners bathed in sweat and businessmen bathed in cologne. And I just wanted to . . .

I jumped in my car and tried to catch my breath. Iris. I needed Iris. My hands were clammy as I reached for my cell phone.

"Hello?"

"I'm going crazy. I've official gone over the edge."

"What?" she asked.

"I nearly jumped Devin, stereotypical gay best friend Devin. Like, tore his clothes off and did him right there on the couch."

Iris just laughed on the other end of the line.

"What's so funny?"

She finished her laughter. "Welcome to puberty."

"What?"

"You've officially been a panther long enough to develop some of their more interesting characteristics."

My brain raced with any thought that wasn't Devin's lips and those creamy biceps. Cats, puberty. Crap. "Am I in heat?"

"Yes, ma'am you are."

"What the hell!" I screamed in my car and hit the horn so

that everyone in the plaza looked at me. "We've got a countdown to the apocalypse. What am I supposed to do?"

"Go home, take a cold shower. Stay away from anything male unless..."

"Iris! I can't. Not now."

"Well, I'm just saying that you're like a beacon for any man right now. And you're young. Have fun with it."

"Hello! End of the world prophecy!"

"Then I'd go with the cold shower."

I fumbled around for my keys and started the car. "You couldn't have told me this earlier? What the hell am I supposed to say to Devin?"

I sat in the tub for the longest time, until my fingers were pruney and my hair was a dried pile on top of my head.

This was not expected. Even after I researched and read about how others control their urges and about the actual nature of large cats, I could not have prepared myself for heat. How crazy was that? As if I needed another time of the month to worry about. But Iris did say that when I truly synced up with my animal, things like this would happen. I had to take the super strength with the super horny.

There was a rustle at the front door and I listened carefully, picking up the sounds of keys and boot steps in the foyer.

"Violet?" Chaz called up the stairs.

Crap. This was not what I needed right now. Whose bright idea was it to give him an extra key? Oh yeah. Me and my "we need to stay together" speech. He must be back from his fact-gathering mission.

The cat stirred again and just the thought of him, his broad chest, his strong arms made parts of me tingle that really shouldn't have, considering our arrangement.

I heard him walk up the stairs. With a sigh, I stood up out of the cold water and reached for my robe: this huge plush thing that you could lose yourself in and look completely unappealing. Maybe four inches of terry cloth would dampen whatever was going on.

He tapped on the door as I tied the belt.

"Violet?" he said softly.

"Yeah." I came to stand with my back to the door, feeling his heat through the wood. With no control over my boundaries, I could feel the outline of his body as he leaned forward, listening to me listen to him. He was probably wearing the same tight T-shirt that he had been wearing when he left to get more information about the prophecy. He was probably wearing those perfectly fitting jeans that made every day hell for me before all these crazy hormones started running through my veins.

"I'm back."

"Wonderful."

He pushed on the door but I stopped it with my foot.

"Vi, what's going on?"

"We've got a bit of a problem."

"Why? What happened?" he said, going straight into protector mode.

He had put a hand on the door right next to my shoulder. If only the two inches of wood weren't between us, his warm hands would be on my . . . "Nothing. I just think you need to go. Find Jessa."

He sighed hard. His hand traced its way down my back to the handle. "Whatever it is, we can face this. Talk to me, Violet," he practically whispered.

This didn't sound like Chaz, or, at least recent Chaz. He had to be affected. The plushy robe and door wasn't enough to keep him from being surrounded by my little bubble of mojo. I licked my suddenly dry lips and carefully put the words together. "I got a new side effect of the shift."

"Okay?"

"I'm going through heat."

He was silent on the other side of the door. I could almost see the smile on his handsome face as he leaned his forehead on the door. "So you're a little frisky right now?"

"And if you get too close, you will be too."

Chaz was quiet. His heat moved away from the door but I didn't hear him go downstairs. God, why didn't he know what was good for him? Why wouldn't he just listen to me for once?

"Did you call Iris?" he finally asked.

"She said that if I didn't want to maim every guy I see to go home . . ."

"And take a cold shower. Did it work?"

Every cell of my body wanted to rip the door off its hinges and take him right there in the hallway. "Not really," I grumbled and I moved to the mirror to see my reflection.

My hair had curled in long curls and my lips were fuller than usual. This was unfair. There was a ridiculously good looking man on the other side of my bathroom door and here I was holed up and looking hotter than usual.

"Going to stay in the bathroom all night?"

"Thinking about it."

Chaz put his hand on the handle, making it jingle slightly. "Can't be that bad."

"I nearly ripped Devin's shirt off."

He took his hand off the handle and left the door closed. "Probably would have made the kid's year."

"You should just go," I started, sitting on the edge of the sink. "Someone needs to go get Jessa."

The air was still, hot and stifling, and I could still feel every ounce of his energy on the other side of the door. I watched completely transfixed in fear and anticipation as the handle rotated and the door inched open.

Why didn't I lock the door?

He stuck his head in and my heart leapt in my chest. He had a black eye and a busted lip already scabbed over. His golden eyes were wide and sad and his hair was in all different directions. The information gathering must have not gone well.

"What happened?" I questioned automatically, moving for the door, my protective instincts quieting my feral ones for a moment.

"Another day on the job," he shrugged with the one shoulder I could see.

He looked wonderful, despite the black eye. And he smelled wonderful too, a mixture of the wind in his hair and his natural musk. I inhaled and before I knew what I was doing, I ran my fingers down his stubbly face.

I snatched it back when I had the urge to kiss him. "You should go."

But his pupils were large and his lips were so very, very moist.

I shook my head and moved away from him to stare back

into the mirror. Think about the worn robe. Think about the clouds moving across the window behind me. Think about anything that wasn't him without his shirt.

"You need to leave now." It was the last ounce of prevention I had left in me.

He opened the door fully and I had to brace myself forward against the marble, my knees went weak with the full scent of him, with the power he radiated. There was a blood stain on his left shoulder and a bullet hole in his shirt that revealed a white bandage underneath. It must have been a really bad day at the office.

"Do you really think that's the best idea," he whispered as he wrapped his arm around me. "With you in the state you're in."

And I was lost, drowning in him and what the cat needed. He brushed my hair away from my neck and kissed the racing pulse in my throat. My knees gave way and he quickly pressed me against the sink counter from behind.

The pain of my hip bone grinding into the marble snapped me out of my hormonal stupor enough to make me push him away and turn in his arms to look into his dilated eyes, the relaxation in his features. No furrows, just long lashes. No borders, just his radiating heat.

Before I could put together an effort to struggle against him, he kissed me. And not in the peaceful, friendly, "let's keep you grounded for tonight" way. It was a deep kiss that only intensified the desire running around in my blood. It was a desperate kiss I felt running all the way down to my toes.

His hand captured my face, holding it, tilting it ever so slightly to deepen our embrace. His mouth, his kiss was full of alarm and confidence and desire and fear and lust and emotions I couldn't find names for as I was flooded in his scent, his taste, that brilliantly hot tongue.

Slowly, he retreated, pulling away, softly suckling my lower lip as he caressed my cheek. I fought to keep my eyes open to keep from surrendering to the drunken spinning in my brain.

He stopped and put his face just to the side of mine, his stubble against my flushed flesh. "Tell me that was a bad idea," he whispered.

I lost all control of my legs and he lifted me to the edge of the counter. One leg curled around his waist, the robe fell to expose my pale thigh. He ran a hand up all thirty-four inches and I could faintly feel him tugging at the cloth belt as the needs of the cat took over.

We were in the bedroom when I resurfaced, gasping for air. My robe was long gone and his shirt was off, the jeans quickly following.

I whispered as he burned kisses into my neck. "Chaz, this isn't real."

I heard the clink of his belt as his jeans hit the floor. A little voice in the back of my head screamed for us to stop, that we had been resisting this for a reason. A world-destroying reason. But that reason was lost as he kissed me again and brought is bare skin against mine.

He didn't give my eyes time to linger over much as he pulled me fully across my lavender comforter with one swift movement. One arm wrapped under my shoulders, he parted my legs with his knees and I couldn't help but open up and wrap my legs around his.

Chaz kissed me deeply. He lifted out of our embrace to look down at me, those golden eyes flashing. "Tell me again this isn't real."

With a grace I'd never experienced before, Chaz slid within me quickly, fully. Once joined, my hips rocked up to meet his, to pull him to me deeper. We stayed frozen together as if taking a moment to match our heartbeats, to swim in the pulsing need that swirled around and through us.

When he did move again, he tried to take his time, be in control as he slid away, but he could not. Chaz thrust within sharply, making both of us gasp. The cat still had her needs and so did I.

I ran kisses along his strong jaw and suckled at his ear. He moaned softly and his fingers on my shoulder dug in with pleasure, his face buried into the crook of my neck. Playfully, I grazed the fleshy lobe with my teeth and felt him grip me tighter.

It was no longer the cat orchestrating us; this was me finally taking something that I wanted. And I had wanted him like this from the first time he brought me coffee.

One raw thrust forced my back to arch, breaking our kiss. I dug my nails into his back. I bit my lower lips as I spun in the sensation of his hands caressing my side, my breast, before curling his hand around my hip to lift me close to him.

I had never been the type to come uncoaxed before, always the stubborn one. But the way Chaz thrust into me was just hard enough to compress that brilliant rose that burst at the slightest provocation. I began to tighten even more around him, feel the heat rising from my inside to sear his skin.

Chaz let out a thick moan as I whispered his name, the breath and words catching deep within my throat.

I spasmed beneath him, crying out softly as the orgasm hit me like bursting through a brick wall. I wrapped my legs around his waist and let him plunge into me as the waves of pleasure flooded my body, wracked my senses and possessed my muscles, making places tighten and surge I hadn't thought had the ability. The spell woven around us had burst as well, evaporated in the pent-up heat now released between us.

Amidst all this, I could feel him, more than just his taut moist body against mine, more than his soft lips as they kissed my throat, my neck; I could feel his power glowing white hot in his chest. Its warmth surrounded me as I closed my eyes and bathed in the brilliance of his raw power.

Just as I was coming off my high, toes just beginning to uncurl, Chaz's back hardened and I prepared myself as he rammed into me, harder than before, wildly uncontrolled as his body took over and he came. I could feel everything in my sensitized state, every spasm, every inch, every ounce of shuttered breath that escaped his lips onto my neck. It was like a second orgasm, my body exploding again with his.

Chaz's coaster of ecstasy slowed, then stopped. He stayed inside me as he kissed up my neck, my ear, and found my still hungry, always hungry, mouth.

I had to be smiling a Cheshire smile. My head spun like a glass of champagne on an empty stomach. I didn't want him to go as he slid away and rolled on the bed beside me. He laid his head down on the arm still around my shoulders and wrapped the other around my waist.

His eyes were soft, his dark lashes even darker in the moonlight that now streamed through my window. He looked over at me with flushed lips and silence.

I couldn't bear to think, couldn't bear to speak. But just let him cover the two of us with the edge of my lavender comforter and allowed him to pull me close to his moist frame. He kissed my ear one last time before sleep claimed us both.

Chapter Twenty-Nine

As I slept, dreams came, blinding and bloody. Jessa's reflection in a mirror. Blood on cement. Chaz crouched in the darkness. The sinister glint of a cat-like eye.

Even in my dreams, Jessa reached out to me scared and in pain. Overcome with roses and raindrops, I woke up and flew to a sitting poison. My hand slapped against bare flesh.

"Vi?"

"Jessa," I whispered as I looked down at Chaz, my hand leaving a red mark on his flawless chest. "I had a dream."

In that instant, he went from satisfied male model to hardened Guardian. It was a sight that drop-kicked my heart into my stomach. Chaz sat up and turned towards me.

"Like a prophecy?"

I bit my lower lip as I remembered everything from last night. Everything that the cat had called for, every line of his body and every curl of his hand around my hip. Everything that she needed and I wanted.

The mojo that possessed us was gone. My borders were back; my thoughts were my own. My heart, not so much anymore.

Chaz's eyes flicked from my lips to my eyes to my ears, back to my lips. Just when I thought he was going to kiss me again, he swung his legs over the edge of the bed and reached for his jeans on the floor. A clear set of nails marred his broad shoulders and though not bleeding, the marks were still very red.

Wow, go me.

He pulled on his pants and only allowed me the briefest of glimpses as he stood and slipped them up.

"Chaz?"

"We have to get Jessa."

I pulled the sheet up to cover my chest. This was suddenly getting very déjà vu-ish.

There was a crash and the sound of breaking glass. I grabbed my sheet and flew down the stairs. Chaz was on my heels. I stopped at the bottom stair and he ran into my bare back. Awash in his scent, I had to force myself to focus on the possible disaster ahead and not the one behind me.

Nothing was out of place. The front door was still closed; no windows were busted. There was the faint smell of coffee from a two-day-old pot in the kitchen.

I slowly moved towards the back of the house as Chaz moved for the front door. On my way, a stab of pain ran up my foot. "Ow," I shrieked as I brought the foot up and hopped around to find what had stabbed me.

"What?" Chaz was at my side with super speed.

A sliver of silver was embedded in the ball of my foot. Where would that . . .

I looked up to the mirror, the mirror that linked Jessa's house to my house. It wasn't just cracked like Kurt said it would be. It was busted out, the pieces spread in a wide arch on the dining room floor.

"Crap," I whispered and ran up the stairs, forgetting the sheet in the dining room.

I threw on what I could find and pulled my hair up in a ponytail. Chaz appeared in the doorway.

"I'm going to Jessa's."

"I'll drive."

"No, you're going to hunt down Spencer. He's been talking to a demon through a mirror. We need to destroy the mirror." Hopping around, I pulled on my Chuck Taylors.

I spun around and headed back for the door. I descended the stairs at a speed that Chaz even had a hard time keeping up with. I snatched my keys from the bowl in the foyer and opened the front door.

"Violet," he snapped.

My entire body flinched as I turned to face him. He'd only gotten his shirt on, not buttoned yet and his golden eyes met mine. Places tightened in ways I didn't ever want to admit as he stared me down. My skin flushed as I licked my lips. More memories came flooding back of his lips around my throat, his hands clenched in mine.

"This is it, Chaz. This is D day. I can feel it. This is what I was made for." I took a step forward and rested my hand on his bare chest. His heart pounded wildly beneath my long fingers. "This is what my mother died for, so that whatever is supposed to happen today doesn't."

I watched as goose bumps covered his strong chest. His dark lashes fluttered closed for a moment.

"Find Spencer and you'll find the mirror," I repeated.

I gave him a long slow kiss and then I was the one who left. This was just great. Save the world, lose the boy.

"Jessa." I called out into Jessa's apartment but nothing responded, just the echo of my voice back to me. She hadn't answered her home phone the seventeen times I called her on the way over and she hadn't answered her cell the fourteen times I had tried that number.

The door had been locked, but looking around, something was wrong. Things were slightly out of place. My eyes jumped to her matching mirror. It was in pieces on the floor.

I sniffed. And smelled dog. "That's not . . ."

And I would have finished the sentence if it wasn't for the blunt force trauma to the back of the head. I was really glad Jessa had sprung for the softest carpet on the market because my face hit the ground really hard.

Chapter Thirty

Blacked out and not naked. A personal best. I pushed myself off the beige carpet and looked around at Jessa's dark apartment. It was deep into the night already. I had been out too long.

Wiping dried blood from the already healed wound on the back of my head, I looked around. They had trashed the place after I was out of the picture. By the wound on the back of my head, these guys were a little heavy handed, but Jessa was no fragile girl. I stretched my neck from side to side. Blood had stiffened my T-shirt and run down my back, pooled in my clavicle.

Part of me panicked. But the other part, the furrier part of me, immediately knew what to do. The truth electrified my skin. This was it. There was no running from the prophecy, there was only standing up to it and kicking its ass.

I took off my jacket and walked back to the guest bedroom. I kicked off my shoes and went directly to the chest of drawers there. I pulled the entire drawer out of the dresser and threw it on the bed.

I had never wanted to have to use the clothes Jessa had

charmed to shift with me, to prevent the ever-embarrassing nakedness that happened every time I shifted. I opened the pink tissue–papered parcel and held out the clothes before me. Bebe? Seriously? She had charmed a track suit from Bebe to shift with me? I rolled my eyes. Save the world one yard of stretchy black velour at a time.

I slid into the suit easily. It felt like a second skin, which is what it was supposed to be, a second skin that would be infected by the magic that surrounded me. The slow slung pants hugged all the right places, but it breathed and moved as silkily as I did. I zipped the jacket up and shook my head as I jammed my wallet and cell into the pockets. Even without her here, Jessa was making sure that I looked fabulous. Bless her pointed little head.

I strode through the apartment and headed back out to my Miata. Despite the cold weather, I pulled back the top. It was the first time since LA I'd had it down, but you can't track someone's scent with the roof up and you just don't look as cool doing it.

The scent of Jessa's Aveda shampoo vanished outside the warehouse. The building was fairly nondescript in the streetlights, one of many antique shops along this line of Industrial Boulevard. I had to park a block away and jump a fence to approach the side of the building. But fences were nothing after climbing around in Iris's barn for two months.

The scene was straight out of my TV show. A dark night with no stars, shadows jumping out of every corner, and the slight scraping of a bare tree against a brick wall somewhere.

And I was just about to enter the lion's den—well, technically the panther's lair.

My cell phone began to vibrate in my jacket pocket. I plastered myself against the nearest wall as I flipped open the little black thing. I gulped when I saw the picture appear on the little screen.

He didn't wait for a greeting. "Violet. He's got Jessa."

But I heard his words on the wind more than from the phone. I snapped it closed and followed the voice.

"Vi, Vi. Damn it, Violet," he cursed as I rounded a corner.

He was crouching behind a tower of palates, swearing at his cell phone.

"How'd you find her?" I hissed as I came up behind him.

Chaz jumped and spun around quickly. "Why in the hell haven't you been answering your phone?"

My body reacted to seeing his face again, warming and tightening, and my panther rolled in my chest. I turned quickly and flashed him the back of my neck that was still encrusted with blood. "I don't know why, but they didn't take me. Woke up about thirty minutes ago."

Chaz's furrow eased. "You okay?"

"Of course I am."

He just looked me up and looked me down, speechless. Maybe Bebe should be my new best friend. "Yeah, I know." I had to smile. "Tell me about the building, about the guys inside."

Chaz gulped, smacking his lips as if his mouth had run dry.

"Um," he whispered. "There's six guys and Jessa. They've got her tied to a chair in the center of the room next to the mirror. I thought you said this was happening on the darkest night. We still have three days."

"Maybe Cristina got her mojo crossed. But sure looks like they're going to try to open a gateway to Neveranth."

I looked around to see how high the windows were and where the entrance was. There weren't any security cameras, not close enough for the neighbors to hear anything. Scenarios ran though my brain, some worked, some were crazy. Jumping in one of the windows was a little out of the question but there seemed to be only one door on the street side of the building and a loading dock in the back with us. And what the hell did I know about ambushes?

"You know this is just to get you here, with him?"

"No shit."

"Violet," he chided.

"I think I'm allowed to be a little jumpy. I'm the only one who can stop this."

His entire body tensed as he quickly turned to focus on the building before us. I watched as his jaw muscles rippled and his fists clenched and then released at his sides.

"That's not a bad idea," I whispered.

"What? Frustrate them to death?" he grumbled.

My brain raced through plot lines. It just might work. Granted, I wasn't a great actress but my panther could do most of the talking. And I already knew what the bad guy wanted, as much as I couldn't believe it.

"He wants me, like *wants* me. What if I walked in there looking to play?"

"You can't," he protested. "It's like walking into a lion's den."

I tried not to smile. He looked slightly confused until he got the joke too and chuckled.

I smiled. Somewhere in the sliver of moonlight, I looked at Chaz and finally knew what I wanted.

It only hardened my resolve that I was going to do whatever it took to keep that bastard from getting what he wanted because he was keeping me from getting what I wanted.

"I'll get in there and then you can get Jessa out when they are distracted."

"How are you going to distract them?"

I unzipped the front of my track suit and slid the jacket off. His pulse raced and his body warmed as I pulled off my tank top. He licked his lips and tried not to stare. "Whatcha thinking about right now?"

He just gulped and tried to keep his eyes up and on mine.

"Exactly. I'm hoping a plate of flattery and a side order of sex and he won't pay attention to you sneaking Jessa out." I slid the jacket back on but only zipped it up to my bra line. The pale lights from the surrounding street lamps made the girls look bigger and frankly they were a little perkier than usual thanks to the chilly night.

Chaz looked at me like he was looking at a stranger. He stuck his hand out between us. "I'm Chaz Garrett, and who the hell are you?"

"Funny," I snarled as I adjusted the jacket a bit more. It was the dead of December and we were facing down what the forecasters were saying was going to be the coldest winter in years. And I was wearing a thin velour suit. No Kevlar, no combat gear. Just me.

I took in a deep breath of the cool night air and slipped my keys and cell in his jacket pockets. In this very close proximity, I had to force the blush out of my cheeks as I matched his hazel gaze. Had to force myself not to take one long, possibly last breath of him to remember.

"This is a crap plan." His hand caught mine as I pulled my hands back to my sides. "You can't sacrifice yourself," he whispered as his forefinger began to caress my knuckles.

I could feel my heart race in my throat, taste the beat of his in the hot air between us. In that moment, I could have fallen into his arms and let him take the lead, let him be the big hero. But it was sentimentalities like this I couldn't have romping around in my brain if I was going to pull this off. I needed calm, I needed focus, and Chaz did neither of those for me.

Slipping my hand from his, I rocked back on my heels to take in a deep cool, un-Chaz-filled breath and explained what he needed to do. "Got a small knife?"

He quickly pulled a folding knife out of his jean pocket.

"I'm going to shift. When I do, hand me that," I said glancing down at the little knife in his palm, still frozen between us. "Give me about three minutes to get their attention and then you focus on getting Jessa out of there. That's your objective."

I tugged at the edge of my jacket and pushed the sleeves up a little. Energy danced across my skin; nervous, anxious energy that I couldn't control, didn't want to control. I ripped out my ponytail holder and pulled my hair back again, catching some of the wispies that had escaped in the cool breeze.

"Violet, I . . ." Chaz tried to say but I didn't let him. I didn't need a confession right now.

"I'm going to distract them." I slipped off my shoes and set them on a wooden stack of pallets. "Take out the mirror if you can. I don't know how hairy it's going to get in there."

I took another step away from him and his warmth faded quickly from my skin.

"Can you do it?" his voice wavered. "Can you shift and stay Violet?"

"Jessa's my best friend, Chaz. I'll do what I need to do. Besides, this is bigger than just me, remember?"

He looked away, down the long dark street. The silence between us was worse than anything those men in there could do to me.

And I *was* pretty sure I could do this. If not, I could rely on the cat to get the job done. She hated Spencer as much as I did. It was all about timing. All I needed was five minutes to distract them. I had faith in Chaz to get job done.

I turned and stared at the path to the front door. "And if all else fails, you know what a well-placed silver slug can do."

"Now who's starting to talk like who?" he remarked.

I fought a smile. Look who became Action girl after all. But I didn't let him see my amusement. Didn't let him know that I was doing this for him. For Iris. For Devin. For everyone who wouldn't have a chance against whatever beastie Spencer could pull from that mirror.

Rolling my shoulders, I took in a breath and felt for the static-like power in everything around me. I reached out and scooped it all to me, gathered the power that allowed me to change form, like gathering in a blanket to your chest.

"Ready?" I said as I looked over at him.

He was already loading his gun, checking the bullets in the chamber. "Always."

I rolled my eyes. *God, that was cheesy.*

I closed my eyes and found the center of power within me and slid down into the inky blackness.

When I opened them again, my vantage point has shifted. I turned my head to see the gun in Chaz's hand. I was me at panther height. I looked down at the large strong paws, the blue-black fur. I was me. As a Cat. No more than just a cat, a panther, a metaphysical beast only told of in legend.

I rock.

I sauntered in the front door of the warehouse and immediately saw the men Chaz described. Lit by the few electric lamps in the antique shop, they really were in a circle around the girl. The men smelled like stale creek water and chewed pig hoof. Good ole mongrels. Knew I hadn't seen the last of them.

I recognized Spencer even in the dim lights; his blonde hair and his tailored clothes a striking contrast to the dingy wardrobe of the mongrels who stood patiently awaiting orders. Spencer was the target, the one who called out to me above all the others—even Jessa, who I tried desperately not to look at.

Jessa was bleeding and her borders were gone. I felt her roses and raindrops prickle across my skin. She sat limp in a high back chair. Her forearm was cut from elbow to wrist and bleeding freely into a silver basin on the floor by the chair.

There was one surprise that I didn't expect. Cristina the psychic was standing next to Spencer with a thick black volume open in her petite hands. Her blood red skirt swished the floor as she turned around to greet the newcomer. Her eyes focused and then jumped wide with fear. Anger chilled my skin and I snarled at her. That bitch.

"Well, who's this?" Spencer questioned, relaxed as I padded into their circle.

Two of the men immediately pulled guns and I could smell the gun powder on their greasy hands. They had pulled the trigger once already this evening and their energy danced around then like they were willing to do it again.

"I think the little kitty wants to play," Spencer laughed, reaching out his hand to me.

I slinked under his long fingers and he ran his hand gingerly down my back. I slithered in and out of his legs for a moment and stopped next to him, leaning in against his leg.

"Spencer, no," Christina warned as she put her hand on his arm.

Spencer pushed her hand away with a snarl. Cristina squeezed the book against her chest and backed away.

"Aren't you beautiful," he whispered as he ran his fingers down my head, around my ears and neck. It felt natural, him touching me like this, the strength of his panther interacting with mine.

"Why is she here?" one of the thugs growled.

Spencer snarled and the man dropped his eyes. To me, it was clear that if Spencer wasn't there, these men were not strong enough to rip a whole in the Veil. So it was me and Spencer. Two men enter, one man leaves.

I left his side and crossed over to Jessa. I flattened my ears back and made a low throaty noise as I stalked around her, nibbling at her fingers long enough to drop the knife into them.

She caught it quickly and curled her fingers around the blade. Stealthy is as stealthy does.

Then I was back at Spencer's side, wrapping my body around his legs. In an instant, a simple thought, I was running my hand up his chest in one smooth movement that brought me around to his back, my lips in his ear. And thank you god, the suit was still in place.

His men flinched but Spencer was too wrapped up in the energy of my shift to be on the defensive. His head leaned back for a moment and his eyes fluttered shut, putting us cheek to cheek. Within his borders, his power played against mine. It wasn't like on the dance floor where he was forceful; this was more relaxed, playful almost. I let my energy roll around him and let his exotic smell fill my nostrils.

"Why are you here, Violet?" he asked.

"I needed to see you again," I whispered in his ear. "Feel your fur against mine. You did something to me and I can't stop thinking about it."

Spencer smiled and with barely a flexed muscle, quickly pulled me to his side, wrapping his arms around my waist. He looked down the front of my suit but his cool blue eyes snapped up and caught mine by surprise. I managed a deep seductive smile and molded against his body, trying to ignore that my panther loved his willingness to play, that he would be strong enough to really play with.

"Thought your answer was a resounding no."

I cast my eyes down and to the side, the intensity of his gaze finally ruffling my calm. "Didn't quite know what you were offering." I flicked my eyes to Cristina who practically quaked with fear. "But it looks like you already have plenty of girls at the party."

"They are nothing. Means to an end, my love." He chuckled and his lips brushed my cheek softly. "But why are you really here?"

I swallowed hard at the edge his tone took. Time to layer on the act. "Your father sent his lackeys to attack me in broad daylight, like I was some sort of mess to be cleaned up. I didn't appreciate it."

Spencer reached up and ran his fingers through my hair, taking out the tie that kept it back. The surprisingly intimate gesture caught me off guard. A little gasp escaped my throat and he smiled and nuzzled his nose into my chestnut locks, taking in a deep breath.

"I knew you'd see I was right. I knew you'd join me. He said you would."

I pushed away at his chest. "Who said?"

Spencer just smiled. "Jovan."

I tried not to gasp as he so casually mentioned the world-eating demon the Neveranth was created to incarcerate. "Jovan?"

Spencer nodded. "He will come and the entire country will be ours."

"He will come and kill us all," I corrected sharply

Spencer shook his head as he dropped his arm from my waist and I was able to suck in a deep breath of clean air. "He will spare whoever I want, those loyal to me. He promised."

The space between my shoulders went ice cold. This was what Chaz had been talking about it. The Cause knew that Spencer was going for Jovan, going for the big payday. And still they did nothing about it. So this really was up to me to save the world. The realization of it sat cold and heavy in my stomach.

"Are you all right, my pet? You look pale."

"It's a lot to take in." I recovered as quickly as I could, thanking the gods that I had watched Jessa charm men for two years. "Being second in command to all that."

There was a small yelp from behind us and we turned around to see Cristina covering her mouth.

"What?" I laughed as I approached her, slipping from Spencer's possessive fingers. "Did he promise you power in the new regime?" I made a small pout and sent a laugh that echoed through the antique crystal around us. "Sorry honey. I'm abdicating your throne."

I ripped the book from her hand and grabbed her throat, shoving her hard into an armoire. Her toes danced on the floor, her anklets jingling, as she clutched at my arm. Tears flooded my eyes as I felt the betrayal run hot through my veins. I saw the tainted light in her eyes, darkened with fear and power that I hadn't even known to look for before. The disgust curled my fingers around her small throat even tighter.

"You have one chance to declare what side you are on, witch," I hissed into her ear.

"I am yours, Daughter of Jourdaine," she gasped. "I swear it."

"Then I suggest you play dead if you want to survive this."

I dropped her to her slippered feet and held the book close to my chest. The book danced with dark energy, the slimy, cool kind that made bile rise in my throat. Cristina held her throat and took in deep shaky breaths. She looked up at me with brown eyes, clear of any persuasion that Spencer had held over her in the past. Untainted as she declared her choice.

I nodded slightly and threw a wall of energy at her that was bigger than anything I had conjured in the past. Her petite body flew up and over a desk and crashed into a full china cabinet. The noise was deafening.

Without flinching, I turned to Spencer with a satisfied smile and swayed back over to him. "Now, where were we?"

Spencer smiled and held his hand out to me. Slipping my hand into his, he guided me to the mirror and the circle. Jessa's head lulled to one side and our eyes met. It was the only time I wished that I could see into her mind, wished I were telepathic and could tell her that everything was going to be fine.

Every fiber of me wanted to go to her, but I couldn't break the façade. But the panther could. A small amount of energy crept forth and stroked her cheek. I could feel her soft skin on my forefinger. Her eyes fluttered closed for a moment and she moaned softly.

Spencer turned around and looked between us. "What was that?" A deep furrow formed between his eyes.

My energy snapped back and my heart raced. Of course, he could feel that. He was as powerful as me.

I licked my lips and lied through my teeth. "She was my friend for years, yet it took your foresight to see what her true power could be used for."

Spencer's jaw loosened. "You do have a way with words, Violet."

"Thank you."

"If you would do the honors, my pet," Spencer said as he

pointed to the book. He slid his jacket off his broad shoulders and tossed it on a table. He began to unbutton his shirt.

"What kind of a girl do you think I am?"

Spencer laughed as he pulled out his shirttails to expose a tan, taut chest. "I need you to carve a symbol into my chest, so that when Jovan comes, he knows who the worthy one is."

"Worthy one?"

Spencer retrieved an ornate silver knife from the table where his coat lay. "He cannot take human form. He must possess a vessel."

"But what about you?"

Spencer smiled. "That almost sounds like concern in your voice, kitten."

My stomach turned on itself when he called me that. I took the knife from his hand and opened the book. "Which one?"

He pointed to a simple rune on a page full of text that I couldn't begin to read.

As I was looking at the page, Spencer took the basin full of Jessa's blood and dumped it down the front of the mirror's silver surface.

Jessa gasped and her fight was renewed against her restraints.

As I expected to see the blood flow down the smooth surface, the mirror seemed to absorb the blood, taking it beneath its surface, leaving only the frame still covered in the rose-scented red.

The surface of the mirror rippled like water and I looked around to see what the next step was. That's when I saw Chaz sneaking in the corner of the room.

No more thinking, my three minutes were up. My brain

kicked into a gear I didn't even know was possible; an instinctual level that didn't filter through my usual levels of cynicism and self-doubt.

The silver in my hand felt heavy and as Spencer turned back to me to start, I rammed the knife into his ribs, all the way up to the hilt. We both gasped as blood spilled out dark and hot over my hand. I tore the knife out and kicked him farther and harder than Cristina. His surprised figure went flying into the darkness behind the ring of old lamps.

The book, now spattered with blood, grew hot and anxious in my hands. I looked at the mirror and tossed it through the surface. The surface rippled happily with the offering. If it was active, then they must have gathered some of my blood when they cold-cocked me.

The nearest mongrel started to pull out his gun. I could smell the oil as I turned around. I ran for him. His brown eyes widened as he raised the gun at me.

I grabbed his arm and pulled his arm towards me. His clumsy weight fell forward and I put him in a flying arm bar that would have made my sensei pee his pants. The mongrel landed on his back with a loud oomph and his head cracked against the cement.

The gun fell from his hand and right into mine. My plan had worked. I scooped it up, and taking shelter behind a rolltop desk out in the middle of the showroom floor, I aimed at the others before they even noticed their friend was on the ground.

I went for the chest. I wasn't sure how many bullets were in this model, somewhere between ten and fifteen. Didn't know if it would be sufficient to take down a shapeshifter, but I didn't even need to hit the bastards. I just needed to draw them away long enough for Jessa and Chaz to escape.

They scattered like birds, not dogs. The showroom floor provided little coverage for the men. They managed to duck behind tables and china cabinets. Didn't stop me from shooting at them, the chaos throwing glass shards and porcelain everywhere. Taking potshots now and then, they blew chunks off of the table next to me and destroyed the desk. As they focused their sights on the crazy cat with the gun, Chaz crept in towards Jessa, a void of calm in the chaos.

"No!" echoed out across the floor.

Spencer launched his entire body at me, knocking the gun out of my hand. My head smacked against the cement floor as his claws dug into my shoulders. He hadn't shifted. Yet. His hands had grown talon nails and his golden eyes flashed wildly above me.

That's all the invitation the panther needed to come forward. I drew more energy from the air around and from him, stealing it easily from his already charged beast. His energy left a bitter taste of disappointment on my tongue, as my human form gave way to the cat. I didn't even know that I could do that, but the panther didn't care where it came from, just that it made me stronger.

My hind legs threw him off me quickly, heels over head and he landed behind me. Like lightning, he was on his feet again as I was rolling onto my four paws.

Keeping low to the ground, I watched, easily predicting his movements. It was all in the timing. He took one step forward and I pounced with deadly aim straight for the jugular. I didn't just go for cutting off air this time, like in the alley. I went for blood, just as he had Jessa's. I went to steal the life that he had stolen from me.

Lightning stabbed into my midsection as we landed. Spencer cried out as my teeth sank deep into his throat with our impact and a knife buried itself deeper into my ribs.

I let go and rolled away, sliding off the small blade. The wound sizzled and smoke poured out like lips smoking a cigarette. I thought of the previous poison he tried to use and forced myself to shift back into the bipedal version. He'd gotten me right between the last two ribs, in the exact spot I had stuck him.

My hand pressed against the wound, blood spilling out from my fingers. I'd always thought that was a cheesy move on the part of the special-effects guys but turns out, that's exactly what happens.

Spencer sat up not four feet from me, blood pumping out of the wound in his neck. His face was already pale with the loss as blood streamed down his bare chest.

"Heirloom silver," he said smiling, holding up the knife. "Really does the trick."

I looked down at the wound. It felt like he'd stuck me with a fire poker that only stabbed again and again each time I tried to take in a breath. "The picture frame."

"You were a cute kid," he said as he pushed himself up and off the floor. "Too bad you turned out to be such a bitch."

"Better than a spoiled prick."

"Oh, Violet," he said as he swayed over to the table where his jacket was. He slid the coat on and sat on the edge of the table. "Aren't we beyond that?"

The wound in my side began to fester and I could feel the

curse burn like poison through my blood. I barely heard Chaz call out to Jessa, the echo of gunshots, as I pulled myself up against a china cabinet.

"What the hell is going on here?" The voice roared through the showroom. It vibrated the crystal, leaving a tinkling echo in its wake.

I smelled cigars. No, tasted ash in my mouth. And then the flash of energy poured over me. Hello, Daddy Dearest.

Because my night wasn't enough of a complete disaster.

Rough hands grabbed my arms and lifted me from the floor. I cried out as the wound spread open and my feet roughly found the ground beneath me. My captor looked at me with black beady eyes. His father's trained dogs.

"Get your hands off me, dog," I spat.

He didn't, just dragged me over to where the mirror still rippled, still waiting for some evil deed. Spencer and the mutts had already been corralled and lined up like naughty children, each with their own body guard. At least Jessa and Chaz weren't here. My body actually relaxed when I didn't see them in the lineup.

Sharply dressed, his hair neatly combed, a silver-handled cane aided Haverty's procession towards us. I straightened as he approached, despite the sizzle in my side. He was power. Like Iris was power. It was old and ancient as it rolled off of him.

The two Havertys stood nose to nose, but Spencer's eyes were downcast. Haverty said nothing to him. He took a step back and struck Spencer with the silver head of his cane. The man behind him held him on his feet as Spencer's knees gave way beneath him.

The mutts jumped and the fresh scent of burning flesh wafted over to me. When Spencer brought his head back up, a long slit on his face highlighted his cheek bone and the wound smoked like mine had. The Haverty's heirloom silver.

"I knew you were stupid, Spencer. But this? Jovan? That's a level of stupidity they don't have a word for yet."

Spencer didn't say anything. He was defeated. It poured off of him. Or could I just feel it because he was my sire? That was a creepy thought. I shivered and when I did, the wound in my side flared to life again and I winced.

Haverty's eyes snapped to me. "And you must be the leftovers he never managed to clean up."

"I'd prefer Violet, thank you."

The man behind me held me tight as Haverty came over to inspect me. He snuck his nose into my neck and took in a deep breath. I flinched until he backed off.

"Didn't expect that." He reeked of cigar smoke and cologne and being this close to him made my skin crawl. "Where's the Key Holder?"

"Far away from here."

He reared his hand back to strike and when it came down, I dropped my weight and the face of my captor caught the full force of the blow, blood spurting out of his mouth. His hands released my arms and I rolled back between his legs and away from Haverty. I was on my feet, but not stable enough for another round.

In the distraction of my escape, Spencer broke from his captor with an elbow to the ribs and a claw to the face. The man cried out and all attention was given to the prodigal son.

As if in slow motion, Spencer ran for the mirror.

"No!" I cried out as I ran after him.

An arm came around my waist and I was pulled backward, my heels dragging on the floor. Horrified I watched as Spencer leapt into the mirror, the silvery surface welcoming him in a shimmer of bright light. As his shoe disappeared, the surface grew calm for a moment.

Chaz pulled me behind an antique armoire. I struggled against him frantically for a moment. Cool fingers curled around my forearm and I looked over to see Jessa sitting next to me, leaning against the wood, weak and pale.

Oh god Jessa, I whispered and I threw my arms around her neck. My heart leapt. "I'm so sorry. I kissed her forehead. I suck at this guardian thing."

"Not from where I was sitting."

I glared at Chaz. "I thought I told you to get her out of here."

"Shhh," Jessa said as she squeezed my arm. I felt her cool magic over my skin, calming me. "I told him I'd turn him into a frog if he took me away from you."

I looked back at Chaz. "She can't really do that."

Chaz put his hands up in surrender. "I wasn't taking any chances."

There was a rumble in the ground and the wood in my back. Thanks to my five years in California, I knew what earthquakes felt like but this was different.

"It's him," Chaz gulped. "He's here."

"No," I corrected. "He can't come to this plane without a host and Haverty's got too much machismo to say yes."

I twisted around to see if I could make out what was going on. The wound in my side flared to life, but I could see the circle. The dogs were scattering. The man who'd been holding me ran like a little girl for the front door.

"Something Spencer-sized goes through the mirror, something Spencer-sized comes out of the mirror."

"Did he tell you that?"

I shook my head. "Those stories that I keep telling you about?"

"Sonovabitch," Chaz breathed. He immediately started loading every gun he had on him.

"Hold on there, killer," I winced as I turned back. My hand held my side. It had stopped bleeding but still felt like Mt. Vesuvius between my ribs. "You have to get Jessa out of here."

Jessa's eyebrows drew into a hard line above her lavender eyes. "I need to close the mirror."

"I'm not facing your mother when she hears you've been eaten."

A roar deeper and louder than anything a lion from this realm could have produced screamed out into the warehouse. Crystal shattered and mirrors broke through the entire building.

I shook my head. "Do I really want to know?"

Chaz scooted out from our hiding position. I watched his face pale and his lips part. His wide eyes flicked to me and then back to whatever was out there. He slid back and looked at me.

"Is it bigger than a breadbox?" I waited. "Smaller than a dragon? I just need a little detail before the imagination runs wild here."

"Clydesdale?"

My head lulled back against the armoire with a dull thud.

The battle began to rage on the other side of the showroom

floor. Men cried out as they were thrown across the warehouse. And I was stuck on the sidelines with a wound that wouldn't heal.

"You've got to get out there," Jesse winced as she scooted around. "Lift up your jacket."

At this point in the game, I wasn't above flashing my best friend. I sunk down on the ground and lifted up the edge of the velour. The wound was red and angry. Jessa unwound the ripped T-shirt from her forearm and held the wound over mine.

I scooted away. "That's gross, Jessa."

"Shut up, Violet. I know what I'm doing." She squeezed her arm and the blood ran freely again. "In theory," she muttered.

I looked away as warm drops of Jessa's blood fell onto my side. At this point in the day, I was up for anything. I was officially down the rabbit hole and the jabberwocky was right on the other side of the armoire.

Chaz was looking down at me, trying not to watch either. "You were pretty good out there."

"In what world is gutted like a fish good?"

He smiled and reached down to squeeze my shoulder. We both flinched as another roar echoed through the antiques shop.

The flaming infection of the wound eased and a cool chill crept up my side. I pulled up my jacket and saw an angry red line where the gaping hole had been. "Hey. How'd that work?"

Jessa was rewrapping her arm. "Do you want a metaphysical lesson, or do you want to get out there and stop that thing?"

I pulled down the jacket and sat up. "Let's go." I moved to stand.

Chaz grabbed my arm and pulled me hard back to the

ground, ramming my butt bone into the cement. Just because I wasn't festering didn't mean that everything was perfectly healed.

"You are not going out there." The crease in his forehead was the deepest it had ever been.

"But I am. I have to."

"Violet. You've never taken on anything like this."

"Yeah? How many evil beasties from the Neveranth have you vanquished?"

Chaz just licked his lips.

"Again," I said as I slid my arm down in his hand and then took his warm palm. "Born and bred for this."

There was another crash and a scream, human this time, or as human as this group got. I smelled blood in the air; it tickled my nose.

"Guys, this thing can't get out. Those things from the Neveranth have been known to eat cities, or worse." Jessa protested from her place next to me.

I stood slowly and Chaz let me get to my feet this time. The armoire was big enough to keep us shielded from the fight. He stood beside me but Jessa stayed on the ground, holding her arm to her chest and resting.

"Here, take this," he said as he pressed a revolver in my hand. It was heavy but felt natural in my palm.

"Silver?" I asked as I slid it into my pocket.

He nodded as he looked at me. His gaze was steady; his eyes were wide and flecked with more gold than I'd ever seen. I could feel him, his warm, golden center slowly beating with his heart. And I got it. He did have a heart like a lion, all golden and fierce.

The memory of my mother's first fairy tale in the Violet saga brought a tear to my eye and I could believe that I was getting all mushy now, at crunch time.

"You survive this." His voice was low and intimate. "Because I will not lose anyone else to this monster. Do you understand?"

"Look whose all Mr. Emotional Speeches . . ."

"I love you."

Chaz reached out and slide his hand around my jaw. It was warm and nervous, slightly shaking. He pulled be forward and kissed me. My brain was frozen until I tasted his honeyed lips on mine. And then everything from the past two months came rushing in. I loved him. I loved that he brought me cinnamon coffee. I loved that he collected college T-shirts. I loved that he called me out when I wasn't thinking straight. And that he chose the most inopportune moment in all of history to tell me.

When he pulled away, his lips were pink and I was breathless.

"Did you decide before or after the sexy velour suit?" I smiled as I bit my lower lip.

He smiled and brushed a strand of hair from my face. "Nothing's easy with you."

"Thought you'd have learned that by now."

As another scream and crash combination echoed through the shop, he shook his head. "I knew the moment you dropped your red high heels in the alley."

Jessa cleared her throat from the floor behind us. Right, saving the world.

I took in a deep breath of him and smiled. "Okay. I'm going to go kick this whatever's ass. You're going to protect Jessa. And when it's all done, you might want to ask me out for dinner."

"It's a date."

We both flinched as something rocked the armoire we were hiding behind. His hand slid away from my face and went to the gun at his hip. My cheek was suddenly very cold, which focused my resolve to not so figuratively kick this S.O.B. into the next universe.

Chapter Thirty-One

This wasn't something from one of my TV movies. The panther in front of me was liquid smooth and smelled of blood and death. Its fur was inky black and, sure enough, it was the size of a Clydesdale and twice as long, not measuring its tail whipping around. Which meant that I would need four Violets to even begin to threaten this thing.

Guess one Violet and one maniacal bastard would have to do.

Haverty was circling the huge cat, still in a mostly human form, but he wasn't winning. The rest of the men were laying around the room like a dorm room full of tossed clothing from a wild night. Haverty's perfect façade was worn, his hair was in all directions, and a trickle of blood ran from his mouth. His canines pressed down on his bottom lip and his nose was wider, darker.

I just stood there watching the beast hiss and crouch and take sweeps at Haverty, who, weaponless and limping, was still fighting. What the hell was I going to do?

"You gonna help or just stand there like a statue?" Haverty barked.

"Figured I'd let him eat you before I saved the day."

The beast swooped his large paw at Haverty who jumped, spun, landed on his good leg, and hobbled over to me.

"Listen here, girl. This doesn't get out."

"The beast or the fact that your brilliant son let it loose?"

He looked like he wanted to kill me. And I knew he'd have his chance.

"Fine. What do we do?"

"Soft spot in the back of the head, where the spine meets the skull."

That didn't sound right. There was something itching in the back of my brain. But what did I know? Again, how many beasties from the other side had I kicked to the curb?

"You distract it; I'll jump on top and kill it."

I nodded. It was a plan. Not a good one, but with a plan, we could improvise from there.

Haverty walked behind me and began to circle around to my left.

I stretched my neck and reached my hands out. "Hey, kitty."

The beast snapped its black eyes to me and hissed. Its teeth were the size of my hairbrush and the muscles around his massive shoulders rippled.

"That's right, beastie. We don't play well with others, do we?"

I slowly began to move to the right and with each step, not only did the beast follow me, but I gathered power. My body hummed with energy by the time we'd spun 45 degrees.

The beast grew tired with me and looked around to find the other play toy. Haverty was perched on top of a china cabinet. Note to self: cripple but still agile as hell.

I called out to the beast. "No you don't."

I can describe it. It was like a psychic smack. As with Jessa before, I was able to stretch out just the power of the panther and claw the beast's nose. When I looked down at my hands, there was blood under my nails.

I'd gotten his attention and when I looked up at the beast, he was pissed. And then he pounced. I was able to scurry from the attack, the beast landing a hair's length before me.

I ran and the beast followed. Ran like a woman chasing a marked down pair of Jimmy Choo's.

I ran in a huge circle, leaping over desks, hurdling over tables. The beast destroyed everything behind me, not being lithe enough to duck anything. I tried not to laugh as I thought I really knew what a bull in a china shop might look like now.

I caught a flash of where Haverty was perched. As I ran, I picked up the heirloom silver knife that had stuck me like a prize pig and tossed it up to Haverty.

And then I stopped running and turned to face it. The beast stopped too.

I crouched down before it and caught his eyes. I got the distinct impression he was enjoying this. The chase, the game of cat and mouse, and I was small enough to be the mouse in this situation.

Shifting my weight from one foot to the other, I leaned forward on my hands and something cold touched my hand. A flash of silver. Out of my peripheral, I saw Haverty's cane just within reach. I reached for it and the handle pulled away from the black polished piece of the cane and a dagger slid from the end of the handle. Sneaky bastard.

I looked up at the beast as I slowly picked up the dagger.

It growled at me and I felt the power hidden within the beast. Just as it was about to pounce and start the chase all over again, Haverty leapt. Landing on the beast's shoulder, he rammed the knife into the base of the panther's skull.

The cat screamed and reared up on its hind legs, exposing its chest.

The world seemed to slow for a moment and I realized Haverty was just going to piss it off. The center of power wasn't in the brain, it was in the chest. Like Chaz's lion heart.

As the beast reared up, my hold on the dagger tightened. I slid in and under the great paws and rammed the dagger into the beast's chest, just under the breastbone and straight for the heart.

It fell forward on top of me, his claws ripping into me as it ground my shoulder blade into the cement beneath.

The beast flailed up again, bucking Haverty from his back. The man went flying, crashing into some unknown piece of furniture.

As the beast fell back down, I rolled away to a safe distance. It landed heavy on the ground next to me and the blood poured out of the relatively small wound place just in the exact spot. The dark eyes were going glassy and the beast moved its head to look at me.

I stood, holding my arm, and stepped closer to the body. Its breaths were few and far between. Moving in a little closer, I reached for the dagger from the wound and as my hand touched the silver, I felt the power within the great beast going dark. The knife came out with a sucking sound and the cat took its last breath.

As I watched the regal beast die, a gunshot echoed around

the antique store. I dropped to the ground and turned around to see Haverty staggering backwards, inches away from me. Chaz emerged from the shadows, his gun still smoking.

Haverty held the wound in his palm as my silver heirloom knife dropped from his hand, the silver clattering loudly in the suddenly quiet showroom.

"All that and you try to stab me in the back?" I hissed as I stood and my grip on the dagger hardened. "No wonder your son was such a coward."

Haverty's eyes burned dark with power—and not just his power. It was the first time that I'd been eye to eye with the power of the Order. It was black and cold and seemed void of any life. Haverty's energy flared out around him and he tried to smother me in it but I brushed it away like dust.

"You aren't worthy of such power," he hissed through intensified canines.

"I worked my ass off for such power."

Haverty lunged towards me and another shot echoed from the barrel of Chaz's gun. Haverty staggered back and a large red stain appeared on his shoulder.

I looked at Chaz whose face was hard and hate-filled. It wasn't a good look for him.

"Don't do this, Chaz. You won't like yourself in the morning."

He made a wide circle around Haverty and stood beside me. "Funny. Feels pretty damn good to me."

Haverty fell to his knees. His shoulder bleeding, his hand held tightly to his chest. He looked defeated. But I knew better. He glared up at Chaz. "You're that Guardian's brat."

"His name was Seth Garrett," Chaz growled.

I would have put my hand on his shoulder but my arm hung limply at my side. Good thing I had another. And that one had a knife in it that could quickly kill a Haverty.

"I took him down like a rag doll, boy, and I'll do the same to you."

Chaz didn't flinch as he pointed the barrel at Haverty's torso and fired another round. I let him. This was therapy. But that's all I allowed.

"Stop," I said as I moved into Chaz's arm.

"That's right, rein in your little pet."

"Oh, be quiet!" I snapped.

"What are you going to do about it?"

I walked up to him and looked down at his crumpled figure. He glared up at me, panting like a tired dog on a hot day. Sweat dripped down his face. Bruises formed on his cheek and his ash-flavored power lapped low but sharp around him.

"I'm going to live a long happy life and kick your ass every chance I get."

"You are nothing." Spittle flew out of his mouth as pain ripped deep wrinkles into his face. "I made you what you are."

"Yeah. Thanks for ruining my life."

"You are my blood. You are my daughter."

"I am nothing like you." I screamed. Pain filled my head and my eyes went dull for a moment.

There was a crash behind me and I looked to see Jessa push over the mirror with a small smile.

Chaz's eyes didn't leave Haverty and his gun still remained clenched in his hand. Then, Chaz flinched. And I knew what was happening before it happened. I turned, prepared for Haverty coming at me.

It was as if the knife jumped into his midsection. Haverty was inches away as the dagger slipped easily between his ribs. I swept his legs and he fell hard. I kept on top of him and drove the knife down so hard into his chest with both hands, the bit embedded in the concrete beneath him.

Panting, I kept the force down on the blade until I knew that he wasn't getting up again. The movement ignited all my injuries, those known and unknown. I fell to my rear but didn't take my hands off the knife.

Haverty didn't cry out; he fought against the sizzling in his chest. He clumsily pushed at my hand, my arms, my face. He kicked and flopped like a dying fish. Burning flesh filled my nose.

"You little bitch," he spat out blood that landed on my cheek.

I removed one hand to try to wipe my face only to find that I was covered in blood. Mine. The beast's. And now his. "You did this to yourself."

Haverty slowly stopped fighting. His arms went slack and his eyes went glassy. I could taste his blood in the air around us as it spilt out of the wound on his chest.

"Take it then. See if you do any better," the man whispered and the light left him.

I looked over him and felt nothing. No victory, no satisfaction, no disgust. Just the knowledge that I had done something that needed to be done. And the day was over.

Slowly, I pried my hands off the silver handle. As I tried to rise, my legs went numb and failed me, sending me sprawling on the cement floor next to him. My skull made a dull thud against the floor and his head turned towards me as the last of his blood trickled out of his lips.

I panted hard, the pain digging into my shoulder. The

room began to spin and I didn't have the energy to lift my head. My eyelids grew heavy and finally closed, as I focused on just breathing.

Silver light filled the darkness behind my eye lids. And then I was warm and everything smelled of golden hay and I was in Iris's barn. Chaz was lying across from me in a wide puddle of moonlight. This was a pain-induced vision, but I didn't care. I just wanted to hold his hand and sleep because I was so tired.

Unfortunately, the sleep would have to wait as I was accosted by the sour cigar scent of Haverty. It hovered around me on the soft hay, gathering strength like a summer storm, becoming thick like humidity. The silver light around me became hot, searing. It pressed down on me like an iron as it seeped into my skin, burned my eyes, until every inch of me felt like the burnt end of a cigar.

I gasped and my eyes flew open. I sucked in deep breaths of the death and dust around me but I was breathing. Knives of pain jabbed upwards and inwards from my torso and then burning white heat flared in my muscles. It burned in my shoulder, in my side, in my head, sent spots into my vision as the power burned through me and then settled.

Chaz and Jessa hovered: Jessa watching me, Chaz watching Haverty's cold body beside me.

I pushed myself up to a sitting position and looked over at the dead beast and then the dead man. The smell overwhelmed me and I grew nauseous. And this was a good day?

Slowly, testing every muscle, I pushed myself to my feet and swayed a bit. Chaz's arm saved me from biting the cement. The muscles in my shoulder were mending, weaving themselves back together at a speed I knew was far from human, with energy from a place I wasn't ready to think about yet.

"I know you can heal better the other way," Chaz said softly as he led me to the door. "But you came in a convertible. Don't think we can explain a panther in the backseat to the cops."

With a painful chuckle, I held his hand tightly to my arm. Jessa rushed to my side, offering a hand to hold. And I did, squeezed it so tight I was pretty sure her fingers might fall off. She didn't flinch or pull away, just squeezed back.

"Do we need to get you to a hospital?" Jessa asked.

"Nah. I'll patch it up when we get home," I managed, though talking and breathing hurt.

"Violet," Chaz started softly.

"Please don't start, Chaz. It's been a rough day." I said softly.

"You really are difficult."

"Get used to it, Wonder boy."

With super speed, Chaz swept me off my feet and held me close to him, my legs dangling over his arm and my head immediately resting on his shoulder.

"I'm going to stain your jacket."

"It's okay."

"It was your dad's jacket," I whispered as I slid my hand under the lapel.

"You can help me pick out a new one."

I weakly pointed out where the car was parked and he carried me the whole way. Jessa rested her hand on my shoulder as we walked and I felt her cool energy running around us, helping me heal.

Carefully, he sat me against the edge of the car door and pulled away slowly to make sure that I was steady.

"I'm thinking we head to Iris's," Chaz started. "It's quiet and safe."

"I'm thinking that we head to my place because I have a doorman," Jessa said, crossing her arms over her chest. Back to good ole Jessa.

"No," I said softly. "We are going to my house."

They didn't argue. Jessa offered a hand to help me into her car.

"Miss Jordan."

The cry for help froze the three of us in place. We turned around to see four men walking towards us. Chaz immediately went for his gun.

My borders were about as intact as my shoulder so I felt them coming. Their energy was low, docile, and as they got close, I could have sworn I recognized one of them. And as they got closer, I knew exactly who I smelled.

"Officer Briggs?"

His head ducked down and his energy was anxious. The men in the long black trench coats all hung their heads as they followed behind Briggs. He was a mongrel. The damn cop was one of those damn dogs. How did I miss that?

My entire body tensed in anger as I thought about the accident and the shoe and the fact that my supposed break-in was not actually a break-in.

"What do you want?" I managed to spit out as I held my arm close to my chest. The cat danced around my chest, angry still, and by the look in Briggs's eyes, he knew that.

"We pledge our allegiance to you, Miss Jordan."

"Oh god," I moaned.

"You just tried to kill me!" Jessa's anger flowed out from her as white hot needles, and I felt it in my side, like a foot coming back from being asleep.

"We were following orders," he said, his eyes still on the cement.

I put my hand on Jessa's arm and calmed her down.

"Guys, she's really not in shape for anything right now," Chaz started. "Give us a few days."

"We don't have a few days," Briggs growled. "We are traitors to the pack, and without a strong leader, the pack will erupt in chaos and war."

"Not my problem," I muttered.

"It is, Prima Jordan."

Chaz shouted. "She is not your Prima!"

Briggs hunkered down even further and if his ears could have done back, they would have.

I took in a long cool breath and licked my lips. "An hour ago, you were trying to rip my best friend to pieces. Why should we trust you?"

My eyes rose to his and I felt the cat settle, felt power in my own stare as I captured Briggs's eyes and held his gaze in mine. There was a prickle down my spine and I knew that this was not my stare but that of the Haverty energy now coursing through my body.

"We betrayed our pack by following Spencer when he was banished. We have nowhere to go."

Chaz flinched but I put a hand on his arm and pulled myself to a standing position. The muscles in my shoulders and back stretched and burned but were already healed.

"Why do you need somewhere to go? Why can't you just be?"

"They are marked with Jovan. I can feel it," Jessa's teeth ground next to me.

I took in a deep breath, testing my own body, suddenly feeling stronger than it ever had before. My shoulder was fine, my head was fine.

"We are pack creatures," Briggs said slowly. "We need a strong leader. You are strong."

I shook my head. "Sure, I can kick some demon ass, but I'm not strong enough to be a leader."

"But you..."

My finger flew up to silence him. "You will go. And if the pack retaliates, it will be fitting all the shitty things you did to me."

Briggs's eyes dropped to the ground and his shoulders dropped about seven inches in disappointment. He backed away and, in unison, the pack turned to go.

It was that damn shoulder drop that got me. Why am I such a sucker for a shoulder drop? "Wait."

Everyone within earshot was as surprised as I was at the order. Briggs dared to look up at me. There was a glimmer of something there that I was too exhausted to analyze.

"There is a woman inside. Cristina. Go see if she is okay."

"Yes, Prima."

"Don't call me that," I snapped. My skin sizzled and I had to take a deep breath to calm down. "And clean up the mess inside. Burn it down if you have to. No one needs to know about tonight."

"Yes, ma'am."

I grimaced. "I think I like Prima better."

Chapter Thirty-Two

After peeling off my suit, I went immediately to the shower. It was 6 a.m. and I was taking a shower after killing another human being.

I didn't know why it didn't hit me harder. I just felt empty. Maybe because I wrote about death every day, maybe because my head had strategized whole dark armies moving against one another in the night, taking out whole breeds of night creatures. I had written the monologues of the characters as they had made their first kills and I had been dead right about the guilt that comes afterwards and how eventually it became a part of the character to make her stronger.

But this had been me. This wasn't a scripted sci-fi scene. I had killed a person—who was harming others. Did that make it right? Did that make it okay because some Power said Jessa was to be protected at all costs, that a reborn warrior must protect her no matter the loss of lives?

I leaned against the now-warm tiles and let the water wash away the blood from the wounds. The physical injuries were healed but the rest of me would still need mending. I looked down to see a flawless midsection and a small red line where the stab wound had been. With a burger in the morning for some needed protein, I should be back to perfection in a day.

After getting out of the shower, I peeked in on Jessa who was already asleep in my bed. It was the most comfortable and the most defendable. And this was my life now.

I put on a soft nightgown and wrapped up in my purple fuzzy robe. The scent of Chaz still lingered and my body twinged as I thought about him downstairs, pacing madly, making phone calls, double-checking the new sliding glass door.

As I walked downstairs, I could smell cinnamon coffee. I looked around and he had cleaned again, cleaned up the broken mirror, picked up some coffee mugs I'd left around the place. Who knew that he would be the type to stress-clean? It was almost as attractive a quality as his washboard abs.

"I smell coffee," I said from the kitchen doorway, jamming my hands into the robe's pockets.

"Thought you might like some after the night we had."

"Love some."

We sat across from each other at my kitchen table like we had before but, this time, I didn't have anything witty to say. Just looking at him made my chest ache. He looked exhausted and he was the one who did this on a regular basis. He had all the answers for all the tough questions that I needed to ask. Finally, after what seemed like an hour, I was able to speak.

"Have you ever killed someone?" I already knew the answer but I needed to hear him say it.

"Yeah."

"How did you feel after your first time?"

He pursed his lips and leaned forward, looking out the kitchen window where it was annoyingly sunny outside.

"Empty for a while, I guess," he said with that warm soft tone he had first used when speaking of my new lifestyle. "Unworthy of having that much power."

"And how did you get over it?"

"My dad explained it to me. It's part of the deal. To live like we do, with the gifts that we have, it's all part of the package."

"Live hard, die young, type of thing?"

"No," he chuckled softly. "Not quite. More like we've been given these gifts because we have the strength to do what needs to be done and taking lives to protect others is part of that burden."

"But I didn't ask for it."

"Not yours for the asking. Remember you were made this way."

Couldn't really argue with him there.

"And you were incredible last night. The way you moved. Like..."

"Something out of the movies?" I filled in, taking my last swig of cooled coffee.

"I was going to say like you finally know who you are."

I flinched as the reality behind his words struck me. I stood and moved to the sink, closer to the window as I looked out at my perfect little courtyard in my perfect little neighborhood and sighed.

I heard Chaz stand and set his coffee mug on the table. His arms slid around me gently and I rested my head back on his shoulder.

"Anything else you want to talk about?"

I knew what he wanted to talk about. What happened between us less than thirty-six hours ago. "Not right now."

"Then you need to sleep."

"I can't. I've got so much crap running around in my head right now. I'm not going to sleep for a week." I turned around in his arms and looked up at him. "That, and you just gave me a full blend Ethiopian."

He smiled and pulled away, taking my hand to pull me into the living room and stopped at the base of the stairs.

"Go upstairs and go to bed," he ordered.

"Go upstairs and take a shower."

Chaz pulled me to him and placed his lips on my forehead. I closed my eyes and felt him again, more this time than I ever had before. He'd dropped the cement borders around him and I reveled in his golden light for a moment. And then I pushed him away.

"Seriously, you smell."

Once there was a warrior in a time of peace. He and his group of men wandered the countryside without meaning. They got into trouble, fought for money to eat, and created havoc in their wake because that's what they did. That's all they were ever told they could do.

The band of brothers came into a small village rebuilding from the war that had ravaged the houses and stables. The villagers were wary as they watched the warriors ride in on their war horses.

"We need room and board and stables for our horses," the warrior told the innkeeper.

The innkeeper wrung his hands. His daughter, a strong-willed girl, stepped forward. "Then you'll have to build it yourself. Your war has destroyed half our village."

"I'm a knight, not a carpenter."

"Well I'm an innkeeper's daughter, but that doesn't prevent me from being the baker as well. If you want to stay here, you'll have to pick up a hammer."

The warrior was aghast at the young girl's willfulness. But he looked at his tired men and sighed, then looked back at the girl. "What do you need?"

In the days to follow, the warrior and his brothers helped the town rebuild their stables.

"See, you can do something other than warmonger," the innkeeper's daughter smiled as she delivered their lunches.

The warrior watched as his men laughed and ate, healthy and happy under the guidance of this new general.

"The inn needs some work as well," she mentioned the next day as she delivered their lunches.

"Yes, ma'am."

My mother stopped her story there.

"Go on," I prompted.

"I can't. There's no more story to tell."

"Why not?"

"You haven't written it yet."

Jessa had to shake me hard from my sleep. I'd curled up in the front window where the sun still streamed in on my favorite reclining chair and I slept like the dead—or the should-be dead.

"What?" I snapped before I could see who it was and what they were doing.

"I need to go home," Jessa said backing away from my curled up position on the chair. I had somehow managed to completely curl up on just the seat with my head on the arm.

"Do you want me to go with you?" I finally responded after I unfurled and sat up, rubbing my eyes and the pattern of the upholstery off my face.

"Nah, I think I'll be fine."

"Don't be silly. Just let me get my clothes on."

"No really, Violet," she said her voice commanding my attention. "You need to sleep. You look terrible."

"So you don't want to be seen in public with me at the sake of your safety?"

Jessa sighed and walked back up to the chair and sat on the arm. She wrapped her left arm around me and leaned her head on mine. "I didn't mean it that way. I meant that you need to sleep and I need my shower."

I sighed and leaned back in my chair. "I'm fine."

Jessa smacked me on the head and then squeezed me hard.

"Do you think life is going to be like this from now on? With all the almost dismemberment and danger?" I asked tentatively.

"Life is dangerous anyway, sacred destiny or not. That's why you have to live every minute like it's your last."

"Wow. That was deep. You okay? Do you need to lie down or something?"

She hit me on the head again and huffed playfully as she walked across the room to grab her keys off the foyer table.

"I'm going to be fine," she smiled as she reached for the knob.

"But if you smell an ounce of trouble you call us, okay?" I said with a wagging finger, something my mother used to do.

"Us? Stalker boy upstairs?"

"You think I looked bad. He still hasn't slept."

Jessa just giggled to herself as she opened the door, letting in the fresh air.

As I watched her walk to her car, I knew she would be fine, at least for today because the universe couldn't be that evil.

The second thought in my head was that my bed was now open. I slowly climbed the stairs feeling much better after my catnap and leaped on the feather comforter, making the bed springs protest under my sudden weight.

I was almost asleep when I heard the handle of my bedroom door turn. The door slowly opened and Chaz's bare shoulder slid in first, followed by the rest of him. He was wrapped up in a towel. It was pretty.

"I need a favor."

"Okay?" I smiled at the possibilities.

"I'm going to have to burn those clothes."

"Yeah, bonfire later tonight. I'm thinking marshmallows."

"Is there any way you could go to my car to get my duffle?"

"Seriously?"

"I think it would look less scandalous, you in your robe than me in a towel."

He was right. Any more calls to the cops or questionable cars and my Homeowners' Association was going to kick me out.

"Fine," I said as I threw the covers off.

I tromped down the stairs making sure that my footsteps were enough of a protest and threw open the front door to my beautiful neighborhood.

His car was right outside and the duffle was in the backseat. I opened it up and picked up the black duffle. A gun slid out of the side pocket and onto the seat.

This is the life that chose me, I thought as I put the piece back into the side pocket and shouldered the bag. Side arms and sidekicks. Guns and guys.

As I stood back up to close up the car, I looked across the street to see four black dogs sitting there. Crap.

They didn't move, just stayed across the street. But I could feel them, feel their anticipation, their need. They were dogs. They were waiting for orders. I could think of several things that I'd like to tell them to do, but then remembered how Briggs looked last night, lost and lonely.

"Go watch Jessa."

The dogs turned in unison and took off down the street.

As I watched them run, I felt something brewing in the air. It quickened my trek back to the house. I slammed the door behind me and locked all the locks.

Chaz was behind me in four seconds, his towel still hung low on his hips. "Everything okay?"

I looked up at him and leaned against the door. "Mongrels were outside. Just hanging out."

His jaw tightened as he took the bag from my shoulder.

"This is my life from now on, isn't it? A full menagerie of problems."

He nodded and shrugged. "Yeah, pretty much."

"Don't sugarcoat it," I pushed him away and went to pout on my couch.

He set the duffle on the ground and came to sit next to me.

He smelled so much better now. "I can't tell you what's coming. I talked to Iris; she only knows so much. But we created a vacuum of power. There will be chaos."

"Oh, god. Iris. Is she going to be okay?"

He put his arm around my shoulder and nodded. "She's going to be just fine."

I thought of Iris and Jessa and Devin. "Oh crap, Devin."

"What about Devin?"

I hung my head. "He was there when I . . . and then we might have . . . Oh god, what am I going to do about that?"

Chaz didn't attempt to answer. He just pulled me into his shoulder and I rest my head on his warm clean skin. "One crisis at a time."

"So there's the Prima thing. The Guardian thing. The power vacuum thing. I'm going to need a white board or something to keep it all straight."

"And then there's us."

My entire body shivered when he said that. I pulled away and looked at him. Taking down a beastie the size of an Expedition, killing a man, becoming a Prima, and the only thing that still floored me was he loved me.

"No witty comeback?" he tried to fight a smile.

I just shook my head slowly from side to side, my brain still spinning wonderfully. I was too tired. It just took too much energy to be pithy and sarcastic and frankly, I needed the energy for more important things now.

Chaz full smile faded sadly. I felt his shift of demeanor in my chest. My heart sunk with the confusion in his eyes.

"I don't know how do to this," he said.

The words were so familiar, like the pain of ripping stitches. My eyes began to water and my skin bristled as some part of me prepared for another fight.

He must have read it in my eyes. "God, no. Violet. I'm never leaving again," he said quickly. "I love you. I've seen you take this curse and make it into something miraculous. It scares the crap out of me because I'm an idiot when it comes to relationships."

The relief in my chest freed a small tear to slip from my eye. He *was* an idiot. Admitting it is the always the first step. I softened because he did have a hard time getting out the next few words.

"And I don't know exactly how *it's* passed on." He was facing his fears as he took my hand in his.

"You don't know if you could be infected," I clarified for him, using the words I knew he didn't like, even though there was no other vernacular for it. "If we were just lucky the first time."

He nodded slowly, watching me carefully.

I knew the answer; it rushed over me like a wonderfully refreshing stream. A certainty I had never had before. A strength I'd never felt before. The world was right again.

"It's okay," I smiled softly up at him, caressing that moviestar jaw of his. Still wanting to touch everything just to make sure that it was real. "I understand."

"You do?"

"Can't have two furries around the house?" I joked, as I tweaked his chin.

He laughed one strong laugh and kissed me. It was still wonderful and I was very glad my toes were tucked beneath my lavender robe, because they were curling more than Christmas ribbon.

He pulled me close as he lay back on the couch, the crease finally gone from between his brows. I relaxed against his bare chest where I could hear the steady rhythm of his heart. I smiled. A real man lying on my couch. And I knew this time he was going to stay.

"Just because we can't do *that* doesn't mean that we can't sleep next to each other and have coffee together and go out to the movies together . . ."

"And take showers together," he suggested.

I nodded approvingly and let my imagination wander for just a few seconds.

"And it may not be forever. We just need more information."

And now it was my turn to laugh as I pulled a blanket over the two of us as I snuggled in for a deep warm nap.

"What?"

"Only I could have a love life that requires research."

Stay Tuned for
Further Adventures in the Life of
Violet Jordan
Coming December 2011

From Amanda Arista

and

Avon Impulse

About the Author

Amanda was born in Illinois, raised in Corpus Christi, lives in Dallas but her heart lies in London. She has a husband who fights crime, one dog who thinks he's a real boy, and another who might be a fruit bat in disguise. She spends her weekends writing at coffee shops, practicing for the day that caffeine intake becomes an Olympic sport, and plotting character demises with fellow writers Wolvarez, Killer Cupcake, and Keith (names have been changed to protect the not-so-innocent).